A CITY IN BLUE

BY: JOSHUA C COOK

FORGEMASTER CYCLE

BOOK THREE

Books by Joshua C. Cook

The Echo Worlds Series
Bridgefinders
Bridgebreaker
Bridgebuilder (Soon to come.)

Canitus

Project: Perception

The Forgemaster Cycle
Blood of a Fallen God
The Anvil of Souls
A City in Blue

The Ascendant Path
Scholar
Solider
Anchor
Caster
Traitor

"A CITY OF MAGIC? A FOOLISH DREAM, A FARCE TO ENTICE THE WEAK AND WORTHLESS. BETTER TO DEVOTE ONESELF TO A TRUE POWER THAN TO WISH FOR SOMETHING THAT WILL NEVER EXIST…"

-excerpt from the journal of High Priest Bracin Monsteen, final High Priest of Amder.

Chapter 1.

Everything was chaos. Chaos and overwhelmingly blue. A dull rumbling sound filled his ears, and a constant drumbeat echoed with it. A loud drumbeat. William took a moment to realize that was the sound of his own heart beating. His skin burned where the poison had traveled up his arms like twisting serpents following the veins.

It wasn't all pain, there were waves of overwhelming pleasure. More than once, his body convulsed as the mix of the two washed over him. His eyes burned in the blue light, and he forced them shut, but that did nothing to help. The light still came through, ignoring his paltry defense against it. Where was he? Who was he? *William. William Reis.*

Taking a deep breath, he regretted it at once as millions of tiny blue specs flew into his lungs. He fought to stop coughing, closing his hands. He clenched them tight, only to have one jerk in a way that he wasn't expecting. Only then did he realize he was holding hands with someone. He relaxed his grip for a second. Duncan? Was it Duncan?

No. Duncan was dead. Am I dead? He remembered bits of a conversation with his cousin, but the physical sensations tore through him again, washing the fragments of memory away. How had Duncan died? It couldn't be him. Whose hand had he nearly crushed then? A name floated through... Myriam.

The name brought a barrage of thoughts. Sadness. Anger. Hate. Disgust. Joy. Love. He pushed it away. It was too much. He was flying through madness. He opened his eyes once more but still could see nothing but blue. It was paralyzing. He could not focus, even closing his eyes took more effort than it should have. He could feel Myriam's hand, but not see her in this insanity. The sound grew, and a vibration shook his very core. A fleeting memory of rolling down a snow-covered slope came to him, a feeling similar to what he felt now.

Contact with solid ground broke every single thought as he hit hard. He gasped in shock; the air fleeing his lungs along with no small amount of pain. He did cough then and struggled for air, as every cough seemed to bring forth a misty cloud of blue dust. He wiped his mouth and couldn't process what he saw. The smear of spittle was blue, but that was to be expected. No, it was his hands and his arms that made him gape with surprise.

He remembered the lines, red and growing, moving up his arms. Thick and heavy, they had burned with agony. A present from that Blood God follower. William tried to remember his name but failed. Everything was still confused, jumbled up in his head. But his skin, red and blistering, moving up, tracing lines. That he remembered. *Poison, Pain.*

But they weren't burning now. He wasn't sure when they had stopped. They had been a moment before, when they had been in whatever that was. It looked like his skin, and it didn't hurt, but… the lines were still there. But now, they were blue. The same bright blue. William looked closely at them. The skin where the lines were was smooth, and if he stared at it long enough, it was almost like tiny glowing dots were moving there, right under his skin. It was deeply unsettling to see things moving like that. *Cut it out, take a knife and cut it out!* He attempted to take a deep breath to calm himself. He was only partially successful, but the panic did fade.

He made a fist and released it, feeling his strength. Still feels the same. He coughed again, trying to clear his lungs. Where was he? He'd been in a cave, then, talking to Duncan, and then darkness. Voices. He remembered voices. Talking to him. His Da, his mother, Master Jaste, Haltim, and more. He had tried to speak to them, but he'd been thrown into that blue chaos, and then he was here.

William sat back on his legs and attempted to clear his mind. *Where was he?* He was on a plain, but not one that looked familiar. Mountains surrounded them, but not ones he recognized either. They weren't the Skyreach at any rate. The colors were wrong. The Skyreach was gray and shades of blue mixed with gray. These mountains, whatever they were called, were redder, far redder. Iron content is high then. If there was a good supply of coal, he could see. William shook his head. It was easy to slip back into being a Forgemaster.

Forgemaster. He reached out, ashamed that he hadn't thought to speak to Amder. Amder had told him he could talk to him once he entered the Anvil, right? Memories came flooding back, pushing away more of the confused haze. Yes, Amder had told him that. Amder. The name brought forth a sense of loss. Loss and... anger?

Amder was dead. Sorrow. Despair. William felt a rush of sadness as he blinked away the rush of wetness that came to his eyes. No, Amder couldn't die again! He'd only just come back. William had sacrificed too much, given up more than he'd ever imagined to bring Amder back to this world, and he was dead, again?

No sound answered his call. No voice to give advice or reassure him. That little presence in his mind, that he'd come to think of as the connection to his god, was gone. Amder. Dead. No. Not dead. The truth came back in pieces. Amder wasn't dead. Amder was gone. Worse. Amder was now part of something else. Something new. Something... that killed me? Nausea overcame him, and he retched helplessly on the ground. That part of his memory returned, and he wished very much it hadn't. He had died. Killed because all of Amder, all of who he was, all of what his god could be, had been forced through him as Amder was destroyed. No, not destroyed, merged. Joined.

How had that happened? William wiped his mouth again, grimacing at the taste of his bile. Regin was dead. He knew that. Another fragmentary memory solidified, as the sight of a flashing spear striking his armor came to him. Regin. Dead. That only left Myriam. Myriam. Some more of his memories came back to him. Myriam was the reason that Amder was dead. Myriam had done something. Myriam. Where was she??

He whirled around, and there; he saw her. Or at least her form. Lying collapsed on the ground, not far away. William pushed himself upright to walk towards her. He had taken three steps when he stopped. Myriam. She had betrayed him. *AGAIN*. She'd been hiding something. Something important. And now Amder was gone. His plan to save Duncan, gone. He patted his clothing, trying to find the circlet. The circlet that was supposed to draw Valnijz out of his cousin Duncan, and into it. The circlet he was then going to bury as deep underground as he ever could manage.

But that hadn't happened. Because of her. Myriam. All his plans. All his efforts to save Duncan. Gone. Wasted. Anger grew. William reached down to grab his hammer. Anger turned to rage. She had broken his heart. She had flaunted her relationship with Regin in front of him. She had kept secrets and destroyed his god, and his last family. It was all her fault. He raised his hammer.

The sunlight glinted off its' gold and blue surface. Blue? William blinked in the sun. The hammer was supposed to be silver. Not gold and blue. He could feel more of his memory fall into place as he lowered his arm. A sob came forth as he fell to his knees. What do I do now?

William was so tired. Just tired. Tired of gods and wars. Tired of betrayals, tired of all the lies and fears. Another long sob came forth as he sat down again, burying his face in his legs. "William?" A soft voice came. Her voice. Myriam.

William didn't want to answer. Not her. Not now. He remembered enough. All his careful planning, all the risks, all the sacrifice he'd done to get to that point. All of it undone by one person. Myriam VolFar.

"William? Are you all right?" Myriam's voice came again, barely above a whisper.

William raised his head and locked eyes with her. Thankfully for him, he was already somewhat used to the changes the magic had wreaked on them. Her eyes. The color of her eyes. Once green, now were the same bright blue as the lines on his arms. And his hammer. Her lips were blue as well. His eyes flicked down to her arms, and yes, the same tracery of blue following what had been the path of the venom.

"I'm fine." William answered, looking away from her. Towards… Behind him. The one direction he hadn't looked. A massive bank of clouds filled the far end of this strange valley they were in. That was not normal. William had grown up in the mountains. And while these weren't the Skyreach, weather should behave the same.

"Your eyes! Your skin!!" Myriam tried to get up and fell back to her knees. "You're blue!"

"I know." Will gave her the smallest answer possible. He didn't want to talk to her. He didn't want to look at her.

"Where are we? Why are you acting like that?" Myriam asked, wiping her mouth herself and making a quick grimace at the blue she saw left on her skin.

William felt his anger rise. "I don't know where we are. This was you're doing, not mine."

"I saved your life. That..." Myriam stopped talking.

"That what? That god? The one YOU brought back? The one that killed my cousin. The one that KILLED AMDER?" William's voice rose to a shout. "The one that killed ME. And then brought me back to just prove that it could?"

Myriam shook her head but refused to look William in the eye. "That's not my fault." "Not your fault? You knew the plan. You knew what I was there for. You and Regin. You also knew that you were going to do something." William hit the ground with a fist. "How long. How long did you keep that secret from me? From Regin. Or did he know?"

Myriam said nothing for a long moment, her eyes never leaving William. She shook her head eventually. "He didn't know. I didn't know. I did not know exactly what was going to happen William. I didn't. I even asked the voice, what was going to happen to you and Duncan. And Amder. It didn't tell me."

"And yet you didn't mention it to us? You still went through with it?" William didn't know what to feel. Maybe she was telling the truth. Or she didn't know. But the fact that she went through with it all anyways and didn't know what was going to happen didn't help.

"I did. It saved my life. In the Gorom caves. It healed Regin, after we captured Valnijz. It said I had to put a crystal on a pillar. That was all." Myriam shook her head. "I didn't know it was going to make all that happen."

William clenched his jaw. "Gorom caves? You had this thing talking to you back in the Gorom caves and yet you said not a thing? Not one?"

Myriam threw up her hands. "What? Yes. I had no idea that was going to be the result. None. I am sorry William. Sorrier than you will ever know."

"No, you're not." William struggled to his feet. "What you want is for me to tell you that you did the right thing. You don't want to hear the truth. That you cost me everything."

"I save your life William Reis. If I hadn't grabbed you, you would be back in the Anvil. Facing off against that thing. What good would that do you? Here you are alive, at least. I asked the magic that... blue crazy pool I pulled you into. I asked it to take us somewhere safe. It brought us here." Myriam looked at the cloud bank. "Though I do not know where 'here' is."

William wanted to scream. He wanted to break something. "You ruined everything I had set forth, Myriam. You did. You want me to agree with you. You want me to tell you were right. But you know what? I will not do that. Not now. Never."

"Riders." Myriam pointed at the clouds. "Riders, coming this way."

William turned the way she was pointing. She was right. Four riders. Moving fast and right for them.

Chapter 2.

William peered into the distance at four figures coming his and Myriam's way. One thing stood out at once. Two of the figures were tall. Very tall. One he could only sort of see they were so short, and one seemed average. At this distance, that was about all he could make out, but that was enough to pique some interest in who these people were.

He pointedly ignored Myriam as she stood. A tiny voice wanted to help her up, but the rest of him quickly pushed that thought away. *I don't care anymore.* He shifted his attention back to the riders, who were much closer now. Their horses were moving almost faster than he could think about them across this plain. He wasn't any eminent scholar of horses, but this was fast.

Within moments, the riders were close enough to see more. Will blinked a few times in surprise. He was sure that the two very tall guards were Trinil. And the shorter one was a Gorom. Trinil? Gorom? Working together? What was this place that Myriam and this odd blue power had brought them to?

The lead guard dismounted about ten paces away, while the rest stayed on their mounts. None went for a weapon, which was good. Will had seen enough blood for a lifetime. He was in no shape to defend himself, either. His eyes did a quick appraisal of their armor and arms, though. They were impressive. He'd have a better idea if he could actually physically touch it, but the stuff looked very well made. Someone had spent a lot of time making each piece identical. All of their gear was the same, silvery armor, helms, and each carried a sword on their hip and a spear strapped to the side of the horse. All sized appropriately for the rider, of course.

The one who had dismounted had one change. Her armor had a single blue and gold strip down one pauldron. The lead figure studied him and Myriam for a long moment, before removing her helmet, and Will got yet another shock.

A Windtalker. She was a Windtalker. Copper skin, white blond hair, and eyes as white as the snow in the reach. What was a Windtalker doing here? Wearing armor? And she was walking. Granted, he'd only ever met one other Windtalker, Lorelei the Mistral, but she had floated above the ground. But this Windtalker was walking around like anyone else. "And who are you? What brings you two, with a boon bursting out of your skin, here?" The Windtalker rested her hand on her sword but made no other moves.

"Where are we?" William asked. He could see Myriam answering out of the corner of his eye, but he didn't trust her answers. "None of this looks familiar to me."

"This is the city. Also known as the City in Blue. I am Ride Captain Julis." The Ride Captain shifted, and William, with total clarity, could see her arm muscles tense with a strength that was obvious. "Who are you?"

"I am William Reis." William answered quickly. "Forgive me, but you are a Windtalker? Those are Trinil, and a Gorom? Wearing armor? Riding horses? What is this city?"

The Ride Captain nodded, and Will could see her arm relax some. *Good.* "Yes. I'm surprised. Very few people from the outside world have ever seen a Windtalker. There are very few in the world. Though I doubt many would even acknowledge my existence." She turned to Myriam. "And you? Your companion here didn't say your name."

"Myriam. Myriam VolFar." Myriam answered. Her voice seemed sad to Will, but he again steeled himself. *She brought this on herself.* He fought back the urge to stand by her side. Better I take care of myself now.

"It is good to meet you two. Questions are going to be asked. But this is not the place. Come. We will take you to the city, let them discover the truth." Ride Captain Julis remounted her horse. "Come, ride behind me William Reis."

Will felt himself flush. "I don't ride." Will hated admitting that. Why couldn't people use carts or wagons? Why all this riding everywhere?

Ride Captain Julis laughed, a sound that for all the world made Will think of chimes. "You have to sit. I'll do the rest." The Ride Captain reached down to help him up onto the horse.

One of the Trinil reached down and helped Myriam up, who, to Will's embarrassment, had no issues settling on the horse. He was sure she even shot him a small smirk. It brought back the anger about everything that had happened at the Anvil. If she had told him, everything could have been different. Of course, she could use that argument as well. If he had told her the truth in the Guild, things could have been different.

Will knew that might be correct, but the situation was much higher stakes in the birthplace of the gods. Not that it mattered. Not now. What was done was done. The only thing he could do was try to make sense of this whirlwind of change his life had become since the day he stole that crystal from the Mistlands.

"Are you going to stand there like surprised oxen all day, William Reis? Or are you going to take my hand and get on the horse?" Ride Captain Julis reached her hand lower.

Will blinked in surprise, and his fading embarrassment flared back into focus. "Oh sorry. Was...thinking." Will took her hand and tried to figure out what to do.

"Put your foot there, on the back side of the foot stirrup and push yourself up and over. I'll pull." Ride Captain Julis explained.

Will did so and almost lost his grip as he was jerked up. This Ride Captain was much stronger than she looked. He managed to get one leg thrown over the back of the horse without looking too foolish, though the total lack of flexibility was clear. He wondered for a moment how the Gorom got on his horse. Or her horse. He'd never seen a female Gorom, so he had no idea what they looked like.

The Ride Captain mumbled something to the animal carrying them, and they set off at a pace far slower than the one the riders had taken to get to him and Myriam. Will wondered if that was because they were being courteous. Will rather wished they were in a wagon, though. Riding on the horse itself felt odd to him, the slight up and down movement, the knowledge that this animal could throw him off without notice. He didn't like it.

"William Reis. You've seen a Windtalker before?" Ride Captain Julis asked as she directed the horse.

Will glanced over at the other riders. The Trinil carrying Myriam was talking, and she was answering, but he couldn't make out the conversation over the sound of the hoofbeats. "Yes. One. Near the Anvil of Souls. She helped us."

"Us? You and your friend Myriam VolFar?" The Ride Captain waved a hand toward Myriam.

"Yes. And one other. Who didn't survive." Will drifted into thought about Regin. He hoped that Regin got the rest he deserved. "Myriam isn't my friend. Well, maybe she is. I don't know. I know little anymore, it seems."

Ride Captain Julis nodded but said nothing for a long moment. They rode in relative quiet, though he could see Myriam still deep in conversation with the Trinil. It somewhat surprised him to see her wipe her face a few times. Tears? The shame came at once. Of course, tears. *Regin.*

Regin. He'd hated the man, then had grown to like him. A good friend. The best friend William had ever had that wasn't family. His whole life, Will had kept an arm's length from most people close to his own age. He'd been friends with Duncan and Haltim. Though Duncan was family, and Haltim was a father figure.

But other young men and women in the Reach? He'd been friendly enough, but never really connected with them. He'd never known what to say, what to do. So, he'd kept working the forge and helping miners. No one had ever disliked him, but there had been this gap. He'd never been able to explain it.

But Regin had been different. Maybe it was because of the circumstances. From being enemies, to being companions, to being whatever it had been once he'd been named Forgemaster. He'd always been straight with Will. Only the situation with Myriam had made him not be. And that for once Will could understand. He would miss him. The counsel, the voice with some experience. The willingness to do whatever needed to be done.

He could handle that grief, though. Losing Duncan, losing Amder, those... he couldn't deal with right now. Those feelings brought waves of sorrow, and more anger towards the one person he still felt was responsible. Myriam.

"The Windtalker you met. Do you remember her name?" Ride Captain Julis broke the silence. "There's not a lot of my race in the world. And even less in the city."

"Her name was Lorelei. Called herself the Mistral?" William remembered seeing her for the first time. That had been a shock, even more so after the sparks burned pit that the Gorom caves and that red flowered tree had been. She'd been a boon beyond measure at the time.

"The Mistral?? You met her?" Ride Captain Julis stopped her horse and turned as much as she could towards Will. Her voice rose with each word. "Are you sure?"

"Yes. But why?" Will wondered if he'd said something wrong. What was the protocol for this sort of thing? "She helped us after we'd gone through some very rough places. Though she left as quickly as she found us."

Ride Captain Julis snorted a laugh at that. "That does sound like her. Forgive me, but for you have seen another Windtalker is strange enough, but to see the holiest of my kin, at least according to that same kin, that's unheard of."

Will almost smiled at the sound of her voice. It felt good for a moment, before everything came crashing down again. He felt that there was one question he needed to ask, something this Windtalker had said. "Ride Captain Julis, pardon, but what did you mean by boon?"

Chapter 3.

"The Boon. Magic. Or as those in the lower city call it, the 'knack'." The Ride Captain fell silent as she spurred the horse to move faster. "Truthfully William Reis, I've seen no one marked like the two of you are. I'm sure there's a story there. But it's not my place to ask those questions."

"Call me Will, or William. Using my full name doesn't sound right." Will asked. Despite the situation, despite all the heartache and turmoil of the last days, he liked this Ride Captain Julis. He pushed away the feelings that rose again in response to his thinking about the last day.

He should be exhausted. The realization made him nearly fall off the horse. He hadn't slept in an unknown number of hours. He hadn't eaten anything in… he couldn't remember. Nor had he drunk anything in an unknown amount of time. And yet, here he was, he should have collapsed. He looked down at the thick blue lines that swept up his arms. A side effect of whatever this was?

"I don't have any magic. I don't know what this is. I was… injured when we entered a pool of power, that strange blue sand like substance. Then it was chaos and madness. Every wound burned, everything hurt. And then it didn't, and we appeared here." Will explained. "I'm not magic."

Ride Captain Julis didn't answer, and the ground moved past them, as the fog that shrouded the city grew closer and thicker as they approached. Will noticed that the closer they got to the strange mist, the more he felt unwelcome, as if he wasn't supposed to be here.

"You should be feeling a ward by now." Ride Captain Julis remarked. "A pressure in your head. A feeling that you want to go somewhere else, anywhere else than here. It will pass."

Will didn't answer. He was too busy trying not to leap off the horse. He had to get out of this place. This was wrong. Very wrong. Will turned to look at Myriam, to find her slumped over, unconscious! The Trinil had grabbed her arms where she had been holding onto him and kept riding. Will couldn't breathe. He had to go! He steeled himself, and with a lunge, he threw himself to the far side, away from the other riders. A moment of weightlessness, and then, pain. He landed hard; on the same shoulder he'd injured multiple times now. A crunch, accompanied by a raw saw blade of pain, cut through him as he tried to breathe.

He heard a muttered curse as the riders stopped and the Ride Captain Julis came towards him. How could he have ever liked her? Trusted her? She was going to kill him, or worse! Will pushed himself up with his one good arm and tried to stumble away. He had to get away. But where? There was nowhere to go.

One glance back towards the Ride Captain spurred him to run. She held a long black rod in her hand, and she was going to hit him with it! Will tried to pull out his hammer, doing so but stumbling at the same time. Which ended up being a happy accident as the black rod tip went cutting through the air above his head.

Remembering Vin's teaching, Will tried to take a decent defensive stance. He noted the other riders weren't after him, only the Ride Captain. His adversary wheeled her horse around, and much to his surprise, accelerated at a speed he'd not even guessed the animal could reach. Before he could even begin to pivot on his hips to add force to the blow, the black rod hit him, chest first.

Ice. Cold, hard ice covered him. A blackness followed, and the last thing he saw was the Ride Captain's face staring down at him.

Myriam fought back a whirlwind of emotion. She was angry, hurt, crushed, and worried at the same time. How dare William blame her for what had happened? After she had saved his life. But yet, in a way, he was right. She hadn't trusted him enough to tell him the truth. About the voice, about the crystal. And now it was just her and him, because Regin was gone.

She wiped her eyes with the back of her hand, not surprised by the wetness she saw there. Regin. It had only been a matter of hours at most for her. She missed him. That way the corner of his mouth crooked up when he looked at her. The way he smelled. It wasn't fair he had died, and yet William had been brought back to life, why hadn't Regin? She would trade… NO. She wouldn't. Falling into that trap wouldn't make anything better. It would make her resent William even more. She was as surprised as he had been when they had arrived here, wherever here was. She had begged to get somewhere away from her mistake. Somewhere 'safe' she had thought. She didn't understand what had happened to them though, not in those long moments of being engulfed in, something. It had hurt, fiery sharp pain. She wondered if she looked as strange as William did to her. The bizarre blue eyes, the blue twisting lines up his arms. Even that hammer was marked.

She never should have listened to that voice. William was right, as much as it hurt her to say it. If she hadn't done what she did, there was a chance Regin would still be alive. Maybe. Maybe not. It was hard to make sense of the order of things now. Her mind was a broken mess of times and dates, mixed together like some mad baker's spice mix.

And now she was here, riding on a horse, behind a Trinil wearing armor, heading into a strange city. None of this made any sense. The Trinil had only asked her name, and she soon found herself talking to the guard as if she had known him her whole life. Explaining what they had done, and why. To his credit, or her credit, it was hard to tell with the Trinil's armor on. The Trinil hadn't interrupted, not even once.

She spared a look mid-sentence to see William talking to that Ride Captain, another Windtalker. William must be enthralled. She had seen the look on his face with that other one had taken them in for the night, and here was another one, talking to him. Not that she was jealous, but still.

Regin. She hadn't been sure since those Gorom caves that any of them would make it out of this adventure alive. They had started this quest as four, and now they were down to two. A memory of a spear breaking, a sound like a tree breaking in half flickered around her mind. But it was gone as soon as she tried to think about it. The sorrow the idea brought though was all too real.

"Myriam VolFar, why did you stop talking? I found the story of your adventure to be quite the sweeping tale." The Trinil spoke, breaking the growing silence that had gripped her.

"Just thinking. I miss the others. I miss Vin, I miss Regin..." Myriam felt a near avalanche of sorrow as she said Regin's name out loud. "Who were they? You said their names, but nothing else." The Trinil asked as they guided the horse expertly across the ground.

Myriam knew he was fishing for information. Trying to get more information out of her, maybe compare it to whatever William was saying. That man needs to learn the benefit of keeping his mouth shut. It didn't matter, though. Neither one of them was in any shape to fight or run.

"Vin. Captain Vin Tolin. War veteran, former Captain in the Palnor army. We, or really William, convinced him to join us at one point during the attack on the Reach by the Valni. He died deep, underground, in the Vinik caves. Regin was a Guildmaster." Myriam stopped talking as she remembered his face. The feeling of being wrapped up in his arms. A sob burst forth, deep and real. Why hadn't he come back with William? *Why? It wasn't fair...*

"Hush. Do not worry. All can happen here." The Trinil seemed to whisper as she heard a clicking sound, and then utter blackness. And the last thing she remembered was wondering why she had opened her mouth at all.

Chapter 4.

William became aware of things around him. A hard floor. It was cool, almost cold. Laying on the floor didn't feel very good though, so he pushed himself up, or at least tried to. He struggled at first to find the strength. What had happened? He'd been talking to the Ride Captain when he'd what blacked out? Will shook his head. No, she had done something.

Had she? He hurt; his side hurt a lot worse now. His shoulder… he reached up and quickly pulled his hand away. That wasn't the shape his bones should make under his skin. Not even close. He should be screaming in agony, but while it hurt, he found himself able to think and function. Will shook his head again, wincing at the small surges of fiery pain that came with the movement, pain bouncing around his head.

The hurt subsided, and he could take in the room he was in. Smooth polished floor, some kind of marble by the looks of it. So not some place poor. Walls smooth gray rock. No windows. No furniture other than a pair of chairs. And a door. A door made of solid metal from the looks of it. It all screamed one thing. Jail. Prison. Oh, a nice jail, but a jail all the same.

He finally hauled himself upright, fighting the weakness and pain that seemed to fill him now. He pulled a chair over to himself and half sat, half fell into the thing. So why was he in jail? He had done nothing to warrant that. At least he thought so. This was all too much. He wanted to scream, cry, and fall into a bed and not get up for days. Every bit of the last few days wore on him. No world altering danger, no dead gods, no anger… only wonderful boring normality.

He realized that he wasn't even sure how this room was being lit. No torches, no lamps, but yet… glows? It wasn't exactly the same, but there were patches of light giving rock in the ceiling of his fancy cell. And it was a cell. Will closed his eyes for a moment but opened them again, closing them only brought a swirling dizziness and nausea that threatened to overcome him.

He needed a healer. A setter would be fine as well. Then a good meal, a lot of water, and a place to sleep. Thinking about what he needed to do helped, it gave him a sense of purpose. A plan forward. Not that he could do anything about even one of those things right now. Why had that Ride Captain hit him with that… whatever she had hit him with? Something about a ward, and then… cold. Deep dark cold. Then here. Sparks burn it, where was here? In the city he guessed. That strange and huge city they had seen. None of this made sense to him. None of it.

He nearly missed the first change when the door opened. If his eyes had been closed, he never would have even known. Silently it opened and two individuals walked in. Nice artistry then on that door. He couldn't help but suppress a slight chuckle at the thought. Once a craftsman, always a craftsman.

The two people who entered couldn't be more different. One he knew, or at least knew who they were. The Ride Captain. She stood watching him with an almost concerned look, but he noticed her hands stayed near that same black rod, and a rather well-worn leather hilted dagger on the other side. The other figure was something or someone Will had no idea about. Almost as tall as a Trinil, but with features much more human. But he was thick, powerful. He was even bigger than master Greenmar back in Ture. This new figure was wearing a grey and blue tunic, but it was the boots and leather apron that drew Will's eyes. Those were forging boots, and thick leather aprons were standard garb for anyone working with heat. Exactly what you use when smelting. Strange though that he couldn't smell any trace of the forge on this new person, even if you could see tell-tale burn marks and singes in places.

"I see you are awake. Good. I apologize for the rod, but the ward hit you hard." The Ride Captain sat down in the other chair, but Will noticed she still kept her hands near her weapons. "Now, William Reis, we should talk."

Will tried in vain to figure out what else he could do, but it was answer her questions or what? Be left here? He was too sparks burned exhausted to worry about it anymore. "Fine."

The Ride Captain removed her helm, her long hair shining. "Good.

Now, before I continue, the man with me is Tarn Rewil Dask. He will ask some questions as well."

Will nodded at the enormous figure. He did not know who this man was, but if he wanted to ask questions, William wasn't about to tell him no.

"The Tarn here is the leader of our crafters. Normally he wouldn't be here for this kind of thing, but your particular background was a subject of some speculation with the other Tarns, so he offered to come." The Ride Captain pointed to the large man. "Please give him the respect to answer his questions."

Tarn? Tarn was some kind of title? Will searched his memory for things Regin had taught about nobles and rulers, but he couldn't remember anything about leaders called 'Tarn' before. Will had only ever been in an apprentice class, though, and that didn't deal with the southern lands at all. Still, he tried to sit up more, masking the raw edge of pain that greeted his moving of the injured shoulder.

"You know what I am? Or what I was, I guess." Will asked, finally picking up on the fact that they knew about his past as the Forgemaster of Amder, for however briefly that was.

"Yes, but what do you mean was?" The Ride Captain sat back in her chair, her armor glinting in… interesting places.

Will shook his head to clear it as best he could. "Well, since you almost know everything anyway… Amder is dead. Again. Gone. But on the plus side, so is Valnijz. I'm not the Forgemaster, not anymore." Will spoke calmly.

The reaction was anything but. The Ride Captain stood so fast the chair fell backward, and this hulking Tarn gave forth a very loud gasp. "What do you mean??" The Ride Captain blurted out.

Will was surprised at their reaction, but then again, he'd been dealing with gods for months now. *Maybe I am getting too jaded for all this.* "At the Anvil of Souls, Amder and Valnijz were… killed. I think. I wasn't part of that. My…" Will paused. His feelings about Myriam were still so sharp, hard even. "The person I was found with, they were involved."

The Tarn stepped forward now. "You are telling me that the two gods of humans are now one? Right as we speak?" The Tarn's voice was deep. So deep as to make the bones in Will's body almost itch.

"I guess. I died; you know. I had all the power of Amder pulled through me into… I don't know what. I died. I am still not sure why, but the new person, new god I should guess, brought me back to life in some sort of attempt to get something from Myriam. I can't remember what." Will wasn't an expert on people, but he could tell this news worried them. Both had turned much paler since the news of Amder's death.

Will kept going. If they were going to let him speak, he might as well say something useful. "Look, I'll be happy to answer questions you have that I can. But right now, I need a setter for this shoulder. Add in a meal, a drink, a bath, and a bed. I just…." Will shook his head and fought back the sorrow that came with a sudden rush. "I can't. I just can't."

Ride Captain Julis gave him a long look and then turned to the Tarn. Something seemed to pass between them, though Will heard nothing and saw nothing other than the two of them looking at each other with a few glances his way.

"Done." Tarn Rewil slapped his hands together, the loud meaty sound loud enough to give Will an even larger headache.

The Ride Captain nodded. "We will take care of your hurts and provide what you have requested. In return you will answer our questions."

"Fine." Will slumped farther into the chair. Why did everything feel so strange? He wondered if she'd hit him again with the rod, but it was still there by her side. At least he thought it was as the darkness claimed him again.

Myriam awoke groggy but unhurt. She'd been talking to that strange Trinil and then, what? She couldn't think clearly. Her thoughts skittered away like water on a hot rock. Did I pass out? Too tired maybe? If that had been the case, she wasn't much better yet. She was still tired. Thirsty. Hungry. And she was alone. The room she was in was as bare as a room could be. White polished stone, light from… glowstones? Hard to tell.

It was cold in here too. All she had on was one filthy tunic and equally unclean pants and boots. There was a door, or at least it might be a door. No handle that she could see, no window, no opening. If it hadn't been spotless, she'd have sworn she was in a jail. The door opened, and in walked that Ride Captain, and an older kind looking man in green robes with a bright red belt. "Myriam VolFar?" The Ride Captain spoke as the older man walked to the far end of the room and leaned back against the wall. His eyes never left Myriam though. They darted around her figure. At first, she wanted to slap him, then realized what he was looking at wasn't her. It was the blue markings that had appeared all over her since that, whatever it had been.

"Your name is Myriam VolFar, correct?" the Ride Captain spoke again.

"Yes. Where am I?" Myriam looked around again, realizing with a jolt that Will wasn't here. "William? Where is he? Is he all right?"

Ride Captain Julis removed her interlocking metal gloves and held up a copper-skinned hand. "William Reis is… mostly fine."

"What do you mean? What did you do to him?" Myriam stood. "You better not have hurt him. He's…" she trailed off, unsure of what to say next. The Forgemaster? No, not anymore. Important to her? Well, no, not exactly.

"Your friend isn't hurt by our hand. He is exhausted and has a shoulder that needs healing. On top of half a dozen bruises and scrapes. Some older injuries hadn't healed as well." The older man spoke up. "He's sleeping, then he will get some food and get a bath."

Myriam nodded. "Good." She didn't know what else to say. As the older man spoke, she realized for the first time how much William had gone through. She'd been there for a lot of it but hadn't put it together. *Or maybe I hadn't wanted to.*

Ride Captain Julis cleared her throat. "Tarn Mikol, may I continue, please?"

The older man nodded. "My apologies Ride Captain."

"We have some questions. Then you will get food, bath, and rest. Or in whatever order you prefer." The Ride Captain paced the room. "Now, you and William's stories mesh well, but I want to get more information.

You used a crystal in the Anvil of Souls to do what exactly? Where did this crystal come from?"

Myriam shook her head. She didn't know what William had said to these people. Of course, she had been babbling as well when she'd been on that horse earlier. "I heard a voice. It… Saved me in the Gorom caves. It saved Regin's life once. I felt like I should do what it asked. All I had to do was put the crystal on a pillar. When the voice told me to. I didn't know what would happen. It all happened so fast."

"Did you ever ask?" The Ride Captain crossed her arms, locking her eyes on Myriam.

Myriam wanted to squirm out of that gaze. For all the world, it reminded her of her father back at the Inn, when she'd done something stupid and gotten called on it. It hadn't happened often, but there had been a few times when she was younger that look had come out.

"Sort of." Myriam shook her head and broke the gaze, looking up at the ceiling. "I don't have an excuse. Sure, I should have looked into it more. I shouldn't have done it. But the voice, this unnamed god, he helped me. He helped those I cared about. I thought I was doing the right thing."

The older man, this Tarn Mikol, started upright then. "Unnamed God? Did you say unnamed?"

"Yes. It wanted me to name it. I never did. I don't know why." Myriam watched as the older man's face lost its kindness for a moment and fell into a serious frown.

"Does that matter? Can someone tell me exactly what is going on?" Myriam felt like she wanted to scream, or cry, or both.

The Ride Captain turned towards the Tarn and while no words were spoken that she could hear, they seemed to communicate somehow. After what seemed like far too long, the Ride Captain turned towards her and smiled. "This is what we are going to do. We will get you fixed up, and William Reis as well and then we will explain everything."

Myriam wasn't sure if she believed them, but at this point, what did she have to lose?

Chapter 5.

Rewil walked in silence away from the holding cells. This day was not what he had expected it to be. He'd been planning on setting a new set of guardian constructs up. He'd finally found a way to increase working time before they had to be brought down to be repowered again. Or at least he'd thought he had. He hadn't actually tested it.

But now, this had changed everything. William Reis, the Forgemaster of the half god Amder, now marked by the magic in ways never seen before, was sitting in a holding cell. And a friend of his, someone named Myriam? As if reading his thoughts, Mikol appeared sitting on a bench ahead of him. *Waiting for me. That's not a good sign.*

He had nothing against Mikol. In fact, of all the other Tarns, Mikol was the one he actually thought was worth the title. Mikol was the Tarn of the Healers. It didn't matter if it involved using the power to make people well again, Tarn Mikol Nese was in charge of it. They didn't interact much day to day. He was the Tarn of the Crafters; they dealt in metal and magic. The only time there was even communication was when a crafter was injured or one of the crafters wares had broken. Still, Mikol had backed him for his role as Tarn. He was a good sort.

"Ah, Tarn Rewil Dask. Just the man I was looking for." Mikol stood, and while he still carried his usual smiling complexion, Rewil noticed he kept glancing down.

"Just Rewil. We are both Tarns, you know that. No need to be formal, my friend." Rewil gave Mikol a smile that did not last long. "And I know why you are here. It's about our guests, shall we call them?"

"Yes. I spoke to the woman, Myriam. Myriam VolFar. Strange names these northerners have. And you spoke to the other one, the man, William Reis." Mikol added.

"Yes." Rewil said nothing else. It hadn't been a question, just a statement.

"Rewil, we have a problem. They did it. You know they did it." Mikol lowered his voice. Not that anyone came near them. Anyone who saw them here in the ring around the lower city turned right around and walked the other way when two Tarns were speaking. "I know. I don't know if I can believe it." Rewil shifted his weight from one foot to the other. He had tried hard to think about that fact. If those two had brought the sundered god back, that meant nothing good.

"They did. But not all is lost. The reborn one named the woman as his namer. And she refused to give him one." Mikol kept his voice low. "We must call a commons of the Tarns. Now."

She hadn't named the new god yet? Mikol was right. And this was worthy of such a summons. A sour taste rose in his mouth. Nollew Loncel wouldn't think so, but that man was a headache anytime. He'd rather ignore the man these days, but being as how Nollew was the Tarn of the Casters, that wasn't really an option.

"I agree. Come, we will go to the chambers now. We will issue the call from there." Rewil spoke quickly and marched off, heading to the quickway.

Mikol nodded and followed, his long green robes somehow not impeding his progress. "Is the man marked? I have to admit, I nearly passed out when I saw this Myriam woman. I've seen no one that the magic bonded to so strongly. Her boon of power is massive, even if she does not know."

Rewil nodded. He'd had the same reaction when looking at that William Reis character. And his hammer. Golden it was, but also covered in a swirling bright blue. Raw magic. Pure raw power. He'd never seen any item ever bond to the power in that way. And to William Reis himself. "The question is, what does it mean?" Rewil replied as the quickway entrance came into view.

"I wish I knew." Mikol shook his head. "I had hoped to never see this day. I would often hope that a future Tarn would have to deal with this. Not me. Not now."

Rewil didn't answer. How could he? He felt the same. This whole thing had been esoteric. Only the Tarns even knew about it. From the founding of the city till now, the rulers of the city had known, if the broken god is healed, ruin will ride forth. When Amder had been reborn a few months ago, that had caused some concern. Enough for the City to investigate, only to discover that Valnijz had been destroyed.

That was fine. Amder was a known figure. And unlike the other gods, being only half a god meant he was someone uninterested in the god's true purpose. And he was at least sane. Valnijz would have been far worse. But now, somehow, the broken god had been reborn.

But the new god was unnamed. This meant he wasn't fully healed. Yet. *And we have the namer.*

Mikol stood in the quickway, watching his fellow Tarn. Rewil was a strange man. Man. Rewil was a crossbreed. Trinil, Gorom, human, and who knew what else made up his background. Not that Mikol cared, He was more interested in an academic fashion. Mikol frowned as he considered the coming commons. He'd have to keep a close hand on Tarn Nollew and Tarn Yulisia. His plans hadn't included this new information, the sundered god remade, but yet unnamed.

Nollew wouldn't greet their information well. And he'd take the information from Rewil even worse, though that was to be expected. Mikol would have to be the main speaker. He'd rather let others do the talking. Then he could observe and add when necessary. Pushing others to the right decision or at least the decision he wanted, reading their bodies as they decided on a course of action. He knew how to read the actions of others.

His thoughts went back to the two currently awaiting them in the holding cells. He hadn't seen this William Reis, but Rewil's description had filled in enough for him after meeting Myriam. He really had nearly fallen when he'd first seen her. The power had bonded itself to her in a way never seen. His own boon only had a small physical presence, a sunburst of blue on his chest. Even Nollew with his blue face markings that appeared when he was working all the power he could call forth was not even half as marked as the woman was.

"What's so amusing?" Rewil's voice interrupted Mikol's thoughts. "You are over there smiling. I'd think the last thing you'd be is happy when they are here, now in this situation."

"I'm not happy. But…" Mikol lowered his voice, just in case. "I was thinking about how much these newcomers' boon of power will annoy Nollew." Rewil sat still for a moment before a low booming laugh escaped the man. "Ha! I hadn't thought about that. He'll be fit to be a sour angry man to be sure."

"Yes. Look Rewil, knowing Nollew the way we both do, I'd better do the talking here." Mikol watched out a narrow window as the quickway sped up out of the ring and over the low city, its warrens of overbuilt buildings and haphazard construction giving way to more order and planning as they got closer to the spire.

Rewil nodded, but a small low growl escaped him. "For the better, yes, but if Nollew gets out of hand, I will give that man a…"

"Let it go Rewil. He's powerful, but that power only goes so far." Mikol reached out with his power, feeling the sharp edges of Rewil's emotions. Anger. Hurt. Shame. Mikol smoothed out the edges, not ridding the man of the feelings, but not letting them hurt him so. Mikol did not need him angry, not right now.

Mikol wasn't supposed to do that, but he'd met no one who was as skilled as he was at managing the emotions of others. He needed Rewil to have a cooler head, and he would not let some minor paltry rules stop him. The tension in his fellow Tarn's shoulders and jaw relaxed. Good. He knew Rewil would be less than happy if he knew Mikol had been poking around with his emotions, but he would never know. No one ever did.

The quickway door flashed green and then opened into the Antechamber of the Tarns. Mikol always found the quickways somewhat strange. Living systems, bodies and minds he could handle with a finesse and the lightest touch. But things like the quickways, the guardian constructs? So strange. Rewil had tried once to explain how it worked, but had given up after Mikol had asked the same question about eight times.

Rewil followed him, as they walked through the antechamber, towards the lone guardian construct. Massive things, the constructs were a melding of magic and metal. So many gears and thousands of parts. They were one of the crowning achievements of the Crafters and Rewil's pride.

"See Mikol? Any living guard might fall asleep, be distracted. But not a guardian. As long as the magic flows, it will be here. Alert. Awake. Doing its job." Rewil's voice echoed in the large, nearly empty room. The guardian made no noise other than a whirring series of tiny clicks as it moved away from the door it was blocking. Mikol was rather glad the things didn't talk. He found the idea of talking machines to be distasteful.

"Yes. I suppose." Mikol finally said, sensing the desire for a response from his companion.

Rewil stopped and scowled. "Nollew is already here. As well as Yulisia. Grib is almost here."

Mikol didn't bother asking how he knew. All the Tarns had their secrets. "It makes sense that Yulisia is here. She and Nollew are intertwined. And Grib is always late."

Rewil grunted in response. Mikol shared the frustration he knew the man was feeling. Yulisia Ecir was the Tarn of Knowledge. If Nollew was the Tarn of the magic and its flow, Yulisia was the keeper of all knowledge. She was supposed to be the most neutral of them all, curating everything from all their sectors. But considering the rumors that Mikol knew were very true, she and Nollew were lovers, and so she played favorites.

Grib Xermom was another matter. The Tarn of the City. The largest section. Everyone who wasn't a crafter, a healer, a librarian, or a caster. Grib didn't even live in the upper city, he held court on the border of the middle city and the lower city. It wasn't that Mikol didn't like Grib. Mikol had been highly influential in him getting his current position, but the man was somewhat maddening in his decisions. But he was the one person he and Rewil needed today.

Nollew would almost certainly want the two problems that had appeared today to be either held, indefinitely, and in total censure at best. At worst, he'd want them sanctioned. Yulisia would vote for whatever Nollew wanted in most cases. Grib would be the deciding vote. The man switched sides as if every vote was a game of catch, and he was trying to both throw and catch what he threw.

Rewil entered the meeting room first, and Mikol followed. He had to convince Grib that the strangers should stay. If not, everything he'd planned would fall apart.

Chapter 6.

Rewil made his way to his chair, refusing to look at Nollew and Yulisia. He knew what faces they would be making. His chair was almost three times larger than the others. He'd made it himself soon after becoming the Tarn of the Crafters. He liked that chair. It was comfortable, and if he was going to have to sit here and listen to the others drone on, he was at least going to do it in comfort.

And for having to listen to Nollew, he'd built in a grip on the side. Something he could squeeze to the greatest power he could, so he didn't punch the man. He truly disliked Nollew. He had utmost respect for the position, but personally, the man was disgusting. Rewil spent almost all his time working with others in the casters when he needed to, which was often. Usually, they were members of the magical experts who Nollew had banished for whatever reason.

In the crafters, a Tarn was an elected position. They met, voted, and the winner was Tarn until either he died, or until the other crafters replaced him. Each section had their own rules though. Rewil did not know how the casters did it. Nollew had been Tarn for a long time and would probably stay that way. So different now than the old days.

They had been friends once, worked together on some projects even. Once. But the man had changed. His mind had gotten full of poison, and then he'd poisoned Rewil's only close friend. Yulisia.

Yulisia. They had been close; she had always been kind and had a razor sharp mind that Rewil appreciated. Even before her raising to Tarn, they had known each other. She had been one of the first to congratulate him upon his own election to Tarn. And for a few months after her own raising, she had been a careful observer and treated everyone with respect. Then, somehow, someway, Nollew had taken her in, and she'd changed.

Rewil even half wondered if the whispers were true, that they were lovers but that Nollew had used some forbidden working to control her. He had no proof, of course. Nollew was petty, mean, and intolerant. But the man was as smart as anyone Rewil had ever met, and more careful by far.

Settling into his chair, Rewil finally looked at the others. Yulisia wore her traditional robes, her nearly white skin melding to the fabric. She was a human, of course, as was Nollew. Her long white blond hair made her skin look even paler. And next to her, Nollew. Rewil wasn't sure what she saw in the man. He looked average at best. Slightly plump, with a nose too large for his narrow face, Nollew was not a handsome man. But his eyes... even from across the table, Rewil could feel the hate. *Hate.*

Nollew was confident, though. A Tarn. And the Tarn of what many thought was the most powerful section, the users of magic. Lower rungs had their knacks, but the main users of the actual power were all under the leadership of that man. A section devoted to finding new ways to use the power. Usually, to kill.

"Tarn Rewil, what a surprise that you would convince Mikol to call this commons. Even though we have a meeting scheduled for the day after tomorrow. That's in two days, if you didn't know." Nollew spoke slowly. He always spoke to Rewil that way. Rewil knew he was only trying to hint that Rewil couldn't keep up.

It was more bigoted nonsense. Rewil did not get to be the Tarn of the Crafters by being slow. But he let it slide. The coming commons would be fraught enough. He was somewhat surprised that Nollew didn't seem to know what was going on, though. It could be a trap; he wouldn't be surprised to find that it was.

Mikol cleared his throat. "Tarn Grib will be here in a moment. But since he already knows of the situation, we can start now."

"What waste of time are we doing now?" Tarn Yulisia asked as she yawned. Reaching over to stroke Nollews hair.

Mikol frowned. The bond between Nollew and Yulisia was growing... But it wouldn't be fixed today. "Strangers. Two new arrivals. As Rewil and I were on duty today, it fell to us to speak with them. And..."

Nollew stood. "You called us here to discuss two strangers? I'd expect that level of stupidity from Rewil here, but not you, Mikol." Nollew reached a hand out to help Yulisia up. "Come, since we are up and dressed, let's go get dinner out." Nollew threw a somewhat lewd smile towards his female companion. "Sit." Tarn Grib came marching in finally. A full-blooded Gorom, Grib was shorter than the rest of them, but stocky. The only one that he couldn't be considered stronger than was Rewil. Grib at least listened, and so far, had shown no interest in upsetting the balance in the city. Far better than his unfortunate predecessor. Nasty business, that.

Nollew for once listened and sat without a word, though his already sour expression got even more so. "Since it's now three to two, I will listen to whatever is so important."

Mikol waved the others to their seats, and all, even Yulisia, did so. "We had two strangers appear today in the valley. Not on the borders, but in the actual valley."

"That's impossible." Yulisia shot back. "The wards wouldn't allow it."

"Yesterday, I would have agreed with you. Yet, they did. And they didn't get here over the mountains. They came here from the Anvil of Souls." Mikol spoke the words carefully, watching their faces.

Rewil, having already known, did not react. Grib's eyebrows shot up before his face settled into a frown. But the faces of Nollew and Yulisia were the ones Mikol was the most interested in. Nollew went from sour to furious, and Yulisia turned even paler, if that was possible.

"That can NOT happen! I made the wards myself!" Nollew yelled as he stood, breaking decorum. "Those wards have stood for hundreds of years; each Tarn of my section remakes them. It is impossible!"

"And yet, they did. For the one thing we have feared has come to pass." Mikol took a deep breath and before the others could speak, launched into his explanation. The return of the broken god. Amder was gone. Valnijz was gone. A new god was born.

Yulisia, already pale, had gone even paler at this news, and slumped back in her chair, Mikol watched her. *Good. She may be under Nollew's spell, but she's still a scholar. She's read the same works I have.* Nollew seemed to flicker from emotion to emotion. Fear, anger, confusion. Mikol wasn't used to seeing the man this way. He rather enjoyed taking Nollew down a few pegs. "So, the two responsible for this return, they are here?" Grib spoke up then, looking down at the table, his face hard to see.

"Yes. Though one was far more involved than the other. One is the former Forgemaster of Amder, the other, the woman named Myriam VolFar, is the one who did the actual ceremony." Mikol paused for effect. "But we have one unexpected turn of events. She is the namer, and she has not given the new god a name yet."

Mikol often had thought about the different types of silence. There was just quiet, or a peaceful silence. And then there was the silence that had covered the room. The return of the broken god wasn't complete. There was a chance. But a chance for what? Each of his fellow Tarns sat still. Rewil had already internalized his own answer, and Mikol knew what his aim was. Rewil wasn't a deep man. He wanted the crafter. William Reis, the former Forgemaster of Amder.

"Sanction." Nollew spoke, breaking the quiet with two spat out words. "Sanction them now."

"Yes, sanction them. Be done with it." Yulisia added, the paleness of her skin turning a reddish hint with her own bloodlust.

Grib said nothing. Mikol had expected that, though. "There's two problems with killing them. One, if we kill the namer, that frees the reborn god to name a new namer, and we've thrown away any chance we have to control the situation. And two, there's the matter of their boon."

"Boon? How can they have a boon??" Yulisia leaned forward. "What are you not telling us, Mikol?"

"When they appeared, they traveled here from the Anvil of Souls via raw magic. It has bonded to them, both of them. As it stands right now, both have a larger gift of raw power than any one of us. In truth, a gift more than all of us put together."

The effect of his words surprised even him. Nollew and Yulisia turned such shades of red anger that Mikol wondered if his skills as a healer were going to be needed. But that wasn't the surprising part. Grib. Grib was the surprising part. He reacted, of course, but it was an act. *He already knew. But how?* The argument went long into the night. And the votes. To let them both in, with William to enter the Crafters section, and Myriam offered a position with the healers. Nollew, Yulisia and Grib all agreed that there was no way for Rewil to get both.

Nollew had made a hard pull to get the woman into either his or Yulisia's section, but had failed. Grib had voted against it every single time. Nollew and Yulisia left together without a word as soon as the final vote had been taken. Both ignored Rewil for a change, leaving the chamber in a hurry. *No doubt plotting how to turn this to their advantage.*

Grib left next, with a nod to both Rewil and Mikol. *I may have underestimated that Tarn. He bears close watching.* Mikol frowned as Grib left.

"Thank you Mikol. I doubt I could have kept my composure when speaking to…." Rewil didn't finish his sentence, standing finally and giving a stretch. "I will see you in the morning at the holding cells. I assume you will get my newest member a healer tonight?"

Mikol nodded as the last of the other Tarns left the room, leaving Mikol alone. He looked out over the city, his city. For Mikol was the true power here. Everybody was playing their part, exactly the way he wanted it.

"Do you think it worked?"

"I think so. He seemed convinced. The others as well."

"He's hard to resist, isn't he?"

"Very. It somewhat terrifies me how powerful he is. We must tread carefully."

"I agree. We play the part until it is time to make our move. Do you think these newcomers will change anything?"

"I am not sure. New pieces to the game, at least. I don't want them to be part of this."

"I hope we made the right choice. Why now? Why these two people? It can't be coincidence that the now former Forgemaster of Amder and the one person who rejoined a god simply appear here, now?"

"I cannot say. But it is troubling."

Chapter 7.

Awareness came over Myriam slowly. Her eyes didn't want to focus, and she had to wipe who knows what out of them, but she was awake at least. She was better. Not anywhere close to how she should feel, but better. She needed a bath still, and the return of conscious thought also brought some serious hunger and thirst pangs. She'd been waiting here when a Trinil had come in with a cot and some blankets. Silently the cot had been setup and then, just like that, the Trinil had gone, without saying a word.

Myriam had laid down on the cot for only a moment. It was more comfortable than the floor, and that had been the last thing she remembered. *I was far more tired than I believed.* She reached down, rubbing the blanket between two fingers. Strange fabric. She'd seen nothing like it. They did not weave it even that she could see. No telltale weft, or the feeling of tiny threads under her fingers. Soft though. One more minor strangeness to go along with everything else here. Wherever 'here' was.

The door opened again, but at least this time accompanied by a knock. Her hunger and thirst nearly overwhelmed her as in walked the older man from the night before, and two others she hadn't seen before carrying trays of food and drink. She didn't know what it was, but the smell of it almost made her leap forward in want.

"Good day Myriam. You don't mind me calling you Myriam, do you? Or would you prefer a different name?" The older man waved his hand as another person entered the room with a strange long bundle of metal poles that, with a twist, seemed to expand into a table with two built in places to sit. Part of her mind was surprised and curious about the contraption, but the rest of her was so fixated on the food, all she could do was open her mouth in surprise and try not to drool. The man's question finally penetrated her thoughts. "Myriam is fine."

"Good. Good. My name, if you don't remember, is Mikol Nese. Tarn Mikol formally. But for now, call me Mikol." The older man waved her over. "Come sit, this is for you to eat you know."

Myriam stood and tried not to walk too quickly to the table. She only recognized a few of the ingredients, and even then, the dishes didn't look familiar, but it all smelled amazing. "Ummm, thank you?" Myriam mumbled out before she took a large cup of something greenish and took a sip. Sweet, but not overly so cold, refreshing. She took a longer drink, a far longer one. When she stopped, well over half the cup was empty.

She didn't even look at Mikol as she tore into the food. Roasted fowl with some herb sauce she wasn't familiar with, stacks of a flat orange bread, a bowl of roasted vegetables, all of it was good. Better than good. She knew it felt that way because she was so hungry. At the same time, it was impressive. Growing up in an inn with travelers and merchants from all over, her parents had invested in a lot of excellent cooks. She knew food. This was good. Very good.

She had torn through roughly a quarter of the food before she slowed down. She wasn't done by any stretch, but the razor edge of her hunger and thirst had been dulled enough that she could think about something else.

"Better?" Mikol smiled and waved for one of the others to refill her cup with more of that green juice.

"Much. Thank you." Myriam fought the urge to burp. She didn't know these people after all.

"Good. We will get you a bath soon as well. But we need to talk now about what happens next. Please, keep eating though." Mikol nodded at the food.

Myriam reached out and then stopped. "You will not eat?"

"Truth be told, I already did. I'm a creature of habit, I am afraid, and I eat at set times." Mikol smiled, the lines from many such smiles obvious on his face.

Myriam smiled back. She liked this old man. He was grandfatherly. She missed her grandfather. Though the gods above would only know what he would think of everything that had happened to her.

"Myriam. Your future. Yours and your companion, William Reis." Mikol leaned forward, his eyes locking onto hers. "First off, let me tell you, you are safe here. The City has rules about refugees. We are the last free bastion of magic in the world, and everyone here either came here for that reason, or their ancestors did. Chasing legends and stories, hints and whispers. None arrived here in such a dramatic fashion as you and William, I'll grant you. Despite that one oddity, you are refugees."

"William!" Myriam sat back with that exclamation. She had forgotten William. "Is he ok?"

"He is still asleep. Once he awakens, he will be healed, fed and bathed." Mikol assured her, his voice calming and low. "See Myriam, the city has a structure. There are five sections. A Tarn runs each section. I am the Tarn of the Healers. Rewil is the Tarn of the Crafters. Nollew…" Mikol paused for a second.

Myriam knew he was doing it for effect. *He doesn't like this Nollew person.*

"Nollew is the Tarn of Casters. Yulisia is the Tarn of Knowledge. Librarians. And Grib is the Tarn of the City. If you aren't a healer, crafter, librarian, or a worker of the power, you are under Grib." Mikol stood with a stretch. "Forgive me, at my age sitting too long makes me stiff."

"It would seem Grib, Tarn Grib, is the most powerful?" Myriam asked as she speared a small fruit, its flesh the color of roses. "I mean that's a lot of people."

"True!" Mikol shot her another smile. "The number of people isn't important. Magic is. How much, and how it can be used. Anyone with any actual strength in the power isn't under Grib, they are part of one of the other sections."

"Makes sense I suppose." Myriam shrugged. "But why tell me all this?"

"You and William. Your arrival is unusual. As are the effects that arrival had on the two of you. I'm sure you've seen the magic. Bonded to you. We call it a boon. The two of you potentially are the most powerful people in the city." Mikol pointed to her hands.

Myriam felt uneasy, and some of her hunger died. She'd tried very hard not to think about those markings. She knew her eyes were blue now, her lips, and her arms. Her eyes traced the fine intertwining lines that the blue made. She swore it sparked in a faint shimmer as she stared at it. "That." She said, her voice low.

"Yes. That." Mikol reached out a hand and she responded. His skin was warm, soft. He traced a line on her hand, examining it before letting her arm go. "It comes down to this. You are both crafters. Or at least inclined that way. But there is no way the other Tarns would let both you and William be under Rewil. It's too much power."

"It's political?" Myriam sat back in her chair again. It made sense, of course. Though it annoyed her, they didn't get much of a say. She still thought it silly, but it made sense.

"Yes. The decision has been made that William will be allowed to enter the Crafters. If nothing else, his status as the, well his former affiliations speaks for him." Mikol finally sat back down. "But that leaves you." The older man shifted back before leaning all the way back into the chair. "I have come here to offer you a place in the healers. Nollew wants you in his section. But the vote was in my favor first." Mikol held her eyes again. His eyes, unlike the rest of him, weren't old. Bright, they pierced her and kept her attention.

"Healers? Me??" Myriam blurted out before shutting her mouth with a snap.

"Yes. You. You attempted to heal your friend, did you not? You have some skill. With your boon, and the right teaching, you could be a once in a lifetime healer." Mikol leaned forward again. "The fact is, I know you'd rather stay a crafter, but it's me or Nollew, at least for now. And while you have yet to meet Nollew, and you don't know me, you would not be happy to be under that man." Mikol gave a small smile. "I don't even think Yulisia is."

"What?" Myriam asked, not understanding the comment.

"Nothing. I shouldn't have said that. I sometimes say things I should think instead." Mikol smiled again, the wrinkles springing to life once more before fading away as the smile faded. "I don't mean to rush, but I need an answer. Now."

"Right now? I can't have time to think about it?" Myriam wasn't sure what to do. She wished there was someone else here to sound off against. Vin, or William. She pushed the other name out of her head. "I'm afraid not. You and William have come close to upsetting a very careful balance of power here in the city." Mikol nodded at the food. "I can give you until you are done eating. Then a bath?"

Myriam nodded as she picked up some bowl, sniffing it. Soup. Seafood? She never ate a lot of fish or anything from the sea. The Inn had been inland. And the Guild had it sometimes, but she had never developed the taste for it. She took a spoonful, trying to look interested in her bowl as she thought.

It was true that she had tried to heal William more than once. She had some rudimentary healing training. But she was a smith, a crafter! Why couldn't she be in the crafter's guild and William go to the healers? *Because he was the Forgemaster of Amder. It's that simple girl.* And she did like this Mikol. Maybe it wasn't permanent. Get some time and then move to a new, what had he called it, section? Was that even allowed?

The soup was tasty, though there was a slight pungency around it she couldn't place. It didn't matter. She was getting rather full, and with sleep, food and drink having been taken care of now, she needed that bath. It wasn't like in the Gorom caves, covered in bug parts, but still the dirt, grime, and sweat of many hours or even days covered her. Her hair needed a good wash as well.

At least here in the city I can have some kind of a routine. That would be the best thing, at least until I get my feet under me. That and not sleeping outdoors, or in caves. Myriam looked up, placing the bowl on the table. "It doesn't sound like I have much choice, but if the options are either the healers with you or the casters? Or whatever you call it with this Nollew person, I suppose I'll pick the healers."

"Excellent!" Mikol broke into a smile, standing. "Now, get your bath, and we will see to your friend. In fact, I'll have you watch, maybe even assist. You have much to learn."

Myriam nodded, standing herself. The room seemed wobbly as she stood, and she almost stumbled to one side for a moment. Had she been drugged? A twinge of fear arrived with that thought. These were strangers, and they had already said her 'boon' would upset some balance. Killing her and William would be the easy way to fix that. "Don't worry. Your body was starved of food and borderline dried out. You put down a large amount of food and drink." Mikol walked over clasping her arm. "You are fine. Now, one of the others here will show you to a bath. We will get you some clean garments, and then go see William Reis, understand?'

Nodding Myriam watched as the older man waved over a robed and hooded servant who gave her a slight bow and motioned her towards the door. Myriam followed the figure as the door slid open, showing her a large and open hallway. The same stone as the room she had been in, rather plain, at least in terms of decoration. But a second look nearly made her stumble.

Everything was made of white stone, but running through the stone, everywhere were tiny fine lines of the same blue that seemed to be part of her now. Tiny blue specks flowed through those lines. *Like veins moving blood.* She snorted for a moment. *Thinking like a healer already.*

There was no one else in sight in the hall, and their steps made hardly any sound. She would have thought it would echo in here, but everything seemed muffled. The tiny blue lines seemed to appear and reappear based entirely on if she was paying attention to them. Another question that didn't have an answer.

In a few moments, the servant, who had not uttered a single word, waved a gloved hand towards a door. "In here. It is a changing and bathing area the outriders use, but we have cleared it out for you." The figure finally spoke. Its voice was decidedly feminine, though Myriam had no idea of the race.

"Thank you." Myriam answered. She wondered if she should inquire more when the servant faded away. Her eyes widened, and she looked around in shock. But no one else was around. What had just happened? She looked at the spot the figure had vanished from and was sure the tiny specks were moving faster there. Much faster. Something with this magic, then?

She stood still for a minute, looking back the way they had come, and then looking at the door the figure had motioned to. No one else was here. The whole thing was strange and unsettling and made her wonder again if her desire for some place safe had been a mistake. She held up one hand, her eyes peering deep into the blue that was most of her skin now, at least the skin on her hand.

"What have I gotten myself into?" Myriam whispered. No answer came, though. No voice in her head, no friend to offer a word of support. She stood still for a moment longer but couldn't think of anything else to do but get that bath. She moved to the door, which opened on its own, silently. *That's so strange.* She stepped into a large room with shelves and benches. A place to change, she guessed. A hint of moisture came from the room beyond. The smell of water and soap. The scent brought an itch to her skin that hadn't been there before. If they were planning on killing her and William, at least she could look presentable while dying, right?

Without waiting she stripped down, the clothes she had on stiff with grime, sweat, and who knew what else. Kicking them off she strode into the next room, the air growing damper as she did so. What greeted her almost made her cry out in joy.

A huge tub, steaming with water. Soap, and even mint, lavender and other plants she didn't recognize lying in neat bundles on the edge of the tub. It had been many a long month or even over a year since she'd scented her bathwater. She might be a crafter, a hard-nosed and tough innkeeper's daughter, and now a healer, but every so often she wanted to crawl into a huge bath and just be. And she was going to do just that right now.

Stepping into the bath brought a tremendous sigh of contentment. She lathered herself up quickly, rinsing off layers of dirt and sweat. Three times she did so until she was sure her skin was clean. Starting on her hair, she repeated the process, before dunking herself all the way under the water. Tiny blue specks seem to sparkle as she closed her eyes as she went under, feeling the water cover her. The last time she'd done this was at that waterfall underground. That water had been clean, but so cold. This was warm, and it felt amazing. Her mind strayed back to the waterfall. Vin had bellowed with the cold. She missed the old man.

Regin had… Regin. Before she could push it away, the sorrow of his loss hit her again. Regin was dead. The tears came then, and she broke the surface, crying and sputtering. For the first time since his death, she let herself fall into grief and blame. Regin was dead, and it was at least somewhat her fault. If she hadn't messed with the crystal, if she hadn't kept her secrets, Regin would be alive right now. She missed his smile; she missed the smell of him. His laugh. She just missed… him. What wouldn't she give to have him here right now with her. Still her tears came, and a sob tore through her. She could still remember the moment. That thin man had thrown a spear at Regin. And just as fast, or even faster, William had stood in front of it. It was chance that Regin had turned just enough that when the spear had shattered, a long sharp piece of the shaft had hit his side, sticking him just as surely as the spear would have.

It wasn't Will's fault either, he'd tried to stop the spear. Even after everything. After she'd hurt him, he'd been a loyal friend. To both her and Regin, when most people wouldn't have been. But Regin was still dead. Nothing was ever going to change that. The sorrow rose once more.

She let the feelings come. She was alone, and she needed to feel this. She *wanted* to feel this. The only other person who might understand was William, and right now he was dealing with his own emotions. And crying to William about Regin would have been fraught with problems. As the water started to cool, her crying stopped. The loss of Regin was still there, but not quite as raw now. It was faceable, even if it hurt. She washed her face off from the other side of the tub and stood, the air cold on her now scrubbed and warm skin.

She dried off with a towel that was there in stacks, noting again at the strange fabric. She had slept, ate, bathed, and mourned. Moving back out into the changing area, she was surprised to see her old clothes gone, and a small pile of new clothes on a bench. She hadn't heard anyone come in, though… she felt a wave of embarrassment. What if they had heard her crying? *Don't be a fool, people cry.* She heard her mother's voice say in her head. She'd been ten and a girl who she thought had been her friend had been mean to her and made fun of her interest in smithing.

She'd hidden and cried till her mother found her. She'd been sympathetic, but also refused to allow her to be embarrassed by her sorrow. *Myriam my girl, feeling things is good. Never be embarrassed by your feelings. Own them.* Dressing, she found the clothes serviceable and comfortable.

Grey pants, some sort of slipper like shoes, a clean tunic, and a light green cloak and robe combination over garment. There was even a brush for her hair and items to clean her teeth, which she took use of happily. The tunic was of the same grey color as the pants, and it contrasted with the blue that marked her arms. *I must look so strange.* There were no mirrors that she could see here though. *Odd.*

Chapter 8.

"Are you ready to go see your friend William?" Mikol was waiting for her out in the hall. She still wasn't sure about the situation, but Mikol at least seemed friendly, and it wasn't like she had a lot of other options right now. Myriam was even less sure of seeing William. He had been, harsh, the last time they had spoken.

"I guess so." Myriam tried to put confidence in her voice that she didn't feel. She hoped that some of the hurt that she knew William had was gone. *He needs to mourn, just as I did.*

"Good!" Mikol smiled and held out his arm for her to hook hers through. Despite her misgivings, she smiled and felt a rush of amusement. *Maybe he is a nice old man.*

"So where are we exactly?" Myriam asked as they walked. It was strange to her that they weren't seeing anyone.

"You are in the City. Also known as the City in Blue. I don't think it's ever had a different name." Mikol explained as they walked down the featureless hallway.

"No, I mean, why weren't there any people here? In this hallway?" Myriam found the place unsettling the farther they walked. Her skin reacted to a chill she wasn't sure was even there as goosebumps raced across her bare arms. She had that same reaction though to the Guild at one point, like something was messing with her sense of perception.

"Oh, well, for two reasons. Right now, we are on the wall. Those who protect the city from the outside work here. There's not a lot of them, since we have no threats from the outside, not anymore. We made sure of that when we moved here. Also, you are with me. I am a Tarn. I didn't want to overwhelm you with everything the City can be, so I asked the hall to be cleared." Mikol peered down the hallway. "Not much farther."

"Moved the city? What do you mean?" Myriam asked, wondering if she had heard him correctly.

Mikol gave a laugh and shook his head. "You are a smart one Myriam, I'll have to watch what I say. Yes, moved the city. All the Tarns together can move the city. We moved it when we were attacked by blood god followers. Many years ago. We moved it here, to this hidden valley."

Valnijz followers? Despite her recent bath and clean clothes, she felt her skin crawl. She'd had enough dealings with those kinds of people. Still moving an entire city? She couldn't imagine that. Mikol's answers made more questions than she could think of.

"Ah!" Mikol stopped in front of a door that, to her eyes, looked no different. "Now, before we go in, I want to explain things. William is currently asleep. Once he awakens, I will heal him. You will help. I will guide you in what needs to be done. After he's healed, you will get to meet another Tarn. Tarn Rewil will join us for before we take our leave."

"Tarn Rewil?" Myriam paused. "The Tarn of Craft?"

"Yes! More or less." Mikol nodded. "Be aware, Rewil can intimidate some people. He's *unusual* to those not born here. Not that we get many new seekers of the power."

Myriam wanted to ask what he meant, but kept her questions to herself. Nothing she'd seen yet had been quite real to her. What was more strangeness? The door opened silently, as normal. There on a cot was William, asleep. As soon as her eyes laid upon him, she felt a great swell of pity. Maybe it was her recent bath and food, but she hadn't noticed how worn out he had looked before. The blue that marked him was obvious, of course, thicker blue markings that went up his arms, blue marked places she could see on his neck as well.

But that was skin color. What really stood out was how thin he looked. The whole time she had known William, he'd been strong. Heavy, solid. He wasn't fast on his feet, and he could be unaware of his own power, but he'd been a constant font of strength. But this man? Lying here? In places his skin seemed a sag. His face should have been unlined. Instead, she could see the creases now. *Maybe it's the dirt?* He was filthy. Dust and grime clung to him. She was no stranger to the smells of the world, but he stunk. It was this feeling of exhaustion around him that was the most striking though. *I guess everyone has their limits.* Will had always seemed up for anything, and in many ways an inexhaustible force. But not now. Even asleep, the man was a study in exhaustion.

"William? William Reis?" Mikol called out, his voice tinged with a sharpness that made even Myriam perk up.

Myriam watched as William's eyes shot open, blue beyond belief in color, but she could also see how bloodshot they were. He sat up, his eyes first covering Mikol before landing on her. They narrowed for a moment and his mouth thinned to a line before he relaxed.

"Yes. That is my name. I see you have cleaned up Myriam." Will looked down frowning. He reached one tentative hand to his still bound shoulder.

"I know it still pains you. I can feel the pain from here William Reis." Mikol said quieter now. "I admit I am somewhat in awe of your ability to function. I have met many in my years who would be screaming in agony if they were you."

William didn't respond but looked up at them again. This time paying more attention to Mikol than the first time. "Setter?"

"Better than that." Mikol answered walking closer to William. "This is the City in Blue, a city built on the power. I am the Tarn of the Healers."

"So?" William closed his eyes again.

Myriam knew him well enough to read him. He was in no mood for any of this. "William, he can use the power of this magic to heal you. Right now." Myriam hoped she was right. That was what she guessed, at least.

"Yes. That's true." Mikol added. He opened his mouth to say more, but apparently decided not to, and let it stand.

Myriam wondered if she had overstepped her bounds, but what was said was said. "William, I know you are in pain. Let us at least fix that." Myriam pleaded. The more she was around him, the guiltier she felt. Maybe it was for the best that she went to the healers after all.

"Fine." William muttered. He rubbed a hand through his matted hair. "If it makes this better, and get's me closer to food and a bath."

Myriam knew he didn't believe it, or her. She hoped Mikol could do what she had said. "It will William. I didn't believe it either, but I feel much better now." Her words made little impression on him, and she wondered if they ever would again.

Mikol nodded. "This will be a lesson for Myriam here as well, so be patient William Reis."

William said nothing at first, but nodded in his agreement. Myriam could see his eyes flick to her and back to Mikol more than once. She wanted to tell him that everything was going to be fine. *He wouldn't listen, not right now.* Myriam saw his mouth go sour, forming a thin line before relaxing again. "What do I need to do, Tarn Mikol?" Myriam turned away from William, hoping that her actions would do what she knew her words would not.

"The power, your boon right now, is raw. Untrained. So is Williams. As time passes and you excel in your sections, that will change. But for now, I will draw power through your boon to show you how it looks." Mikol rubbed his hands together as he spoke.

"Now. I'm sure you seen the sparks? The tiny lights that make up part of the power? I've seen your eyes narrow as you examine things." Mikol turned to her fully.

"Yes. What about it?" she replied. The things still made her slightly uneasy.

"Try it again, but hold that, hold seeing the sparks. But look at your hands. I'm going to take both your hands in one of mine. My other hand I will put on William's major injury, his shoulder. We will start his repair, his healing, right there." Mikol reached out one of his hands.

Myriam nodded and took his outstretched hand in both of hers. His skin was soft, warm, and calmed her. She instantly liked him more. Trying to remember what she was supposed to do, she peered at her skin, pushing herself to see the power, this magic.

There! The tiny blue sparks flowed right under her skin. Or was a part of her skin. It was hard to see either way. But they flowed and moved, swirling in a strange dance, a pattern that she knew had to be there, but she couldn't quite follow all the way.

"Good! Good. Now, watch." Mikol said as he rested his other hand on William's shoulder.

She could feel at a distance all the hurts and pains of William's body. The avalanche of feeling left her gulping for air for a moment. *I did not know how much his body hurt.* His shoulder was the worst, a fiery pain mixed with an older dull ache. But all over his body cuts, scrapes, not healed bruises, even a trace of a redglow still brought hints of older injury.

Her attention shifted as she felt a strange pull. The sparks now moved as one, flowing through her, into her hands and into Mikol. She could watch them change as they moved from her body to his. At once the random patterns vanished, replaced with a twisting swirling dance, but organized. It flowed swiftly, entering William with a rush. The effect was immediate.

William took a huge inhale and gasped as his body trembled. She could see the power rise up in his own body to force the power flowing from Mikol away but to no avail. It was almost like watching a huge and powerful man fight a quicker and far nimbler fighter. With deft swirling, the power from Mikol pushed away or outright seemed to avoid whatever the power in William tried to do.

"Relax William Reis, there is no need to fight this." Mikol said in a low calming voice. Then without another word, the power from Mikol flowed back into Williams arm. At once Myriam could see more of the problems. The bone was cracked in four places, a tendon had broken, and the flesh around the bone was a mess of ugly raw red and dead blood. The power flowed around it, avoiding anything not alive.

She watched in near awe as first the bones flowed back together, and within moments they were whole, as if they had never been injured, ever. Then the tendon was reconnected and with a momentary blue flash, the broken ends reconnected. Finally, the red flesh relaxed, the old blood faded away. William shuddered and gasped as this happened, but the moment the last of it was done, he relaxed, his shoulders dropping nearly an inch. Myriam hadn't realized how tight he had been, but seeing him now, she saw a hint of the old William still there. But Mikol wasn't done, and to her watchful gaze she saw the power flow through him, seeking each area that still gave forth any pain, repairing it, calming the feeling, and leaving the areas repaired. It was an incredible sight.

Mikol lifted his hand from William, breaking the connection, and then dragged his hand free of her grip. Myriam let out a small breath at the break in contact, feeling the power flow again in unpredictable patterns. "That was… I've seen nothing like it."

"You will learn how to do that yourself; I know. But let's make sure our patient here is functioning better. William, you physical ailments are now taken care of." Mikol waved a hand for William to stand. "Get up, let's see how you feel."

William finally opened his eyes; they were wet with tears, but he was smiling. He hesitated for a moment, then stood upright fully. "Well, I…" William said and gave a small smile. "I feel great. Better than great."

"Not quite yet, you don't. There's a matter of food and a bath. But we have fixed your physical pain. Your other pains are ones you must take care of, yourself." Mikol tapped his nose. "But I can tell we are about to be joined by a visitor. Tarn Rewil is almost here."

"I'm glad you are better, William." Myriam added and waited for his response. William's eyes fell on her, the intense blue they were now searching her face. She wasn't sure what he was thinking or feeling, but it was obvious he was struggling to think of something to say.

"Thank you." William finally said and purposefully looked away from her.

Myriam felt a twinge of regret, but let it go. Things would have to be that way for now, she knew. Maybe they could be friends again one day.

"Now. Tarn Rewil will be coming, and he and you have much to discuss. But I think for you a bath first. Rewil has more of a sensitive nose than I. Because of his heritage." Mikol turned to Myriam. "Would you wait here, please? I'll take your companion here to the baths."

Myriam nodded. What else could she do? William wasn't ready to talk to her, and the fact was right now she kind of wanted to be alone. She had to think about everything she'd seen. In her mind, she was already comparing what she had *felt* when Mikol had healed William with things from crafting. The ornate detail of inlay and jewelry work and how it compared to the tiny veins and connectors, how the bone fixed itself.

Mikol ushered William out of sight as she leaned against the wall, enveloped in her ideas when the door opened and entered simply the largest person she'd ever laid eyes on.

Chapter 9.

"You are not William Reis." The enormous man said, cocking an eye as he looked her over. "But you have the same boon. You must be the other one, Myriam, correct?" The man's voice was deep and almost seemed to echo out of his mouth.

"Yes? Yes. Sorry, Yes. I am Myriam VolFar. And you are Tarn Rewil?" Myriam pushed herself off the wall and unconsciously pulled her clothes down, trying to keep them unwrinkled.

"Tsk. Yes. Be at ease, I'm not here to judge you. But where is William Reis?" Rewil narrowed his eyes and seemed to flick one large finger around the room. "This is his room, is it not?"

Myriam only nodded. "Tarn Mikol took William to the baths, he thought he should be bathed before he met with you."

Rewil laughed, shaking his head. "Mikol knows I don't care about that. He did it so you and I could meet. I like Mikol, I do, but the man plots within his plots." Rewil pointed a calloused finger at her. "Don't forget that Myriam VolFar. Mikol always has something up his sleeve. He hasn't been the longest serving Tarn in all the city ever without a reason. But he is a good man for all that."

Myriam looked away and looked in the direction that Mikol and William had gone in. How long had they been gone? Her eyes flicked back over to Rewil, trying to figure out why his features seemed off, not including his physical size.

"Oh ask. You know you want to." Rewil rolled his eyes. "Yes, I am not human, not... fully. I am a product of the city."

"What does that mean?" Myriam did not know what the man meant. Was he not alive?

"Ask Mikol, he loves to talk about it." Rewil settled down into a chair, giving it a careful look as the legs gave a slight groaning noise as his weight settled into it.

"You are going to be a healer, I take it? I would have loved you in the craft as well, but politics is politics." Rewil crossed his arms. "I have never been to the famed Guild in Palnor. What was it like?"

"Oh…" Myriam thought back. It all seemed so long ago, though not even a year had passed. The madness of the resurrection of Amder, the mad flight to save Duncan, the trip in the black pit of the Gorom lands, the revelation of the Vinik, the tragedy at the Anvil, now here. So much had happened.

Rewil cleared his throat, and Myriam refocused on him. "Oh sorry. Well, for as long as I was there, it was good. My grandfather was a Guild Smith. I didn't want to be an innkeeper like my father and mother, so I followed in his footsteps. I specialized in jewelry and inlay work, Fine detail stuff. I learned a lot, but I was only there for a year, the situation changed."

A snort was her only answer at first. "Politics. It's everywhere." Rewil muttered. "So, inlay and jewelry work? Bah! I wish I had known you had that skill. I would have fought harder to have both of you in the craft. Once you are in the city proper, you will see wonders beyond thought, all brought by the craft. And with the boon you have, and your companion of course, the wonders you might make."

Myriam blushed at the compliment. "Thank you, Tarn Rewil."

"Just Rewil. Come, lass. Let's talk about the joy of making something while we wait. I get bored easy waiting around." Tarn Rewil motioned to a chair nearby, and soon their conversation filled the holding room.

William sank into the water with a pleased flush of warmth. He tensed for a pain that didn't come as he did so. He didn't know how to even think about what had happened. He'd been able, though barely, to keep a lid on all the physical pain and ailments that he'd had. He hadn't even sure if he'd ever pick up a hammer again with his shoulder the way it was. Before Myriam and that Mikol, Tarn Mikol, had appeared he had been sinking deeper into those thoughts. His shoulder was busted, everything hurt, and with everything else, Amder was gone, some new god who… who knew. Then, like some sort of bedtime story, Mikol had used *magic* to heal him. Magic. Magic wasn't real. It was some made up thing that parents told in stories. Priests would say magic came only from the Gods, and then very rarely.

In truth, he'd felt a tiny bit of that in the short time he'd spent as Amder's Forgemaster. Forgemaster, what a waste of a title. Yet, here he was. Alive, healed, and despite a great hunger and thirst, alive, and bathing. Every physical hurt was gone. As soon as Mikol, who hadn't said a word, showed him the bath, William had gone in and moved his shoulder, as if he was warming up for weapons practice with Vin.

A splinter of sadness poked him at the thought, but he pushed it away. He'd expected pain, or the somewhat familiar crunching feeling that seemed to echo in his own head. But instead, there was nothing. It felt, good. And the bath felt almost better. He sat in the steaming hot water watching the dirt, blood, and dust float off his skin. He tried hard not to think about everything else, and instead studied the room. The artisanship here was incredible. Everything was perfectly made, lines were clean, polish was done with a skill few had. He'd even examined the spouts for the water carefully as they were forged bronze. A simple metal, but the work was perfect.

His eyes picked something else up about himself. He'd changed. William had never been a small man. Thick, strong, a slight level of padding here and there. The travels and trials he'd been on since the day he left the Reach, had changed all that. The padding was gone. He was still thick, still strong, but muscles that before had been hinted at were now in sharp relief. A growl from his stomach reminded him how hungry he was. *Maybe too sharp of a relief.*

He was hungry. But right now, the urge to stay in the bath still won out. *For now.* He washed with a nearby oblong thing that he hoped was soap, at least it smelled like soap. Even washing his hair felt fantastic. By the time he was done what once had been clear water was a soapy greyish black. It had been far too long since he'd felt clean. Still, he felt better, but not perfect. The growl in his stomach came again, louder this time. This time he decided to listen to it. Standing he went around the corner to find his clothes were gone, though the armor, his god forged armor, was still there, along with the hammer, and oddly enough the circlet. William picked up the circlet, and nearly dropped it in surprise. Now that he carefully examined it, he could see the dark grey had the same tiny blue specks in it that he could see in himself.

Magic. But why blue? Why not yellow? Why not… did it even matter? William threw the circlet where it had been sitting, somewhat surprised when it made a normal metal pinging sound and not some strange sound that signified it's changed appearance. His armor still looked the same, except for the long gouging tear that still was there from the spear. *Sparks burn it, I wish Regin was here.*

He searched around, looking for something to wear when to his surprise a cubby nearby opened on its own to show a set of clothes for him. Very similar to whatever Myriam had been wearing, but the colors were different. Slight variations but still noticeable.

Getting dressed, William felt normal, except for being hungry. He looked at the armor, the hammer, and the circlet. Would putting them on break protocol? What was protocol here, anyway? He tried to think of what Regin would say. He missed Regin. It was strange that friendship. William would have expected himself to be bitter at the man still, if only for the whole situation with Myriam.

But Regin had done nothing wrong. Neither had Myriam for that matter. She had fallen out of whatever feelings she had for William and those for Regin had grown. He had simply felt the same about her. But he could use the advice Regin would have offered. Finally, he put the armor and other items back down. If nothing else, he was supposed to meet this Tarn Rewil again, and he didn't want to show off.

Everything fit, though looser than it was designed for, he'd lost some weight, not that he'd been after that result. He avoided examining the hammer or the armor any more than he had to. William still wasn't sure what to make of all this, this place. The existence of this power, this magic in the items he'd made was both amazing and intimidating. The less he thought it about it right now, the better. He felt better, but he wasn't sure he could deal with the mental strain.

William paused, not sure if he should wait here, or leave and look for someone to help him. That Mikol person? He knew Mikol was important, and he didn't like all this attention. Powerful people paying attention to him and Myriam made Will far more nervous than anything else. They were leaders of their sections; they had called it. And yet, here they were personally attending to him and Myriam. The more he thought about it, the more uneasy he became.

His hunger pushed those thoughts to the side though, after a short while. Exiting the baths, standing there in the plain hallway, was Mikol again, waiting for him.

"Better? How's the shoulder feeling now?" Mikol asked, motioning William to follow him as he walked.

"Far better than it has felt in a very long time." Will followed the older man. "Thank you again. I left my armor and a few other things in the bath. I wasn't sure if I should wear them or what."

"We will take them to your quarters, I promise." Mikol explained. "You're holding up well. I hope the simulacrum didn't frighten you. I could tell how much you wanted to get a bath, and I had something I needed to attend to. That was the fastest way."

"The what?" Will was confused. "Oh, you mean the man who vanished?"

"Yes. Though it wasn't a man, not exactly. A short-term magical copy, you might say. Or a simulacrum." Mikol explained. "We don't use them much anymore, but in a pinch…"

Will tried to make sense of what he was hearing but gave up. "Well, thanks for healing me. I feel…"

"You were injured. It was my duty to heal you." Mikol set a steady pace. "Normally one of the other healers would attend to hurts, but you and Myriam are special cases."

Will fought off a spike of worry that made his stomach drop. "Ah…"

Mikol shook his head. "Do not worry, you aren't in danger. It is simply because of the information you brought us."

Will nodded but didn't respond further. He hated this kind of thing. Nothing for him had gone right since the day he'd taken that crystal from the Mistlands. Nothing. *They always said it was cursed to do so, how right they were.*

"Ah, here we are!" Mikol stopped at a door that did not look any different to Will than the other half dozen they had passed. He stepped forward, and the door opened, showing the room he had been in, with two key differences. One, Tarn Rewil was there, his vast size making the furniture in the room, including a table look almost comical in comparison, the other was the food. Glorious amounts of delicious smelling food.

Will nearly tripped over himself, trying to get into the room as fast as he could. Tarn Rewil turned and smiled as they entered the room.

"Ah, there you are. Clean and healed, I see. I've been waiting to eat, so come sit. We shall eat and talk. My conversationalist friend here will need to be going with Mikol, anyway." Rewil pointed to someone that Will couldn't see until they stood. Myriam. She'd been totally hidden by Rewil's size.

"Yes. It was most interesting speaking to you Tarn Rewil." Myriam gave a short nodding bow and walked towards the door. "You look much better, William." Myriam gave him a smile and lowered her voice as she passed closest to him. "Don't worry, Tarn Rewil seems like a good person."

Will didn't answer, but felt some of his stress leave him, at least for now. "You two are leaving?"

Mikol nodded. "Yes, but you will see each other again soon, I am sure."

"Come William Reis, let's eat, I am starving!" Tarn Rewil pointed at the seat that Myriam must have vacated.

Will watched and Mikol and Myriam left, neither giving a glance back before he settled into the seat. His stomach growl grew to a near painful cramp at the sight of everything. Sausages, roasted meats, breads, some kind of white-yellow soup, the vegetables were unknown. And the smells, his mouth watered at every whiff.

"Eat, eat. I am not one to make a man wait to eat when he's starving." Rewil waved him to start before he started filling his own plate. "But as we do this, let's talk about the craft. What is the best material do you think for the making of strong and light mixtures to be in gears?"

Chapter 10.

Mikol closed the door with Myriam right behind him, but his boon was still probing William and Myriam. William Reis was a strong but traumatized young man. The amount of pain he had been carrying around was a surprise, even for Mikol. Useful though. Myriam as well. The only thing that had surprised Mikol about her was how her boon adjusted to using it for healing.

"Myriam, how was your talk with Tarn Rewil?" Mikol sent out little feelers, only to detect if she hid anything from him. "Did you like the man?"

"Yes, he's impressive, but… He's not human. He explained that his background was unusual, but he wouldn't go into more detail." Myriam followed close behind. "Where are we going, Mikol?"

"Ah… well, he wouldn't. And the informality is fine with me, but it's better if you call me Tarn Mikol. Some in the Healers section get touchy about such things." Mikol could sense her quick flush of shame. "I can explain his background, and what it means here."

"Yes, I think I'd like that. If it doesn't break any rules or anything." Myriam paused. "Tarn Mikol."

"Rewil is a mix. A crossbreed. That's not a mark of shame here. Well, for most, it isn't. The power that suffuses this place makes things possible that aren't possible anywhere else. Gorom and Trinil can have children here, together. A human and a Windtalker, it does not matter. Not here." Mikol paused, glancing at Myriam to make sure she understood, and then continued.

"Let us get to the quickway. And for as for where we are going, the healers section. Or as one new healer called it once long ago, the Hall of Pain. No, I don't know why it had such an overly dramatic name. But it's been called that for so long, I don't think it would do much good to try to change it." Mikol kept a small feeler out on her for lies, but removed the rest. It was interesting. Her boon made his detection fuzzy. He'd have to figure a way around that.

Mikol had no regrets about getting her into the Healers, but she would bear watching. Her boon of power was far more powerful than he had thought. Maybe because of the way she had gained it, jumping into a pool of raw magic in the Anvil of Souls. If you had told him anyone could do that and survive, he would have never believed it. And yet, two people had.

The question, was why? Was it something he didn't understand about the nature of magical power? Or was there something different about these two? They certainly were not normal, average people. One had been the Forgemaster of Amder. One was the proverbial 'mother' of the new unnamed god. Had that association somehow made a difference?

Questions for another time. The hallway stretched before them, and now, those kept out due to the strangers were returning. He wondered what Myriam thought as they walked, as Gorom, Trinil, Humans, and even rarer races walked around, doing whatever they needed to do. In truth, most of the city was those three races. They were the most common out in the world and made up the bulk of the city. But the call of the power could come to any people, and sometimes it came to odd ones.

There was even a single long-lived family of Lerusin in the City. Boar like humanoids, but gentle, and lived for many years. Only one of the group had died since they came here. Mikol regretted that death, but he needed to study them. Turning, he glimpsed Myriam's face and stifled a laugh. Her eyes darted around like a watching a flea bounce from person to person. She kept a straight face though. *Good.* "Ah, here we are." Mikol paused in front of the quickway door. "In we go."

The door opened to a large single carriage. Private. It was a Tarn only carriage, and it gave them some level of privacy.

"What is this Tarn Mikol? You called it a quickway?" Myriam stepped into the carriage looking around carefully.

"Yes. Quickways are fastest way to get around the city. One of the many wonders of the crafters. Usually they have many riders, but this is a Tarn only unit, so we can talk privately. Quickways ride the air in lines. Some combination of metal and the power that I do not understand. Rewil could give you a three-hour lecture on it. I know it works, it's safe, and will get us to the Hall in a quick time. A great deal faster than walking." Mikol waved to a blue and red velvet covered seat. "Sit, and we will talk and ride. I think you will like what you see." Myriam sat carefully, leaning forward with her hands clasped tight. "So, Tarn Rewil is a mix? May I ask what?"

"Yes, but first I want to see your reaction in one moment..." Mikol trailed off as the carriage took off and emerged into the falling daylight and into the City in Blue.

William sat back in his chair, full, clean and almost complete. Almost. He was working hard to ignore the blue skin that covered his hands and arms, the specks of bright blue that sometimes appeared in the corner of his eye, then vanished. And he'd had a long and frankly enjoyable conversation with Tarn Rewil.

Talking about the craft, techniques, metals and their properties was near perfection to Will these days. No calamity, no talking about gods, or danger, or death. Just the craft. "All this talk about working the forge... makes me want to grab a hammer and get to work." Will admitted as he took a long drink of some juice they served here.

"HA!" Rewil laughed a deep and loud thing. "Spoken like a crafter. Well, what are we waiting around here for? Let's get you to the crafters section. I want to see what you can do. And I have wonders to show you, things beyond your experience. While we do work the forges, there's a lot more to being a crafter than a hammer and anvil."

Will smiled in response. For the first time since his conversations with Master Jaste, he felt like he belonged. He fit. This was normal, even if the place was very different from Palnor.

"Your friend, Myriam VolFar, pleasant woman. Are you close?" Rewil stood, wiping a loose crumb of some bread off his shirt.

Will paused and took a last sip out of his cup, feeling some of the contentment leak away. "We…. It's… strained." he struggled to find the right words. He found that he somewhat regretted his words when they appeared here. The truth was, if she had told him what was going on, everything would be better, he was sure of it. He knew she had her reasons for keeping it all from him, though. And while some of those reasons were weak, some weren't. "Well, I'm sure you will see her again soon. The healers come around often. If only because some apprentice usually gets hurt doing something stupid. I'm sure you will see her again soon." Rewil gave a stretch of his back. "Come, let us go."

Will followed Rewil out into the hall, to finally see it rather busy, which was a relief. It made this place seem more real. "Where did all these people come from?" Will watched as groups and clumps of Humans, Gorom and Trinil, walked by. Some in mixed groups, others not.

"We closed this section of the long hall; it goes all the way around the city. Just in case." Rewil pointed ahead and began long steps, eating up the distance to whatever location he was going. William found himself in a fast walk to keep up with him.

"Are we walking the whole way?" Will was better with running now, he'd done enough of it, but he still would rather not be at a fast pace like this after an enormous meal.

"No, no. Heading to the quickways." Rewil waved him forward. "Come, I'll explain how they work."

Will listened as Rewil talked but lost some of what was explained by virtue of working harder to stay close to the man. Something about two metals, given the power that kept one from touching the other. He didn't understand it, but it sounded interesting.

"And here we are." Rewil finally stopped in front of a door that, to Will's eyes, looked like any of the half dozen doors they had already passed. "We had somewhat of a longer walk, Tarn Mikol and your…" Rewil paused for a moment, glancing at Will." Companion? Took a closer quickway."

Will considered how to respond but said nothing. His attention was taken up anyway by the door that opened in front of them. Not the door so much as what lay beyond it. A strange room, long and rectangular.

With couches lining the walls. What was stranger was the walls themselves. Lots of windows that looked at, walls?

Every window showed a wall. A close wall. None of it made sense. Will watched as Rewil entered the long room and settled into a couch, pointing at a nearby one for Will to sit at. The man was smiling too. Will knew that kind of smile. *He's hiding something.* Nothing bad, Will thought, but like there was a surprise coming and he was having a hard time keeping a plain face.

Will sat down and the door closed behind him. Odd. He'd gotten used to those doors already. The first time or two he'd wondered how they knew to close and open, how the system worked, all that. Now he accepted it that they worked in some mysterious way.

"What is this place?" Will asked. "You called it a quickway? This room?" Rewil nodded and his smile grew. "Just watch."

Will wondered what that meant but didn't wonder for long as the room seemed to lurch forward. Scrambling, Will grabbed the couch in panic. "The Room! It's moving!" Will yelled before realizing that Rewil wasn't worried. *The Tarn knew this was going to happen.*

Light flooded into the room as the windows, once blocked by a wall, now showed a sight that Will had a hard time accepting as real. A city. A massive, enormous city spread out below them. Vaguely circular, the outer wall was far larger on this side than the outside. Three times larger. Below it sat roads and buildings, all older looking though, rougher. The room moved in a straight line towards the spire that stood over the city.

A spire that tore a shining white line, straight up. A spire that outshone anything he'd ever seen, including the Guild back in Ture. It caught the light of the sun and the light that seemed to come from parts of it. Even at this distance, it was stunning.

"Welcome William Reis, to the City in Blue." Rewil spoke now. "Below us is the old city, also known as the lower city. Laborers, common people, the unskilled. Tarn Grib is in charge there. It's not a place we go much." Rewil snorted for a moment as his eyes took the lower city in. "Usually dangerous. I must talk to Grib, though sometime, looks like a fair amount of material we could make use of."

Will wondered for a moment what the Tarn meant, but his eyes were drawn to the outside again. They were passing over a huge canal like river that curved in the same shape as the walls. One side was this low city, on the other was a nicer, cleaner part. The streets were wider; the houses looked nicer. Unlike the buildings in the shadow of the walls, there were no torches or smoke about.

"The middle city. Tradesmen, bankers, most merchants. Mixed management." Rewil explained as they traveled over a view that took Will's questions away with his breath. Will couldn't tear his eyes off the view below. Something about it tingled on the edge of his awareness. "Horses! There're no horses. No animals at all!" he blurted out.

"No. Everything in the middle city is done via the transport constructs. You simply load them, either with cargo or people, and say where you want it to go, and it takes you there. Magic and machinery. Faster, and far cleaner than any animal could work. All powered by the source." Rewil answered him.

Will looked up for the first time. "Source? Constructs?"

Rewil shifted in his seat for a moment. His eyes darted around. "I am not at present able to say more, thanks to the politics around you and the other one, but yes, the source."

Will knew enough to let it go, at least for now. They were approaching the spire now at even faster speeds. And he could see these pale fine lines, wispy, as if they were almost not there crossing the sky. "What are those?"

Rewil, if anything, looked surprised after that question. 'You can see them?"

"Not fully. It's as if they aren't... there?" Will peered at one line, and it seemed to fade away as he tried to study it, only to snap back as he looked away. "Those are the ward lines. Usually, you need a special scope to see them." Rewil stood. "Will look at me."

Will turned away from the view to look at the Tarn, a huge imposing figure.

"William Reis, we are about to enter the craftsman section of the spire. Down at the bottom. Let me do the talking." Rewil pointed at the spire, which was larger still.

Will could see the Tarn was right. However, they were still moving forward but also dropping, approaching an enormous door in the spire's side, near the base of the structure.

What have I gotten into now? Will wondered as the golden doors opened into a sight for very sore eyes.

Chapter 11.

Will threw down his hammer onto the workbench. Flexing his wrists and elbows, feeling the muscles tense and relax. His right elbow gave a loud crack as the joint popped. Will's eyes were locked on what was in front of him. He had finished his third attempt so far on making his own construct. None had been successful, but he'd gotten closer each time. He'd been in the crafters section now for four months. Four months of relearning everything, four months of learning how to use this boon of his, the magic, in his crafting.

He still didn't feel comfortable using the power. The only good thing was that the blue stain that once had been bright and fresh against his skin had faded and faded a lot. He'd been here for almost three weeks when he first noticed it. He wondered at first if that meant it was leaving him. He'd almost felt relief at that thought, but that wasn't the case.

In a way for him, it was sort of like when he had Amder riding around in his head. There was this…. force in his mind. He usually kept it as far from his thoughts as he could, but yet, when he needed it, the power would flow forth in a massive torrent. The only real reminders now were the ability to see the power, and of course its mark on the hammer and the circlet. Those hadn't faded at all. The bright blue clung to both objects, swirling with the gold of the hammer and the dark silver of the circlet in patterns that made his head hurt if he looked too hard at them.

He'd tried using other hammers, but it seemed he needed this one hammer if he wanted to use this power. Normally he'd be happy to do so, but not for this. A construct by design needs the magic, it was a meshing of metal and the power. A machine that could think, follow commands, orders, all that. And of course, he wasn't supposed to make one.

"No mere first year crafter, regardless of their boon, or skill can make a construct. But since I already know you will argue, please, go ahead and try." Tarn Rewil had said while giving forth one of his huge booming laughs.

Will had to admit so far it was far harder than he had expected. He was still learning a lot here, so his first attempt had been very crude. His second had been little better. This try was going well, at least so far. There was a lot more to do, of course. This was the start of the core of the thing. Following the plans laid out made his eyes glaze over. Rewil's plans were far more detailed than anything the Guild back in Ture ever had shown him. Still, there were similarities. Rewil reminded him of some of the nicer Guildmasters, the ones that cared about the craft, not the politics. And the guild itself had that same somewhat shifting feeling in the air. Like the Guildhall, the crafters section felt larger inside than it did from the outside. Though, unlike the guild, no one slept here. Will had a small room two flights of stairs lower in the tower. It only held a bed, some clothes and his old armor and gear, and that was it. It had a small bathroom attached. Very plain, very simple.

His eyes looked up at the ceiling, somewhere up there, in some other part of the spire was the healers section and Myriam. He hadn't spoken to her since she left with that other Tarn. Tarn Mikol. Four months and not a word. Of course, if he admitted it to himself, he hadn't reached out to her either. *Maybe it's better this way.* The thought of her brought back more memories of the Guild, and their time there. Memories that no longer brought pain or joy, they just…were. *Yes, it's better this way.*

"Nice work Will." Martus's voice shifted Will's attention from the past to the now. Will liked Martus. A new crafter as well, Martus was friendly, and didn't seem to care much about Will's past or whatever level of power Will might have. Others, while friendly enough, seemed fairly reserved around Will, enough so that he could tell at least.

"Thanks. Third try on that part." Will flicked a thumb at the collection of gears and rods, some moving, some not. And the small bright blue and green crystal that made it all move, though Will still didn't get *how* exactly.

"Better work than most. I'm sure Tarn Rewil would approve." Martus eyed the contraption carefully. "I'm no expert, but shouldn't the third rod here on the upper junction be joined to the upper movement gear, not the middle?"

Will grinned. "Yes, but that made little sense to me. If I do it this way, the ratio of movement to power usage will give more flexibility." Martus was a stickler for following plans, and the idea of deviation was not one that he entertained.

Martus frowned and gave a shrug before shaking his head. "Your project, your problem. Come on, it's getting late, let's get some food." Will grabbed his hammer off the table, hooking it into his belt loop. "Might be a good idea." He cast one look at his work. "I'm going to get this right." "Yes, yes." Martus agreed with a long drawn out eye roll. "Very nice work. Food. Now."

Will entered his room, full and relaxed. Food here was interesting. He wasn't sure exactly where it came from, or who made it, but it was good. Still, he missed some of the flavors of home. Everything here was still too spicy for his tastes. *More Myriam's style than what I like.*

Will remembered the first dish she'd ever made for him, some chicken dish, back in the Guild. He was sure his sense of taste would be ruined forever after the first bite. He'd kept eating though, if only because at the time he was falling deeply for her. If he closed his eyes, he could almost feel the memory around him. The smells and feelings of the air, the solid worn stone under his boots, the sense of peace that seemed to float everywhere in the Guild.

Will sat down on his bed, closed his eyes and laid back. He needed a bath, and to get some sleep, but remembering the Guild made this place seem less strange. No magical powers, no reborn gods, none of that. He'd been in the Guild under an assumed name, but that danger seemed so minor now, somehow. Will felt himself slipping into slumber and didn't fight it. He drifted off, his mind full of memories of the Smithing Guild of Palnor, and a smile on his face.

Master Reinhill slammed her hand against the nearest wall. Her feet gave way before she focused and righted herself.

"Again?" Master Greenmar whispered as he helped steady her.

"Yes. Worse this time." Reinhill answered back, her voice unsteady.

Clearing her throat, she tried again. "Yes. It's getting worse. I almost got sick over the whole new apprentice class yesterday." "Master Trie Reinhill, you did not!" Greenmar answered in an exaggerated fashion.

Trie smiled as Greenmar tried to cheer her up. Or at least take her mind off how she felt. It failed. "Three months. Three months since this started. First the changes in the building, then the issue at the anvil, and then the sickness." Trie shook her head. All related to the change that happened.

"Well, at least we don't have to deal with that bastard Bracin. That's a good thing, right?" Greenmar let go of her arm as she waved him off.

"Of course. But that doesn't solve everything, or really anything. Amder returned, Bracin gone. All the Priest blessed items minus a few lost their power, and then Amder vanishes. And William Reis, the newly appointed Forgemaster who was supposed to come here, vanishes. No word, and then…" Trie shook her head.

"I was there, remember?" Greenmar closed his eyes.

She knew what he was thinking about. It had been a normal day in the Guild, though everyone was still on edge about recent events. It had proved impossible to keep that information out. Amder was back. There was a new Forgemaster. The youngest ever. The Apprentices and Journeymen had been mostly excited. Most Masters were happy as well, but a few of the older ones were more worried about loss of status.

But things had gone on, even though there were more than a few questions about where William had vanished off to. Then that day… One entire wing of the Guild, the nearly limitless building, had simply vanished. And anyone in that wing had vanished along with it. Thirty-five souls. Two Masters, seven journeymen, and the rest second year apprentices. All gone.

The Guild had erupted. Trie Reinhill had to come up with something, anything, to say. And she lied. She simply said Amder had needed them for special duty, so he had taken the part of the guild they were in and would return it when he was done. Along with the people, of course.

To her surprise, it had worked. She'd lied not to cause a panic. The remaining Masters had met and had agreed with her decision, though all hoped there was something, anything, that Amder could do. But then more things had gone wrong. Rooms seemed to be less real. The calm serenity of the Guild was sometimes now on edge, tempers flared far more often. And for the first time in memory, two apprentices had fought, both sustaining severe injury. And for her, personally, that day had marked the start of the nausea. "Are you really going to be all right?" Greenmar reached out another arm for her to grab a hold of.

"I'll be fine. But I have to clear my head." Reinhill looked around, thankful there were no students anywhere nearby. Not that it would make much difference. *Come. Now.* A voice echoed through the halls. Reinhill jerked upright in surprise. One glance over made it clear she wasn't the only one to hear it. Master Greenmar, the 'Maul' himself, had turned near white.

Come. The voice vanished.

"Was that… Amder?" Greenmar turned to her, his face still pale with the lingering surprise, but the smile that had broken out was one screaming of the relief he must be feeling. She was feeling it herself. Whatever had happened, Amder was back to being here. She instantly felt… Not better. That was strange. But no mind, Amder was back!

"The Anvil…" Reinhill felt a pull to that room. Strong and powerful.

"I know, I don't know how I know, but I know." Greenmar walked with her. Soon they were joined by droves of other smiths. Masters, Journeymen, even Apprentices. The murmurs and whispers around her mixed to form a joyous noise. Amder was back. And whatever had been going on was over. It had to be the God, who else could it be?

Chapter 12.

The anvil room was crowded, very crowded. Master Reinhill got the chaos organized, at least getting sections set up. That everyone could fit was more confirmation to her that the message had to come from the God of Craft. Even with all the troubles, there was no way the room should fit everyone.

In the middle sat the huge Anvil, glistening in the light. "Does the Anvil look normal to you?" Greenmar whispered next to her.

"No. It... "The glistening made it look wet? Slick? It was strange. The thing was God made, though, who knew what secrets it kept. "It looks different." Reinhill shrugged.

The room grew still, as a presence seemed to flow in. More than a few apprentices fell to their knees, and a few masters and journeymen as well. Reinhill bowed her head. She hoped when this was over, she could talk to Amder, alone. *She wasn't the Forgemaster, of course, but being the head of the Guild must mean something, right?* The presence flowed to the middle of the room, and a figure grew there, tall, regal, and... not Amder.

"I am that was meant to be. You were expecting Amder. He is part of what I am, a flawed part. I am more than Amder. More than Valnijz. Know this. In the distant past, I was... broken. Two halves. One Amder, One Valnijz. I am reborn now. Fall to your knees and worship me. Now." The figure raised its arms, clad in shimmering golden armor, and with a single fist struck the Anvil, hard.

A sound that reverberated around the room and through the walls and floors made Reinhill wince. Loud echoes reverberated around the room. Like the snapping of a metal brace. But the horror that came after. She opened her eyes to see the anvil, broken! Trie blinked in confusion. "My..." She didn't know what to say.

"I am your god. But I am not... complete." The figure spoke carefully, its words echoing around the room. "I also do not have the inclination to explain it all. I am what was supposed to be. Behold..." The figure, its face unable to be seen from the glow, faced the now destroyed Anvil.

Trie desperately wanted to do something, but what? How could this be happening? Yet, the safest course was to let this go, at least until it was over. Anything, any creature, that could destroy the Anvil that readily warranted caution. And fear. Shattered into several large chunks, the Anvil released a nearly imperceptible shimmering essence into the air that the figure, this new god, breathed in. "I take back what was removed. My guild. You have a job for me. "

The figure reached down and took the broken anvil and forced the metal back tighter. A horrible grinding and tearing sound filled Reinhills ears. Master Greenmar next to her grabbed her arm and squeezed, painfully. One glance could tell he was in great pain, blood was streaming from the man's ear closest to her, and his mouth was open in a silent rictus of terror.

The metal pieces were forming back into another Anvil, but nothing like the first one. Amder's anvil had been a thing of beauty. An aura of peace had laid upon it and the room. This was squatter and plain, and it held a feeling that she could only call twisted. Wrong. As if a flaw existed, deep in the metal. A flaw that would one day spell the end of the thing.

"You will make weapons. Spears. Hammers. Armor as well. We are going to war." The figure pointed his finger a scant length from her face. "You. You lead this place?" Reinhill found herself trying not to be sick again the closer the figure got to her. Was this the cause? This… whatever it was? The nausea she'd been feeling was stronger the closer the thing came to her. And it was a thing. She refused to believe it was a god. Amder was their god!

Reinhill struggled to speak, her voice failing her as she tried to tear herself from the vision in front of her. "What have you done?" She heard Greenmar manage to speak, his voice nearly a growl. "What have you done?" Greenmar wiped a finger through the blood on the side of his face. "We don't understand. Where's Amder? Where is the Forgemaster?"

The figure turned to Master Greenmar. Its face shone brighter. She wondered why the thing shone with such beauty, but felt so wrong. No, not wrong, unbalanced. The same feeling this new anvil gave off.

Twisted. Like something was wrong, deep inside. "Greenmar, don't…" Reinhill whispered.

"What I have done is reforge the Anvil. I am a god. I am the TRUE god of your race, human. You should bow your head and worship me. Forget Amder. And I have no need of a Forgemaster." The figure turned its attention back to Reinhill. "I will ask once more. You are in charge?"

A fleeting thought came to say no. To shake her head and look away. But only for a second. The barest of facts were simple. If she did that, she would be turning the guild over to whatever came next. Maybe, just maybe, with her there, something good could come out of this, something decent. "Yes." She said, her voice low, fighting back her sickness again.

"Good. This is what is going to happen. You will make weapons. Lots of weapons. Every weapon will be struck three times against this anvil I have made. Do you understand? Fulfill my orders and you will be rewarded. Do not, and the punishment will be severe." The figure touched this new anvil, and the feeling of something not quite right intensified for a moment.

"And what…" Greenmar asked, forcing himself upright. "What do we have to say in this?"

There was silence for a moment as the glowing figure said nothing. Then, with no other sound than the air splitting from the quickness of the movement, this self-proclaimed god touched Master Greenmar on the forehead. The reaction was immediate.

Master Greenmar, known as the 'Maul', was thrown backward with a force that shattered his skull. Blood and bone fell on Reinhill and the other Masters nearby. She could sense the room fill with terror, but no one screamed. She couldn't scream. The sound was stuck in her throat.

"You have no say. I am not a cruel god, except to my enemies. He made himself my enemy. Do what I ask, and the Guild survives. There will be changes, of course." The figure traced a finger against the new anvil. "I will be watching."

Master Trie Reinhill, head of the Smithing Guild, blew out a breath, forcing her terror down. She wanted to scream, yell, and wash the blood of her dearest and oldest friend off her skin. But she couldn't, not yet. She needed answers. Answers that this… being, had. But she had to be subservient to this thing, or she would end up like poor Greenmar. And so would a great many other people.

"Forgive me, but… what do we call you? Where is the Forgemaster? William…" her voice died once again as the hand slammed forward again, not touching her but even closer than before. *I didn't even hear it move this time.*

"I will tell you my name when… it is time. Do not mention that *person* again. I have my own plans for the former Forgemaster." The figure lowered its arm. "You will serve, or you will die. Go, make my weapons. My rebirth brings a crusade, one long needed on this world." And with a lack of any warning, the figure vanished. Leaving a hushed and terrified crowd for Master Reinhill to deal with.

Myriam pondered the man before her. He was ill. Her sight could tell her that. She had trained that aspect of being a healer with this magical gift to a fine point. In was intoxicating to see what anyone's body was doing. She had to concentrate, but she could see how each part of the body worked. She had spent hours studying every single living being she came across. Humans, Trinil, Gorom, even rarer people and mixes. The more she used the sight, the more she understood. But the man in front of her confused her.

His muscles were breaking apart. But he wasn't doing anything. He was a scholar, yet every aspect she could see said his body was breaking from hard work. Muscles were made of tiny fibers, in a way it reminded her of making cloth of gold. Thousands of tiny strands woven together. His muscles shouldn't be unraveling but they were. Even now as she used the sight, she could see there, in his right shoulder, a tiny snap as two or three fibers broke.

The man winced and rubbed the area, not knowing what she was seeing.

"Well Healer Myriam? What's wrong with me? What do I do?" the man asked.

She wished she could remember his name. There were so many people to remember now. She had thought Ture was massive. This place, this 'City in Blue' dwarfed the capitol of Palnor. "I have an idea." Myriam finally answered. She placed her hands on the man's shoulders. Her prior crafting experience sometimes came in handy, and this was one of those times. If muscles reminded her of tightly woven cloth of gold, maybe she could use the boon, her power, to fix them the same way she would fix cloth of gold. *Maybe.*

Her skin, which had faded away from the blue over the last few months, burst into a glow, startling the man. "What?" the man managed to ask before the power flowed from Myriam and washed over him, leaving him unable to speak.   In fixing cloth of gold, you take a tiny speck of gold, and force the fibers into it and then respin it into thread. So, she reached out and took the muscle fibers and did the same, instead using the power to force them together. The man howled and shuddered as his body reacted to this forceful change. But it was working. She could see the formerly broken fibers reform, smooth, and rejoin the others in the proper shape.

The power flowed as the man screamed, but Myriam continued. The screaming was distracting, but sometimes to heal, things had to hurt. But still… with an unthinking push she turned off the vocal cords of the man, stopping them in mid motion. He still tried to scream, but nothing but air came out. *Good, I can concentrate now.*

The man, she thought he was a scribe, but she wasn't sure, thrashed around. It made her working harder, so with another push of her power she froze him in place. She could feel the fibers reforming stronger, better. *Better? No, they need to be the same.*

Myriam blinked, somewhat surprised by the sting of salt that came to her eyes. With effort, she ignored the sweat that was already moving down her face. Just a bit longer. She turned down the power, making the new muscles much like the old ones. Finally, the new fibers stopped growing. As far as she could tell, he was healed.

She removed her hands from the man and could barely move her arms. She hurt. Her own strength was weaker now. It would return, but healing was hard sometimes. Still, she wiped her forehead finally with her sleeve, and her face. Why wasn't the man moving? Oh right! Myriam released her control and expunged all connections between her and the man. He let out a groan, lapsing into a painless oblivion.

Tarn Mikol frowned. Myriam VolFar was advancing. Quickly. He had watched with some interest as she had examined the patient he had given her. She should not have been able to heal the man. It should have been far beyond her abilities. Only he, the Tarn of the Healers, should have been able to. It had been a simple test, to see how far she was progressing. But not only had she had figured out how to do it, but also how to silence the man. And how to stop his movement. That was dangerous. Mikol had spent years making sure that no one else could even think about approaching his level of power and control. She hadn't shown an aptitude to tweak emotions yet, which gave him some solace. *She can't do everything.* But to already be at her level of control and ability, he was sure that would come, and soon.

If she could match his skills, she could be a threat to him. He had little doubt that she wouldn't agree to his continued plan to run the city. No, she was dangerous. He liked her; she was a nice enough woman, but he was not about to let his control slip. He had spent years making his position safe and pulling the strings of power. No mere outsider was going to be allowed to change that. But what to do?

His lips curled upward as he thought about the problem. There was a way. He could reduce another Tarn's power and fix his issue at the same time. *Yes, that would work.*

Chapter 13.

Myriam dried her hair again and pondered the letter she had written to William. She had avoided contacting him for a while, wondering if he would make the first contact. *Foolish thought on my part.* Even back in the Guild, the man could not make the first move. Man. He'd been a boy then, but now, he really had grown into a man. Not that it mattered. Myriam threw the towel down over the back of a chair and sat down, reading the letter again.

William,

So, since you've not done this first, here I am, contacting you. How are the crafters? I liked Tarn Rewil; he reminded me of the Maul back in the Guild. Maybe because of his size. Smart though, talented. The healers have been good. I'm learning a great deal. Have your, well… lines? Have they faded off a lot? Mine have. I can see them if I try, but otherwise they can't be seen. Tarn Mikol says that's because the boon has formed a full joining with the body. It's so strange to have these powers, these gifts. I don't think the people who live here realize how strange their life is. The quickways? The Constructs? The way water comes from a pipe in the wall at a touch?

I keep thinking about how much Regin would love this place. He'd find it fascinating, though I'm sure he'd gain weight on all these exotic foods. Not sure Vin would like it much though. I miss both of them, and truth be told, I miss you. I know we have our differences William, but we went through a great deal with each other. Can we at least try to be friends?

--Myriam

It wasn't all that good. She wasn't sure what to even say in it. William had been in a dark place when they had split apart. It was her actions that had done it. Why did I do it? Why didn't I say something to William and Regin? Why? *Because I didn't want to. I was so focused on avoiding being anyone special, that in running away from things, I ran straight into them.* That thought was the one thing that kept her up at night. If she had sat down and SAID something. Would Regin still be alive? Myriam picked up the letter and frowned. Was this the right choice? Maybe this was a conversation to have in person. It wasn't as if she was forbidden from leaving the healers and going to see William. She had been so busy. And she was sure he had been busy as well, William wasn't one to shy away from work.

No, it would be better to talk in person. With a curt nod, Myriam ripped the letter in half, and then in half again. Getting dressed in her robes, Myriam appraised her appearance in the mirror. The robes were far different than her old crafting leathers. Plain light green, with a bright red belt. She'd been told that only healers wore that belt, so they could be spotted in an emergency.

It was time to ask Tarn Mikol about going to see William. He wouldn't mind, she was sure of it.

Tarn Nollew closed the tome with a loud thud, getting more than a few looks from others in the impressive library of the city. Though none looked twice or said anything upon seeing his gold sash. He was the Tarn of the Casters, after all. If he wanted to slam a book closed, no one was going to tell him no. Chewing his lip, he stood and went back to searching the tomes, trying to find the answer.

The written history of the city was rather complicated, with sizeable gaps here and there. The largest resulted from the attack of the Valnijz cultists. The ones they had moved the city to get away from. He wished he had been Tarn then. To feel the city shuddering with that much raw power. That kind of working must have been intoxicating? That wasn't the right word. Maybe breathtaking? Nollew stopped chewing his lip and rubbed his face, feeling the slight stubble there. For a moment he thought to remove them with a quick wave, but stopped, a smile on his face.

Yulisia liked the stubble. She'd often tried to talk him into growing a full beard, to which he'd refuse. He'd leave it, at least for now. His searching continued, trying to find anything that might have the correct records.

"You know, I can help you with that?" Tarn Yulisia's soft voice came from the other side of the bookcase.

"You can help me with a great many things, but I'm not sure I want you to, for this." Nollew whispered back. Yulisia came around, her robes cinched with a white sash, her symbol of office. "Are you saying you don't want the Tarn of the Library, the center of the city's wisdom, to NOT help you look for a book?" her eyebrows cocked up a short distance.

Nollew shrugged. "In truth, I don't think what I want is here. There are so many missing records."

"Well, we aren't perfect." Yulisia picked up a nearby tome. "City records, Plains period, the River." She placed it down where she got it from and frowned. "Nollew, I know what you are after."

"Well?" Nollew leaned against the wall to their right. "What is it?"

"You are looking for evidence. About Mikol. About how long he's been here. And his part in the city." Yulisia paused, making sure no one was nearby. "That's dangerous, you know that."

"I know." Nollew let his gaze wander down the long table. It was getting late here, and the library was clearing out. And ancient history sections weren't heavily used, anyway. As a result, they were alone, as alone as they could be. "His pushing is getting worse. I don't know if my counters will continue to hold them back much longer."

"We have to. If he even suspected that we knew of his tampering, I have no doubt that he would get rid of us." Yulisia lowered her voice even more. "Should we talk to Rewil? Or Grib?"

"No." Nollew walked over to the table and sat on its edge. "Rewil is convinced we hate him. That was hard enough to pull off. Even if it was exactly what Mikol wanted." He could still feel the emotions that Mikol had tried to push into him. "And he firmly believes that Mikol is his friend."

"That still leaves Grib." Yulisia joined him at the table. "He knows a lot more than he lets on. And he's still open to listening."

"I know. But there is something about Grib I don't trust. He's…too apart?" Nollew shook his head in thought. "He keeps himself away from the rest of us. And I wouldn't be too sure about his connections to Mikol.

He might not be directly influenced by him yet, but there are very much some ties there."

"Well, he is the Tarn of the City. He doesn't live here in the spire. He lives in the middle city and does whatever it is he does. He even goes into the lower city I'm told. I've never even been to the lower city." Yulisia shifted, sliding back on the table.

"The lower city is a rough place. Or can be. I've only needed to be there twice myself." Nollew stood, grabbing another tome. "No, for now it's safer that we keep this between us. I'll find a way to strengthen our protection. Maybe I'll take a trip to the source."

"You want to go there? That place always feels strange to me. Dangerous. I know it's useful, but still, I don't like it." Yulisia gave a shudder.

"Want to? No. But being close to the source makes my work easier." Nollew opened the tome in his hands. "Oh look, forty years ago, there was an oversupply of grain in the lower warehouses of the spire that were sealed by my predecessor, how fascinating." A snort escaped the man as he placed the tome back on the shelf.

"Tarn Mikol. May I have permission to go to the crafters? I wish to see William. We've been here months and I've not heard from him." Myriam stood still, her eyes lowered from the desk that Mikol sat at, though only because of the bright light that streamed in behind the man from the huge window behind him.

"You could write him a letter, you know?" Mikol answered, but stood and walked over to a corner, away from the direct light. "Sorry. I know that sunlight is a bit much to take. Some predecessor thought it made him look intimidating. It makes it easier for my old eyes to see though." Mikol sat down at a small table with two chairs and waved Myriam over to the other one. "Come sit." Myriam made her way over, sitting down carefully. She still wasn't used to sitting in robes. It was sort of like, but

not fully like, sitting in a dress. A thick dress. "I thought about it. But....
William is a person who it might be better to talk to in person."

"Oh, do I detect a story there?" Mikol paused. "Tea. I want some tea.
Would you like a cup?"

Myriam shifted, wondering how much to say. She wasn't sure how much
Mikol knew already. "Yes, tea would be good." She didn't like tea that
much, but she also didn't want to annoy the Tarn. Not that he would be
annoyed. *Manners.* She could hear her mother's voice. *Good manners!*

"Good. One moment." Mikol stood and walked out of his office. She
heard some muffled conversation with an attendant before he returned to
his chair. "One of these days I need to have Rewil install a fartalk."

"I could ask if I go see William." Myriam threw it out there, hoping
Mikol wouldn't say no.

"I've noticed something, young Myriam. You always call him by his full
name. William. It's never Will. Why is that?" Mikol sat back, his eyes
locked on her. Those eyes might be surrounded by wrinkles and the
ravages of time, but the eyes themselves were sharp, bright, and cutting.

"I…" Myriam paused. She knew why, of course, but it was hard to put
into words. "I guess it's because when I trusted him, he broke that trust.
Sort of. He had significant reasons, but it was hard to get past, and calling
him Will was something he wanted. I was mad, though. So, I refused to
do it."

"Don't you think that's a little… silly?" Mikol asked, his voice calm and
kind.

"Yes." Myriam shifted again, but not because of the robes. "Now that I
say it out loud, it is kind of childish." She cast her eyes down but felt a
rush of relief when a robed attendant entered the room with the tea.
Anything but thinking about this right now.

She watched as Mikol took the tea, movements steady and careful, and
poured her a cup. No shake in his hands. How old was Mikol? He
certainly was older than the other Tarns from what she understood. She
hadn't seen the others though, only heard about them. Tarn Nollew and
Tarn Yulisia, the Tarns of the Casters and of the library respectively, were
lovers apparently. And bigoted, or at least the rumors said so. They

disliked anyone not human and hated anyone of a mixed background. Myriam had been surprised by her own reactions to that fact. Mikol had told her, but hearing it and seeing it were two different things. It just never happened outside the city. There was an entire group of healers devoted to studying that, but all were far more than simple apprentices.

Her own shock had been one more born of surprise than any animosity. The first time she'd seen a Gorom and Human couple she'd caught herself staring, and quickly looked away in a flush of embarrassment at her own reaction. It hadn't helped that the Gorom was Grib. The other Tarn, this Grib, lived outside the spire, and only ever came here for their meetings, or commons as they were called, or something like that. She knew almost next to nothing about Grib, no one ever seemed to talk about him.

"So, as we were talking... Will. William Reis." Mikol took a long sip of his steaming tea, his eyes cast down at the cup giving a small smile. "Ah rosehips and farnio, my favorites."

Myriam took her own cup with a hand she hoped was steady and took a sip to avoid having to talk right away. *HOT!* She felt her tongue burn as the hot liquid burned it. She quickly pushed a tiny bit of power to the injury, washing the pain away. The taste was pleasant. Sour, almost, but not bad. She had no idea what farnio was, but it must be the aftertaste, a spicy sweetness. Nice.

"Yes. William." Myriam said faintly, as she saw Mikol watching her, one eyebrow cocked. "Sorry, Will."

"It's nothing to me either way, Myriam VolFar. I noticed it. And for someone who came here with you, who based on everything we know you traveled with, fought with, mourned with, you two stay very far apart from each other. It was noticed." Mikol took another long sip but kept his clear, piercing eyes on her.

"Our relationship..." Myriam trailed off. "Fine. The truth is, I don't know what to say to him. As I said, I screwed up. I was so desperate to stay Myriam VolFar, innkeepers' daughter that I hid from anything else I could be or was. William, Will, I was almost in awe of him at one point. How could he still be this straightforward man from the Reach, and still be the Forgemaster of Amder? And then, then I took it all away from him."

"Amder is gone because of me. Duncan is dead because of me. Will is no longer the Forgemaster. There will never BE another Forgemaster because of what I did. Who knows what the Guild is like now, what Ture is like. What all Palnor and beyond is like? All because I kept a small golden crystal, and the voice that came from it, to myself. I avoid Will because I'm embarrassed. I'm ashamed." Myriam closed her eyes and sighed.

"And Regin. Regin died because of me. I don't think about it or try not to." She took a small sip of the tea this time, thankful for its warmth, now that it had cooled some.

"Would he have still died, though? From what you and William said, it was a blood cultist who killed Regin. Before you put the crystal on the pillar." Mikol reached out and touched her arm. "I will not say you didn't make mistakes. But blaming yourself for Regin's death is too far."

Mikol's hand felt warm, strong. She was grateful for the contact. "Maybe you are right. I don't know. But I guess I'm reaching out to William now, because if I don't, we might never speak again. The longer this distance goes on the more likely that becomes. And I don't want that. The idea of never seeing him again, never talking to him again, I don't like."

"Well then. Finish your tea and go!" Mikol removed his hand and held up his cup. "Far be it from the Tarn of the Healers to tell someone not to heal a relationship."

I do like Mikol. He so reminds me of my grandfather. Nicer though. Myriam smiled at the thought of her Grandfather. Not that he wasn't nice, he had a lot of sharp edges. Nice underneath, but a temper that could shake the Inn if he was mad. After taking several long drinks of her tea, Myriam finished it off . "Thank you."

"Of course. Go." Mikol waved a hand to the door, putting his now what must be a cold cup of tea down. "I will see you tomorrow. You show great promise, Myriam…" Myriam fought the urge to hug Mikol and left the office, heading to the spire quickway.

❖

Mikol watched as Myriam left. The tea should kick in soon for her. If he'd had it dosed correctly, and he was sure he had, she'd be unconscious when the quickway would malfunction. No way for her to use her boon to heal herself. And he didn't want her to suffer. She was a very nice young woman. If she wasn't so talented with the power, she would have lived. But she was strong. Too strong to let live.

He had taken her in, not realizing just how strong she was. Or how fast a learner. He would miss her. Her death would shock the spire, of course. The quickway breaking would tarnish Rewil's reputation as a craftsman. A few well-placed stories and rumors, courtesy of Grib, would seal the belief. Rewil would fall in influence and power, Mikol wouldn't have a threat in his own section. Simple and clean.

For a moment, he considered the fact that she was supposed to be the namer. If she dies, the unnamed god could pick another. Mikol wasn't like the others. He held no god in any fear. This was the city. It had fought off many bandits, armies, and worse over the long centuries. What could a newborn god do against the might of the power of the City of Magic? They had fought off the Blood God's followers, they could do the same with this new one. Mikol was sure of it.

Chapter 14.

Will pondered the shoulder assembly before him, mentally checking through a list of gears and ratios in his head, with only the occasional glance at the long list of parts that were in Rewil's notes. He'd been at this construct for days, and these parts were hardest. He'd thought the Smithing guild was the pinnacle of craftsmanship, and in some ways, it was. The artistry of simple things was, in fact, perfected at the Guild. But this, this magic and mechanical crafting was something else.

The first time he'd ever seen the inside of one of these constructs, he'd felt a thrill. *A challenge.* Something to throw himself at, one day. He'd gotten the chance far sooner than he'd expected. Rewil had first given him permission to try, and then a few days later after looking at Will's preliminary attempts had shown up with a pair of thick notebooks and left them on Will's workbench. Tarn Rewil hadn't said a word, but he didn't need to.

If Rewil was willing to let him use the notebooks, then Will was doing better than expected. If nothing else that pushed him forward. For a while that had been enough. But now, the design bothered him. The typical construct had four arms, and a single large ball shaped base. There were exceptions of course. Some had a set of spider like legs. And a small number of the things that rode the quickway lines, keeping them clean and repairing any damage.

The ball wasn't the problem. The arms were. The design was too complicated. Too intricate. It worked of course, but... Will took some parchment out of a drawer and a marking rod and began to sketch out his thoughts. If he could remove the third interlocking gear, and instead connect the small flywheel for movement here, and he'd need a way for the power to get to the elbow and beyond...

Will drew at a quick pace lost in his thoughts. The marking rod flew as his notes filled the first parchment, and he took a second, then a third. Taking a stack of thin, transparent sheets of planning paper, he started drawing his thoughts clearer, layers upon layers to make a new image. A new way. His fingers hurt, and his hand felt sore, but he pressed on.

At last he threw the marking rod down. His lamp was sputtering needing to be refilled, and he'd been at it for hours, but his notes were done. He flipped back and forth, following the patterns. *It would work.* He had made a new plan. The shoulders were simpler to make, and yet offered the same range of motion. And with the changes he'd made, his plan would offer more power to the upper limbs. His construct would have two upper stronger limbs and two lower limbs that weren't quite as strong, but had two elbow joints, instead of one.

Stronger on the upper set, and nimbler on the lower set. Perfect. Will stood and realized most people had already left. Where had everyone gone? When he'd gotten in, the place had been full, as normal. Now, besides himself, there were only two other apprentices and one older crafter. How long had he been at this?

Will stretched, noting his back was sore from hunching over the table. *I should get a healer to look at it.* He hadn't had any actual injuries since his healing when he first got here but sitting for so long did still make him ache some. But a healer might mean Myriam.

Will put out his lamp and cleaned up his workspace. He'd get some rest and come back to this tomorrow. He was in the middle of his cleanup when a shudder convulsed through the room. Will dropped his notes on the workbench as a sound of metal under pressure giving way echoed through his ears.

The two other apprentices dropped whatever they were doing as everyone turned around in surprise, trying to discover the location the sound was coming from. The one older crafter jumped up, face pale and waved an arm, shooing them all away.

"QUICKWAY LINE BREAKING." The older man yelled. "TAKE COVER."

A quickway line?? Will hadn't studied up on those much, but he had learned some since he'd been here. The metal the lines were on was a special alloy that Rewil had been involved with. But even Will knew the lines were not supposed to break. Never.

"TAKE COVER!" The older crafter yelled one more time before a huge peal of sound tore through the room. Will had once heard a crucible fall in the Reach. A huge empty one. The smelter had cut corners to keep costs low and hadn't done proper maintenance on the support structure. The only blessing had been it finally gave way when it was empty, not full. It had crashed to the ground with an echoing sound as if a thousand bells and been rung so hard they broke.

This was worse. Far worse. Because the sound was followed by a wave of raw power, released from whatever had given way, the power smashed into the spire wall and then through it. A huge chunk of the wall was thrown through the room, carried by the unguided magic.

One apprentice, a person named Jun, was standing there with a stunned expression when the wall section hit him. Jun was gone, just like that. Tables flew, papers flew, and whatever anyone was working on was thrown into the mix, becoming deadly and thankfully inaccurate missiles. Will had gotten as low as he could when he heard more of the wall give way.

He was thankful because, as the newest apprentice, he'd gotten one of the farthest workbenches from the center. Not out of animosity, it was only because the nearer ones had already been assigned out. That simple fact had placed him and his workbench out of reach of most of the flying debris.

Mostly. Because to his shock, his completed notes were flying as well, and in the chaos, burning, as several lamps caught fire, the raw magic igniting them. Will's arms burned as well, as the power that had bonded to him responded to the released wild magic. He gritted his teeth as the sound continued, and the pain grew.

Even his eyes burned, as the released power became visible to his sight. No mere sparkles. It was more like flame, roaring and tearing. It passed over the room, partially built devices and constructions firing up and failing as their incomplete nature failed them. A proper fire broke out on one workbench, as some series of bottle and tubes exploded. And then, as suddenly as it came, it vanished.

Will slumped down to the floor. Even the floor was glowing to his eyes. The sound might be gone, but his ears still rang, his skin burned, and his eyes felt as if he hadn't blinked in hours. He'd worked a smelting once in the Reach where the wind had shifted, and he'd gotten a face full of fumes. It had been his own fault for not wearing a shield, but his eyes had burned for days after, and he'd been terrified he was going to go blind.

This, this was worse. He could see, but everything sparked and glowed. Will closed his eyes tight, trying to soothe them. It didn't help. If anything, it made it worse. Blinking in rapid succession all he managed to do was generate a single tear and that was it. "Quick. Everyone get out." A booming voice echoed across the crafters section. He knew that voice, Rewil.

Will struggled to stand, the combination of burning and tingles in his skin joined by a pool of ever-growing nausea. He really did need a healer now. Maybe Myriam. She'd know, or at least might now, how he was feeling. Sparks, he felt horrible.

"William! How are you…" Tarn Rewil approached him his voice ending suddenly.

"I… I don't feel so good. But I'm alive, I guess." Will rubbed his eyes once. "My eyes hurt, my skin hurts, and I think I'm going to be sick."

"Lad, your skin." Rewil pointed down at Will's arm.

Will looked down and felt his stomach fall, increasing his desire to get sick somewhere. His arms were nearly black with the power. A deep dark blue spread from his hands up most of his arms. Unlike when he'd gotten here, it didn't trace veins and the like. No, this was uniform. And he instantly hated it.

Both hands and arms were the same. "By the blood god's dead soul." Will muttered under his breath. He reached a single finger out and poked the dark blue arm with his other hand.

Pain. Fire erupted at the touch. Literal fire. With a popping rush, a small flicker of blue flame rushed from the point of contact before dying in the air. Will nearly fell to his knees but managed to slump over enough to stay upright.

"What is wrong with me?" Will asked the Tarn, but realized the tarn wasn't looking at him anymore.

Rewil stood, shoulders slumped, looking at the section of wall that had hit Jun. Will could see Jun's body now, his neck obviously broken, his face staring outward, and blank. "Source be cursed. How did this happen??" Rewil growled, his booming bass echoing around the mess.

"Heard a sound, the older crafter. I don't remember his name said a quickway was breaking… then… Everything." Will tore his eyes away from Jun's face. The lifelessness of his form disturbed his vision even more than the magic did.

"Quickways don't break. They aren't supposed to. How did this happen?" Rewil grabbed a workbench and sat on it, his hands going to his head.

"Will. Get yourself to the healers. Can you do it alone or do you need help?" Rewil sat there, his face blank.

"He can't." the older crafter who yelled the warning crawled out from some rubble. "The quickway that broke, that was the one from the Healer section."

"What??" Rewil stood, his voice cracking. "I crafted those lines myself!"

"I'm sorry Tarn, but yes." The older crafter pointed. "Go look for yourself."

"I will, Mytin!" Rewil picked his way across the room and left through a ruined door.

"Thank you for the warning, Crafter Mytin." Will said as he closed his eyes again, fighting pain in one hand and nausea on the other.

"Hmmmmm." Was all Mytin said as he turned to his workbench. "There goes months of work."

Will tried to ask what he was working on, but failed, as the combination of burning skin, eyes on fire, and the sickness in his stomach combined to overtake him. The floor rushed up to his head as his knees gave way. *At least it's not glowing now.*

Chapter 15.

Myriam tried to move but gave up as a simple shift brought pain that she wasn't expecting. *What had happened?* Noise. Massive and overwhelming noise. A roaring sound, breaking metal and then... then nothing. She had tried to do something, anything with her boon, this power that allowed her to heal. It had failed. Why had it failed?

Trying to push away the pain, she reached out again and the power... it was there. She could feel it, but she couldn't do anything with it. Directing the magic seemed confusing. What had happened to her? She tried again to move, but the pain that came was as strong as before. Her eyes weren't even opening. At least she didn't think so.

Was the room dark? Her thoughts were disjointed, shattered almost.

"Quiet." A voice came out of the darkness. "You've been hurt. In truth, I'm rather surprised you're even alive. I did enough to save you, but it wasn't what I'm good at. Sorry."

Myriam tried to ask what had happened, who the voice was, anything, but at best, a hissing croak was all she could make.

"Quiet I said." The voice wasn't angry. It was tired. If she could tell anything about it at all. "You have had a great deal of hurt, and if my informants are correct, you were drugged before sending you on your way to die."

Die? Drugged? Myriam wanted to laugh. The idea was ridiculous.

"I know you don't believe me. I didn't believe it either when he did it to me. He tried to kill me. I bear the scars of that attempt still. I survived and hid. It was Mikol. Mikol is smart, but too sure of his plans. That arrogance allowed me to escape. To be free. And now, it should allow you to be free." The voice stopped as a series of coughs erupted from whomever was talking, finally tailing off after a good while.

"My apologies. My... body doesn't work quite right anymore." The voice still held a slightly rough sound, like a man speaking with a chest sickness. "But I should introduce myself. My friends call me the Downtrodden Lord." A brief laugh, sharp, erupted after that. "It's a joke, you see. I'm laid low, and we have no lords in the city. More is the loss. I was once a Tarn. Until I impeded Mikol's plans."

Myriam didn't understand. What was the man talking about? A former Tarn? What? Then, with a tiny flash of memory, someone saying something early on about the former Tarn of the City. The laborers, the normal people. About a Tarn dying.

"Don't worry. Whatever Mikol gave you should wear off soon. Then I'll try to find you help. We can't use a real healer of course and healing oneself I've heard takes a huge amount of the power and is basically impossible, so that's out. But we will come to that. Rest. Know you are alive. You are safe."

He doesn't know who I am. To her surprise, Myriam found that thought comforting. As much as she could find anything comforting right now. Whomever this so-called Lord was, he didn't know her. He wasn't trying to use her for anything, she wasn't a piece in some game he was playing. She had more than enough of other people pulling her life this way or that way.

"Rest. You have a long way to heal." The voice broke into another cough before she heard the sound of a creaking chair, a rustle of cloth and the opening and closing of a door.

Myriam did her best to steady herself, trying to remember things she had been told in the Healers' section about reaching her boon. *Stay calm, feel the power in your mind.* She still felt fuzzy, and things were hard to deal with. She was thankful for one small thing benefiting her for once. If she stayed as still as she could, it didn't hurt as much.

I must get to the power. She didn't have to be a healer to know that healing whatever had happened to her would be a lot simpler and less painful if she did it now, versus later, when it had healed naturally. That was one lesson she had seen in person early on. A border guard had been out on long patrol, which meant they were gone for a month before they came back to the city.

On the third day, or least early on, the guard had managed to cut his leg, somewhat badly. But rather than return to the city, the man had hidden the injury, and tended to it as best he could. By the time he had gotten back to the city, the wound had been weeks old. Scarred and thick, the healing with the magic had been ugly and painful for the man. Everything had to be removed that had healed on its own, and that wasn't a pretty sight.

And based on how bad she felt, if any of this really healed this way, fixing it herself might kill her. And if that Downtrodden Lord person was right, and Mikol had tried to kill her, there was no way she could ever return to the healers for help. But that was silly, there was no way Tarn Mikol Nese had tried to kill her. There would be no reason!

For a moment she almost laughed. Left the Smithing guild, afraid for her life, and now out of the healers, and trying not to die after. Either way, she did not have a wonderful history when it came to getting trained to do things. Being an innkeep would have been a better fit after all. Her life wouldn't always be in danger at least.

She pushed again for the power, and finally felt a tiny trickle that she could work with. It wasn't enough to do much, and only a splinter of what she normally could work, but it was at least something. *My eyes.* Eyes first. She wanted to see where she was. And if possible, how injured her body was. *Maybe I don't want to see that.*

She took the trickle of power and sent it on its way, using it to trace out the connections in her eyes. She didn't understand eyes all that well. One of the great advantages of the healers section was they taught you everything about the body. Human bodies, Trinil bodies, Gorom bodies, and down the line. How they worked. Every difference and even similarities. She'd only begun those trainings.

Still, she could do a pass to know what was broken. It didn't take her long to figure it out. Thankfully nothing internal seemed to be wrong, but her eyelids were battered and bruised enough that they had swollen shut. If my eyelids are that bad, I really don't want to know what the rest looks like.

She pushed the power that she could summon and felt the eye lids get smaller. Keeping her breathing calm, she fought to ignore the feelings it brought. Ice. Ice and sparks under the skin. It burned as the blood returned to the tissues. It went on for a while, the trickle still only a tiny fraction of what she normally could do, but it was enough. At last, the burning and ice feeling faded, leaving her eyes normal, or at least as far as she could tell. She had yet to open them, and braced herself for more pain, or just simple inability. She relaxed the power, fighting back the tide of exhaustion that came as soon as she did so. *I have to try to see. I must.*

She tried to open her eyes, and to her joy, found they did so. Tears formed as she adjusted, but she could see! She blinked, wanting to wipe away the moisture, but unwilling to try to move her arms much. *Won't be able to see most of the room lying down, but don't have much choice there.*

Her eyes focused at last, and the room took shape. It was, she decided, very underwhelming. Stone, old and black with torch smoke and who knew what else, lay above her. Torch smoke? Here in the City? That meant some of the oldest sections of the city, the poorest sections.

And that was about it. She cast her eyes down as much as she could but could only see her own cheeks as her face seemed to have gotten four times larger. Swelling. Her skin, or the tiny part she could see of it was an unhealthy mix of blue, green and yellow. *By the sparks, I look a mess.*

She could see, though. A minor victory, but a victory all the same. The tiredness that had clung to her hunted her still, and she gave in. Sleep now, and then see if I have access to more power. *Just sleep*

"Who is she?" Ralta pushed her chair back, rocking on the two back legs. "I don't know. But, if Mikol wanted her dead, that's good enough for me." Jinir sat in his own chair, a rather oversized affair, patched and faded, but ornate all the same. All to live up to the title he was known as. Downtrodden Lord. He still considered it rather ridiculous, but it kept his name, his real name, off the lips of those he didn't know.

"Don't you think that's being kind of risky? She could go back to the spire, you know, and if they questioned her…" Ralta cocked her head for a moment and lifted the chair to balance on one leg. "Show off. I know your knack, Ralta, you know that." Jinir felt the rattle in his chest as he spoke. He hated that feeling. Ralta was right that it was a risk. If this woman wanted to go back to the spire and she talked about him, Mikol could figure it out. The man might be manipulative and power hungry, but he wasn't dumb. He could connect the 'Downtrodden Lord' to the former Tarn of the lower city. A Tarn that was supposed to be long dead.

"I know it's risky, but we couldn't leave her to die there. I don't even know why Mikol wants her gone. And in such a dramatic fashion. Making the quickway line break? If he wanted her simply gone, he'd find far less grand way to get rid of her. No. Mikol is plotting something. Something has changed." Jinir wheezed out the last word as a new series of coughs came. He hated this. This life. Scarred, broken lungs, joints that didn't heal. A far distance from who he had used to be.

Tarn Jinir Yallow. Strong in body, handsome in looks. A powerful man. His boon had been the gift to repair things. He'd almost been a crafter, but that wasn't his talent. He could take something, anything, and fix it. Even an entire building, though that would have tired him out for a day or two. As long as he knew what it was supposed to look like, how it was supposed to work, he could fix it. His boon was suited to that. Repairing what was, not making new.

Could.

After Mikol had planted false information about a place that needed his help, everything had changed. He'd gone to an abandoned building that had once been used to dye cloth. Huge vats had lined the walls of the main workroom. Vats with broken pipes and not working taps. He could still remember that day. At least before the vat that was supposed to be empty had erupted in reaction to his working.

And covered him and by virtue of his sudden yell, his lungs with a highly caustic liquid fabric cleaner. Some chemical made from a mix of urine and some powder. He'd never wanted to find out. Why bother? He knew the effects. His skin had blistered and torn, he'd screamed, and the fire had gone into his lungs, bringing the coughing and blood. He should have died. He'd wanted to die.

And yet, one of his people, shocked, had the forethought to drag him away after he'd stopped screaming and cover him with water. He'd lived.

But never truly healed. His talent had almost died that day with him. Working the power brought him back to that moment, and he'd break down. He knew it was all in his head. He KNEW. Knowing that didn't help the feelings that came. The loss, the pain, the anger.

Jinir let his eyes move towards the room where the mysterious girl lay. He knew she was a healer. Her robes, ruined and blood soaked as they were, had given it away. If she could heal him… even a little.

"What are you thinking?" Ralta's voice brought him back to the room. He liked the Trinil. She was tall, thin, lithe, and smart as a whip. And about the only person he trusted anymore.

"Remembering. I need you to do something. Go out, into the city. Get as close as you can to the spire. See what people are saying. I need to know what's going on." Jinir sat back in his chair. "Please."

Ralta shook her head but returned her chair to all four legs and stood, a full head taller than Jinir. "Spying? Oh, all right. At least it's not doing your laundry or anything." Ralta gave a full and mocking bow. "My Downtrodden Lord."

"Stop. Now go. Please." Jinir smiled in deep recess of his hood. He wasn't sure if Ralta had even seen his true face, but he wasn't going to show it now. "Go. I need information."

Ralta said nothing, but left the room, ducking her head as she left. Jinir watched her go with some growing excitement. Mikol was up to something. He was sure of it. And this girl played a role. Maybe, just maybe, Jinir would get what he wanted now.

Chapter 16.

Light. Light accompanied by pain. Throbbing pain across his head. William groaned and felt like he was getting sick again, but that feeling faded. The pain, however, did not. What had happened to him? He remembered being in the crafter section, then a noise. The quickway, the quickway had broken. The memories rushed back, only occasionally disjointed by his throbbing head. He remembered falling, and then… being here. Where was here?

The room was the stark polished white of most places in the spire, and the bed he was lying on was softer than his own. The healer's maybe? The air was soft almost, if air could be soft. Cool at least in temperature. He never complained about being hot anymore, but in his heart, he'd give up a great deal to have a brisk cold mountain blast wash through wherever he was most days.

Half sitting up, the pain jabbed his head hard enough for him to wince, but it faded quickly again. It must be somewhere in the healers. The room was clean, spotless. And there was a faint smell in the air, soap and beeswax. His arms! The memory of the skin being dark blue, something about the released magic from the quickway washing over him and reacting to the boon given by the wild magic of the Anvil.

Yet, his arms looked, thankfully, normal. He shifted his sight for a moment and the surge of bright blue sparks that his ability to see the power brought both relief and some discomfort. Am I getting used to this already? It had only been months, and yet the magic seemed part of him. Strange how something he'd spent most of his life believing was a made-up thing was now accepted.

'Ah hello there young crafter." An older man clad in brown with a red belt and sash entered his room. *I know him*. Mikol. Tarn Mikol, leader of the healers.

"Tarn Mikol! Forgive me for not getting up, I'm not feeling myself." William spent a moment trying to decide if he should try to sit up, but gave that thought up and laid back down with a sigh when the decision did not bring any added pain with it.

"You're a patient. I wouldn't ask you to get up so soon after injury." Mikol pulled a simple white chair up next to the bed. "Now, how do you feel? While I will check, of course, I like to know how a patient interprets their own injuries." "My head hurts. A fair amount when I move it. Other than that, tired. Very tired. Worn out. At least now." Will wondered if he should add the bit about the blue skin and the rest, but let it go. Wasn't worth mentioning.

"Understandable about the head. You landed hard on it when you collapsed after that tragic event." Mikol reached out a hand but stopped short of touching William. "May I?"

'Yes. Of course." William let out a long breath and braced himself for, well he didn't know what, but something."

Mikol's hand was cool, almost cold. But it brought with it even something colder, as the power leaped from the Tarn into William's head. A tremor flew up Will's back as his body reacted to the shock.

"Steady. There are a few damaged parts in here. Nothing serious, but I can fix it, but stay still. This isn't a place to have me make a mistake young William Reis." Mikol closed his eyes as he spoke.

Will suddenly couldn't move, his body locked other than his breathing. He couldn't even blink. He wanted to ask what had happened, how were the other crafters? How was Tarn Rewil? But he couldn't. Even his breathing wasn't under his control, or least he felt like it.

"Calm. I've stopped you for a tiny amount of time. And… there." Mikol removed his hand and William felt his muscles return to his control as he slumped back into his bed. "My apologies, but when working the power on someone's head being totally still helps."

Will tried sitting up, and to his relief, the pain was gone. Just a slight throb so small he wasn't even sure he was imagining it. "Thank you, Tarn Mikol."

"You're welcome." Mikol pushed his chair back. "Now, my lad. I have to be the bearer of some bad news."

"What? Did something happen to other crafters? Is Tarn Rewil all right?" Will looked at Mikol, a slight knot of fear in his gut.

"No. Though Rewil is..." Mikol paused and shrugged. "No, my news is about your friend. Myriam VolFar. Young Myriam was on the quickway that day, when it broke. She was coming to see you. She felt that your friendship seemed to have been lost, and she wanted to try and fix it. I blame myself; she and I spoke that very day about it, and I gave her permission to go see you. But when the quickway line snapped... she was gone." Mikol shook his head. "Such a sad event. She was a supremely talented young woman."

William tried to focus on the words, and not the feelings that they brought. Myriam? Dead? That couldn't be. She... couldn't be dead. Will felt the tears start to form before he even could say what they were. Myriam VolFar. Dead. She had fled the guild for him, helped him bring back a god, and traveled to the depths of Alos. On her own brought back another god. It was...

Sorrow flushed over him. "Please leave me for now." Will managed to choke out. Myriam gone?

"Of course." Tarn Mikol stood and left the room. Leaving William to his sorrow.

Mikol closed the door behind him, hoping he had made the right choice. He had been very tempted to rid himself of this William when he was fixing his head. Mikol had nearly yelled in surprise when he'd touched William this time. He had thought the man strong with the power he and Myriam had arrived, but now... Somehow the power that had run amuck when the quickway broke had been absorbed and now was part of the man.

This made him dangerous. He half wondered if he had made a mistake. Let Myriam meet with William and then make sure both were on a quickway before it had an accident. No, that would raise too many questions. And breaking the quickway had taken a great deal of work to make happen. He wasn't sure if it would even be possible again.

He did not understand those constructs well enough. He had only discovered that certain ones could, if he used the right kind of power, could be influenced by him. But not much. And only the oldest constructs. None of the newer ones reacted to him at all. He'd tried several times.

Mikol approached his office, not sure of his next steps, when one of his attendants stopped him. "I am sorry, Tarn Mikol, but Tarn Grib is waiting for you in your office. He refused to listen when we said you were busy."

Mikol felt his mouth tighten involuntarily. Grib was a useful tool, but not bright enough. In some ways, the old Tarn of the City had been better. Jinir had been smart and talented. That intelligence had made him popular, and then a target. Grib was never that bright.

"Mikol. You will hold fast with your end of the bargain? The quickway explodes, kills more than a handful of my people on the ground, and not low city wastes, either. Good middle city people." Grib stood as soon as Mikol entered.

"Yes Grib." Mikol shut the door quick. "But can you please keep your mouth shut before I close the door? I don't know what was overheard."

"Forget them. I know you keep a tight leash on your people. Mess with their minds. You have made me many promises, Mikol, and yet the time is always not right for your action. It would be a shame if things became known. Yulisia, Nollew… maybe even Rewil. Could you stand against us all?" Grib took what to Mikol was a comedic pose, arms crossed, chest puffed out. *Silly.*

Mikol walked around the Gorom and sat as his desk before answering. "Yes, that would be a problem. What is it the esteemed Tarn of the Commoners wants?" spitting the last word.

"Find this 'Downtrodden Lord.' The low city is becoming troublesome. Whomever this person is, they bring headaches." Grib pointed out the window. "I can't be bothered to search the whole low city, can I? I'm a Tarn."

"But yet you are asking me to do it for you?" Mikol lowered his voice to a monotone. "You need to be sure that this is what you ask of me."

To his credit Mikol watched as Grib became more aware of his words. His skin once flushed, paled at a rapid pace. "Now Tarn Mikol, all I meant was that you have access to skills that I do not. I would assume finding this Lord person would be far easier for you than me."

The corners of Mikol's mouth curled up for a moment watching Grib back down. *He's mine, and he knows it.*

"I will look into it Tarn Grib. But if you will please excuse me, I am dealing with the fallout from the tragic accident that struck the spire." Mikol turned away from his fellow Tarn and stared out the window. He found it amusing the see the faint reflection of Grib shake with anger for a moment before leaving Mikol's office.

In truth this 'Downtrodden Lord' was something that Mikol did need to get to the bottom of, but not for Grib. Anyone that had a base of power already was worth looking out for and if need be, handled. Mikol would gather a few lower city types and make sure they were bound to him and find out what he needed to know.

Chapter 17.

Myriam awoke to a sharp and sudden pain in her left arm. Her natural reaction to grab the site of the pain with her right hand helped nothing. The pain grew as what probably was a broken bone or three rubbed something inside, bringing a new stab of red-hot agony. She lowered her arm, thankful that at least her shoulders or at least one shoulder didn't seem to hurt, at least not much.

Clear your mind. Reach for the power. She pushed the pain away, though it wasn't easy. Working like this was harder than she ever imagined. Still, the power was there, and to some relief on her part, she felt like she could access more of it after she had slept.

But what to do? *First, find out what's wrong.* The voice of the elder who trained first year healers whose name she never could remember entered her mind. Not all that different than smithing. When repairing a piece of work, first figure out exactly what went wrong. Then fix it. She had done a pass before, and nothing inside seemed deadly, and she considered going with that.

But… she hadn't been as able to focus then, and she'd had access to less of her boon as well. *Knowing my luck, I'd fix the broken bones and fall over dead from a damaged liver, or something worse.* No, she wanted to be sure she was not about to die. Even if most of her seemed to want to give up right now.

She pulled as much of the boon as she could and released it in a wave through her body, as she had learned. Anything damaged or injured would respond to the working. And a response she got. Both arms had broken bones, and both had already started to heal, and heal badly. Her right shoulder had torn muscles. Three teeth were almost totally out, and her lips were both busted. The wave passed over her chest without reaction. But there, in her stomach, a slight reaction.

The wave passed onwards. One leg had a minor fracture the length of the bone, and the other was fully broken in two places. The cords that kept her ankles working were torn apart, badly. *I must have landed hard on my feet.*

That idea was reinforced by the fact her feet lit up fully when the wave reached them. Multiple broken bones, and the skin… Myriam wasn't the squeamish type, but her feet looked more like the remnants of the cook's work on a roast before it hit the fire than someone's feet. Add in that all over her skin reacted with various cuts, scrapes, and more bruises than healthy skin. She was surprised she was still alive.

Turning her attention back to the inside, she sent another trickle of power to see what the small sign had been. There! She didn't know the name, but in a small tube thing, a shard of metal had struck through her skin and was lodged in it.

Well, she knew what she was going to have to handle first then. She reached out with all her might and gathered as much of the power as she could. It was nothing compared to what she could do when healthy, but it was more than before. Much more.

She wasn't sure if she should risk a pain deadening working. She needed to be clear headed, and she'd never tried to do that on herself. In fact, no one had ever even asked if was possible when she was around, or at least when she was paying attention. She very much hoped that she hadn't missed some important information while she'd been drifting off. In some of her classes she'd developed a bad habit of only looking like she was paying attention. Only in the ones where some of her fellow students asked many questions that had obvious answers. Now she wished she had paid attention more.

So, no pain killing then. *This is going to hurt.* Myriam closed her eyes and formed her power into what in her mind was a line. A strong thin line. Drendel steel. Strong, tight. She held one in her mind and the other she placed on the shard of metal stuck in her body. Even that brought a slight ache. She squelched the feeling with some effort. She was sure this was going to hurt, and too much pain might break her working. Letting out a slow breath, she gathered her power and pulled.

The pain burst forth, white hot and raw. She wanted to flail, but at least some part of her recognized in her current state, that wouldn't be a good thing. Still, her reaction was powerful enough for a few shudders and flops, enough to bring more agony. Myriam could feel her control slipping but forced her mind to keep a hold of it. But it worked. The metal shard, some copper hued thing, pointed and sharper than a razor, flew free, cutting her skin again on its way out.

She grit her teeth and bit back the scream that wanted to come. *Stay quiet. Stay quiet, Myriam.* She didn't know who these people were who had her. She wasn't sure she wanted to know. Still, a grunt escaped her, but it did not seem to attract any attention. She worked quickly, first sealing the cut in whatever part the shard had been stuck in, and then healing the skin before she bled too much. The pain had almost been more than she could handle. For a moment the feeling of falling had come near, falling in a blackness that would have swallowed her whole. If she had fallen unconscious like that, with the wound unclosed, she could have been in far worse shape. That would have been bad. But she hadn't. And she could still use the power. It hurt, and she felt worn out, but there was so much to fix, and she didn't know how long she had. *I can do this. I must do this.*

Will sat slumped into the chair in his room. He hadn't bathed in two days and had refused any healers who came into his room. He didn't need a healer. He had picked at some food they had brought him, but he had little appetite. Myriam. He had thought himself past her. Past any feelings. But now, he wasn't so sure.

How could this have happened? He didn't understand. For all the adventure and danger they had been through, for her to die like this? His thoughts were interrupted by a knock outside his room. "I'm not hungry." Will half yelled, half growled. He was in no mood for yet another well-meaning healer to come check on him.

"I'm not bringing food." A familiar deep voice came.

Rewil! Will stood and wished he had taken a bath. "Ah yes, come in Tarn. Sorry."

Rewil entered, ducking as he often had to do. Will was at first somewhat taken aback. The Tarn of the crafters did not look like himself. His face was somber, and he looked exhausted. "Sorry to bother you like this William. But I wanted to talk to you, in person."

"Not a problem at all, Tarn." Will waved Rewil toward the only chair before sitting on the bed.

Rewil cocked one eye at the chair and shook his head. "I think I should sit on the bed, and you take the chair."

Will realized that Rewil was right. The chair wasn't built for anyone close to the size of Rewil. "Sorry." Will stood and sat back down in the chair as Rewil sat on the bed, making sure it could hold him.

"No need to apologize. If anyone needs to apologize, it's me. The crafters main workshop is in shambles, the quickway that I made with my own hands and plans exploded, and your friend, the one you came here with, is dead. Not to mention the handful of people who died when everything fell to the ground." Rewil shook with an enormous sigh. "I still don't understand."

Will wanted to tell him it wasn't his fault. But he didn't. He wasn't sure what to say, if only because he wasn't sure what he felt. The silence continued for a long moment, before Will decided he needed to say something. "What caused it?"

Rewil threw up an arm, nearly bashing the ceiling. "That's it! I can't find a reason. I've not slept and barely eaten anything since the accident happened. I've gone over every inch of the quickway rail I can get my hands on. I have gone over my plans and reports when I built the thing so much, I can repeat them from memory, and yet I still cannot find a reason."

Will nodded, his mind pushing the emotions away to concentrate on the problem. "That would be frustrating. How much survived the explosion? I mean, was it an explosion?" Having a problem to fix had always helped calm him.

"Not a lot. Or at least not a lot of large pieces. All quickway lines are in a state of tension. The metal is an alloy I made that can hold on to the power. The alloy allows much of the wonders you see here happen. But the quickways were the original use. Holding onto the power though makes the alloy... not brittle but adds stress to it. But the levels of the stress were manageable. Like hardening steel." Rewil crossed his arms, lowering his head in thought.

"Either I made a mistake in the planning, or there's a flaw in the alloy itself. And that worries me even more. The alloy is used in any place we need to move the power around in large amounts. If there's a flaw..." Rewil shook his head again.

"Then large parts of the city are in danger." Will finished the thought. "What's the name of the stuff? I mean what you call it."

"Ha. Spoken like a former smith. It's called Honnim. But most call it the alloy. It has become that popular." Rewil paused again before rubbing his eyes. "I came here to apologize. And ask for your help."

"You may be only a first-year crafter, William, but you have the skill. You also have a huge connection to the power. In fact, that ability you and Myriam have to see the power? That's almost unheard of. Few have the skill or the boon necessary. I was hoping you might help me figure out what happened." Rewil raised his head and looked William in the eye. "I need the help."

"But you're the Tarn! Why would you need my help?" William wasn't sure how he could help. He had talent, he knew that, but this was a whole new thing to him.

Rewil stood, his head nearly brushing the smooth white ceiling. "William, let me be open and honest with you. I'm being blamed for this. Before I invented the alloy and the quickways, there were other ways to get around the city. But my work changed everything. Now, I'm being blamed for these deaths, and a host of things that I've never even heard of. I need an extra person to help me clear my name. To clear the name of the whole crafters section."

Rewil pointed towards the door. "Out there they are whispering now. I know how this goes. Whispers become talk, talk becomes yelling, yelling leads to anger and violence. Look at me. I'm a... mix. A hybrid. Most people in the city right now don't care. But those who DO care and hate me for it are already pushing that as a reason. I need you to help. You might be a crafter, but you're still an outsider. You're recent to the city. Which means you, at least for now, are considered to be neutral."

William frowned. He had never really thought about the fact that people didn't like Rewil because of his background. Why would they? He was proud of the fact that his Da and his mother both had lectured him and Duncan when they were small that all that mattered was a person's actions when it came to judging them. Rewil was a good, talented man. Anything else was stupid.

"And I thought you might want to find out who or what caused the death of your friend. The quickway carriage hit some other things when it hit the ground and burst into flame. Fire powered by magic burns hot, very hot. There was nothing left but small pieces of the carriage on the ground for a large area. We haven't been able to recover any... remains." Rewil held out a hand to William.

"What do you think? Help me with this? I could order you, of course. But I'd rather ask." Rewil's hand was steady, waiting for William to decide. William looked at the outstretched hand, but only for a moment. It was a simple choice. Shaking Rewil's hand made Will feel better still. Having something to do helped. He could throw himself into this, and maybe get the answers he truly needed. He couldn't save Myriam, but maybe he could do something to make sure it never happened again.

Chapter 18.

"I know that couldn't have been an accident." Tarn Nollew paced around his section of the spire that was reserved for his living quarters. He hated the stark white of everything in most of the spire, so his quarters were paneled with dark woods, metal, anything other than white. Yulisia had once told him he did it to be mysterious.

"It could have been. And that new healer, a prodigy from what I understand, was killed. As well as the poor souls on the ground." Tarn Yulisia lounged on a sofa; arms crossed.

"Do you think Rewil of all people would make that kind of mistake? Rewil might be boastful at times, but he is a genius when it comes to mixing the power and machinery." Nollew stopped pacing for once and turned to Yulisia. "A prodigy you say?"

Yulisia shrugged and paused for a moment before speaking. "From what I gather, she had already outstripped other healers who had been there for several years. But remember, the girl was fairly overflowing with the power. A trip through the magic from the Anvil to here marked her and that other one."

"Do we still not know how they survived?" Nollew sat down next to Yulisia, lifting her legs and putting them across his lap. He liked her legs.

"I have searched the records several times. Everything I can find says it should have killed them both. Torn apart by the raw chaos of it. But remember, even before their trip, they were both marked in different ways. He was the Forgemaster of Amder. And she is the bringer of the unnamed god, and the namer still." Yulisia paused for a moment. "And speaking of which… I was going to bring this to all the Tarn's attention, but there are rumors out of Palnor. The unnamed one has done something to the Smithing Guild there."

"What?" Nollew's eyes drifted across her legs before her words sunk in. "Trouble?"

"We don't know. You know how difficult it is to get good information out of Palnor, or anywhere in the north. All I can say for certain is that the unnamed god did something at the guild. If I had to guess, he made his presence known." Yulisia covered her legs with her robe, cocking an eye at Nollew.

"Wait… if this girl is dead, doesn't that mean that a new namer can be chosen?" Nollew stood suddenly, thrusting Yulisia's legs out of the way. "That is bad. Terrible. And if there is activity in the Guild…" Nollew rushed over to a large desk. "We must call a commons."

Yulisia stood as well. "Wait. If there was a new namer, that name would be everywhere. The unnamed one wants a name, wants it bad. He wouldn't hesitate to make a new namer. But he hasn't. Which means…"

"He can't. So, she isn't dead. But where is she?" Nollew sat at his desk. "I know Grib went to see Mikol right after the incident. What is Mikol up to? Where does Grib factor in?" Nollew thumped the desk with a fist. "I hate not knowing."

"Well, if the girl is still alive, whomever is hiding her or wherever she is, she's safe for now. And that's good for us. And her." Yulisia poured herself a large glass of honeywine. "The library has ears everywhere, my fellow Tarn. We will find her."

Nollew knew she was right. The library, besides its store of knowledge, ran the largest and most complete spying enterprise in the city. Only a few knew that. Most of the spies didn't know it. They thought they worked for other factions. But all the information ended up with Yulisia, one way or another.

"You know, if Mikol tried to have her killed, then he made a mistake. A rare mistake. Can we take advantage of that?" Yulisia sat back down on the couch, her robe falling in interesting ways around her legs again.

"There's a chance. But how? Let's say we have evidence he tried to kill her. Would Rewil believe it? He thinks we hate him. I know we play that game on purpose, but now, considering this, maybe we should end that game and bring him into our confidence." Nollew sat down by Yulisia. "First though, we have to find the evidence."

"Well, I will start looking. I don't think she's anywhere in the spire. Which means the middle or lower city. Hard to track." Yulisia took a long drink of her wine, the slightly glowing amber liquid clinging to the goblet at first before its power faded out. "Good honeywine."

"Thank you. I had it made for me, at least this batch. There's more coming." Nollew sighed. "I don't know Yulisia. The more I think about it, the more I'm sure something big is coming. There's too much pent-up pressure around here. Even the power is acting different, I think. I'm going to the source tomorrow. You should come with me."

Her lips downturned at that. He was sure Yulisia was going to say no or find some other excuse. She hated going to the source. He'd had others say that as well. It was… disconcerting being that close to it; he agreed with that. But to him it always seemed like a living thing, some strange hidden life, but still alive. He kept that observation to himself, however.

"Fine. But only because YOU asked." Yulisia took a last sip of her wine, placing the goblet down nearby. "Now, Nollew, what do we do meanwhile?"

Nollew laughed and pulled her towards him.

Jinir awoke, coughing again. A fit engulfed him, muffled only by his sleeve, which failed to make much of a difference. Once it was over, he glanced down to see the telltale red stains. *Blood again.* It never healed. Even more reason to see if this healer could help him. He felt somewhat sorry for the girl. Her healing would have to take place the slow way, and he knew just how painful that was. He needed to get her a setter at least, so her arms and legs could work. There were a few of them in the lower city, cheap home cures and the like. Ralta would know who the best of the lot was. He would make sure to ask her when she returned.

He stood slowly, his skin always felt thin, stretched in places after he awoke. It took some time for the feeling to fade away. But he needed to check on his guest. Shuffle walking, he made his way down the hall. The light, such as it was, threw off strange shadows. Such an old building. He was sure when this house was built; the city was a very different place.

Back then, the city had no spire, no sections. Just a group of people from various races who had one goal, one desire, to use magic. Countries were young, and Valnijz wasn't even a mad god yet. At least the earliest records from the library when he could still go there had said so. Jinir couldn't imagine it. A few hundred people. Humans, Gorom, Trinil, Mastri, Sea mistresses, whatever else, here to learn magic. Learning how the boons work. How to grant a boon. How children born here would have one automatically. It must have been an incredible time. He wished he'd been there.

But like most things, people got in the way. Some had stronger ties to the power than others. That led to more authority, and then to some being more important. And the sections were made. And over time, the current version of the city had been forged.

Jinir didn't think those former leaders had any idea the city would end up like this. They wanted to be in charge. Never any thought for what comes next, just what comes now. Short-sighted foolishness.

He stopped outside the door to his guest's room, as a strange feeling came over him. His skin tingled. It felt like… the power! Jinir pushed the door open. It wasn't locked. Why would it be? His guest was broken, unable to move, injured and…. Lying fully healed on the slab. The air was thick with lingering power. He'd never felt such levels before.

"This shouldn't be possible." Jinir whispered. The girl was still out, but her face was healed. She had the look now not of injury and near death, but of someone exhausted. She was pretty, with clean, strong, features. Though she was healed, her skin still had large amounts of dried blood on it, and her hair was a mess, but still. She was whole. But how?

"Jinir? Are you down…" Ralta spoke quickly and then stopped, the shock spreading across her features.

"So, you see it as well?" Jinir asked. "A healer can heal their own minor injuries, but even then, it's taxing. But this is beyond anything I ever have seen. Or dreamed of. It shouldn't be possible."

Ralta didn't respond. But he knew her well enough to see that she was studying everything. She wasn't as strong in the power as some, her 'knack' being the impossible balance and the tricks she's learned with it. But the way her eyes darted around, he knew, she could at least feel the air thrumming with the magic. "You feel it too?" Jinir asked, keeping his voice low.

"Yes. It's something, and dangerous." Ralta turned to him face to face. "We should get rid of her. Now."

"What??" Jinir nearly spat the word out. "You want to get rid of the most powerful healer I've ever seen? She could fix me. Fix ALL of me. I was hoping to not cough up blood anymore, not to feel like I had inhaled broken glass when I wake up. But with her power? I could be whole again. Not this broken shell."

Ralta shook her head. "Anyone that powerful is dangerous. For you, me, all of us in the lower city."

"No. I will not get rid of her." Jinir fought back a cough, half choking on his words. "If I am whole…"

"You will be even more of a target." Ralta interrupted him. "People from the spire are asking questions about the Downtrodden Lord. If you are healed, fully healed, how long do you think it would be before Mikol finds out that the former Tarn Jinir is alive and well?"

Jinir held up a finger to his mouth in thought. He didn't like it at all, but Ralta had a point. But he hated this. He had to be whole. Not this shell. No more pain. Yet if Mikol found him alive and healed, who knows what that man would do.

He smothered another cough and looked down to see blood on the finger near his mouth. "I am far from well, and you know it. But fine. For now, she fixes my lungs, and cures the cough."

"If she agrees to do that much." Ralta turned back to the woman. "She may not."

"She will. She must." Jinir walked into the room. "It's time to talk to her."

Chapter 19.

The unnamed god sat in a throne-like chair, a complicated affair of metal, bone, and cloth. He didn't like it, but until he had a name, he couldn't make it be anything else. At least in the time that had passed, he had made his plan to force the namer to give him what he wanted. He never should have given that human any power over him. It had seemed simple in the Anvil.

A slight tingle in the air was the first thing he noticed. So, one of his siblings was coming to visit. Probably Grimnor. He tried to remember if there was any reason for the visit. So much of what was came back foggy. A gray mist clung to his memories still. Sometimes he remembered things clearly. Others, it was like trying to look through poorly formed glass. But no, he could tell now. Not Grimnor, but who? A scent, like tall grass, came next, grass and the open fields.

Taltus? Of any one of the other gods, he expected Taltus the least. One, they didn't like each other much. What fragmentary memories he had of why were old, ancient. From another world, before they came to this place. He did not know if it was the world before or farther back. And two, of all the other gods, Taltus was almost always considered the weakest of their number. Grimnor wasn't strong either, but Taltus? Weaker by far.

Reaching out with his mind, the unnamed god built a better room to be seen in. The flat blue gray plain now sprung into an existence a dais, red stone with veins of silver and gold. The air held an echo of the sounds of the forge, and he formed a goblet of black stone set with bloodstones to drink from.

He could see Taltus now, moving fast towards him. Taltus was always fast. The figure drew closer, and he could see his fellow god for the first time since the rebirth. Standing upright on two hooved legs, skin covered with black hair that faded into white on the limbs, and a black stallion's head. *Typical Taltus.*

"Greetings Taltus. To what do I owe this unrequested and unwanted visit?" The unnamed god sat back on his throne, taking a long sip from his goblet. He nearly spit it out but forced himself to swallow it, wine and blood. *When had he ever wanted wine mixed with blood?*

"Greeting's brother. I came to speak with you. I am concerned that things have not been made clear to the rest of us." Taltus bowed, but a half bow, and never let its eyes leave the figure on the throne.   "Oh? You speak for the group that left me broken? Split in two? Sundered? And not for a year or ten, but centuries." The unnamed one felt a flare of something travel up his back as he spoke. A sound like shattered stone came suddenly as he realized he had squeezed the goblet to the point where it gave way, spilling its dark red contents on the stone dais.

"None of that was intentional. In all the worlds and all the timelines, that had never happened before. We did not know how to save you. But you have saved yourself." Taltus snorted and stepped around the edge of the stones. "Still full of anger I see though."

He doesn't want to step on the dais; he doesn't trust me. "You all, every one of you, did not even try. As a result, my people are split. Instead of one human kingdom and race, my people are fractured! Northern lands distrust the south, the south doesn't trust the north. One land is a blasted ruin filled with creatures that prey on my creations, and on top of all that, you all have let a group of mortals have access to MAGIC!" The unnamed god stood and threw the crush goblet, now little more than a shredded and broken ball at Taltus.

The horse god dodged it easily, stepping back from the dais. "You did most of that. The two halves were broken in their own ways. One became fixated on a single craft, and the other became hate and violence itself." Taltus took a step forward, the edge of one hoof a grass blades thickness away from the dais. "But know this brother, we could have wiped your people out, but we did not."

"You could have tried." The unnamed god waved his hand. Images of great human cities from across Alos sprung into being. "Even in my weakened and broken state, my people are still wonders to behold. They are more numerous, stronger, and skilled than any of the rest of your creations." The unnamed god smiled at his brother god. "And what of your people? Weak and ineffectual as always? We let your playthings rule a world once to shut up your whining. What happened? Do you remember?"

Taltus said nothing in reply at first, though the unnamed god could see the muscles in his fellow gods' arms tighten and flex before finally relaxing. "Where was this anger brother in the Anvil? You were almost cordial after your resurrection." "I had accomplished my first goal, fixing what was broken." The unnamed god sat back down. "As for my plans, why not ask, Grimnor? He's aware of at least part of them." Taltus surprised the unnamed god by breaking into a laugh, though coming from Taltus it was a harsh, grating sound. "Grimnor? He doesn't talk to any of us. Never has. I do not understand why he speaks to you, not that it matters." Taltus smiled then. "But if Grimnor is involved, I can guess what you are up to."

"Fine." The unnamed god didn't like this turn of events. Taltus wasn't taking the bait and letting his anger get the better of him. *The fool has learned, I guess.* "Yes, the Vinik, those vile things will be the first to taste my wrath for their actions."

"There are hardly any of them left." Taltus stomped on the ground with one hoof. "The Gorom wiped most of them out, and what they didn't kill they enslaved, or something. I don't look into it, it's all underground, anyway."

"There are enough. But they won't be the ultimate target." The unnamed god pointed a finger at Taltus. "But that's not the real problem. Again, why would you let MORTALS have access to the raw magic of this world?"

Taltus shrugged. "It's one city. And this world, what do the mortals call it again, Alos? Do you not remember the discussions before we came here? The last world we came to was weak in the power. This world was drenched in it. It will be many years until we have drained this planet dry and move on to the next, as it always has been. We decided it was better to let them be for now, when we have taken everything else, the city those mortals built would be last."

The unnamed god shook his head. "That does not matter. It never does.

Mortals should only get power through us. That was the pact. We never should have come here. We should have only gone to worlds that had magic but no life."

"We came because it was too rich to ignore. You agreed. Or the old… version of you." Taltus shook his head, his mane leaving a fair shimmer of silver as it moved. "But you have named your second target now, the city. That place the mortals have built using the power. That is dangerous, you know. We don't provoke them, and they don't fight back. An attack will upset that balance. If your forces even survive. We know about your god blessed weapons, taking a page from your other self?" The unnamed god smiled at Taltus. *The trap is sprung.* "More than that." Reaching out into the gray void, the unnamed god took a gauntleted hand and pulled a tall thin rod out of nothing. Black and shiny, it seemed to suck in the surrounding air. "This will stop the city. This, and others like it." Taltus stared at the object. "What is that? It feels… wrong."

"Take it." The unnamed god tossed it to Taltus.

Taltus reached out and took the rod. The reaction was immediate, and powerful. Taltus broke into a scream, his body wrenched itself and contorted before he finally went down to his knees. The unnamed god watched with a wide smile and deep satisfaction as the rod pulled the power that ran through his fellow god into it.

"Does it hurt Taltus?" The unnamed god stood again, and without moving, was suddenly right in front of his fellow god. He reached out and grabbed Taltus by the throat while Taltus writhed and tried to free the rod from his grasp.

"There are worlds where my people ate horseflesh, you know that? I have wondered sometimes what it tastes like." The unnamed god got closer to Taltus. "You stink of the plains, though. The rod absorbs magic. It is an anchor of sorts. Any power used in its area will go into it and then back into the world itself. When my forces attack, that accursed city will use the power, I'm sure. I will drain every speck they have stolen, and then my forces destroy the source of their power. And any who stand in my way will die. **Every single one.**"

Taltus tried to respond and even stopped trying to pull his other hand free of the rod to pull at the unnamed god's hand at his throat. Writhing, the horse god kicked out with his large and powerful legs, but the angle was wrong, and they kicked the stone dais, hard. A large flake broke off, but quickly it dissipated into the mist that everything was truly made of here.

Without warning the unnamed god released his hand and pulled the rod from Taltus's grasp. "Don't be so dramatic, Taltus. You will not die by my hand. We are brothers, are we not? You and the rest are my family! We agreed all those long eons ago."

Taltus gasped for breath but said nothing, dragging himself away from the dais. "Go Taltus. Tell the others, it makes no difference. I will have my revenge on the Vinik, and I will do what must be done and remove any trace of the mortals who dare to use our power. But know this, if you stand in my way, I will remove you. The pact is almost broken as it stands since none of you did anything to help me when I needed it." The unnamed god went back to his throne and smiled as he watched Taltus retreat into the gray void, leaving the unnamed god alone. "And when I have my name, the rest of you will know." The whisper echoed across the dais, as the rest of the stone crumbled into the misty nothingness it was made from.

Chapter 20.

Myriam could hear them, two people out in the hallway. She had heard one of those voices before. Her mind, exhausted from the healing she had performed on herself, struggled to make connections. She couldn't hear them well. The room seemed to suck all the noise into it. It was all she could do anyway, to keep the power flowing, to fix everything she could find wrong.

She was close. Very close. Then rest. She wanted to get up and run, but this healing had been harder than anything else she had ever done. No amount of forging, even helping William bring Amder back hadn't been this exhausting.

"You are quite a surprise." A voice spoke from above her. She was clearer now about who was speaking. That man from before. He called himself a Tarn, yes? Former Tarn. The 'Fallen Lord' or something. No, not Fallen, Downtrodden.

"I had heard that it was impossible for a healer to heal themselves that much. But you... But based on the power flowing through this room, I would think impossible was something you did every day." The voice was raspy, fluttering between clear and weak.

"Careful. Is she even awake?" A higher voice, a woman? But there was a strange feeling to it. She was fighting to even find the strength to open her eyes. She wanted to see these people. But it eluded her still. If she did so, she was sure the power would slip away. It was taking everything she could muster to hold on to it as it was.

"She is awake, Ralta. She's listening. I'm sure of it." The raspy voice came again, joined by a few coughs, hard and deep. "But she isn't responding. She's scared, I'd bet. Of us, which she does not need to be."

"Of course, she's scared. She should be. If you or I were dragged out of the wreckage and ruin like she was, we'd be worried as well. Maybe she should be though." The other voice, this Ralta, spoke. "I still think this is a mistake."

"You think everything is a mistake." The raspy voice spoke. "I am Jinir, former Tarn of the Lower and Middle City." "Fool." Ralta's voice came quickly. "Now she is even a greater danger." "I and my friend Ralta here saved you. Though I did not know you were this powerful. I saved you since Mikol wanted you out of the picture, a piece removed from the board. That was enough of a reason for me. But now, this... this changes everything." Jinir coughed again, hacking coughs that came in a long spurt before fading into a gasping breath.

The sound of a chair being dragged across the room filled the air. "Sit Jinir, please." Ralta spoke.

"Fine." The response came as the sound of someone almost collapsing into a chair seemed to come. "Open your eyes, let go of the power. We aren't a danger to you." Jinir spoke again.

Myriam struggled for a moment. This Jinir person sounded sincere, but the other one, this Ralta, she wasn't sure about. *Do I have a choice, though?* She knew it would be hours if not a few days before she would have the strength to run. *If I ran, where would I go?* If Mikol really had tried to kill her, a large if in her mind, she couldn't go back to the spire. And she didn't know anything other than the few places in the outer ring and the spire. And only the healer's section at that.

Myriam slowly released the power, feeling the tremendous weakness spread across her as she did so. *So tired.* But she had made her choice. Slowly she opened her eyes, looking up at a dingy and old ceiling and an even older and dirtier torch holder.

"Over here." Jinir's voice came from the left.

She turned her head to see the two figures there. One, a man, human. His face, as it was uncovered by the large hooded robe he wore. His eyes were bright, but the rest of him... His skin was almost melted in places, horrible old scars smooth but twisted covered what skin she could see. A fleck of blood on his lips. *From his coughing.* He was not a well man then.

The other, the one called Ralta was a Trinil. Tall, thin, and even though Myriam had never seen her before, she was sure this Trinil would kill her without a second thought. Ralta's eyes locked onto hers in an almost challenge before Myriam dropped the gaze. Ralta was standing next to this Jinir, almost protectively.

"Hello." Myriam managed to force out, her voice weak. "Thank you for… saving me. Do you think I can trouble you for some water? Clean water, to drink." She knew water in a place like this might be suspect.

"Of course." Jinir turned to Ralta. "Please go get water for our guest."

"I'm not sure I should leave you here alone with her." Ralta kept her eyes on Myriam. "What if she does something?"

"I am too tired to do anything other than talk, and even that, not for long." Myriam managed to give a clear voice to her words, watching as the Trinil's eyes narrowed in thought. *I wonder if she can still see if I'm lying or not?* Myriam knew that most Trinil in the City lost that ability over time, one of the side effects of this place. This Ralta, though, stared at her as if she was trying to force a hole into her head to see.

"Good." Jinir waved Ralta towards the door. "Please, water."

Ralta didn't argue this time, but let her eyes narrow one last time before turning to leave the room.

"Don't mind Ralta. She's protective of me." Jinir shifted, the chair creaking with age as he did so. "So, your name?"

"Myriam. Myriam VolFar." Myriam saw no reason to lie about her name, at least to this man. He'd figure it out eventually, she was sure. Better to be honest when she could.

"Myriam. Unusual name for the city. And your accent. The north?" Jinir leaned forward bring a new set of creaks from the decrepit chair. "So, you're one of the two new users of the power, then I'm guessing. I heard rumors of course but didn't think…" Jinir stopped talking suddenly. "Ah. So that's his game."

"What?" Myriam struggled to make sense of things. She was so tired. So tired. "Game?"

"Mikol. Your Tarn. I see why he tried to kill you. It's the same reason he tried to kill me. Almost succeed, both times it seems." Jinir held up a somewhat shaky hand. "Let me explain."

"This should be good." Ralta said as she reentered the room holding a large and smooth metal cup. "Sorry, I had to make sure it was a clean one. Jinir, you need to have someone do your dishes more often. It's disgusting."

Jinir ignored her comment and took the water, handing it to Myriam. "Drink, while I tell you a story."

Myriam took the cup, surprised by its chill. *Ralta might not trust me, but at least she's courteous.* "I'm listening."

"I was the Tarn of the Commons. Mikol laid a trap for me and nearly killed me by making a vat of caustic liquid explode in my face. He did so because he felt I was a threat to him. I was popular, and much loved by the people of the lower and middle city. It was a stupid fear. I had no plans to run the city at the time, especially not the way Mikol does." Jinir broke into a cough again.

Myriam listened to it carefully, remembering what Jinir had said. He must have gotten whatever it was into his chest. Surprised he lived through that. Painful.

"Forgive me." Jinir wheezed out after the fit subsided. He took several deep breaths, or at least as deep as he seemed to be able to muster. "While tradition states that the city is run by the five Tarns, sometimes one Tarn gets… more control. Mikol is that person now. And has been, for a very long time. No one is even sure how old Mikol is. No one says anything for two reasons. One, Mikol is the Tarn of the Healers. Everyone loves the Healers. Two, Mikol makes those who might ask questions, or what he thinks is a threat, go away. He makes them no longer be a problem for him."

"Dead. He makes them dead, Jinir." Ralta crossed her arms. "But why her?"

"Don't you get it, Ralta? It's the power. She's strong. Very strong. Stronger than Mikol was ever or will be. Look at what she did! Healing herself of that level of injury in that short of time?" Jinir pointed at Myriam. "She's a direct threat." "I am here, you know." Myriam took a long sip of the water, its chill refreshing her, but only a fraction of what she needed. "But why? I am a new healer. I am nothing."

"You are nothing NOW. But in a year? Two years? You already have the raw power to eclipse anything Mikol could even imagine. But you don't have the knowledge, the skill. Eliminate you now." Jinir paused. "Ah… two targets."

"What?" Myriam asked, trying to keep her eyes open.

"He engineered the quickway accident. Kills you and lowers Tarn Rewil. The Crafters are also highly respected. And Rewil while he's a crossmix, has a lot of support. I'm sure Mikol has worked his brief hints into the minds of some, making people wonder if Rewil is up to the task of running the Crafters." Jinir sat back once more, shifting in his voluminous robes.

"What about the other one?" Ralta was frowning now. "The stories said there were two."

Myriam tried to answer, but the exhaustion she'd been fighting rose and overcame what resistance she had. "Will" was all she said before her vision faded to black as everything rushed away from her.

Chapter 21.

Will surveyed the pile of scrap in front of him, unsure of where to start. The constructs had cleaned the debris up and piled it all here, in this large empty room in the spire. He wasn't even exactly sure where they were in the spire. To get here, Rewil had taken him through what seemed a never-ending series of stairs, hallways, and more stairs. He was tired, and he wanted to sit down, and they hadn't even done anything yet.

"Tarn Rewil, where are we? What is this room for?" Will asked, as he felt a sense of dread settle over him looking at the pile. Why am I afraid of it?

"This? It's an older storage room. It's out of the way and hasn't been in use for a very long time. Less chance to be disturbed. I know it's somewhat of a far walk, but with the quickways out of commission for the time being, we have to deal with it." Rewil picked up a long piece of twisted rail, frowning. "I don't get it still. I've gone through the design a thousand times; how could this have happened?" Rewil dropped the twisted rail. "Don't be afraid. The constructs didn't find any trace of the girl. Which is unusual. I don't want to speculate about why, at least not yet."

Will still didn't like it. The idea of moving something and finding. *No, stop thinking that way. Myriam was missing, but you don't know.* "So where do we start?"

Rewil crouched down and picked up another piece of scrap, some mess of twisted metal that Will did not know what it was. "I am not sure. Seeing it like this, I don't know."

Will forced any thought of Myriam out of his head as best he can. "There's too much. Too much chaos. Maybe, can we have the constructs sort the pieces? Maybe make piles? Rails in one place. Parts of the cabin in another, and so on. Or a pile where it's not clear? Just to organize it, find a place to start."

"Good idea." Rewil stood, brushing his hands against the thick gray leather apron he wore. "Give me a few minutes. The constructs guarding the door should be able to handle it."

Will watched as Rewil stepped out for a moment and brought the two large units into the room. Four armed, strong, and fast. These two constructs also had a brass and copper tube on their back. Will did not know what that was, but he hadn't examined the guardian constructs much. The basic design was the same for almost all the units, but based on the job, there were changes.

Rewil was speaking in a low voice, so low that Will could not hear it. He still didn't like to talk to the machines. It felt strange to him, like he was talking to his hammer. But Rewil, being their creator, didn't have that unease. And before long, both guard units rushed into action and began moving pieces around, far faster than any person could.

Rewil approached him. "There. That will make quick work of the pile. And if they find anything that was… once was living, they will stop and let you leave the room." Rewil laid a heavy hand on Will's shoulder. "You need not have to deal with that."

"Thank you." Will dropped his voice. "I've seen death, lots of death in the past. I've seen the Valni kill, but I don't want to see her, not like that."

"I understand. But remember, she's missing. The odds are that based on the amount of power that was released all at once, there isn't anything to recover." Rewil smiled. "You have nothing to worry about!"

Will frowned in response. "Thank you, I think." He knew Rewil was trying to help him move on, but Will wasn't ready to. And attempts at humor right now did not sit well with him. Even though he knew Rewil's heart was in the right place.

"Sorry Will. I'm not good at this sort of thing. I'm a crafter. I make things. It's not what I do, it's who I am." Rewil rubbed a hand through his hair. "But look, they are making fast work of it." And the constructs were. There were already half a dozen piles on the room's far side. And the mass that before had looked an impossible task was already down by a third. Will watched as the machines moved, rolling around.

"Tarn Rewil, what was here before the constructs? I mean, what did this kind of thing before you invented these machines?" Will turned to Rewil. "How long have they been in use?"

"Ah. The story of the constructs." Rewil walked over to a far wall and sat down against it. "Sit. It's an interesting story. And my knees aren't getting any younger." Will joined Rewil, watching the constructs continue to work. "They are... It's strange. I'm so used to them already. A few months ago, a year ago if you had said I'd be seeing this, I wouldn't know what to say."

"That's somewhat by design. But we are jumping ahead." Rewil paused for a moment. "I've been Tarn for eighteen years. Before that, I was a crafter for nearly thirty. I came up with the first construct soon after the creation of the quickways. In fact, the first constructs were designed to make sure the quickway rails were in good order. They are, or at least were, still in use. It's another mystery why they didn't detect whatever happened before it happened."

"To answer your first question, before the constructs, there was a combination of things used. People did most of the guard duty, but for things like this, we used to mostly use power made simulacra. I think that's one reason Nollew hates me so. His section used to summon these power wrought fake people to do things like this." Rewil shook his head. "He doesn't like to remember that we made the first of the constructs together, before we were Tarns."

"How so?" Will shrugged. "I really don't know anyone from that section. From an outsider's perspective, the divisions here stand out. On one side you have the Crafters, on another you have the Casters and the Librarians, and on a more... neutral side are the City and the Healers. You'd think you all would work tighter together more."

"I don't consider you an outsider, Will. Not anymore. But that's not the point. And in fact, the casters do have some... interactions with us. Most of the power sources we use require a caster to form the links from the source." Rewil paused. "I'm not doing a great job explaining this."

"No, but it's interesting." Will's attention shifted again to a construct that was pulling a large, twisted rail out of the pile. "So why make them?"

"Well, there were a few reasons. The main reason was the casters were always complaining about making their simulacra. See, they were patterned after people. And their abilities mimicked the abilities of the person for a while. That was useful, but for things like this, you'd need a large group of casters and workers. It was helpful, but slow. And as I said, the first constructs were really the old rail riding kind. No worker, regardless of if they were a Human, Gorom, Trinil, or whatever other race or hybrid they were, was going to do that job quickly." Rewil shrugged. "The first constructs were powered by a simulacrum. The power bonded to the frame and stayed. The echo of the person they were based on was a pattern for the power. It wasn't like we were enslaving people or anything. I say that because it got asked, a lot."

Will nodded slowly. "I understand. Sort of."

"We don't do it that way anymore. Now the casters use a changed form of the working to forge a link with the principal source and use their own mind as a template. Sort of. I don't fully understand the power side of things myself. My boon and skills are elsewhere." Rewil shrugged. "None of the Crafters truly has that much skill in using the power. We all have the boon, of course, but in Crafter's the expression is different. It's one reason I was happy to have you in my section."

Will paused for a moment. He'd wanted to ask this question often but hadn't. But this was as good a time as any. "Tarn Rewil, what is the source? Everyone talks about it, or at least mentions it, but no one says what it is."

Rewil sat back, his eyes widened slightly, before laughing. "You're right! I forget sometimes that you weren't born here. You wouldn't know." Rewil eyed the shrinking pile. "The source is… where the power comes from here. Unlike where you were exposed to the magic in the Anvil, here it is more controlled. Less wild. Everyone born here at the age of fifteen, or if they find their way here, is brought to a chamber under the spire. Only once for most people. It is bathed in the power. There, they are given their boon, or knack. Whatever you want to call it."

"A rare few are born with their boon. A very rare few. We don't know why. But Tarn Nollew was one of those. Almost always those who are born with it become part of that section."

"Boons. Some seem, limited. Like a certain thing they can do with the power. Others can shape or change the power in particular ways. Like a healer, or a crafter. Why?" Will pushed with his questions. Something in

Rewil's answer didn't add up to him.

"Hence the great divide in the city. Some are given a particular skill a solo ability with the power. They all are part of the middle and lower parts of this place. For the most part they use their 'knack' not very often. I once met a very capable leatherworker from the middle city, his knack was to make milk turn purple. Only milk. And only purple. Nothing else about it changed but it's color." Rewil shrugged. "We don't know why."

"But for those with a true boon, it's different. There's a much greater link to the magic. Crafter's use it to make things. Healers use it to heal, obviously. Caster's use it directly. To protect, to kill, to do other things as well. The Librarians use it to gather knowledge and keep it. I once met a librarian who had used the power to memorize every plant in the ocean. Every single one. Useless, but still impressive. Truly, if you're given a boon and you're not one of the others, you get put in the library."

"How does this chamber work? Where does the power come from?" Will pushed again.

"The chamber was built by the first to come here. But it moved with us when we moved the city." Rewil stood. "Ah! They are done. And…" Rewil turned to Will. "Let's get to work."

Chapter 22.

The Unnamed God hated talking to Grimnor. He'd only been partially truthful with Taltus, Grimnor didn't speak to him much either. He couldn't in fact remember anytime that Grimnor had spoken more than four words at once since they had come to this world. Not that his memories were all that clear. Since his return to being whole, he'd had trouble sorting out the conflicting images and pasts of the two halves that he had been.

Most of what he had from dealing with Grimnor had come from Amder. There were a few fragments from Valnijz, but fragments, and ancient. From before, that shard of him had gone mad from the truth. Amder had actually spent time with Grimnor, which made sense with the overlap that had formed.

And even with Amder, Grimnor didn't speak, usually. Grimnor often only made these sounds that were so low that more felt them than heard them. If he was angry, the volume rose to a crescendo. And right now, the crescendo was being reached.

"Calm down, brother. You alone still have the right to call yourself my brother. But the first part of my vengeance is here. These Vinik will pay for what they did to me." The Unnamed God almost winced as Grimnor's voice crashed into him.

"I know your Gorom punished them. But that was long ago. They still scraped by, deep in their tunnels. And… the ones you use. But they struck at ME. And I will have my due. "The Unnamed God pointed at his brother God. Grimnor did not look all that different from his creations. He never did. The only notable differences were his size and the colors of his skin. Standing six spans high, Grimnor towered over his Gorom. That and the blue white glyphs that covered his body made sure that anyone who saw him knew the truth.

The almost plaintive rumble would have been amusing if the subject wasn't so serious. "All of them. Even the creatures your precious Gorom enslaved. They all must die." The Unnamed God hefted a two-handed hammer, its head covered with a series of small pyramid shaped spikes.

"Your people will be spared, as long as they don't interfere."

Grimnor complained again, but the Unnamed God didn't bother to listen. He turned his attention to the deep places in the world. Deep in the Skyreach mountains, he could still feel the traces of the nest the Namer and the other had found. A nest that would soon be eradicated. Every Vinik in the world of Alos would die before he was done. And then, the ultimate target. The City in Blue.

He could feel it tickling the edges of his mind. The Unnamed God didn't hate the City. Nor the people who lived there. Hate wasn't the right word for it. He hated the Vinik. No, the City... the City had to be destroyed because of what it allowed. What it represented.

A world, a place where magic, where power, could be wielded by mortals. Where he and the other Gods had no sway. He still did not understand why the place had been allowed to continue. They had all agreed to the pact. No creature could wield the power except through them. Magic had to be controlled by those with the wisdom and knowledge to use it. And no mortal ever would have that wisdom. They could not have it.

Magic was power. And power was dangerous. And power should only be held in the hands of those who could wield it as it needed to be wielded. If not by the Gods, then by those with knowledge and wisdom. But the nameless magic wielding people of the City in Blue... they had been allowed to keep this great power. And it could be used by those who did not have the right... the ignorant. And now that power was turned at them. But the Unnamed God had no intention of letting it go. That City and everything it stood for had to be destroyed at whatever cost.

"I am going now. Do not try to stop me." The Unnamed God forced himself forward, from the half world of the gods, into the physical world of mortals. It was harder than it should have been. If only he had a name. His old name, the one from before, was lost. He wasn't that anymore. But being split into two for an eon or three and then being remade changed everything. Myriam. He knew she was in the City. That was the other reason to go, to take it. She had to name him. He would be complete then.

The tunnel formed around the Unnamed God. Flat stone, pale stone. He could feel the nest nearby. He'd only been a minor presence the last time he was here. Confined to a tiny crystal. An echo of what he was now. But it had been enough. When these creatures had admitted their involvement with his splitting, he had raged, but he'd been powerless then. Not so powerless now. The sound of uncountable clattering feet came to him. Echoing down the hall. Good, they wish to try and fight. Hefting his hammer, the Unnamed God waited and smiled.

Myriam could more feel the light on her face than see it. She was still tired. Everything ached now. Not the sharp pain of injury, but the dull ache of exhaustion. But her body was making demands of her that had to be answered. She was thirsty, and hungry. Her stomach reminded her of its needs with a spasm of pain, and it furiously seemed to try to digest itself.

"Ah, she awakens." Ralta's smooth voice came, for the first time not sounding quite so annoyed.

"Water?" Myriam managed to croak out. She had taken that one sip to be sure earlier, whenever that was, but she needed more. "Water and food." She managed to say.

"Hmmm…" was the only response she heard, but the sound of liquid being poured came to her ears, a wonderful sound in her current state. Slowly opening her eyes, and ignoring the sleep that clung to them, she reached out for the metal tumbler that Ralta held, getting her first full look at the Trinil.

Tall and thin like all her race, Ralta had unusual hair for a Trinil. A fiery red. It arched up in some strange fashion that Myriam had never seen. "Before I hand you this, we must come to an understanding." Ralta dropped her voice. "An understanding that Jinir will never hear of, or this water and the food you desire will never come."

Myriam wanted to be angry at this turn of events, but she couldn't quite work up the energy to care much. "Fine. Talk."

"Jinir, the Downtrodden Lord, is special. You will not harm him. You will not hurt him. If you can heal him do so, but do not give him false hope. Do not pursue him, do not seduce him. Do you understand?" Ralta's question was nearly whispered.

Myriam wanted to laugh. She had no interest in getting entangled in anything like that. Why did this Ralta care so much? Myriam debated trying to use the power to see if there was real care in the Trinil's words, but the lack of food and water made the idea of working the power that much more distant. "I have no interest in your Lord."

Ralta stared at her for a long moment before finally proffering the tumbler filled with ice cold water.

Myriam could have kissed the glass. She drank, taking huge gulps that drained the tumbler, fast. She could feel life flowing into her, brought by the water. She wanted more. She needed more.

"Easy," warned Ralta. "It's not my fault if you choke, and it's an awful way to die." Still, she refilled the water to nearly the rim.

"Thanks." Myriam said automatically and drank another careful sip. Ralta blinked oddly and frowned, pushing a plate with various foods on it towards her. Myriam felt her stomach rumble. The first bite forced its way down her throat, and lay there for a moment, unmoving. Then the second bite happened. And the third and the fourth. Myriam was ravenously hungry. The meal continued, the food disappearing almost as fast as the water had.

For the first time in a while, Myriam actually felt somewhat normal. At least she was starting to. Not all the way back to usual, but still the food and water had, in fact, made a huge amount of difference. She sat up slowly, feeling the kinks and protesting muscles after laying down on what amounted to a hard wooden table for so long.

"Thank you again." Myriam said, unsure of what to do next. She wasn't sure where she was exactly. Somewhere in the lower city. She doubted it was anywhere near to the spire. She tried to remember what the other one, Jinir, had said to her, and slowly remembered. More healing then.

"Do you remember what happened to you?" Ralta sat down and leaned back, perfectly balancing the chair again on its two back legs.

"I was going to see my friend Will. In the crafters. Then, a noise, loud… and then I was here." Myriam had a vague and deeply unsettling remembrance of falling to go along with it. And she had tried to use her power for, well, something, but she couldn't. That was it.

Myriam stood in sudden shock as something else returned from her memory. Mikol. Mikol had tried to kill her? No, there was no way that was true. Mikol was Mikol. Tarn of the Healers. More like her Grandfather than anyone who would try to kill her.

"Ah. So, you remember what he told you then." Ralta shook her head. "No, I can't read your mind, but there are very few things that could make you startle like that."

"It's true? How do you know it's true? Mikol? I can't believe that." Myriam winced as muscles in her legs complained about her putting weight on them again after that long.

"Tarn Mikol. The sweet old man who runs the Healer section is also a cunning, powerful man. He is the secret power who runs this place. Anyone who might threaten his power, like you, a young healer bursting with magic, bright, very talented, is a target." Ralta shifted and much to Myriam's surprise, the chair now balanced on one leg.

"The Downtrodden Lord was popular. He's a good man. A great man. Mikol removed him, replaced him with Grib, who is wholly subservient to Mikol." Ralta stared at Myriam, her eyes narrowing once more.

"He was injured, right? I remember something about healing him?" Myriam held Ralta's gaze. She didn't know this Trinil, but she knew enough about people in general to realize that Ralta didn't trust her and was very protective of this Jinir person. This Downtrodden Lord. "I thank you for the food. I do. But I need a bath and something else to wear. I can feel my skin being pulled tight under all this…" Myriam waved her hands over the dried blood and dust that still clung to her. Ralta did finally smile then. "Yes, of course. We don't have fancy bathhouses here in the lower city, but I can provide clean water, soap, cloth to clean yourself, and a towel to dry with. And a clean robe and other clothes." Ralta stood and left the room. "That will do just fine."

Myriam called after her. She was ready to remove the last of this grime from her. It would almost be nostalgic to get clean this way. True to her word, Ralta reappeared in a short time with everything Myriam would need. Ralta left, giving her some privacy. Myriam wished there was a mirror here, but she'd manage. Washing felt good, and by the time she had gotten dressed again, Myriam was ready to deal with the situation she found herself in. "I'm done Ralta." She said, knowing the Trinil was waiting just outside the door. Ralta came back in, giving her a nod. "Better?" "Much. Now about Jinir, how long ago was he hurt?" Myriam needed to know.

Ralta frowned and nodded. "Yes. He's...." the Trinil stopped midsentence and turned toward the entrance to the room.

"Ah! She awakens at last." A voice, broken and gravelly came from the doorway as the man they had been speaking about stood there. Slightly stooped, one shoulder noticeably lower than the other, and a face hidden in the depths of his hood. "And yes. It is my sincere hope that you free me from this." Jinir pulled his hood off. Myriam swallowed at the sight. The man's face was more like a half-melted candle than a normal human face. A few thin patches of hair clung to his scalp, wispy and white, blond. One eye was bloodshot, but the other was clear. In that eye Myriam saw the man inside. A strong, talented, man. And one who was now pinning every hope he had on her.

"Ah, I apologize for my appearance. It has not been an easy time for me. But you can fix that. I know." The man said with a light voice. It was strange how a man whose face had been so melted and set afire could sound cheerful.

Myriam swallowed. Healing him would likely exhaust her and be extraordinarily painful for him. Those were old injuries.

The older the hurt, the harder the heal. That had been one of the first lessons the Healers in the spire had pushed on her.

This, this was not going to be easy.

Chapter 23.

Will rubbed his hands together for the thousandth time since they had started. This metal, this Honnim, was ice cold to the touch. He did not know why. Whatever it had been made to do made it act like no metal Will had ever worked with in the past. He'd tried three times to get an idea of how the stuff was made out of Rewil, but the man had shaken his head and told him to ask when he was a full senior crafter.

But the other strange thing that still bothered Will about all this was the odd buzzing sound in his ears anytime he held a piece of the wreckage for more than a few moments. It got progressively more annoying over time. He had started to say something to Rewil about it, but realized quickly that Rewil didn't seem to hear it. The man was gripping a piece of rail in one hand, trying to find the other end in a pile of rails the constructs had sorted out. The same piece for more than an hour.

"Look, Will, come here." Rewil held up a random piece of rail in the air with his free hand. "See this?"

Will could only guess at what Rewil was pointing out. It was an off bronze and gold-colored piece of rail. It looked like all the other pieces. Broken like the rest. "I am not sure." Will said, trying to figure out what Rewil was trying to show him.

"Look lad. The edge. This side is twisted, bent. The other is broken clean. Like a shard of some crystal." Rewil ran a finger along the edge, jerking back suddenly as a small red line appeared. "Sharp too."

Rewil was right. It looked different, but what did that mean? "Ah, I see. But what does that matter? I mean, it's metal. Metals have a lot of crystalline features, you know that." Will felt like he was being patronizing. This WAS his Tarn he was talking to. But his head hurt from all the buzzing, and they were getting nowhere. And the whole reason he had come was for Myriam. And there was nothing to help him close that chapter of his life.

Rewil gave him a long look, a frown appearing for a moment before he laughed again. "Sorry Will, I forget you weren't always here and one of us. This shouldn't happen with Honnim. Not with the way it was made. It's almost as if there was a resonance." "A what?" Will was confused.

"Ah." Rewil thought for a moment. "So, have you ever heard someone break a glass with the sound of their voice?"

"No." Will smiled for a moment. "That's impossible."

"No, it's not." Rewil paced, waving the oddly broken rail around as he talked. "If you can hit the right sound, the right way, the sound can make the glass flex, and then shatter. It's difficult. I only ever met one person who could do it. A Saltmistress." Rewil pointed to the broken end. "If something setup a resonance, the right frequency, the right way, at the right time, the rail would shatter like glass."

Will had never heard of this, but it made some sort of sense. Vibrations could do a lot of damage. He'd been in a mine in the Reach once when a boomer had happened. He'd been lucky to escape. *Fearsong.*

He tried not to think about that singular sound, and the effect it had on him and his friends. *I guess it's not so strange to think a sound could break glass, or this Honnim alloy.* "How would that work, though?" Will asked.

"I have no idea." Rewil threw the rail back into the pile, and the other one he was carrying. "The rails only carry the carts, and the constructs keep them in shape and clean. There's no way anyone could attach anything to the rail and leave it."

"So, wait." Will pulled the idea together in his mind. "You're saying something like a small explosion happened on the rail. Hmm." Will studied the piles in front of them, saying nothing else for a long moment.

"So, Will? What do you think?" Will was brought out of his thoughts by Rewil, who, for once, seemed serious.

"I haven't got a clue." Will looked up from the mess. "I mean, it's something."

"Yes." Rewil frowned. "I had hoped we'd find the answer today. People are talking Will. I've heard rumors that anything the crafters make is now suspect. Not good enough. That maybe it's time for a new Tarn. Slow down the pace of change."

"That's ridiculous!" Will blurted out. Rewil was one of the most talented smiths and craftsmen he'd ever met. He outstripped every Guildmaster <u>Will had</u> ever met.

"Kind of you to say lad, but..." Rewil's shoulders slumped. "Let's go. Get some rest and food, sleep on everything. Come back in the morning."

Will nodded, if only because the buzzing still annoyed him. *What could cause that?*

I really don't like this place either. Nollew entered the chamber under the spire, feeling the age and weight of the place bear down on him. Lit by the blue glowing light that sprang up from the well-like hole in the middle of the room, it wasn't day bright, but it was strong enough to make him shield his eyes. The walls here were bare stone, gray and black with age. Marked with ancient torch smoke in a few places as well.

That was all fine. But what bothered him the most here was the feeling of the magic. The power felt bound. It always had to him. As if what spilled into this room, what powered everything in the city, what gave everyone their boon, it was a tiny echo of the genuine power. At least it had always felt like that to him.

What lay at the bottom of the well was a mystery to them all. Anyone who entered the well died. Anyone who tried to tunnel under this chamber died. Anyone who tried to make anything to investigate the well died. It was remarkably direct. Death greeted anyone who investigated past this room.

Ruthlessly efficient, he had to admit. "How long do you think this has been here?" he asked aloud. Yulisia stood next to him, already watching the stone well that had been put in front of the hole.

"Longer than any kept records for." she sighed. "Maybe longer."

"Hrm." Nollew let out a low rumble that might have been a laugh. "They say the Gorom were here. Sometime in the past."

"They say." She agreed.

"You ever wonder if they were right?" she asked. "I hear the Gorom were convinced there were creatures that lived down here."

"Like what?" Yulisia let out a long, slow breath. "No, I don't think..." Her head shook, and she continued. "I mean, why would the Gorom have special stories about this place? Besides being the Gorom and always wanting to be special."

"I don't know. Doesn't it bother you we don't know?" Nollew reached out with his boon, feeling the giant sweeps of power that flowed here. The source both was nerve-wracking and near ecstasy at the same time. To be able to control that much of the magic would be wonderful. And terrifying.

"No." Yulisia frowned. "Why are we here, other than you wanting to bathe in the power?"

"Well, this is one of the few places I can drop the defenses. Mikol can't touch us here. Too much of the power in the way. I can relax. Keeping him out some days is hard, and as of late, it's gotten harder." Nollew felt the tension in his mind melt some. "And I think we are going to have to talk to Rewil. I can't think of another way."

"He will not listen. In some ways, our act was far too good. He truly thinks we hate him." Yulisia turned away from the Well, her face more shrouded and darker now. "But I think we should talk to the other one. The other one that came with the girl."

"What?" Nollew released his mind from the power, and the nagging feeling returned that there was so much more that he couldn't touch. "Why?"

"He's untainted. He likes Rewil, but he's not been here long enough to have any real set ideas about this place. He's smart." Yulisia held up fingers as she touched on points. "He's as talented as the other one was. Or is since we both think she's still alive. I've read his interview, have you? He understands pain. He has lived through betrayal." "But he's not a Tarn. We need Rewil!" Nollew shook his hand in dismissal. "What good would a barely trained crafter be?"

"Rewil trusts him. Get this William Reis to listen, and then HE can talk to Rewil. I don't think there is anything we could say that would convince

Rewil ourselves."

Nollew nodded slowly, picking up a small rock off the chamber floor. "You see this? You don't see them often here. A tiny rock. It's infused with the power. I can feel it. But if I take it out of the valley, the power will drain away. Fast. If I throw it in the well, it will disappear. We don't know why either of those things happen."

"So? What does that have to do with our situation? With Mikol and Rewil?" Yulisia frowned at Nollew and arched one of her impeccable eyebrows.

"Everything and nothing." Nollew knew he was grasping, but it gnawed on him. "We've waited too long, I think. This!" Nollew held up the rock. "This is what we should try to figure out. How to use the power farther away from the source. Why we can't ever get closer than this room. That's what we should worry about, or at least working on. Instead, we are neck deep in plots and killings for political power."

"And your point?" Yulisia held a long, slender finger against Nollew's chest. "We didn't have to start down this path. I told you that when we realized Mikol had killed Jinir. When that man started trying to put things in our head. We could have handled this differently."

"How? Why?" Nollew threw the stone, watching it fly until it struck a wall, a tiny flash of blue-yellow light erupting at the impact. "It doesn't matter. This is the path we are on. I will make time to find this crafter, William, and talk to him tomorrow."

"You will do no such thing." Yulisia rested a hand on his shoulder. "I will speak to him. I can be much more persuasive than you ever could."

"Why you?" Nollew studied her face, looking for some clue in her expression. "By the source, you aren't planning to seduce the poor lad, are you?" The slap that came was more shocking than painful.

"Nollew, if you ever say that again you will find yourself in a great deal of discomfort." Yulisia cracked her fingers, making a fist and glanced down at a very specific part of his anatomy. "No, I will speak to him because I am much better at being sympathetic than you are. And the fact is, everyone believes you are the one who hates hybrids here. That I'm the woman who loves you and goes along with it." Yulisia smiled. "And I do love you, so that part is correct at least."

Nollew smiled and then glanced at her fist, feeling some of the smile leak away. "Fine. But please do it soon. You don't have to be a Tarn to feel it. Things are coming."

Chapter 24.

Will sat on his bed, trying to make sense of the day. They had found nothing so far in the quickway's wreckage. Nothing. Rewil had been going on about the edges being wrong, but it didn't seem like much of a lead. And he still had no answers on Myriam. Was she alive, injured somewhere in the city? Was she dead? Blown apart by the release of magic so strong she utterly just ceased?

He hated the idea that she was gone. Even thinking about it made his stomach flip in ways that almost forced him to lie down. "She can't be gone. She can't be." Will whispered. The sound of his own voice seemed flat in this cold, empty room. Maybe it was the shock of the thought of her being gone, but he looked around the room and realized he didn't like the City much.

Oh, he loved being a Crafter. He loved the power that comes with making things, creation. The rest of this City? No. Everyone was so focused on power and how powerful they were or weren't. Even the 'sections' here all seemed pitted against each other all the time. Power. Magic. Will shook his hands in the air, focusing hard to see, maybe, tiny blue flecks in his skin.

He didn't want this. They never should have come here. He should have followed Amder's order and gone to Ture. If he had gone to Ture with Regin, Vin, and Myriam, one wouldn't be missing, and the other two wouldn't be dead. All because of him.

Will scowled at the door as a knock came. "Yes?" He snapped. He was in no mood for anyone to visit him, not even Tarn Rewil. Rewil had gone off to wherever Tarn's go to think about what they had and hadn't found in the wreckage, without much more than a sigh and a back slap.

"Message for you." The voice came.

Will didn't get many messages. Or any, truly. He opened the door to see a young man in the bone white and gray sash of the library holding a folded piece of paper. Actual parchment. "Yes?" Will worked to keep any annoyance out of his voice.

"Message for you." The man thrust the folded message at Will's face. Will leaned back, blinking in surprise but taking the message. "Who is it from?"

The man, however, was already gone, quick walking down the hallway. Will had had little or no real contact with the librarians. The Crafters kept their own records these days, and he hadn't been here long enough to need to go anywhere else. He wasn't sure he'd be welcome anyway, with all the plain enmity between Tarns.

The parchment was new, slick almost to the touch. Opening it, Will read it once, then unsure if he was clear read it again.

"William Reis,

I have information for you regarding the recent vanishing of your friend, Myriam VolFar. I need to speak with you and speak with you in a safe place. Come to the chamber of the source, tonight at four bells. Bring this letter with you, it will get you past the construct guards. I wouldn't mention this message to Rewil. He wouldn't approve.

Tarn Yulisia Ecir"

Yulisia? Tarn Yulisia? The Tarn of the Library? Who along with Tarn Nollew hated Rewil? Will wasn't sure if he should laugh and throw it away or take it to Rewil, or even do what it says. What plausible reason could she have to talk to Will? And why at the source? He'd never been there, and he had to admit he was curious about the place.

Only the Tarns had full access to the source. So, there was that idea, being able to see this mysterious chamber. Yet, he didn't like it. Sneaking off in the early morning to meet in secret with someone who hated someone Will liked and respected deeply? There was only one thing to do, show it to Rewil. Even though the letter told him not to, that made him want to more. He was done with sneaking around. He wasn't good at it, anyway. Duncan was great at it. He had the right kind of physique, and more than the right kind of attitude for subterfuge.

Will took the letter in hand and began searching for Tarn Rewil. He didn't know where he'd gone after they had said goodbye earlier, and the crafters section wasn't a small place. Searching through various workshops, he finally found Rewil sitting at a large workbench alone, toying with a small gear, deep in thought.

"Tarn Rewil? Sorry to bother you, but there's something I need to talk to you about and show you." Will glanced around as he spoke, but the room was empty as far as he could tell, apart from them.

"What?" Rewil's head snapped up and broke into a smile, if a tired one.

"William! What are you doing here?" Rewil stood grasping the gear in his hand tightly. "Lad, go and get some rest. I know you're a hard worker. You don't need to prove anything to me by working late."

"No, that's not why I am here. I got a letter, just now. A letter you should see." Will held up the parchment.

"A parchment letter?" Rewil frowned. "Those are only used by the Library. Why would anyone in the Library send you a letter?"

"Take it, and you will understand why I brought it to you." Will proffered the letter once more.

Rewil frowned and took the letter opening it and reading it quickly. Will saw the man's shock come over him. His eyes went wide, then narrowed into slits. His color changed as well, first dropping to pale, before rushing back.

"What game is this?" Rewil thrust the parchment back to Will. "Yulisia wants to meet you in the small hours of the morning, in the source? And not to tell me? What is her game?" Rewil frowned, his face becoming set that way. "I don't like that idea." "I don't know what to do. If I go, and it's a trap or dangerous… but why would it? I mean, what have I done to them?" Will threw up his arms. "I don't want to get involved in whatever fight you all seem to have."

Rewil flipped the gear in his hand. "Too late for that Will, the moment you entered this place, you became a piece in the game. But how would Yulisia have information on Myriam? She was a Healer, not a Librarian. And why meet with you at the source? There are lots of better places to meet than that chamber."

"Should I go?" Will held the message tight.

"No." Rewil shook his head. "There's no reason. She will try to set you against me. Yuli may have written that note, but I'd bet Nollew was behind it." Rewil tightened his hands into fists. "And Nollew wants only one thing, for me not to be a Tarn."

Will took a few steps out of the room, but turned around and stopped. "Tarn, why does Nollew hate you?"

"Ha." Rewil shook his head. "You know, lad, I do not know. We were friendly enough once. He became Tarn, and Yuli and I were already in our positions. In those early days, we spoke often. We made the constructs, and the quickways. Did you know that? He was the one who figured out melding the power into the rails. Not to mention half a dozen other magic and craft made items. There was a time when Yulisia was one of my closest friends, and by extension, Nollew. Then it all changed." Rewil opened a fist, revealing a bent and broken gear.

"I don't know why or even exactly when, but they both turned their back on me. And Jinir, and Mikol." Rewil threw the bent gear in a reuse bin nearby. "Jinir was the Tarn of the City before Grib. I liked Jinir. Then, he died in a horrible accident. It was right after that when things changed, or it was then that I noticed it." Rewil sat back down in the oversized chair that was nearby.

"So don't go?" Will wanted to ask about this Jinir person more but felt like this wasn't the right time.

"I wouldn't." Rewil shook his head. "Maybe I should call a commons again. How could she have secret information on the vanishing of your friend? And why there? The chamber of the source? There is no reason to meet there." Rewil shook his head. "Go on. Go back and get some rest. And Will, thank you."

"For?" Will wasn't sure why he was being thanked. As far as he could tell, Rewil was about twice as pale and more on edge than he'd been.

"For telling me." Rewil leaned back, his face showing that his mind was concentrating on something else.

Chapter 25.

Myriam paused for a moment, collecting both her thoughts and her strength for what was coming next. Jinir and, by extension, Ralta were waiting for her in the next room. She was supposed to be healing, or at least starting to heal Jinir. Based on the tiny look she'd had so far, though, this was going to be both exhausting and very dangerous. And if something should happen to the man, Ralta had made it very clear that she would take it badly. A feeling that probably came with knives.

She wanted to leave. Run away and get back to the spire. She didn't believe that Mikol could be behind the accident. There was no way. She didn't quite get why these two were so hung up on hating the man. But she had come to realize in her short time in the city that infighting seemed to be a way of life here. This group hated that group, and this other group didn't like either of them. It was a minor wonder the place hadn't erupted into actual fighting to hear the way some talked about the other sections.

She wanted to run. But she couldn't. For one, she wasn't exactly sure where she was, other than in the lower city. She could get out and make her way to the wall, but she'd bet any amount of money that Ralta would be watching that way. And the other reason was simple, for all the unease she felt about her current situation, Jinir and Ralta had saved her life. There was no doubt that if they hadn't brought her here, she never would have survived. They had pulled her from the burning twisted metal of the collapsed quickway. She owed them her life.

Myriam blew out a long breath, and with one motion knocked and turned the handle.

"Come in." Jinir's rasp answered. There was a new tone in his voice, excitement.

"I'm here now." Myriam entered the room, walking slowly, and examining her patient's skin and general shape. Her first impression had been correct. Jinir was more scar than skin. Huge ropes of shiny skin badly healed crossed most of his torso. One shoulder was hunched over as bones had set improperly. His face as well, twisted and pitted skin, a few small tufts and wisps of hair. Only his eyes were uninjured, eyes that watched her carefully.

"Yes. I know. It's not a sight to make women swoon." Jinir gave a small smile, the skin pulling tight. "I don't know, I rather like it." Ralta joined in. The Trinil stood, leaning next to a table that held several flasks and bowls. Myriam didn't respond, trying to figure out what to do first. And exactly how painful this would be for the man. "I will need to do a working, to check what's inside. Is that all right?" Myriam addressed Jinir. She would not be drawn into conflict over her patient with Ralta.

"Yes. Of course." Jinir gave her a grin that made her shudder. He twitched and his jaw clenched.

"What is that doing?" Ralta was staring at her, curiosity clear on her face. "You're not adding anything to his burden Myriam, I won't allow it." Myriam had ignored Ralta yet again. "I have a lot of work to do before I do anything." Myriam focused only on her patient.

"Burn it! What's going on? What are you doing?" Ralta turned to Myriam, her mouth frowning. A knife appeared in her hand, small and silver, and by the looks of it, deadly sharp.

"I have to check what's wrong inside as well. I said that. You can either stop asking questions I answered or leave the room." Myriam put on her best healer voice and stared Ralta in the eye.

The Trinil, to her credit, lowered her eyes first and turned away, saying nothing else. Yet the knife vanished just as fast as it had appeared. Myriam felt her muscles relax, if only a little. She didn't want to get on Ralta's bad side, because if this was her good side....

She turned her attention away from Jinir's assumed protector and to the man himself. Taking hold of her power, she sent thin tendrils of magic towards him, feeling his form. Almost at once, she felt a wave of nausea and pity come over her. How could this man stand it? Almost everything she touched had not healed properly, if at all.

His lungs and throat were still raw, evidence of the injury that had given him the cough and his rough voice. Bones, twisted and reset in awkward positions, rubbing against other parts that they shouldn't ever touch.

Myriam could *taste* the pain flowing through the man. Enough that she struggled to keep a firm hold on herself. Her own recent injuries had been bad enough, but this man lived this way every day.

"Well Myriam? How bad is it?" Jinir asked, his voice even more rough sounding than usual.

"Not good." Myriam finally replied, having made a mental list of everything that was in awful shape. "I don't know how you stand it."

"It's difficult." Jinir whispered, eyes downcast. "Some mornings are bad. Terrible. I wake up from what little sleep I can manage and wish I had died in my bed. Every breath hurts."

"Hush Jinir." Ralta said, but for the first time, Myriam heard the warmth and sorrow in her voice.

"It's fine, Ralta. The healer needs to know." Jinir tried to clear his throat and grunted as he did so. "I'm tired Myriam. Exhausted. But that doesn't matter now. You are here. You can fix... this." Jinir pointed to himself. "You can make me the man I once was."

"I can. But you need to understand, it will be painful." Myriam locked eyes with her patient. "You live in pain now, but that's old pain. Pain your mind has accepted. Made part of you. This pain will be new. Everything that has healed wrong will have to be undone and healed correctly. You will live every moment of pain you had the first time all over again. And then the sped-up healing will kick in, and the pain of things regrowing, fixing themselves will start."

"Jinir, you don't have to do this." Ralta leaned close to the man, resting her forehead on the side of his head. "It doesn't matter to me."

"It matters to me Ralta. It matters to me a great deal. I will not let Mikol have this prize. I will leave this building whole and well, and spit in the man's great plan, or I will not leave this building at all." Jinir took another croaking breath. "What do I need to do?"

Myriam waved Ralta back, and the Trinil followed her request without attitude for once. Does he realize how much he means to her? Myriam watched the two of them. Ralta's eyes never left Jinir, a wetness clung to them, and the sadness she must be feeling was naked on her face.

Jinir for his part kept his eyes on Myriam. His pupils were dilated, and a wisp of a smile played on his twisted face. "Well healer?"

Myriam nodded. "I wish we had some Cloud, that would at least make it easier on you."

"Cloud?" Jinir had a confused look cross his face.

"A... drug. A medicine sometimes as well. Blocks you from feeling, well... anything. No pain, no happiness, no joy, no anger, no nothing. It gets abused a lot, but it has its uses in healing." Myriam remembered that Will's cousin had abused Cloud, but that had been..... That was another life. It didn't matter now.

"A strange thing. Never heard of it. Probably for the better. I never knew it existed." Jinir shook his head. "No, I know what this will take. It is worth the pain."

Myriam turned to Ralta. "A few things before I start. One, I don't care what he does, you will not touch him or move him. This will hurt him, but you must let me work. Two, bring me several tumblers of the coldest water you can get. For both me and him."

Ralta snorted but left to get the water. Myriam watched her go with an amused feeling. *Ralta, at least, was getting easier to handle.* Turing back to Jinir, she took and let out a large gulp of air. "Are you ready?"

Jinir nodded. "I have been ready since we pulled you from the wreckage and brought you here. But can we not fix everything? I dream of being whole. Being me again." "Do you have the strength?" Myriam locked eyes with Jinir. "That much healing at once could kill you. We can stretch it out." "No, just do it. I want it done. Ralta may argue, but I need this, Myriam. *I need it.*" Jinir coughed again, the spasm wrenching the muscles in his neck. "Please."

"We begin." Myriam said, closing her eyes and reaching out again with the power. Working not to detect, but to heal. The parts that had never healed, his lungs, his throat, those parts first.

Her power struck hard, as Jinir stiffened in shock. Holding him steady with a flicker of thought, she began to fix his long-ravaged lungs. Pushing out tiny, unseen shards of glass, and some caustic liquid that his body refused to absorb. Yet it somehow stayed, slowly tearing any new tissue apart. For a long moment it seemed the damage fought against her, defying her will, before, with a rush, a wave of old clotted blood and tiny fragments of metal and wood erupted from Jinir's throat.

The man's retching was not pleasant to hear or see, but she had to get the stuff out of him, and that was the quickest way. She was rather glad Ralta hadn't seen it, though. For all her acquiescence before, the sight of the man she was clearly in love with throwing up blood might have been too much for her to stand.

Another gout came, but smaller this time, as her power forced the never healed wound to finally close, forcing the tissue to grow. Myriam watched in some satisfaction as Jinir finally took a long breath, hearing the change in how the air moved through his body.

"I can breathe!" Jinir whispered, his eyes shining. "Thank you. Just, thank you."

"Don't thank me yet." Myriam said before Ralta came into the room holding a box with nearly a dozen large metal tumblers full of water. Myriam could hear the gasp from the woman as she surveyed what had been a clean room a few minutes before.

"I can breathe!" Jinir said again, for Ralta's sake, Myriam assumed. She heard the change in his voice as well. What had been broken and rough was now much freer, and his body was responding already to not having to fight for each breath. She could see the color return to his skin, now not so starved for air. "We aren't done yet Jinir. We have only started." Myriam closed her eyes and reached out again, hoping she didn't pass out before she was done.

Chapter 26.

Will made his way back to his room, gripping the parchment tightly. Had he done the right thing in bringing it to Rewil? He found himself standing in a hallway crossway. If he went straight, he'd end up at his door, his room, his bed. If he turned left, he'd end up in the workrooms, and his now ruined construct prototype. But if he turned right, he could find himself at the great stairwell. Now that the quickways were somewhat out of service, the stairway was getting a great deal more use.

It ran the whole spire, from the very top where the Tarns held their commons, to the base. Where the door to the chamber of the source was. Well-guarded of course. But which way to go? His room would only bring him rest, but not much of that. He was tired, but too much was on his mind to sleep. He'd only lay there and stare at the parchment.

Going to the workrooms would at least keep him occupied. Though after today he didn't feel the urge, the need to create anything. Not since the day the whole wall exploded, and Myriam vanished. That only left the way he had come, and the great stairs. He had time; it was still early enough in the evening. Will read the letter again, as if reading it once more would change anything about it.

Finally, he looked right, and turned and faced his rooms. He forced himself to slow his walk. He'd made his decision. He'd get some rest, but at 4 bells, he would be in the chamber. By the sparks, he had to have answers. Or at least different answers than the ones he had now.

The night passed in fits. Will would sleep some, then start awake, thinking about explosions, and a great blue wave of power ripping through him. Sometimes in the dream he was alone, sometimes Myriam was there. Either way, he'd wake up taking a great gasping breath. *It feels like drowning, every time.*

Will had almost drowned once. Like most Reachers, he didn't swim, there wasn't any place TO swim. The few ponds and lakes that formed when the spring melt hit the mountains were cold enough to get a thin sheet of ice overnight, even in the late spring. No one wanted to swim in those.

That only meant it was the place of choice for bullies to toss other children. Will had been picked on once, right after he and Duncan had been left alone by the death and disappearance of their parents.

Two boys, older boys, Lenit and Rolph, had grabbed him and dragged him to the pond right outside of town. It had recently formed, there was still snow most places yet. Lenit had accused Will of stealing money for food and wanted Will to give him every bit of coin that he and Duncan had stored up. Will had struggled, but he'd not come into his growth yet. The two older boys had tossed him into the pond and walked away. He still remembered the shock of cold that hit him, then nothing. He'd lost all feeling. Some minor part of his brain had registered this as a terrible thing.

Will had tried to move to the shore, but his muscles refused to move. The ice-cold water had covered him. He remembered the surface shining above him; the light filtering through the clear water, his chest burning for air, and the realization that he was about to die. And then Duncan was there.

He'd hauled Will out of that pond, both gasping at the end, though Will was sure his had been far more panic driven than Duncan's had been. Freezing cold, but at least still alive, they had made their way back home. Duncan had got it out of him who had done it. Duncan had only come looking for him because he'd heard that someone was going to beat Will up. Two days later Lenit and Rolph had appeared with more bruises than skin, and both refused to say what happened.

Will hadn't thought about that in years. *I guess I owed you for that as well, Dunc.* As for Lenit and Rolph, Lenit had always been a bully. He'd died in a mine accident some years later. No one in the Reach had been sad about it. Rolph had actually become a good man. He'd died in the Valni attack, and Will remembered helping bury him, or what was left of him.

Will heard the faint chime of three bells. If he was going to go, he had to get up now. For a second that seemed to stretch out, Will paused. Was Rewil right? Should he forget this? It very well could be a trap, it sure seemed like one. A hard to get to location, a nighttime meeting with someone he'd never met but had a hatred of someone he respected. And mysterious information that anyone would know that he'd have a hard time ignoring.

But what was the worst that could happen? He didn't feel like there was violence brewing. Even Rewil hadn't given that impression. The worst Will could think of was that both Tarns, Yulisia and Nollew would be there, and they would do… something. He couldn't think of any reason not to go other than Rewil didn't want him to, and the fact that they hated Rewil.

So, he had to go. He stood, and dressed quickly, simple clothes. He did not wear the traditional leather apron of the crafters though. Why remind them of what he was and who his Tarn was? He did expect both Yulisia and Nollew to be there though, if it was a trap.

He made his way down the hall and started down the great stairwell. To his surprise, it was not deserted. Even now, in the small hours of the night, he passed a few people here and there. A few couples who were in different sections passed him, stealing what moments they could at night. One construct, a spider legged one, came clacking by, headed up on some unknown mission. Will shuddered at the sound. It reminded him too much of the Gorom tunnels. He'd made his peace with the Vinik, but he still found the insect like nature of them highly unnerving.

Soon however he was deep enough that he was the only person here. The base of the spire only held storerooms and of course, the way into the chamber of the source. It was darker here as well, the glows here much farther spread out. Still enough light to see by, but shadows grew the deeper he went. The construction changed some as well, at least to his eye.

What had been smooth and hard stone, was now, not quite as well fitted. It was all clean and tidy, but the color wasn't as bright as before. A feeling of age, of something old and waiting settled into the air around him. Finally turning the last spiral, he stopped, standing at the bottom of the staircase.

In front stood two huge constructs. Larger than any he'd ever seen. And in between them was a door, unlike any other door he'd seen here. This door was polished stone, but there wasn't a speck of white in it. Mottled brown and blacks, with veins of shocking blue, the door screamed of power, and waiting. That feeling, of age and patience had now become nearly overwhelming.

Will let out a breath he hadn't even realized he was holding and approached one construct, holding the parchment letter up like a shield. He had no idea if this was how to do this. The letter hadn't said. His eyes darted to the arms of the thing. Each was not only huge, but instead of two force cylinders, theses seemed to have six. He'd seen what those things could do. Even one was enough to crack stone. Two was enough to tear metal. One hit from six would be enough to end his life many times over.

The constructs, which hadn't moved at all, sprang into action. Both sets of arms cocked themselves into a ready stance as Will approached. Maybe this was a trap. Send him here to have the constructs kill him. Make it look like he was trying to break into the source. Will nearly turned and ran but forced himself to keep coming closer.

A single drop of sweat rolled down his face and onto his cheek. It wasn't warm here, but he was becoming more worried with each step. *This was a mistake.* Will was about to turn and run back to the staircase when, without warning, both constructs relaxed. Their deadly arms, just moments before ready to kill with a single trigger, fell to their sides, and they both rolled away from the door in unison.

Wills jaw hurt, and he realized he'd been clenching it. He lowered the parchment and stood before the door. A single handle, tarnished black stood in the middle of the thing. Will stole one more glance at the construct guards, and then, lowered his head and pushed the door open.

A tunnel greeted him. One carved out of natural rock. The smell of earth and stone floated forth, a smell that Will knew well. His skin felt a slight chill, made greater by the sweat that now was cooling on his skin. Sweat brought on by fear. A faint blue glow was at the far end of the passage, a glow that seemed to hum in Will's ears.

"No time to waste." Will whispered to himself. If he really did get information about Myriam, it would all be worth it. If.

Chapter 27.

Will felt strange. The air in the tunnel made his skin prickle in waves. It wasn't good or bad, it simply was odd. A tingle made the hair on the back of his neck stand up, and he found himself giving a shiver. The air smelled of age, of something sleeping, waiting, wanting. It made little sense to him. The tunnel ended, and he stood on the edge of the vast chamber. Far larger than it had any right to be, based on where he felt like he was in relation to the spire above.

It was almost empty, though. Walls of bare stone, worn shiny smooth down low, but rougher the higher up you looked. A few tiny patches of silvery moss clung to these upper areas, reflecting the only light in the room. A light that held that same blue Will had seen under his own skin, that shade of blue that had made him uncomfortable ever since he'd first seen it.

The light sprung from a well like looking circle of stone in the middle of the room. Strong, steady, and pure, it filled the chamber. The floors were also worn smooth, but the closer you got to the center, the rougher the floor got. It was obvious no one went near the opening much. Yet Will soon stood at the opening's edge. The feeling of waiting, of ancient age, and something else, something Will couldn't quite understand, wafted over him.

He could see down to the bottom of the well. It was like standing in a pit, a pit with another world beneath it. The opening went on as far as he could see, and was dotted with points of light, lights that danced around. It was actually quite beautiful, and to his surprise, it seemed to call to him. *If I jumped in, what would happen? Would I fall? Would I drift down into a blue abyss?*

"Careful. I doubt Rewil wants to lose you this early." A woman's voice came from behind him, a voice full of rich tones and some humor.

Will turned and, to his somewhat surprise, only saw one person. Yulisia. The Tarn of the Library was clad in a white robe, which glowed blue in the available light. Hair unbound, it moved with her as she walked. Will couldn't help but notice the way the robe clung to parts of her body. *Steady Will. Steady.* "What do you mean?" Will managed to say, tearing his thoughts from where they had gone.

"That I am surprised. I don't think I've ever seen anyone go so close to the edge before and not jump into the well. You don't feel it calling you? It's hunger?" Yulisia stopped a good fifteen paces from him, one eye cocked upwards as she studied him.

"No. Not that… I feel, age. Waiting. A desire for something. I don't know what." Will glanced back at the Well. "Why?"

"I forget you haven't been here. This is the chamber of the source. This is as close as any of us can get to it. If you get too close to the well, you jump in and die. If you tried to dig into whatever is below us, you die. If you try to cap the well, you die. It's all very simple. Their bodies are blown apart by the power, and they are gone. Bloodless, painless, but still dead." Yulisia shook her head. "I have only been as close are you are once. I had to be dragged back by a rope. I wanted to jump in. It was all I could think about or want. I craved it. I clawed at the rope, trying to free myself of it. I broke four fingernails and one finger, trying to get free before I got far enough away. And yet, there you are. Just standing there."

Will didn't know what to say. The call he felt was not that strong. Just a light desire, not anything overpowering. Mostly all he felt was age, a weary feeling of countless time passing by. "Why did you want to come here?" Will finally asked, deciding that whatever this mystery of the source was, he wasn't going to find any answers right now.

"Ah, to the point. Like a Crafter." Yulisia paused. "Fine. Let's talk about your friend. Myriam. The Healer."

"What about her? She's dead." Will almost winced when he said the word dead, almost.

"She's not." Yulisia paused. "I don't know where she is, but she's not dead. She's somewhere in the city though. But I want to talk about the accident, and who is responsible."

"Tarn Rewil had nothing to do with it!" Will snapped at the woman. "I know you and the other Tarn, Nollew turned your back on Rewil years ago, turned your back on a friend but…"

"I know Rewil had nothing to do with it. I wasn't going to say he did."
Yulisia looked down at the stone floor, her slipper clad foot tracing a
cracked line in the floor. "And we didn't turn our backs on Rewil, not
really." "I know what is said by you both about him." Will frowned
though. What game was this?

"We say what we must." Yulisia looked up at Will. "Rewil is a good man.
I hope one day he will be a good friend again."

"Say what you're here to say, get to the point. I don't like this not saying
things." Will threw his arms up. This kind of thing drove him crazy.
Mostly because he was terrible at it himself.

"Tarn Mikol of the Healers killed Myriam. He engineered it. I am not
sure how yet. Neither is Nollew." Yulisia looked back at the yawning
tunnel behind her. "As for why meet here? This is one of the few places
where Mikol can't read people. He's a very dangerous man, William
Reis."

Mikol? Kindly old Mikol? Will nearly laughed at the audacity to claim that
Mikol was a great evil man. "That's the silliest thing I've ever heard." The
smile from Yulisia gave him pause, though. It was a weary smile, one that
screamed that she had expected him not to believe her.

"Mikol is a very dangerous man. He can twist your words into things you
never meant, shape your thoughts into lies you never spoke." Yulisia
kicked a small pebble that had gotten lodged in the crack she'd been
tracing before. "Do you know how old Mikol is?"

"No." Will didn't know. "Why does it matter?"

"No one does but Mikol. No one really knows how long he's been the
Tarn of the healers, either. I am the Tarn of the Library. We keep all
records, every scrap of knowledge that the city has. We even have copies
of all the Crafter information you all think we don't know about. Yet, if I
try to think about Mikol, the thought fades away and I lose all interest in
the subject. Only here, if I concentrate, can I think about the questions
that surround the man." Yulisia pointed at Will. "Hear me out."

"Mikol killed Myriam. She was a threat to him. A young, very powerful
healer? One he couldn't really control well? A danger. Rewil was also a
growing threat. Under him, the Crafters have become well known, even

loved. Though Rewil wouldn't do anything with that growing power, to Mikol, it was a threat. So how to fix both things? An accident. The quickways. Destroy the girl and destroy the reputation of Rewil." Yulisia gave the pebble one last push with her foot. "Do you know why Nollew and I appear to hate Rewil? Because Mikol wants us to. We have been playing the part for a while now. At first, Mikol's influence was true. Then, Nollew had to come here for some research. The man loves to tinker with the power. And here, he uncovered the influence that Mikol had laid on us both. How he'd twisted us. Made us hate. Do you have any idea what it's like to know that your own emotions have been bent to hurt someone you consider a friend?" Yulisia looked at Will, the question hanging in the air.

"Since then, it's been a careful game. We say horrible things while Nollew keeps the appearance up for Mikol. Conversations like this are hard to hide, so coming here was the best bet. Mikol probably isn't awake, and he can't very well order me not to come here. I am a Tarn. I have free passage in the city." Yulisia stopped talking then, her eyes focused on Will.

Will didn't know what to say. Mikol? Part of him found the idea silly. Mikol reminded him of Haltim. He missed the old Priest badly when he allowed himself to think about him. But Mikol? Kindly friendly old Mikol? Yet Will could tell there was something to what she had said. It made sense, in a twisted way. "Why do you think she's alive?" Will finally asked. "Myriam, why is she alive?"

"Ah that. It's simple. Your friend was made the namer of the unknown god. If she were dead, he could choose someone new for that role. He'd have a name as fast as you could think. He's probably desperate to be complete. But he hasn't got one. Which means, she's still alive." Yulisia tore her eyes from Will to stare at the Well.

Will could see the bright blue reflect off her, a necklace shone in response. "Tell me this since no one has ever explained it to me well. Why does he NEED a name? Or a namer?" Will felt a new taste in the air, a pensive feeling, like someone listening from far away. No danger though, only curious attention.

"Ah. Well, the Gods are a strange bunch. The best we know when they came here, this world was different. Each god made a people, and from each group they picked a namer. While the records do not say why clearly, it is said that each god needed a link to its people, a link to this place. Until then, each god while powerful, was not fully of this world."

"To hear the Vinik say it, they still aren't of this world." Will blurted out before catching himself. He had no idea how much these people knew of the Vinik, and their place here.

"Ah. So, you do know that story. Yes. Very few know of it, but again, I am the leader of those who keep the knowledge. The Vinik were of the before time. When this world was flush with the power. You came from the Anvil, right? The sights and sounds you saw there are a tiny fleck of what this world once was. Before the gods came and imposed their order on all this." Yulisia glanced back once more to the tunnel. "We don't have much time. I will need to return to my section soon."

"Listen. Warn Rewil. We did not think he would listen to us directly. But he may listen to you. Mikol might have tripped when he decided this course of action. What his final goal is, isn't clear. But he is setting up the city for something." Yulisia turned back to the tunnel stopping right before entering it and turning back to Will.

"Warn Rewil. Find Myriam. Be on guard. And Will…" Yulisia gave him a smile. "It was very nice to meet you."

Will watched her enter the tunnel. It took a moment for her to disappear into the darkness before Will finally began his own return to the spire above. His heart was heavy, and his thoughts were confused. And by the sparks, when he stepped into the tunnel, all he could feel was a silent goodbye from the chamber.

Chapter 28.

The Unnamed God stood at the edge of the cavern, looking at the Gorom City. He had killed more of those disgusting creatures, the Vinik, than he'd thought possible. Nest upon nest of the things. Thousands of crawling Vinik had fought back. He'd enjoyed that part. His new shield reflected his victory. He'd made it himself, a trophy of sorts. A backing of what they called 'Drendel Steel' now and the front, a carapace of swirling gold.

The Vinik he'd taken it from had dared to talk to him. As if the creature had anything worth saying. They had attacked him, HIM, at the moment of his entry into this world. There was nothing they could ever say. They had brought this upon themselves. And now they were gone. He'd hunted every nest, every place they had hidden themselves in the deep places of the world, and crushed them.

Hefting his hammer, the Unnamed God was pleased with it. The sound of shattering shells it had made was pleasing. He knew a few worthless drones had fled into the darkness. But all the others, the egg layers, and tenders to the young, they were all gone now. He rather liked the thought of those few last Vinik, alone, terrified, knowing that when they died, their race would be gone and forgotten.

But he wasn't done. There was still the Vinik that had been captured and trained by the Gorom. He found the idea disgusting. Had they not moved against him when he came to this world, he'd have ignored them as he had any other race that existed before he and the other Gods came. It had happened before. It wasn't common, but they would every millennium come to a place where life had already appeared, and sometimes, life with a will and a mind of its own. They never lasted, though. As the power was drained from the world and was filtered and fed upon by him and his kin, whatever existing minds there were vanished. Unable to adapt to a world without magic. It was the way of things.

But to do what these Gorom did? He didn't condone it. He never understood why Grimnor allowed it at all. Turning intelligent, knowing minds into nothing more than meat and milk producers? Disgusting. It was time to end their misery. All Vinik must die.

A single pale figured came into view. Head uncovered, its skin white as ever, except for the thousands of geometric lines and shapes tattooed upon its skin. A Gorom. An elder Gorom. Coming to talk to him, he guessed. They knew then. He was sure Grimnor had warned them what was to come. Not that it would help or make a difference.

He waited though, his mind watching not only the Gorom approaching, but many other things. The Guild in Ture, producing weapons by the day. The soldiers, drawn from every northern land, drilling, practicing for the assault on the city. He took no pleasure from the thought, though. He was doing what he must do. Mortals were not to have access to the power. It was simple. The City broke that rule. Thus, the city must be destroyed.

But many of his people would die in the attack, of that he knew. He knew what power the city could wield, and what it could do. Hence the anchors. But losses would be great, and he did not like the thought of that many of his people dying.

His attention was drawn back to the Gorom who now finally had made it to him. The thing was trying to decide if it should bow or not. *It matters not.* "Well?" The Unnamed God spoke first, ending the Gorom's attempt to make up its mind.

"Grimnor has told us of your arrival. Why you are here. I have come to tell you, do not do this." The Gorom spoke, his words rushing out. But it did not look him in the eye, keeping its face downcast.

"You are telling me? Telling? Or asking?" The Unnamed God hefted his hammer, eyeing the top of the Gorom's bald head.

"Asking. Without them we may have starvation, death." The Gorom raised its eyes. "We helped them. The ones that brought you back. We did. We guided them. Surely that pleases you."

The Unnamed God knew that. It had been these Gorom, in this place, that had brought his namer and her companions to the far side of Alos. He'd only been able to watch them. He'd led his namer out of danger, but the Gorom had helped. "I know. Which is why I offer the choice. Kill them all. Yourselves. Do it and tell the other holy cities of your kind to do the same. If that happens, I will leave. If not, I shall have to do it myself." The Unnamed God smiled then, a toothy thing, a smile that promised pain and a rage that would cleanse the cavern of everything alive. "But." The Gorom stopped short, his head cocked to one side before suddenly appearing even paler. "Fools!" The little creature yelled.

A sound unlike any the Unnamed God had ever heard came blasting out of the sacred city. It brought forth images of his death, images of being broken once more. Of tearing and clawing, of the Vinik overwhelming him. And… it did absolutely nothing to him. He was a god, and that, was just fearsong.

The Gorom backed away, his eyes wide, staring at the hammer and shield that the god carried. The Gorom attempted to say something, but in his panic, stumbled and rolled down and off an edge into the deep gorge below. The sound of his body hitting stone took a surprisingly long time.

"Fine." The Unnamed God muttered before hefting his hammer. He'd do it himself, and if any of these Gorom tried to stop him again, well, there were always other holy cities.

Myriam took a long drink, not water this time. Soup. She needed both liquid and some sort of sustenance. Jinir lay cold and pale on the makeshift bed they had made on the table. His breath still came though, each one clear, each one true. Even now, the changes to his body were remarkable. Where twisted shiny skin and badly healed bones had held sway, now clean pink and smooth skin covered bones that lay in their proper place and angle.

She was tired, though. Exhausted to her bones. And she wasn't even done yet. She knew acids could destroy a person, but she'd never seen the true aftermath of what it could do and what a natural healing would look like. The more she worked, the more she held Jinir in esteem. The amount of agony and pain he had withstood both after the accident and now had been far larger than she'd thought anyone could have taken. She had wanted to dull it with her power, but she found she needed every scrap to fix some of the things that had never set right. "How is he?" Ralta's voice was quiet, only above a whisper.

"He is asleep, which is good. He is tired and drained. Each healing tears at him. I wish I could do more to help, but some of the healing takes so much of my boon, I need every scrap." Myriam cast one eye on the Trinil while still trying to keep the other on her patient.

It was obvious that Ralta would do anything for this man. Her protective nature nearly had her threatening to kill Myriam if Jinir moaned in pain. She'd been worried about healing him with her here. One of the early lessons at the healer section had spoken about that. *Always make their family, friends and loved ones wait somewhere else if the person is seriously injured. They will only make it harder for you.*

Any idea of telling her to go elsewhere, however, died the moment Myriam saw the look in her eyes when she looked at Jinir. *I know that pain.* When Regin had fallen for the first time, she'd been shocked. Killed by a strike from the Blood God, she'd not been able to process it. Just as fast he was brought back by the shard of the Unnamed God she had been carrying around then. His second death had been no less sudden, but at least she had time now to process it. And she knew Ralta would not go anywhere. "He is good, Ralta. He is good."

"Is there anything I can do? Anything at all?" Ralta asked as she lowered her face. "I doubted you. I accused you of things I had no evidence of. All because I wanted to keep you and Jinir apart. But you have shown who you really are. And I must make amends."

Myriam nodded and fought the urge to hug Ralta. Not that she feared her, but the Trinil still carried half a dozen very sharp knives on her person, and well, Myriam wasn't a fool. "No. Let him rest. I will finish my soup and eat some bread before trying to fix again. But soon I must rest."

Giving a single silent head nod, Ralta stood and kept careful watch on the sleeping man. She reached out, and brushed a wisp of blondish hair off Jinir's forehead. "Will his hair come back?"

"In time. While I have fixed the damage, I cannot make hair grow faster than it wants to." Myriam took another long drink of her soup. One more oddity for her to keep track of. Soup here was thin. The vegetables and meats were diced so fine as to be nearly a mashed whole. She wanted something of substance, something to sink her teeth into. But she'd take whatever she could get right now.   "How do you know?" Ralta looked up. "How do you know what he looked like? Before? You had never seen him."

"I don't have to. His body remembers." Myriam finished the last of the soup, a few thin dregs clinging to the inside of the tumbler. "Every part of you has a memory. It knows how it's supposed to be. Part of being a healer is finding that image and using the power to let the body put itself right."

"So, he's healing himself?" Ralta frowned.

"Yes and no. His body knows how it's supposed to be. But it lacks a method for changing it. That's where healers step in. We act as a conduit between the power, and what the body remembers as itself." Myriam wiped the inside of the tumbler with a piece of pale yellow and brown bread before eating the now damp piece, savoring it. "I'm sure I'm not explaining it well." Myriam chewed up the last crust of bread and finally, this time, took a drink of water again. She sort of wished it was an ale, even a watered down ale. But there was still work to be done, and she didn't know in her state how that would affect her.

"No, I think I understand." Ralta smiled again at the man. "At least he remembered how handsome he was."

Myriam didn't see the attraction, but for her, Jinir was a man to be fixed, and cured. Not someone to love. Not that I do the best job picking those men either. First William, or as he had been called, Markin Darto, then Regin. One hated her, and one was dead because of her.

"He will sleep for a while more I think." Myriam yawned herself. "Can you rouse me when he wakes? I want to see how he is feeling before wrestling the last of the old hurt out of him."

"Yes, of course." Ralta had the kindness to blush. "I am sorry. I did not think to tend to other needs other than food."

"It's fine." Myriam said as she yawned again. There, in the room's corner, was a long bench. She wasn't sure if it was all that clean or not, but as she was not about to complain, Myriam laid down, gathering the cloak around her like a blanket.

Chapter 29.

Mikol read the report he had been given with a careful eye. His few connections in the lower city had done their searching, trying to ferret out this 'Downtrodden Lord' character. What they had found was somewhat disturbing. And Mikol did not like disturbing.

One, the mysterious Lord had appeared only fifteen years ago. No one ever saw his face, they only ever heard his voice, a voice that was broken and harsh. He was always accompanied by a Trinil who was quick with her knives and had a boon for balance and speed.

Two, he was loved by the lower city dwellers. He organized feeding people, kept the sections where he operated clear of crime, and made it a far safer and better place to live. And he wasn't setting himself up as some sort of crime leader, which made what businesses that stayed around down by the wall love him even more.

So popular, guarded, and mysterious. All those were a problem, but that wasn't the main reason Mikol did not like the report. He was more worried about the timing. Fifteen years ago, would place this "Lord's" appearance right after the death of Tarn Jinir. Killing Jinir had been a masterstroke. The man had gathered much love from the lower and middle city and had forged connections in several of the sections here in the spire.

Killing him had been needed, and the accident had been perfect. But his body was never recovered from the tannery. After that vat of blacklime had exploded, the place had burned down. Mikol had always assumed the body had been destroyed by the combination. But... then this robed, hidden figure appeared soon after.

Coincidence? Mikol wasn't sure. And the fact that he wasn't sure did not make him feel good. Myriam's body had been destroyed as well; he was told to believe. But now, maybe not.

"Tarn Mikol?" His assistant stood in his door; his eyes downcast.

"What? I asked that I not be bothered right now." Mikol shoved the report under a set of scrolls in the corner of his desk. "I am sorry, Tarn, but Tarn Rewil is here. He'd like to talk to you." His assistant lowered his voice some. "He is very agitated."

Rewil? Here now? Mikol frowned. No, there was no way he could have traced what happened back to himself. "Bring him in then!" Mikol said and added a kind smile.

His assistant, whose name he never learned, left quickly. The sound of approaching feet came. Heavy footfalls. Rewil. The Tarn of the Crafters burst into the room, his face etched in deep lines.

"Rewil! Good to see you. Though you don't look good, my friend. You have not been sleeping enough, I can tell." Mikol proclaimed as Rewil entered the room.

"We must talk Mikol. I don't know what to do." Rewil scratched at his beard, settling himself down into the sturdiest chair he could see. And while the chair grumbled and made a small sharp crack sound as something gave up in trying to hold him. But the rest of the chair stayed together.

"What is wrong, Rewil?" Mikol settled down as well, giving Rewil his full attention.

"What's not wrong?" Rewil settled back and Mikol could see how much the recent events wore on the man. His large frame was already looking thin, stretched. A few weeks ago, the only lines on his face had been ones from laughing, now pallid skin and dark circles under his eyes accentuated the deep wrinkles that were showing through.

"I can only help if you say what it is." Mikol kept his voice calm but couldn't help but feel smug. This, at least, was working exactly the way he wanted it to.

"Fine. So, William, the other one who came here from the Anvil? He and I have been going through the wreckage of the quickways. Trying to find the reason, trying to get an answer as to why Myriam died. But nothing, it's like… I don't get it. I've gone over every inch of that rail we could find. And after Will came to see me about that other mess, I went back and went over every scrap of the quickway carriage I could find. And still, nothing!" Rewil threw his hands up, his voice rising. "I don't get it!"

"Calm Rewil. I'm sure there's a reason somewhere." Mikol sat back, making sure to look concerned. "It's a tragedy, yes. Myriam VolFar was a wonderful young woman, and as talented a healer as I've ever seen. My section, and the whole City are worse for her having died."

"I know. And I wanted to apologize to you. I wanted to find an answer for you. You're the only other Tarn who even talks to me. Grib was never openly hostile, but now, since the quickway accident, he's been angry. I know some of his people died in that accident as well. And you know how Yulisia and Nollew are. They hate me." Rewil lowered his head. "Maybe I'm not cut out to be Tarn. If people are going to get hurt like this, it would be better if I stepped down."

"Nonsense." Mikol stood, turning to look out his large window and overlooked the city. "Rewil you are the finest crafter I know. You have a good heart, an even better mind. I, for one, will fight any attempt to remove you as a Tarn."

Rewil said nothing for a long moment, and Mikol could hear the large man shift in his seat behind him before a long sigh came. "Thanks. I just... I don't get it. And I hate not understanding things."

"It's not a problem." Mikol turned back around to face Rewil. "What was that about the other one? Will? How is he holding up? I know he and Myriam were friends." Mikol fought hard to keep the smile off his face. Rewil would stay, but now he would be indebted to him. With his more direct control of Yulisia and Nollew, and his power over Grib and now Rewil, Mikol could consolidate even more control over the City. No more deaths, no need for more damage. Mikol knew that too much of that would raise way more questions than he wanted to deal with. No, this was best. Keep the tension between Rewil and Nollew and Yulisia and keep everyone under his thumb.

"Oh, William? He isn't taking it well. Poor lad. You can see it on his face if you mention her, writ loud and clear as lampblack on new snow. And that Yulisia business didn't help matters any." Rewil rubbed his eyes with one large hand. "By the source I am tired."

"Yulisia business?" Mikol sat down to hide the shock. A quiver of fear came. *Why would Yulisia need to talk to William?*

"Pffftt." Rewil made a dismissing sound, standing now. The chair made another noise in response to the weight being removed. "We should probably replace that." Rewil said as he looked at the chair, raising one eyebrow.

"Yulisia?" Mikol asked again. He had to walk a line. Push too much and Rewil will want to know why. *But what did Yulisia have to do with anything?*

"The horrible woman. She sent a parchment letter to him, claiming to know something about Myriam's death. Wanted to meet in the Chamber! At four bells! And not to tell me about it at all." Rewil ran an idle hand over his beard. "Being a good lad and a smart Crafter, he brought it to me. I told him to ignore it. Trying to stir something up, I am sure. Her and Nollew."

The quiver in Mikol's stomach turned ice cold. That made no sense. What was going on? "Do you have the letter? I'd like to see it."

Rewil shrugged. 'I gave it back to him to throw away. Why keep it? Don't worry about it. He didn't go, I'm sure of it."

Mikol gave a small nod but choked back what he really wanted to say. *The thrice bloody fool!* He needed Rewil to leave. He had to find out what was going on. Yet, the man stood there, staring at the chair again. He counted something off with his fingers, making some mental note about how to replace the thing, as if the chair mattered!

"My apologies Rewil, but I do have some things I need to go and take care of." Mikol gestured towards the open door.

"Oh sorry. Crafter mind kicked in." Rewil took a few steps before turning back to Mikol. "And thank you. You're a good man, Mikol. If you weren't a Tarn, I'd step down fast. But with you here, I'll stay."

Mikol watched as the large man left. Rewil's words normally would have brought a great deal of satisfaction to him, but not now. Not after learning about that letter. What were Nollew and Yulisia up to?

The one downside of his influence on them was distance. He needed to be close to set up the workings. So that meant getting them nearby. He could go and see them, find a reason to have a meeting with only them. But that held its own dangers. If they had found a way around his work, being one on one with the two other Tarns would be foolish. He wasn't overly worried about Yulisia. Her power was strong, of course, but her boon was of a more practical sort.

No, he was worried about Nollew. Of all the Tarns, his use of the source for direct action was the strongest. The man was constantly finding new ways to use the power to do what he wanted. He suspected Nollew was far more powerful than he let on, and quite possibly more powerful than he himself thought he was.

So, a one-on-one meeting wasn't the best plan, at least not until he was sure he was safe. That left a Commons. But what excuse to call a commons? Mikol sat back in thought when his eyes fell on the report he'd been reading. *Perfect.*

Chapter 30.

Grimnor's wrath was loud and full. The Unnamed God stood in the ruin that had been Heartsteen. He'd grown annoyed by the Gorom trying to get him to stop killing their Vinik. It was almost sad, the Vinik here. The creatures had welcomed death. If they hadn't been the race that caused him so much pain for so long, he would have freed them all out of pity.

As it was, he killed them. They had all been silent during the slaughter. Not the Gorom, though. Many versions of their 'songs' had been tried on him. Fearsong, Ragesong, Confusionsong, even a Sicksong. All had been for naught; he wasn't a mortal. But it had grown to annoy him. And so, he killed them as well. They were only Gorom, they weren't his people.

Grimnor, however, was furious. He could feel his brother's rage swirling around him like a storm on the sea. "They brought it on themselves, Grimnor. I warned them." The Unnamed God braced himself, in case Grimnor decided he would try to attack. He didn't think it likely or even all that possible, but still, he'd never be caught off guard again.

The wave of feeling and sound that came back at him was still full of anger, but it carried with it a hint of something else. Fear. Grimnor was afraid. The Unnamed God pondered this development. He'd wiped one of the holy cities of the Gorom off the underworld of Alos. Grimnor was weakened by this. Not fully, of course, but still weakened.

An idea played around the Unnamed God's mind. One that would solve his problems and increase his own power. An idea that might work. It wouldn't work on the others, but Grimnor had always been a coward with direct action. "Hold brother. I will spare the other cities. IF, they kill the Vinik they have. The same thing I offered these Gorom." The Unnamed God smiled. "I will even make this offer. If they do so, I will have my people, and the lands they have provide your Gorom with replacement food. Your people will not starve, and my revenge upon that thrice hated race of bugs will be complete."

The presence of Grimnor was silent but could still be felt. The Unnamed God waited, hoping that Grimnor would take the bait. Then a single curt feeling of acceptance came. He could tell that Grimnor did not like it but would accept it. *Now. Strike now.* The Unnamed God cleared his throat. "For this to work, though, I must have assurances you will not seek revenge. So, you, and your Gorom, must swear…" The Unnamed God searched for the right word for a moment. "Fealty. You and your race will swear fealty to me and, by extension, to my people, the humans."

Anger boiled forth almost instantly, and to his surprise, Grimnor appeared. Grimnor did not like taking physical form, he remembered that much. He preferred to dwell in his rock and stone, a presence. *I may have pushed too hard.*

The air around his brother god grew hot, and waves of heat came off him. The very rock he stood on glowed with the rage the god was obviously feeling. A faint orange glow at first, but increasing. Grimnor himself was like a larger version of a Gorom. But his skin was more rocklike, and he was hairless. His eyes, though, his eyes glowed with all the colors of this underground realm.

"Now brother. Do you want to do this?" The Unnamed God readied his hammer and shield again. "I am seeking assurance that no revenge will be taken. But if we come to blows, I will make sure that every Gorom will be the enemy of man. Every scrap of trade will end, and we will seal your people underground, after they march here and kill the rest of the Vinik. Do you want to risk that?"

The rage that came back was white hot now, and lines of blue and orange flame appeared in cracks over Grimnor's body. But yet, he did not attack. But neither did he show any deference to the Unnamed God. Instead, he made a series of motions and melted into the stone from where he had formed.

So. That was it for now. Grimnor would order his Gorom to kill whatever Vinik they had, but would not swear any kind of pact to serve him. Grimnor was proud, though the Unnamed God had never quite understood why. Over a hundred worlds and uncounted ages, Grimnor had followed the same pattern.

His people, regardless of what name they had been given, were always very like what the Gorom were here in this place. Short, sturdy, lived underground. Sometimes more, sometimes less. Always good at craft, but the same attitude, the same edge.

Grimnor was the one brother he actually liked, and the Unnamed God wondered why. Maybe it was because Grimnor knew his place. His people had never tried to challenge his for control of anything. There had only ever been a small handful of worlds where Grimnor's creations were common. None of those worlds held much of the power, much magic for them to feast on. No, Grimnor was predictable. Maybe that's why he liked him. He was right; he had pushed too hard, too fast. But it didn't matter. As the Gorom starved, Grimnor would remember his offer, and would agree to his terms.

One way or another, the Unnamed God would win.

Myriam awoke with a jerk. She'd had a horrible and strange dream. She'd been underground, back in the Gorom tunnels. Captain Tolin had been with her, and they had been running. Running over and over while the sound of something scrambling over hard rock echoed around them. They had burst out of the caves into an impossibly enormous cavern to see a city in ruins. And in those ruins stood the God she had brought back.

She shuddered again, trying to think of anything else but that face staring back at her. Her body thankfully supplied a way to stop dwelling on the dream, as the aches and pains of sleeping on a hard wooden bench appeared. Her neck hurt, and her shoulders hurt. Not a serious pain, but the normal grumbling of tendons and sinew that didn't like whatever position she'd slept in.

By the sparks, she had been tired. She still was. When was the last time she'd felt well rested? Full? Relaxed. She was having a hard time remembering that. Would she ever feel that way again? She blinked a few times before her thoughts turned to what was actually important. Jinir!

She stood, jolting upright to see her patient still asleep. But he looked better. Much better. Skin that was pale and almost thin when she'd fallen asleep, was now a much healthier pink. Even his breathing was steady. Yes, he was much better. Not fully healed yet, but far better than before she'd fallen asleep.

"Your awake. Good. Here, food and drink. Plus, I brought a mirror and a brush. I must apologize, I have not been the best host." Ralta's voice came from behind her.

Myriam turned towards her, the smell of food, proper food, making her mouth water. A clenched knot in her stomach she'd not even paid attention to made sure she was paying attention to it now. She wondered if she'd ever be full again either. All this work, all this healing had turned a healthy appetite into more of a ravenous pit in her guts. "That smells…." Myriam didn't have the right words. "Thank you."

Ralta dipped her head in acknowledgement and placed the tray on a small table by the bench. "He looks better."

Myriam nodded. "Has he stirred any?"

"No, but I could tell you were going to awaken soon, so I took a chance and got you food. But he seems better. Is it normal for him not to have awoken yet?" Ralta's voice caught, just a tiny bit at the end of her question.

"Yes. His body is still catching up with what has been done. It was all as exhausting for him as it was for me, if not more so. He had to deal with the pain as well." Myriam examined the tray Ralta had brought. Meats, roasted pork? Chicken? She wasn't sure. Breads, fruits, a huge chunk of yellow white cheese. More water, but this time fruit floated into the water as well. And true to her word, a mirror, and a brush.

Myriam had never been overly concerned about her appearance. She didn't even care too much when her hair had been hacked away, when all that bug slime had got in it. The memory of the caves brought back sorrow, and she pushed it away again. *Now was not the time.* Still, effort deserved to be made, right? Myriam picked up the mirror and brush, but one look in the mirror and the brush clattered to the floor.

"What?" was all she could say. The face that looked back at her was not even close to the one she felt like should be there. It was all wrong. Her face was thin, and her skin looked… stretched. As if you really tried hard, you could see the bones in her skull. But the worst, the worst, was her eyes. She didn't have eyes that color. No one did!

 For her brown and green eyes were gone, even the more recent blue was gone, and all that was left now was silver. Silver eyes, flecked with that same bright blue, looked back at her. Who was this person? It was her, but it wasn't her. "Myriam?" Ralta reached down, taking the brush from where it had fallen. "Are you all right?" "I have no idea." Myriam looked down at herself and didn't know the body she was in, at all. "I really have no idea."

Chapter 31.

Will awoke, his mind a jumble. He'd had a rough rest of the night after leaving his clandestine meeting. He'd arrived back at his room right as everyone else was getting up. The noise in the hallway, of other crafters awakening, talking had brought him nothing but annoyance. His mind was whirling with the thoughts that had come up since talking to Tarn Yulisia. Mikol? And Myriam? Not dead? He was worried about her. Now very worried, if Yulisia was right. And yet, all he could hear was cheerful chatter and crafters talking, laughing.

Finally, the noise had died down, and he'd fallen back asleep. He had not meant to, but he had never been one for getting up when it was dark and he was tired. His dreams were full of explosions and falling. Nothing he wanted to think about. Rising again, he washed and got dressed. Wearing his crafter garb, including the thick leather apron this morning, he wondered what he should do.

Rewil had said they would start over today, but the man hadn't come looking for him. Which meant either he was busy with something else or didn't want him there. Go to one of the craft stations and see what he could salvage out of his work? He liked the idea of making something again. It seemed like ever since he had left the Reach so long ago, he'd never had a long stretch of time to do the one thing he loved, the one thing that made him, *him*.

Yet, the conversation gnawed at his thoughts. If Myriam was alive, where was she? How on earth would he ever find her? Did she even want to be found, or found by him? They hadn't spoken in months. There was a lot of regret there with the way their last conversation had ended. She was the one link to his old life, the only one left. Well, the only one anywhere near enough to matter. He was stranded here far to the south, in a distant land, surrounded by incredible things made by incredible people.

Myriam should have been a rock in his life and he in hers, something for each other to cling to in the insanity of this place. But he had turned his back on her. And to some extent, her on him. But it was his fault, he was sure of it. He had been so angry. Everything he had done, broken by her action. But she hadn't known how it would all turn out. How could she? He wished she would have told him about that crystal, but would anything have gone differently?

Will shook his head. It didn't matter. If he did ever see her again, or could think of a way to find her, he'd apologize. But the first thing was trying to decide what was true. Mikol was either a kindly and wise healer, or a powerful and immoral man who ran the city with an iron fist. A fist encased with a velvet touch. Myriam was either dead, blown apart by the unleashed power when the quickway came apart, or she was alive and hiding for her life.

Which meant that based on everything they had evidence for, that Yulisia was right. The only reason he could think that Myriam would not come forth was she was scared or in danger. Which meant someone had tried to kill her, and she knew that. Or someone had her. Will didn't know much about the criminal elements in the City. The spire seemed free of that sort of thing, and 'spire folk' were discouraged from going into the City. So really, the question was, where was she?

Will still didn't quite understand all this naming talk. A name was a name. But not apparently for Gods. Why it mattered, though, he did not know. How could having a name give the Unnamed God power? But standing here, in his room dressed in his crafter garb, would not make anything happen.

He headed out, deciding that he would find Rewil first, or at least try to. He wasn't sure if he could even get back to the warehouse that held all the wreckage by himself. The route had been confusing enough with Rewil to lead the way. First though, Rewil's office.

The Tarn of the Crafters didn't have an office per se, only a large workroom with two massive worktables. One usually covered with paper, marking rods, ink, and a handful of mechanisms and glowing things that William could only guess the function of. The other was normally reserved for whatever project his Tarn was working on.

But today, no Rewil. He had heard that other sections had guards, or people assigned to be the assistant to the Tarn. But not there. Rewil didn't want such things. There were enough constructs around to work as guards if anyone tried anything violent. And Rewil didn't seem to have much use for anyone waiting on him.

The downside to this was, of course, that no one ever knew where Rewil was most of the time. He'd appear randomly all over the section, checking the work, discussing ideas with senior crafters. Will found this part exasperating. Where could Rewil be?

Finally, his stomach growled at him enough for him to realize he had not eaten or drank anything since getting up. Making his way to the almost empty mess hall, he was greeted by the one person he had been looking for. Rewil. "William!" Rewil's booming voice came as soon as he entered the room. "Come. Sit. I only have a short time. Mikol has called a commons, so I will leave the work in the warehouse to you today."

Will felt his skin chill at the mention of a commons being called by Mikol. "A surprise commons?" he asked, trying not to sound curious.

"Yes. But there's rarely any other kind. There's a standing one every three months, but it seems as of late we get an emergency every week. But it's Mikol calling it, so there must be a good reason." Rewil took a long drink of some slick looking black drink that was popular here. He'd heard one older crafter call it 'The Oil', but to him it was disgusting. Thick and tasted of coal. At least to Will's taste.

Will wondered if he should say anything right now about what he was told last night, what Yulisia had told him. He found himself somewhat reluctant to do so. He had gone against Rewil's wishes, against his direct orders. Though if Mikol was as amoral as she had said, he owed it to Rewil to say something. But still he hesitated. Would Rewil believe him?

The question got its own answer and quickly. "Here, I'll have a construct guide you to the warehouse, and then guide you back when you are done. I know this place can confuse people sometimes." Rewil took another long gulp of that oily black liquid and grimaced. "Not the best tasting drink, but it keeps me going."

Rewil stood and walked over to a small panel hidden behind a shelf covered with plates. He did something Will could not make out, and within moments a smaller many legged construct appeared. Rewil spoke to the machine for a few minutes, and then came back to Will. "All organized. Get some food and then tell that construct you are ready. It will guide you there, and back." Rewil yawned, a huge thing that made his frame seem even larger.

Will nodded but realized that all this was taking a toll on his Tarn. Rewil looked tired, thin. The man didn't complain, at least not to him, even so, the exhaustion was obvious. "Sounds good." Will said when he realized Rewil was standing there, waiting for him to answer.

"Good, good." Rewil smiled. "All right, I have a long climb ahead of me, so I better get started." Rewil looked upwards in thought and gave a chuckle. "Do you know why I invented the quickways in the first place? Have you heard that story?"

"No." Will hadn't. He hadn't had time to dig into stories like that, or any other stories.

"Ah." Rewil smiled. "I can tell you this one, it's short."

"I hate stairs. I hate climbing them. Up or down. I hate stairs. They are never big enough for my feet. And stairs sized for me are too big for everyone else. So, the quickways." Rewil lowered his eyes for a moment. "I hope my quest for laziness doesn't disappoint you."

Will laughed. "I am not fond of stairs either. Or running."

"Then you get it!" Rewil glanced up again. "I'd better get started. It's a lot of stairs."

Will watched him go and resolved that when he had figured out where Myriam was, he'd warn Rewil about Mikol. He needed more proof than whatever Yulisia said. But now food, and then back to work. Will looked at the construct waiting for him. A feeling of sadness came over him, watching the automated thing standing there, waiting.

Will remembered what Rewil had said about early constructs being based on some magical copy of a person. That felt wrong to him. Though he had also said they weren't made that way anymore. Still, the idea of a copy of someone, a magical short-term copy being forced into a metal shell and made to work forever, or until they weren't needed anymore, was very unpleasant.

He wasn't sure though if he had the details right. Rewil had said something about based on a pattern. Or something like that. In truth, Will hadn't been paying the closest attention at the time. Grabbing a meat roll and a cup of hot tea from the long table where quick food was left, he walked over to the construct. He examined it with a crafter's eye.

It was a newer model but not the newest, of that, he was sure. It had those kind of unnerving spider legs, or what he thought of as spider legs. He could see the power source in it as well, the blue green orb stuck in the middle of the unit. That also showed its age. He knew from his studies that anything made in the last few years had that covered up. There had been an accident where an orb had gotten cracked and there'd been an explosion. Not a huge one, even so, big enough. Some people had gotten hurt, though he didn't think anyone had died.

Explosion.

Maybe? Will's mind went racing. If one of the rail constructs had gotten damaged, and its power source exploded, could that have started the events that led to the ultimate destruction of the quickway? The rail riding constructs were old. They were the first constructs made. For the first time since he'd been caught in the aftermath of that tragedy, Will felt like he had made progress. He was going to find Myriam, one way or another, and this might help get him one step closer.

Chapter 32.

"I have called this meeting to discuss a situation in the lower city." Mikol stood up from his seat at the table of the commons. His eyes looked at each of his other Tarns, measuring them. Rewil looked attentive, if worn. And he was utterly ignoring the people seated to his left.

Yulisia and Nollew sat there, their hands touching, fingers intertwined. He would get a gage on them soon. It was easier to nudge and figure things out if they were talking and distracted from him. Still, he examined them with a practiced eye, but saw nothing that showed any deviation from the working he had placed on them. In fact, Yulisia was ever so slightly turned away from Rewil, who sat next to her. Both she and Nollew looked bored, which was normal for them. As for Grib, the man was leaning forward, eager. Mikol had sent him a message that he was going to call a commons about his 'Downtrodden Lord' problem.

He would have had Grib called the commons himself, but he would have made a mess of it. No, it was better coming from Mikol. He could embellish. Grib would go along with anything he said and most likely Rewil as well.

"Who cares about the lower city? The only one here who does is Grib." Nollew gave a slight yawn. "If this concerns him, why didn't he call this meeting? And why did this warrant an emergency meeting? We have too many of those now."

"I asked Mikol to do it. I have a suspicion if I did so, you'd find a reason not to show up." Grib replied, the words coming quick. "And what happens in the lower city affects all of you, one way or another. Or do you forget where your food comes from? Where the people who make this spire work, where they live? It affects everyone, and that's why the emergency meeting."

Nollew didn't reply, and somewhat, to Mikol's surprise, he didn't throw in a characteristic eye roll or sigh. He rested a hand on Yulisia's arm and gave Grib a blank look. Mikol cleared his throat. "I called this because through Grib, we've learned more about this 'Lord'. And none of it is good in the long run. No one knows what the man, and we do think it's a man, looks like. No one knows if the voice we hear is his real one. But he controls a large section of the lower city, and even a sliver of the middle city. And his influence is growing." "And?" Yulisia asked quickly. "So, a lower city resident is popular in the lower city. I've done my own listening to this problem. He feeds hungry people, helps families find homes, and generally helps people out. This is not an emergency."

"He's undermining my authority." Grib growled and slammed a fist down. "What if he decided that the spire was off limits? And no lower or middle city residents could come here, or work here?"

"Then I'm sure our…. *Friend…* Rewil here would make some magical creation to do their job **FOR THEM**." Yulisia's voice rose to the same volume as Grib's had been.

"You don't understand." Grib lowered his voice, flushing red. "But then again, why would you? You're either neck deep in some dusty tome, or neck deep in a pile of pillows on Nollew's bed…"

Nollew stood, pointing a finger at Grib. The finger and arm it was attached to threatened to wipe his fellow Tarn off Alos. "Watch your tone, GOROM."

Mikol stood now and raised his voice. "All of you. **SILENT**. I called this meeting to discuss what could be done, not so the rest of you could bait and threaten each other." Mikol sent a fraction of a tendril of power, small enough not to be noticed, to Grib, calming the Tarn. The Gorom was a thrice blunted fool to make the comment he had. He'd have to have a conversation with him to remind the Tarn what his position was.

The only Tarn who said nothing so far was Rewil. He sat there, a slightly bemused expression on his face. Mikol appreciated Rewil's calmness. He'd wondered a few times if he should have gotten rid of Rewil the same way Jinir had met his fate, but he was happy he'd kept him around.

"The fact is this, there are far more people in the lower and middle city than there are in all the sections of the spire put together. *IF* this Lord has designs on being more than a doer of good deeds in the lower sections, he could do much." Mikol held up a hand. "We know he is guarded by a Trinil nearly every moment, a Trinil with the knack for speed and balance."

Nollew had sat down, but his face was still flushed with anger. Mikol didn't need to feel him out to read his emotions. They were obvious. But the man was distracted by his anger. *This was as good a time as any.* Another tiny tendril sped out, touching Nollew and then Yulisia, joining them to each other, and both to Mikol himself. Two things became plain very quickly.

One, the suggestions and distrust of Rewil that he had spent so long building in his mind were gone. And had been gone for half a year. And two, Nollew was very careful to have put a false working to make him think things were still in place. Mikol would have never known if the man hadn't gotten angry at Grib.

Mikol could feel the difference between the genuine anger and the false one he'd been fed. So, it was true then. Mikol paused. This was a dangerous turn in his game. He doubted he could pull the same trick twice on them. Nollew would be attuned to it now, and he would have placed deep layers of protection on himself and his lover Yulisia. But there was still a chance he could turn this to his advantage, since Yulisia and Nollew didn't know he'd discovered their deception. A fleeting idea came that it might be time to use the other plan he had with these two. It was a dangerous plan. One he'd never actually put into full use. He'd targeted them, and Jinir back before the 'accident'. Though with all the new information he had, he probably should have used it. But... no, it wasn't time yet. Still too many variables.

"What do you propose we do?" Rewil finally spoke. "We are informed now, but is there a plan of action? Something for us to do about it?"

Grib spoke before Mikol could answer. "I'm asking for the power to sanction the man."

Mikol tasted the sourness in his mouth. *Yes, it was very much time to remind Grib of his position.* "Are you sure that is necessary?" Mikol tapped on the table as he spoke, his voice low. "We have not given any Tarn the power to sanction anyone in a very long time."

"I won't hear of it." Rewil shook his head. "He hasn't done anything yet, by your own admission. You want the power to kill the man because he

MIGHT be a threat? No."

"Rewil, listen to reason…" Grib started to say, but Nollew and Yulisia stood and headed to the exit.

"We will not listen to this nonsense. We are leaving. NOW." Both of them left together, quickly leaving the commons.

Interesting. Mikol hadn't expected that. His touch on their minds had found little anger outside the comment from Grib. What was their game?

Rewil stood as well. "I will not be a party to death like this. No. My apologies Grib, but until this Lord person actually works against us, I cannot agree to a sanction." He walked out as well, and all Mikol could feel was… confusion.

The commons chamber was quiet for several long minutes, leaving Mikol and Grib alone. Grib said nothing, his face like stone. He stared at the table, his fists clenched, stewing in his anger. Mikol watched him before finally clearing his throat. "A nice mess you made of this, Grib. You know that?" Mikol paused and grimaced. "You should know, I have an excellent idea of who this person is, and you won't like it."

"What?" Grib raised his head. "It's Jinir. I knew that."

Mikol felt a cold jolt move up his spine and run through him. Grib was far cannier than he'd thought. "How do you know this?"

"It makes sense. That's why I wanted the sanction. If the others discover Jinir is alive, what would that do to the balance of power here? I may not live in the spire with the rest of you, but I know, I see. You have kept everyone else at each other's throats. I owe you everything. But Jinir not being dead? That could upend everything for me, and for you."

Probably. It could also do the exact opposite and bring him the power he desired. "Oh?"

"Yes." Grib leaned forward. "We need to act now, while the rest of the Tarns are not paying attention. And capture him. I want him brought here to me, with restraints."

"Do you have a plan for that?" Mikol was genuinely curious. "You do not have the power to command anyone to do that."

"I may not have it now, but I will." Grib locked eyes with Mikol. "I will do what you couldn't."

Mikol would have taken him seriously, but the Gorom forgot Mikol knew what he was feeling. Tarn Grib was terrified. *This is a gambit.* A ploy to see how much he can push. Mikol sat back in his chair. "Do what you think you need to do. But remember this, even if this is Jinir, he's not the same man he was. I'm sure I can find ways for you to not be the same man you are now as well."

Grib paled, and the sticky taste of fear clung to him as he stood and left the chamber.

He knows.

Are you sure?

Yes, I'm sure. When Grib made that comment and I got angry, Mikol struck. I wouldn't be surprised if he put Grib up to it. So, he knows.

Interesting. I was somewhat surprised by Grib's comment, and more by your reaction. He had no business saying that.

My dear Nollew, it was true, though.

Chapter 33.

Myriam stood in front of a full mirror for the first time in months. Or maybe it was years. They didn't have any in the Guild. What was the point? Her mother had one in the Inn. That was the last time she'd actually looked at herself like this. And what she saw confused her and worried her more than anything else.

She didn't recognize herself. She had always been fine with her size. She wasn't a slim, tiny thing like from the ballads. She had worked in the Inn and swung a hammer at a forge. That brought strength and toned muscles. What she saw now looked like she'd been starved. Her hair, while torn up still from her recent almost death, was far lighter than she remembered. It shone a near pale silver white, and only tiny streams of her normal auburn could be seen.

But the strangest was her eyes. When she and William had arrived here, her eyes were full of blue. The blue of the magic they had absorbed. Raw power. That had faded over time to her natural green and brown. But what she saw now was silver. And not a tarnished dark silver, but a bright shining silver. Eyes you could see across a room.

What had happened to her? How had it happened? Panic formed in the pit of her stomach. This wasn't her looking back at her. It was someone else! The kernel sprouted and sweat formed on her forehead. The beads of sweat running down stung her eyes, bringing pain that she tried to blink away. She hoped each blink would fix the image and make it the way it was supposed to be.

A still rational segment of her mind fought back. No, this WAS her. The shape of her face, while thinner than she'd ever seen it, was the same. And oddly enough, the tiny nick of a scar on the underside of her chin was still there from her time with Regin in the woods, right before the Anvil. She felt the warmth rush to her cheeks at that memory and felt some relief that her reflection showed the same color.

The panic began to fade away. Replaced with a lot of questions. Maybe it was something with the explosion? Or something about the healing she had done on herself? Healing yourself was difficult. Maybe it changed you in some way. It could be a combination of both even. As the last vestiges of the fear left her, she took a long-ragged breath, and felt one final tick of relief that her reflection breathed with her. After everything she'd been through, some part of her half expected her reflection not to join in.

"Is everything all right?" Ralta entered the room without a warning. Myriam repressed a flash of annoyance. The Trinil almost never knocked. Though it was her place, not Myriam's. Maybe that was normal for her, or normal for Trinil. Myriam had met Trinil before but couldn't say if she'd ever been around one for any period of time. All the Trinil she'd met had been traders, and they had little time for a human girl who mostly wiped the tables down. Her father had spoken to them more than anyone else.

"Myriam?" Ralta asked. Her voice rose a fraction as she asked the unspoken addition.

"Fine. I'm fine. I just, I don't, I am not who I was." Myriam gave the stranger in the mirror one last look. "Maybe I never will be again."

"Jinir is waking up." Ralta didn't respond to what Myriam had said. The annoyance returned at Ralta's obvious uncaring of the predicament that Myriam found herself in. But as quickly, she pushed it away. Ralta had never seen her before the accident. She had no way of knowing that she differed vastly from what she'd been before. At least in the way she looked. She still felt like herself. *For now.*

"Well then, I need to be near my patient." Myriam forced the uncertainty and strangeness out of her mind. There was no time for that. Ralta led her back to the room where she'd been working on Jinir. When she entered, she found him propping himself up on one elbow, blinking in the room's light.

"You did it." Jinir whispered. His voice was firm now. The horrible raw tone of a never healing wound was gone. A powerful voice. A clean voice. Myriam watched as he raised a hand, eyes traveling up the arm, the wonder in his eyes bringing a wetness to them. "Not everything. Not yet. And you did a great deal. I am still surprised at how much pain you survived. How much every breath hurt you." Myriam meant it; she'd never met anyone as able to live with pain as Jinir.

"I'm whole." Jinir didn't say anything else. His fingers traced his face, pulling back several times as if he was scared to touch it, sacred to feel it. "Mirror. Please, a mirror."

Ralta with a small smile, handed him the mirror Myriam had used earlier. Myriam was struck by the expression on Ralta's face before she realized what it was. Kindness. Love.

Jinir took the mirror and stared at it. His free hand touched his head, and for the first time a tinge of a scowl crossed his face.

"It will grow back on its time. Hair seems to be impossible to make grow on its own." Myriam explained as Jinir's hint of a question died on his lips.

"I'll have to shave what's up here off. Start fresh. That's fine." Jinir took a deep breath, a grin breaking out as he did so. "Power, save me, I can breathe again!" He put the mirror down. "Thank you. Thank you. There is nothing I can give that could ever repay this."

"We aren't done." Myriam cautioned. "I have a few things left to heal. And check. One I must do now, then you must eat and drink."

Jinir closed his mouth in mid-breath. "All right, let's get it over with."

Myriam smiled. "That's the attitude." She pressed her hands to his stomach and closed her eyes. She could feel it, a half-healed section of his stomach. It had bothered her when she'd felt it the first time, but there had been so many other things wrong, it had fallen down the list. Now she could turn her attention to it properly. It was strange; it didn't seem to be related to the incident that had wrought so much other destruction to the man. It was a different hurt. She stretched her power out, feeling her way to the wound. A tiny gasp escaped her.

"What?" Ralta sprung up from where she'd been watching.

Myriam ignored her. This wasn't a wound. This was something else. A tiny ball of something. A something that made her sweat. Poison? The ball was small, smaller than a drop of metal that had fallen into a quenching tank. But it had been sealed somehow, sealed and placed where it wouldn't do anything. But why? Why poison someone and then seal it away?

For later.

Myriam understood then. It was a backup. If nothing else, whomever had done this, could release the toxin if the accident didn't kill Jinir. The odds were if he'd been returned to the spire, he would have been horribly injured. Taken to the Healers, it would only take a tiny flick of power to release this, killing him for sure.

The thought she'd been going through raced into her awareness. The Healers. And the one thing Jinir had said, that she'd not believed. Mikol. Her skin prickled, a thousand tiny bumps spreading across her skin. Mikol had done this. And her accident, Mikol again. This proved it. Mikol had tried to kill Jinir AND her. Some small part of her didn't want to believe that. But the facts were here.

"What?" Ralta asked again, more insistent this time.

Myriam was happy that Ralta knew enough about healing, though, to not touch her, not bother with her while she worked. Sealing the ball of poison twice over, she pulled at it, healing the place where it had lain for quite some time. She pulled at it, hearing a grunt from Jinir in response. Pulling again, she concentrated. The only way to get this out was to pull it through his skin. "Knife. Now. Clean." Myriam spoke to Ralta. "See it? Don't cut it but make a slit so it can leave." Myriam had her eyes closed, but she could feel it with her power. The small, rounded ball, pushing against the skin.

"What is that??" Ralta reached out with a finger but jerked it back. "Do it Ralta." Jinir growled.

Myriam could feel his pain, though she was blocking a large part of it.

Ralta took a thin blade, and ran it through a candle flame a few times, then with precision, she cut a tiny slit in the skin. Deep enough for the thing to leave, but not far enough to damage any muscle. The ball, brown and black, popped out, falling to the floor with no sound that Myriam could make out.

"Leave it." Myriam ordered, turning her mind to the cut. It sealed fast, the cut having been clean and precise. Releasing her power, Myriam opened her eyes again. "That was unexpected."

"What is that?" Jinir looked down at the tiny ball. "Was that stuck in me?

It doesn't look like anything I've seen. It's not wood, or metal."

"No. It's, well, I don't know what it is made of. But it proves you were right. About Mikol." Myriam felt repulsed looking at it. It felt wrong. She had no idea what the poison could be, but the mere fact that someone would do that, and a Healer at that, was wrong. Very wrong.

"How does it do that?" Jinir asked. "I'm glad you believe me, but how did that make it so?"

"It's poison. A poison placed inside you. Carefully. Secretly. Waiting. My guess is it was set there in case the accident didn't kill you and you ended up back in the spire. Horribly injured, but alive. It was sealed with the power in some way. I can't think of anyone other than Mikol would have that ability, that level of control." Myriam looked away from it, and at Jinir. "I am sorry I had a hard time believing you."

Ralta touched the ball with the tip of her boot. "So, if I hadn't carried you here, you'd be dead."

"Yes Ralta, I would. Another debt I owe you." Jinir reached out and grabbed Ralta's arm. "Thank you, my friend." Myriam saw the flash of sadness in Ralta's eyes. Eyes that met hers right after, begging her not to say anything. "Well, you can eat and drink now. The only things left to heal are minor. Your large toe on your left foot has some joint damage. It might cause you some pain while walking. And your knee on the same side. Other than that, and your need to regrow some hair, you're as healthy as I can make you."

Jinir smiled, rubbing a hand over his very patchy scalp. "Well, Ralta, I may ask you to shave this off, and then we feast. All of us."

It wasn't until many hours later that Myriam realized they had left the poison on the floor. She returned to the room, now empty, to find it missing. A hollow feeling entered her chest at the sight. Her mind told her one of the others must have gotten rid of it, but it took her far longer to fall asleep than it should have.

Grib waited for his men to arrive. Mikol was being a fool. He owed everything to Mikol, Grib knew that. Even so, the man was being a fool. Jinir was alive, and that meant nothing good for Grib. He'd never liked Jinir, even when he had been his Tarn. Always concerned with the lower city, and not where the real power lay. Which wasn't the spire. Let Mikol and the others play their games of who was in charge.

Nollew was too infatuated with Yulisia to make any sense these days, and Yulisia loved the attention. Grib didn't see the attraction to either of them. Nollew looked like a middle-aged clerk to him, and Yulisia was too thin. Grib leaned back at his tall table, making sure that when his searchers arrived, he'd be a full head taller than them.

That left Rewil. Grib actually found Rewil to be tolerable. Maybe it was his Gorom blood, but the man was smart and capable. His fundamental flaw, though, made him worthless to Grib. The man had no ambition. He was content to be the Tarn of the Crafters. Nothing else drew him in.

Grib did not regret his actions in placing the blame on Rewil when the quickway had gone up. He regretted the need for losing his people on the ground, but sometimes sacrifices had to be made. Or at least sacrifices that actually did something, because it appeared to him that Mikol had screwed this one up as well. Grib calmed himself as the door opened, and in walked three men. Two normal humans, and one odd looking man with rough features and pointed ears. Grib couldn't begin to guess what his background was, which races had mingled to make him. But it didn't matter. They had a job to do.

"The three of you have sworn yourself to me. By the blood and the power. I have a simple task. Jinir is alive. I need to know where he is." Grib watched each man's reaction. All of them had been part of the city section long enough to know Jinir.

The pointed eared one snorted. "Even if we could find him, if he's alive, that means Ralta's alive."

Ralta. Grib wanted to end that Trinil's life, personally. She'd been the whole reason he'd never moved against Jinir himself. Anyone who ever tried ended up dying on a knife. At least anyone in the lower or middle city. Spire folk were outside her range, which was why Mikol had done it.

The other two men shifted from foot to foot, each looking uncomfortable. The one on the left spoke, breaking the silence. "Tarn Grib, we will do as you have asked, but Ralta…"

"You will do as I have ORDERED. Not asked. And forget Ralta." Grib looked down at the three men. "If you're so worried about her, then find the other one. Find Rauger."

The pointed eared fellow looked surprised for a moment. "The word in the lower city is he's around but working against this Downtrodden Lord person. Whomever that is."

"That's Jinir." Grib interrupted. "And if they aren't working together anymore, then even better. Find him."

Chapter 34.

Master Reinhill stood before the anvil, her stomach lurching. In the time since this new god appeared, her beloved Guild had changed drastically. What was once a sacred place to create and share knowledge had become not much more than a weapons factory. She had dared to hope after the fall of the Priesthood that maybe now, finally; the Guild become what it truly was meant to be.

Amder had returned, there was a new Forgemaster, and Bracin and his power were broken. Everything had been working out exactly as she had dared to dream. Then the first cracks had appeared. Ture was thrown into turmoil. The King and the Nobles, long regulated to figureheads by the power of the Priesthood and the Heart of Amder, had proved as powerless as she had always feared.

No one listened to them. The city guard included. A few honorable men had tried to whip things into shape and failed, and usually those failures were deadly. The evil of the past had been long entrenched, and it would have taken the Forgemaster to set it all right. And he hadn't come. He'd vanished. Amder had made a single appearance but had solved nothing.

Without the Forgemaster, the city had fallen into warring factions. And then, the new God had appeared. And made an example of Greenmar. A deep twist in her heart betrayed her loss of her friend. Dead. All because he'd asked questions of this new god who claimed to be the remade god, made of Amder and Valnijz. She longed to leave, to run. But she knew others would pay the price. So, she stayed, trying to protect all she had known.

She could see little of the God of Craft in this new thing. And a lot of the Blood God. But they had done as he had ordered. Piles of weapons filled storerooms now. Spears made up the vast bulk. Spears were easy to make, fast, and fairly easy for a commoner to use. Elsewhere in the city, the new god had raised an army. How he'd managed it; she wasn't sure. But somehow this new god had reforged Ture into something else, something new.

Each spear had their last edge hammered on this anvil, this new anvil. Then sharpened. The edges were sharper than anything else she'd ever made. And didn't dull. Or if they did dull, she wasn't sure how long that would take. There were hammers, shields, armor as well. The guild was still the guild and could craft like no other place she knew of. But everything felt wrong about it. Everything was slightly off. *Polluted.* Yes, that was the word, polluted. And the feeling came from this new anvil in waves. Even being near it felt wrong.

"But it's not Master Reinhill. It is perfect." A voice she had only heard once before filled the room. The Unnamed God.

"If you say so." Trie Reinhill forced the words out and turned to leave, not wanting anymore contact with this entity.

"I did not dismiss you." The voice carried an undertone of violence. "You may be the Guildmaster, and I am giving you the benefit of that office by not ending your place and your life right now."

Trie said nothing. What was there to say? This was a god.

"We will march to war soon. I will open the way, and my army, with your weapons, will march on the City in Blue. Have you ever heard of the city?" The voice came louder, and the presence solidified. There, standing on the other side of the Anvil, stood this new god. He was different now, though. For one, he carried a hammer. But it was a hammer of war, not creation. He also carried a shield, a strange thing, Drendel steel she recognized, but the cover she did not. It was shiny and covered with a swirling, almost organic pattern of gold.

"I have not." Trie lowered her head.

"A dangerous place. An evil place. A place where mortals dare to use the power, unfiltered." The Unnamed God thumped a heavy hand on the anvil. "A place that defies the order of the world."

Trie Reinhill had no idea what this thing was talking about, but since it wouldn't let her leave, she wondered if she should say something, anything. "I don't understand." She finally managed to say. And she didn't understand.

"Mortals cannot use the power. Magic. If that makes it easier to understand." The heavy sound of a hammer hitting a flagstone echoed in the room. "But… didn't the Priesthood do that? Didn't the anvil do that?" Master Reinhill backed up as the feeling of anger flicked around the room. She had no idea what this presence was mad about, but she'd annoyed it, somehow. "Doesn't this current anvil of your creation do that?" The anger cooled.

"No. Not at all. Those examples were accessing the power through me. Or parts of me. What the City does is evil. Mortals cannot use the power. Not directly." The sound of the hammer hitting the floor came again, accompanied by a horrific cracking sound. "Look at me."

Master Trie Reinhill, Guildmaster of the Smithing Guild of Palnor, was never someone who scared easily. She, in her long time at the Guild, had faced down nobles, merchant lords, other Guildmasters, and even High Priest Bracin a few times. But this feeling of nearly overwhelming command made her raise her head.

"Better. I do not hate you, Master Reinhill. You have done exactly as I have asked, and to impressive effect. This is to be commended. Not punished." The figure spoke in calm tones. Warm, and friendly. The kind of voice you'd listen to, and do anything for.

Master Reinhill found breathing was hard to do now. The figure glowed in front of her, a beautiful glow. A kernel of love swelled up in her, a devotion to this glorious figure. Her sorrow and revulsion at Master Greenhill's death skittered away, vanishing. The man had questioned their god, and while his death was a sad turn of events, it was not unwarranted.

No. This was a divine being. It was not to be questioned. Only loved, worshiped. If this City was wrong in its working of magic, then it was wrong. Master Reinhill could see it now. It was all perfect. Whatever this God wanted was what she and the Guild would do.

"Yes." The Unnamed God spoke again. "You understand now. I am more than Amder ever was. I am the protector of humanity. I am the true God of my people. Violence happens, but obey me, follow me, and strike where and when I say, and there will be no hand raised against any of you by me."

Master Reinhill went down, kneeling. A wetness slid down her cheeks. "My Lord, I am sorry for my doubts, my fears."

"There is no reason for sorrow. You were lost, and I have found you."
The Unnamed God rested a hand on the anvil in front of him. "I will give
you, however, a task."

"What task?" Master Reinhill stood, blinking away the last of the tears. "I
and the Guild exist to serve."

The Unnamed God pulled from what all the world looked like nothing
but air, a long iron rod. It was black, shiny; the air seemed to twist around
it in unsettling patterns. "This will be our way to remove the blight of the
City from Alos. And you will make them, as you have made the
weapons."

Trie Reinhill studied the rod. Long and slender, it seemed to drink in the
light that came off everything. "What is it?" she finally asked. She'd never
seen it's like. Making a rod of iron was simple, but this wasn't a normal
rod, or even really iron, the more she looked at it.

"This is an anchor. When the battle comes, these will protect our soldiers
from the power. It will draw the magic into them. Transferring it away,
into the very ground they walk on. But they must be made with care. It
takes time and skill. I will show you how, and you will make them. You
and a few others. I will give you leave to choose whom." The Unnamed
God pointed to the Anvil. "Place your hands upon my creation."

Master Reinhill did so and sucked in a chattering breath. Cold. Intense
cold. The method of making the Anchors flooded her mind. The
materials, the process. The cost. She tried to push it away, to keep a
rational mind, but she could not do so. And then she stopped wanting to.
The truth of the anchors filled her.

"You will make many of these. Do you understand Master Reinhill?"
The Unnamed God spoke, his tone clear.

Master Trie Reinhill smiled and nodded. She only lived to serve. Her
god's voice filled her mind with joy and strength. She would need that
strength. Her first step would be to share this great blessing with those
who were worthy to learn it. Then the metals needed, and finally, the
guards in Ture. For she needed all the parts, and with the right sort of
people to help, the slums and poorer parts of Ture could provide that
one needed material that was harder to get. A soul.

Chapter 35.

Will paid closer attention to the hallways and staircases they traversed this time. It was easier since the Construct didn't move as fast as Rewil did. Will didn't think the man knew how quick those long strides ate up distance. He mentally checked boxes as they walked. *Left hallway, then open fourth door on right. Down a narrow staircase, three flights. Take the smaller door on the right. Then down another hallway till it ends, then take the left passage that will end in another staircase. Take this down....*

Will doubted he'd be able to remember all the twists and turns. But if he could get most of it down, he'd be happy. Finally, after several more turns and doors, the door in front of them opened to show the same few steps down and into the large warehouse storeroom.

The piles still sat there, a motley mix of that golden metallic alloy, Honnim. Pieces of singed cloth, broken glass, and other things he couldn't begin to know what they were. It gave him a strange feeling to look at it. He knew on some level that Myriam really did have to be alive. But to see all this, and the damage wrought, a sliver of fear stayed, a sliver that poked at him, hard.

But enough introspection. There was a mystery to solve. Will examined the piles. The largest comprised of the broken and shattered quickway rails. Followed by the wreckage of the carriage, and then the piles showing destroyed constructs. Finally, a small pile was off by itself. A pile of things that Will had no idea what they were part of. Whatever it was, the humming buzz noise was the strongest near it.

Will turned to the construct, which hadn't moved since it had led him to this room. "Can you separate out the parts of the rail, carriage, and constructs that were near each other when the explosion happened?"

The construct rose on its spidery legs but did not move for several minutes. Will scowled at the thing, wondering if it could even help, when, though at a rate far slower than the other constructs had done it, it started sorting the piles again. Forming a new pile that Will hoped met his criteria, or at least something useful.

Will began talking to himself. It helped him think, and there wasn't anyone else here, anyway. "Now, if the explosion came from a construct's energy source, what would that look like? The orb would have to be damaged; I would guess." He wished Rewil was here, the man could answer the questions that Will had bouncing around in his head.

What did the rail riding constructs look like exactly? Was there a telltale sign that an explosion was caused by the release of all that power? He'd seen the rail riders, but only at a far distance. In a city of wonders like this place, they were a minor thing. He realized the construct had stopped adding things to the pile. It was far smaller than he'd expected, and his annoyance grew larger.

"Is that all? There's no more?" Will asked the machine. He knew he wouldn't get a response. None of the constructs could talk. He'd heard once that they had investigated it, but the idea proved both very hard to do and unnerving for most people to deal with.

The construct didn't move. Not even a quiver. Will pushed his annoyance aside. It wasn't the fault of a machine. Maybe his idea was faulty. But the more he turned it around in his head, the more he felt like he was on the correct path.

"Ho Will, what's all this about?" Tarn Rewil's voice echoed around the warehouse as the large man ducked his head as he moved through the doorway. "What's the new pile for?"

Will was happy to see him. "I had an idea. Maybe the explosion wasn't caused by the rail breaking, well it was, but maybe the start of it wasn't."

Rewil raised his eyebrows for a moment and frowned before nodding. "Well, maybe. But how?"

"The constructs. The rail riding ones. You mentioned them this morning, right? What if one of them was damaged? If its power source had gotten cracked, then the explosion happened, and it was enough of a release to snap the rail, releasing vast amounts of the power…" Will trailed off. He could see Rewil mulling it over.

"It's an idea that fits. But there is a problem with it. One, the rail riders don't use power sources like most constructs do. Remember, the riders were the first. For those, we bound a simulacrum to the machine. They don't have a permanent power source. They must return to a special alcove and be refilled with the power after a few trips." Rewil pointed to the new pile. "But what is that?"

Will's stomach dropped. So much for his grand idea. He had been sure he was close to getting this right. "I had the construct here make a new pile, only the parts that were near the point of the explosion."

Rewil's face turned pale before he erupted into laughter. "Why didn't I think of that? Let's examine that pile."

Will felt his mood brighten at the sound of Rewil's laughter. There wasn't enough laughing in this City. "I see nothing all that useful."

Rewil didn't answer and was already at the pile. Kneeling, he started examining pieces and mumbling to himself. 'Tolerances aren't right. Why is this here?" and something about "force array."

Will didn't say anything. He had no idea what the Tarn was looking for, and while he was a fast learner, Rewil was the inventor of almost all these items, Will wasn't about to seem like he understood it better than him.

Finally, after a good quarter of a bell, Rewil stood. "This is strange."

"How so?" Will prodded for more information.

"There was a construct there when the explosion happened. So, you still might be on to something. But…" Rewil shook his head. "Overcharged maybe?"

"How can you tell there was a construct there?" Will tried to study the small pile. He didn't see anything that looked like a construct in the wreckage. Or even part of one.

"Here." Rewil held up a single gear. It was warped, as if from great heat. Will had thought it part of the carriage.

"And that is?" Will didn't know exactly what he was looking at. What he did know was that the strange buzzing sound was much clearer since Rewil had held up that gear. Was that the cause of the noise?

"The lower impulse gear that governs the rail lock on a first-generation construct." Rewil smiled now, a big grin. "That it is here says everything."

Will didn't share the renewed enthusiasm that Rewil was giving off. If the explosion wasn't caused by a power source being damaged, what did it matter if a construct had been there or not. "I don't see why that's important now. You said they don't use power sources like regular constructs."

Rewil held up the gear. "The answer won't be here. We need to go to the construct charging area."

"The what?" Will asked. "Where the rail constructs get power? But if they didn't explode, why go there?"

Rewil pointed a meaty finger at Will. "You are giving up on your idea too soon. I said they didn't have a power source like the newer constructs. I didn't say they couldn't explode."

Will's skin prickled as he considered this. Rewil was right, as usual. He had given up too easy. "But what could make it explode like that, if it exploded?"

"I am not sure. But my best guess is maybe if a construct somehow got overcharged, it might happen. And the only way to answer that is to go to the station where they recharge." Rewil pocketed the gear and, with a sharp sound, flexed his fingers so his knuckles cracked. "I will tell you, it's a... cramped location. No one really goes there. It's all automatic. I designed it that way."

Will wondered if Rewil meant it was cramped for himself or for Will as well. He'd see soon enough though, as Rewil had already started walking again, even faster than usual.

Will hustled to catch up. Rewil led him down a series of sloping hallways and stairwells again. But this time, the last few stairways stood in stark contrast to everything else he'd seen. The bright clean white was gone. These were raw blocks of gray stone. Simple granite. Not that high polished white stone they used literally everywhere else in the City. Will half thought it should be the 'City in White' based on the looks of the place.

"Over here." Rewil had paused again, but this time he was pointing at a spot on the wall. It all looked like smooth stone to him, more granite.

"Here?" Will couldn't see anything. No door, no control, nothing. Just wall. "What's here?"

"They are recharging. The power is given through here. Here." Rewil slapped his hand on the wall. A small section of the wall swung out, exposing a hidden passage. Will gaped and then followed him in.

It was dark. Will paused to let his eyes adjust. The passage ended, but other than that, he could not see much. He couldn't see anything except a small slice of a room. His eyes strained to see in the black corners. A new sound entered his ears; a low hiss and a loud buzz that grew louder as he watched.

Chapter 36.

"I know I'm not supposed to follow the Gods, but by all the gods, alive or dead, that was amazing." Jinir grinned and wiped his mouth, chewing the last bit of the enormous meal he had downed. "Food has been tasteless and bland since the attempt on my life." He took a long drink of some golden yellow beverage. "Damage from whatever was in the vat."

Myriam cocked an eye at that. "Be careful. Too much wine could make your recent healing still tender."

Jinir held up the glass in question. "It's not wine, do not worry. I have much thinking to do and planning. It's honey juice."

"I have no idea what that is but be careful." Myriam found herself smiling as well. Jinir was strange, but he was good. Myriam had met his type before. They seemed to make everyone around them happier. But there seemed a wound in there, somewhere. Not one of the body, but of the mind. Every so often, a flash of it would enter his eyes. Anger, sadness, and some fear.

"You've never had honey juice?" Ralta shook her head. "And they say the spire is a place of wonder."

"Should have I?" Myriam shrugged. "I never paid too much attention to any of the food."

"Bleh." Ralta made a small, disgusted sound. "Boring. Food is one of the four great pleasures in life."

Jinir poured a small glass of this honey juice and offered it to Myriam. "Here. Thank me later."

Myriam sniffed the glass. A slight scent of flowers, or spring? A clean cool wind, something like that. She couldn't place her finger on it, but it relaxed her. Raising the glass, she took a sip. Her eyes shot up, and she took a second longer drink. It was amazing. A feeling of happiness, of forgotten joy, filled her mind and body. Her first kiss in her father's inn with the stableboy, the smell of Regin's shirt as she hugged him. Even older memories came of riding on her father's shoulders, the wild joy of a child being up so high.

Jinir smiled back at her. "Honey juice is a magical drink. It brings forth your best memories. Your true joys and best feelings. But the feelings fade quickly and drink too much of it and it will no longer affect you." Jinir took a last sip. "I haven't been able to drink it since my injuries. Every time I tried it burned like the accident was new."

Myriam finished her small glass. Her mind was a rushing wind of happiness and pleasure. She wondered how anyone ever could drink anything else. "This is…" Then the feelings faded, and part of her instantly searched for the bottle. She wanted to drink it all and drink it now.

"Ah, you see the trap." Ralta pointed at the bottle with one of her long thin knives she kept hidden somewhere. "Honey juice is potent stuff. But if you drank all that as you are now, you'd never be able to have that feeling again."

The feelings ebbed to the point where Myriam could think clearly. She was in a better mood though than before trying this wonderful drink. The overwhelming joy had retreated into an almost contentment. "I could see why people might drink it all."

"It's not uncommon. Honey juice is expensive as well. I procured it at a high cost." Jinir smiled, settling back in a large padded and patched chair.

"You bought it?" Ralta asked, arching a long eyebrow. "I seem to recall being the one doing that particular deal." She took the knife she'd been holding and balanced it, point first, on the tip of one long finger. "With Hitmal. And you know how much I find him to be a pain in my thin Trinil behind."

Myriam watched Ralta and wondered if she ever cut herself on those knives. She'd never examined one up close, but they seemed as sharp as a bone setter's knife. They didn't use things like that here in the Spire with the Healers. She wondered for a moment what some of her fellow Healers would think of the way healing was done outside these walls. The shock and horror she imagined almost made her laugh, an effort that was hard to stifle being as how she was still somewhat under the influence of this honey juice.

"I stand corrected. It isn't wine." Myriam finally said, "Even so, don't overdo it too much."

"There is a wine too, but it has different effects." Jinir smiled and glanced at Ralta, who blushed.

"Never mind that. You said he still had a few things to heal?" Ralta turned her attention to Myriam and began tossing the knife without looking at it.

Myriam wondered if she was doing this yet again to try and intimidate her. She need not have bothered. Myriam already considered Ralta one of the most dangerous people she'd ever met, regardless of race or gender. "Yes, the toe and the knee."

Jinir leaned back. "Feel free please."

Myriam reached out again, marveling still and how much faster this kind of healing was than anything she had done before. She still considered it a kind of forge work, only with blood and flesh, not fire and metal. It used a lot of the same skills, though instead of a hammer, she used the power. Magic.

She corrected the tiny flaws that remained. It was simple work. Neither of the remaining injuries was all that serious, but Myriam liked to make sure she completed her tasks. "You are as healthy now as I can make you. Stand and walk around?"

Jinir jumped out of his seat, flexing his knees, and walked a loop around the room. Then, with what Myriam could only call a joyful shout, he ran around the room, his robe flying behind him. Myriam didn't suppress her laugh now, though one glance at Ralta almost stopped it. A look of longing and nearly overwhelming sorrow crossed Ralta's face, not for long, but long enough for Myriam to be sure of what it was.

"Jinir…" Ralta's voice stopped the man mid run. "Don't you think it's time to talk about next steps?"

"Yes. I don't know what to do now. I believe you about Mikol, though I still have a hard time thinking about it. He's…" Myriam struggled to find the words. "I understand the struggle." Jinir sat back down, slightly out of breath. "It took me several weeks once I was aware enough to really think to come to grips with the fact that Mikol, the kindly old healer, was this kind of man? Maybe that's why he's so good at it. If he wasn't a

Healer, he'd make storyteller for the ages. He spins a world around everyone. And you want to believe in him so bad, you willingly turn away from any hints that he's corrupt to the core."

"But…" Myriam shrugged. The last of the honey juice had worn off, and now the uneasiness returned. "Is he evil? Does he enjoy this?"

"I have asked myself that same question, Myriam. Often. And the best I can come up with is that he doesn't care. I don't actually think he actually hates you, or me, or anyone else he disposes of. We are all things that get in his way." Jinir wiped a tiny bead of sweat off his forehead.

"He's evil." Ralta spoke now, and while she had put her knife away, her fingers twitched all the same.

"No Ralta. Well, maybe. It depends on what your version of evil is. Let's say you're walking down an alley. A group of feral cats is eating something. You need to pass, but they threaten and hiss. You push this out of the way with your boots. Maybe you, in annoyance, kick the food away, leaving them hungry and mad. Are you doing evil? Not to you. But to them, maybe." Jinir sighed. "I don't think it matters though."

"What does matter then?" Myriam locked eyes with Jinir. "You both saved me. And I can't thank you more for that. But I healed you. I did what I was brought here to do, more or less. So, what now? What becomes of Myriam VolFar?"

Silence filled the space for a long series of heartbeats. She watched as Jinir and Ralta exchanged glances that said a great deal. She couldn't read the Trinil, but she still had enough power in Jinir to at least get a feeling about where his emotions were. There was a thin layer of guilt, then a fierce burst of what she could only call determination.

"I wanted to kill you." Ralta finally looked away from Jinir. "Before you healed him. I thought, even if she fixes everything wrong. It's too dangerous to leave her alive." Ralta looked down at the ground. "I am ashamed of that. But there is the fact you know who he is. You know his face, his name. I am sworn to protect him. Forever." Myriam's hand went clammy as Ralta spoke. Kill her?? For a moment, she wondered if that drink had been poisoned. Was she already dead? "And now…?" Myriam forced the words out and tried to delve into her own body, a desperate scramble with the power to see if they had done something to her. The fear washed away quickly when she couldn't find anything.

"Now, that isn't an option." Jinir spoke now. "I trust you. We are both wanted by Mikol. We are both in need of hiding. And in fact, you can help a great deal. I can influence even more of the lower city and even the middle city with a healer with me as well. No one must see our faces or know our names. If I am the 'Downtrodden Lord' we need a good name for you."

"What is Ralta known as?" Myriam asked. She wasn't sure if she liked the idea Jinir had presented, but she also had little in the way of options.

"I am called the Protector, or the Guardian. Or just Ralta." The Trinil smiled at that, a genuine smile.

"It needs to be something… strange. Powerful." Jinir thumped the chair arm. "I have it! The Hand of Mercy."

Myriam wasn't sure she liked it. It was grandiose. But she guessed that was the point. "Fine." finally answering after Jinir kept looking at her with a grin that showed his excitement.

Chapter 37.

Will couldn't process everything he was seeing and hearing. This room was, he didn't have words for it. It was so foreign to everything he'd seen, even in this City. The constructs and the other wonders in this place were enough to make him feel unsteady if he dwelt on it too much. Even more when he considered how the outside world worked and lived. But this strange little room made his head spin. This buzz only helped the feeling of unease.

The constructs all sat in these alcoves, each one touching a blue line. Though most of the lines were dark. One empty alcove was present as well. He wondered if that was where the one construct that had been destroyed in the explosion had laid.

But that was the strange part. When they had entered the room, the hissing sound died at once. And even stranger, each construct had turned their heads, or what Will thought of as heads towards them. It made his skin feel cold, and a deep uneasiness crept over him.

"I haven't been here in a long time." Rewil pushed them into the small room. "Still a tight fit. Tighter than the last time I was here."

Rewil did not seem to find this place strange in the least, much to Will's surprise. "I could wait out in the hallway." Will offered, hoping his Tarn would agree.

"Nonsense. I'll need an extra pair of hands. I'm going to take that alcove apart, see anything strange is going on. That's got to the be one I need." Rewil pointed at the empty one. He lowered his head and shuffled over to the empty unit. "I made these in a workroom and then placed them here. I should have paid closer attention to how small the area was. I was excited to see it all working."

Will kept his eyes down, trying not to look at the surrounding machines. Normal constructs didn't give him the strange feeling that these did.

"Why do you need extra hands?" Will asked, trying to concentrate on the task at hand.

"I'll need you to hold a panel up and a few other things while I examine it, hard to do it one handed. I could take it back to the section, but then I'd have to disassemble a lot, and I don't want to have to do that, unless I have to." Rewil pushed the dark blue unlit line in the empty alcove, and then moving his hand up. A smooth metal door opened, revealing a strange mix of metal tubes and strands. Will recognized a lot of them, though some were shockingly rare. One stood out to him right away, though. Wight Iron. A good long thin piece of it. He couldn't see either end of it, so what it was doing, he had no idea. *Wight Iron.*

His hand brushed down, touching his hammer. But it wasn't the same. His eyes fell to the tool at his side. For a tiny second, he wondered where HIS hammer was. But no, this was the golden hammer made by Amder himself and handed to him. After he'd had to take his hammer, his wonderful Wight Iron hammer, the one he'd made with Duncan and a shard of Amder's blood and made shackles for the Blood God out of them.

The hammer at his side was a good hammer. A very special hammer. Despite that, it wasn't his hammer. Not fully. It never would be either.

"William?" Rewil asked, loudly.

"Oh sorry, lost in thought." Will stopped looking down. "You need me to hold that up?" Will pointed to the covering that Rewil was holding up.

"Yes. Please." Rewil gave Will a strange look for a moment. "Is everything all right?"

"Yes, sorry. I saw the Wight Iron, brought back memories." Will held the panel up easily. Though he needed both hands to Rewil's one for the job. "What are you looking for, if you don't mind me asking?"

"I don't mind at all. In fact, I'd be annoyed if you didn't ask." Rewil pointed to the strange mess of metals and such. "This moves the power into the constructs. It was a serious headache to make work. But thankfully, I made a way to see how long it took each construct to recharge, if you will. So, I could know when setting all this up how many constructs we would need to keep everything working."

Will got the basic idea. "Useful."

"Very." Rewil turned to the opening and began to tinker, his fingers, which were frankly twice as large as Will's, were far nimbler than Will's as well. "Ah ha!" Rewil pulled a marking rod out of a pocket and a scrap of paper. He scribbled something down and then stepped back. Will pushed the panel back in place. "Find what you were looking for?"

"Yes. And it's strange. You were right, though not in the way you thought. The construct here took nearly three times too long to recharge. But I could see no reason for the extra time. Which meant it was overcharged." Rewil tapped the alcove with his marking rod. "But, I don't think it actually exploded itself." "Why not? It would fit." Will looked around the room, each of these constructs still faced them, and the buzz remained, annoying him. "Just because of how the power is stored. It's not centralized like in the current machines." Rewil tapped a nearby rail rider with his marking rod. "I really should remake these things, it's a poor design." "Then… I was wrong." Will did not enjoy being wrong. He'd been so sure he'd hit the right answer. "No. Maybe. Look, remember what I said? About resonance? I think the extra power caused a resonance in the rail. It moved up the metal, full of power, and when it hit the carriage, everything broke." Rewil paused. "I think at least. The construct probably got pulled along with the resonance, so that's why its wreckage was there as well."

"So, the extra power, where did it come from?" Will finished the thought. "Why did the construct not stop charging?"

"I have no idea." Rewil frowned. "It shouldn't work that way. These older constructs took a certain amount of the power every three bells. It's an exact thing. I know, I made it. So why would one take in far more of the power, go onto a rail, and cause that particular event? And why when a carriage was there?"

"Is that important?" Will hadn't thought about it, but did the constructs ever go on the rails when a carriage was there? He couldn't think of an example when they did, but he also never paid it much attention. He had been so wrapped up in his life in the crafters section, he'd not ridden a quickway, but one other time after he'd arrived.

"Yes. They aren't supposed to be anywhere near the carriages. It makes it almost impossible for them to do their main job, inspecting the rails for damage or to help fix a rail if it needs it." Rewil poked at his paper with a thick finger. "It doesn't make sense."

Will agreed. One look at the constructs by him made him feel strange again. "Can we go now? It's warm in here." Will hadn't lied exactly. It was warm. The main reason was that infernal buzzing, it was like a small army of voices, all talking very fast, very loudly.

"Ah yes, you Reachers, always getting hot." Rewil joked for a moment, then thought better of it. "Sorry."

"It's not a problem." Will answered, the words spilling out in a rush. We headed back to the door they had come in from and exited the area, taking a large breath of cooler air as he did so. "Better." *And a lot quieter.*

"I know what you mean, it is warm in there." Rewil spoke to the air as he walked with his head down, his eyes trained on the paper. "We can't have people baking in the heat. That will ruin the work, so that's why we made it that way. No people need to be involved."

The tunnels weren't empty, as Will had expected. Workers, tradesman, and others could be seen. Snatches of conversations could be heard, but Will couldn't make them out. He realized this was the most he'd seen of regular people. "Rewil who are all these…" Will waved his hand around.

Rewil looked up from his paper and then looked at Will with a surprised face. "Oh! Well, the spire has many people who actually work there. Cooks, cleaners, those who handle the mundane details of life."

"Yes, but why am I seeing them all now?" Will never saw the people who did all that stuff. Which was strange to him. But thinking back, he'd never looked or thought about it. His food sort of appeared. He'd given no thought to how it got there. If the floors were polished white stone and clean enough to see your reflection in, then that was the way it was. He felt a flush at that thought. He didn't like that his mind had gone that way.

"Well, these lower tunnels like this they use to get around. The spire is riddled with passages and hidden doors. That way they don't bother the people in the sections." Rewil looked back at his paper, but looked up after a moment. "Too loud in here now. Come on, let's get back to the Crafter's section." And with that Rewil headed out, mumbling to himself about storage of power in older metals.

Will followed but felt sadness as he did. For all Rewil's kindness and brilliance, the man didn't see the problem with what he'd said. Anyone not of the sections was separate. No one ever said they were lower, but they didn't need to. Most of the things the crafter's made stayed in the spire. The books here stayed in the spire. The Casters had nothing to ever do with the lower and middle city. Even the Healers kept their work in the rest of the city to the lowest point they could.

It made Will sad. And as they walked, they left the hallways and passages that the 'knackers' used behind. Knackers. Spire slang for those who live in the middle and lower wards of the city. Will didn't like it the more he thought about it, though. He gave one last look behind him and followed Rewil up into the white polished world of the sections.

Chapter 38.

Myriam watched with a reserved acceptance as the man left her. His healing had been typical of the last few months. He'd been stabbed in an alley, robbed by some desperate person in the poor lower city. Jinir was working to find out who had done it, and swore he'd make sure the criminal was brought to justice. Justice. Myriam knew the justice here in the lower city was a hard thing. It usually ended up with someone dead, or at least never seen again.

She'd taken this role as the 'Hand of Mercy' for the 'Downtrodden Lord' because she had no other options. And she stayed because nothing had changed. She healed those hurt, those brought to her or those who got here on their own. The only sticking point had been the early insistence of Jinir and Ralta that she hide her face. And only heal those brought to her by his followers.

The first she had done, though not without complaint. Ralta had shown up with a set of pale blue robes in an unusual cut and fit after she had agreed. Myriam had to make some alterations for them to work. They were not suited for a human sized body, though what exactly they had been made for she didn't know. Ralta refused to talk about them when asked. But they worked, and even if they didn't fit completely right, they were very comfortable. Soft, and cool to the skin, and they didn't take dirt or, more importantly for her, blood, very well.

But as the second point, that she only heal those brought to her by Jinir and his followers she had refused. If she was going to do this, she was going to help anyone who needed it. The fight had not been a pleasant one. She had won, sort of. It came down to her being able to see anyone who got to her for help, but because she had to stay in places controlled by the 'Lord', most of those not part of his organization didn't try.

And so, it had gone now for months. Healing, eating, drinking, and sleeping. Day in and day out. Every few weeks, being moved to a new location, based on some rumor or hint that Ralta heard somewhere. Information that Ralta never shared.

Myriam pulled the hooded robe back and wondered if there was any of that stuffed bread left. Healing still made her hungry. That was the only other truly annoying thing. Food. She was totally dependent on whatever Ralta brought. And based on the light outside, Ralta was running late today.

This did happen sometimes, usually when Ralta got busy with her other duties, namely being Jinir's protector and enforcer. Myriam didn't ask what those tasks entailed; she really didn't want to know. The grumble in her stomach reminded her that she was getting hungrier as she waited. A quick search proved that not a scrap of food from yesterday was left.

There was water, and a small bottle of honey juice, and that was about it. Myriam hadn't touched the honey juice since that first time trying it. She used it when she had a patient who was more emotionally upset and physically upset. It seemed to work fairly well, and she didn't like forcing people to keep still. It felt wrong.

The sun moved lower still, and still no Ralta. Myriam found herself by the front door. She had no money, and she didn't know exactly where she was in the lower city, but the idea of leaving was enticing. When she moved from house to house, the robe and hood had to be up. It kept the illusion, but made it hard to get her bearings.

Pouring the freezing water into a tumbler, she took a drink and wondered if she could leave. Just walk out. Did Jinir and Ralta have someone watching wherever she was? Did they do that? She didn't think they did, but who knew for sure. Ralta would want to, she knew, but would Jinir let her? Another growl came, this time with a sharp pain. She did need to eat, and soon. Looking around, she spied the small bottle of honey juice. She could trade that for some food. Ralta could get her more. She'd say it spilled, or something.

Her eyes shifted between the bottle and the door. Could she leave? *Sparks burn it. She would leave.* Oddly enough, that thought came to her in the voice of William. She had tried not to think about him much. She wasn't sure if he was even alive. If Mikol had tried to kill her, what would he do to William? She'd mentioned it once to Jinir and Ralta, only to have Jinir shrug. Myriam grabbed the bottle and opened the door a little, peering outside. The door opened into a stone cobbled street, but one that had seen far better days. Most of the stones were cracked, and more than a few had tufts of a greenish brown grass growing in it. She could see people, though no one close. Even the surrounding buildings that she could make out were, old. Run down. Not ruins, but far from their best days.

But more important for her, no one seemed to pay any attention to her. Opening the door all the way, Myriam felt a sense of accomplishment. And a hint of something else, excitement? She had a hard time putting her finger on it. But it felt good. Maybe because she'd felt for the last few months more a prisoner than a guest in hiding. Doing something that she wanted to do felt good.

Pocketing the small bottle of the honey juice, Myriam squared herself up and left the building. Closing the door behind her, she noted the building she'd left. She'd need the information in case she got lost. It was plain looking, but there was one thing that stood out. By the door on a bottom stone was a small hand in white paint, or what looked like paint.

So that's how they find me. It made sense, but she was somewhat disappointed that in a city of wonders, the answer was a simple painting. Myriam looked either way down the street she was on. There was still enough daylight, so no torches were lit. No glows here. She rather liked all the torches though, it felt, real. Solid.

Finally, she decided to go down the road that had the most people on it. It was a risk, but she'd rather walk with others than alone with the night coming, and there was a pack of children playing farther down that way, so it should be safer, right?. A few of the people she saw were short enough to be Gorom, and one was as tall as Ralta, so it had to be a Trinil, or have Trinil blood. But it didn't appear dangerous, at least not from where she stood.

As she approached, she could see a few merchants hawking wares. Not many, and it looked like more had already left. The smell of food wafted to her, but she had a hard time deciding on where it had come from.

Trying to follow the scent and evade interest proved to be harder than she thought. She stood out. Still far thinner than she felt herself to be, with silver eyes, wasn't a normal thing. Even here. One child pointed at her and said something low to the woman that Myriam assumed was his mother, who answered the question and also pushed his pointed finger down with a look that silenced the child.

Myriam smiled at that. Even here, mothers taught their kids to have good manners. The smell was getting stronger, and the sound came now. Sizzling fresh meat. The smell was amazing. Maybe it was her hunger thinking about it, but it drew her like a moth to a flame. Now only if the merchant might trade.

She stood in front of the stall, drinking it in. It was a simple thing. A low rectangle full of coals and turning on a spit, large haunches of some roasted meat. A small series of spreads were arranged in jars, and a truly massive dozen loaves of some dark bread stood nearby.

Perfect. The grumble in her stomach grew at the smell, again coming with a sharp lance of pain. Enough pain for her to wince, at least. "How much?" She asked, mouth already watering.

The man who turned around was like no one she had ever seen. His face looked like he slept face down on a book it was so flat. He had a wisp of a beard, but long tapering ears that rose like points, almost above his head. "What?" he said, spitting the word.

He must be a hybrid of some kind. Myriam couldn't help examining him with some interest. Hybrids were only possible here, in the City. At least that's what the Healers taught. It was the influence of the mysterious 'source' that made it possible. She'd never seen the source and thought the whole thing rather strange. But she couldn't deny that there were things possible here that were not possible anywhere else. She realized the man was waiting for her to respond. "How much?" she asked again, covering up her momentary lapse of attention.

The man gave her a long look, his eyes darting around, and locking onto hers. "You have never been here before. I would remember. Why are you here?" he finally asked.

Myriam wasn't sure how to answer that exactly. Better to go with the simplest answer. "I was hungry and smelled the food." She didn't want to get into anything right now involving Jinir and Ralta. She was nervous that Ralta would appear at any minute and force her back to the safe house she was in. Knowing Ralta, sharp knives would be involved.

"Humph." The man grunted. "Never seen anyone with silver eyes before. And that's saying something here. What's your knack?"

Myriam almost left right then. If she hadn't been so hungry, she would have. But the lure of food kept her here. "Um…" Myriam paused, trying to think of the right answer. Finally, she saw the man had a slight burn on one hand. A tiny thing. From the coals, she was sure. She reached out a single finger and touched it and healed it.

"What??" The man stepped back, looking at his hand and then back to her. "Spire healer??" he said now, in a whisper, his eyes glinting in a way that was decidedly not friendly.

"No." Myriam answered quickly. And it was true, sort of. She wasn't, not anymore at least. "That and minor cuts is all I can heal." That part was a lie, but his reaction had surprised her.

"Ah. A knack like mine." The man smiled now, the fear and anger that had glittered in his eyes now gone. "A knack not good enough for those spire fools."

"Why, what's yours?" Myriam asked. In truth, she cared little, but she didn't need him getting any more suspicious, and besides, she'd already invested time in this. Better to get what she wanted than leave now.

The man turned to the coals and waved his hand over them. Instant heat came blooming out. "That's all I can do. Start fires and light coals. Nothing huge, nothing powerful." The man grumbled. He returned to looking her over. Appraising her not for her looks, but for how much to charge her, she was sure. She'd seen enough of those looks from merchants. "For you? Three copper bits."

Myriam thought that sounded fair, though she had no money at all. She didn't even know what the money exchange rate was around here. "Would you take a trade?' She asked as she pulled out the small bottle of honey juice.

The man's face changed in an instant. Eyebrows shot up to the height of his ears, then plunged back down, scrunching his already flat visage even more. His eyes darted around back and forth, as if searching for someone or something. "Honey juice? You want to trade that bottle of honey juice for a meal?"

Myriam could tell that the juice must be worth far more than the simple meal, and she cursed herself for showing her hand so fast. He would be suspicious now, and he'd know that she wasn't from around here. "Yes." She finally answered.

The strange man drew himself up straight and nodded. He held up four fingers. "Four meals. One now, and three whenever you want them." The man snatched the honey juice out of her hand, and in a voice barely above a whisper. "Do not let yourself be seen with that kind of thing around here."

He went to work, slicing thick pieces of the sizzling meat off the spit. He added three slices of the brown bread and after giving her a look, slathered a thick red and yellow sauce over most of the meat. "Here." Was all he said and turned his back on her, going back to whatever he had been working on before.

"Thank you." Myriam said, but her voice was low. She had no idea if she had done the right thing or not. But she was hungry, and for now, she was free.

Chapter 39.

Mikol stared out his window, stifling a yawn. These last few months had been a tiring waste of time. He knew that Nollew and Yulisia weren't under his control, but he couldn't do anything about it. But they still acted as if they were under his control. It was, he had decided, maddening. He'd never foreseen the idea of Nollew breaking through his control. He should have, of course, but retrospection was always like that.

Add in reports of this Downtrodden Lord still circulating, and now, someone being called the 'Hand of Mercy' who was a healer, and Mikol's list of problems kept getting longer. The odds were that this hand was Myriam VolFar. Which meant she was alive and knew of his involvement, or at least suspected. If not, he was sure she would have come back to the spire. He did not like it at all.

Grib had avoided him as well ever since their fight over Jinir. So, he had failed both times to kill who he had marked. Jinir and Myriam. Even though both lived, he had still gotten what he wanted out of it. And he didn't hate either of them. He didn't hate anyone. They had been obstacles, that was all. Dead or not, they were now out of his way.

He took a long sip of his tea and continued staring out the window. He had others under his control, and he would always end up on top. This fact made him smile, a smile that continued when a knock brought him around. One of his assistants stood there, head bowed, with a handful of parchment. Good. Information.

Mikol took them and ignored the man who left as soon as Mikol turned around. Yulisia might not be under his influence anymore, but he made sure others in the library were. He did not waste power on them, pure bribery and favors bound those to him. As a result, every scrap of information from the library's spies came to him as well.

The first parchment had information about the upcoming marriage and alliance of two middle city families. Useless drivel. The second was a report of the power vacuum in the western lands that had grown since the fall of the Valnijz cultists. And a sighting of the Mistral again. Again, useless drivel. But the third drew his attention. A description of this protector of the Downtrodden Lord. The description painted a very dangerous picture. A Trinil, which he knew, but whose knack should have put her in the city guard. How it had been missed, Mikol did not know. Her knack gave her impossible levels of balance and speed. She combined that with a set of knives and a lot of practice. She had killed a group of men who tried to jump this Lord person last week. There had been nine of them by the report, and she had killed all nine before any had even started to run.

Very dangerous. And more interesting was the information that she was utterly devoted to Jinir. But that was all. Still worth knowing. The next parchment reinforced his belief that Jinir was the Lord, and this Hand was Myriam. It laid out recent changes in the Lord's voice, walk, and behavior.

It all pointed to one thing; Myriam had healed the man. That WAS a problem. With Jinir hurt, and forever unhealed, he was limited in what he could do, even with a protector. But healed fully? Mikol's face fell. A healed Jinir could do a lot more. So far, it did not appear he had taken full advantage of this. He still wore the robe and hid his face, but his influence was spreading. And spreading more and more each day. Myriam must have been exhausted. Her own injuries he was sure were grave, and healing a man like Jinir with old injuries? Mikol had to admire her talent. Old wounds of that nature, acid, and fire, those would be hard, very hard.

Of course, if he could get close enough, he could use his contingency plan. He'd have to be right up on Jinir for it to work, but at least no one would really investigate. After all, Jinir was already dead. But getting that close would be difficult. He'd need someone to help, or the right opportunity to strike. Which he had neither of right now. The same plan had been put in place with Nollew and Yulisia, of course, but they were still far too useful for that course of action.

The last parchment was useless, like other ones dealing with the outside world. Palnor was apparently stockpiling weapons. And a noticeable portion of the poor and any criminals had vanished from Ture and the surrounding areas. So Palnor was training its undesirables to be front line fodder. They would invade some other silly northern country. It did not affect the City at all; he wondered why Yulisia even wanted information gathered about that sort of thing.

But he wasn't a Librarian. Knowledge for the sake of itself was a shallow and poor enticement to Mikol. Power. Power and control. That was useful. "And it always will be." Mikol murmured, deciding what to do with this batch of missives.

Mikol took another sip of his tea and crumpled up the parchments. He threw them in the fireplace, rarely used, lit it, and watched them burn. He had a feeling the next few weeks were going to be very interesting. These last few months had been a dull, dull time. He had been idle for too long. He imagined he was like a lion cooped up in one location, waiting. Now he was ready to hunt.

But first some preparations.

Nollew tested yet another pattern of the power, a trickle of power though. Enough to see the effects and study the reactions. He was testing, experimenting. Too much power now could be dangerous. Early on, he had one time forgotten that maxim. He'd injured a fellow caster section trainee. Nearly removed half of his skin. It had all been a horrible accident, and the boy had been healed, but Nollew never forgot to watch how much power he was using. Ever.

"Are you going to spend ALL day doing that?" Yulisia appeared, holding a parchment tightly. Even white knuckling it from what Nollew could see.

"Why not? I'm the Tarn of the Casters. Or what was that word we found in the old records again?" Nollew wasn't as into old lore as his love was, but searching old records for notes that other casters had made was useful sometimes. More so when things were dull. The last few months were perfect examples of that.

Nothing had come from the meeting with that William Reis person. Either he had said nothing to Rewil, or Rewil hadn't believed him. As a result, everything stayed the same. Nollew hated it. Everything made him feel on edge. That nothing of interest seemed to happen made it all worse. Like the City was taking a huge breath.

"Thaumaturge" Yulisia gave him the answer. "But I came here to show you something."

"Oh?" Nollew grinned, looking her up and down. "I only see robes."

Yulisia cracked her knuckles loudly. "I'm serious Noll. Take your childish boy jokes elsewhere."

"Fine." Nollew pulled away from the power, letting his working vanish. It wasn't going the way he wanted to, anyway. So, a failed experiment in underground water control. "What is it?"

"This." Yulisia held up the parchment. "Remember the last commons?"

"Of course. Grib wanted permission to sanction someone. Sanction. A pleasant word for killing. All because he was afraid he might lose power." Nollew walked over and pointed at the parchment. "What's that got to do with it."

"This gives a huge clue who this Downtrodden Lord is. AND a clue about what happened to Myriam VolFar. Remember me mentioning how the lower city had better names than we do?" Yulisia Put the parchment on a nearby table and sat down. "Specifically, this 'Hand of Mercy' person?"

Nollew sort of remembered. He had been listening, but he been tired. The words had sort of floated around him, not making sense. "Yes." He didn't elaborate. Yulisia didn't seem in the mood for their normal banter.

"Well, if I am right. And I am right. I know who the "Lord" and the "Hand" are." Yulisia paused, grinning. "Jinir and Myriam."

Nollew jerked back at the names. Jinir? Tarn Jinir? "But Jinir is dead. Dead and gone for years. Mikol got rid of him long ago."

"That's the story. But I traced it back. The times match up. This "Downtrodden Lord' appearance matches up. And he's obviously been healed recently. You and I both know healing old wounds is very hard. Myriam VolFar with her connection to the wild magic of the Anvil is one of the few I would guess who could do it. Painful in the extreme for Jinir, I would guess. But she could do it." Yulisia pointed at the parchment.

"It's the same Lord, but his voice and walk have changed. That means healing. A healer vanished right around the time the hand appeared. Myriam. It all fits."

Nollew could see where she was going with all this, and he agreed. "Yet what does that mean for us? For our plans, such as they are." Their plans were somewhat loose. A silent stalemate was the best way to describe it.

"We contact Jinir. I didn't know him well; you knew him better." Yulisia paused. "Find out what he wants. Revenge? His seat back? Something else? I don't know. But we need to talk to him."

"What about this Myriam VolFar person?" Nollew sprawled out on an oversized cushion nearby.

Yulisia sat back, looking up at the dark wood paneling. "I don't know. She is of no use to us and our plans directly. But she is important to William Reis and the namer. Bound by Wild Magic. Those two together may be of some use. And if she's important to William, then she's important to Rewil. My information says that Rewil has made the young man practically his shadow."

"That could help make him come to our side of things. If we can get both Jinir and this Myriam safe, and somehow arrange a meeting with Rewil and William…" the words spilled out of Nollew before he took a breath and paused. "There is a lot that could go wrong." He finally said.

"Yes. But it might be worth it. I can tell how much you've been on edge, my dear." Yulisia locked eyes with her fellow Tarn. "I have been as well. A meeting and conversation could be the thing to get things moving again."

"And then…?" Nollew asked quickly. "I agree. Mikol needs to be gone. He's an amoral menace. But what happens after? I don't want to be caught unawares if something suddenly happens and Mikol is gone, and we have no plan past that."

"We will figure it out then." Yulisia smiled as she spoke. "You worry too much."

"No." Nollew stood now, pacing. "Without Mikol's hand behind everything, there's going to be an unstable City for a time. We need to be prepared. If we can find Healers who could step in for Mikol's role, AND aren't already under his influence, I'd feel better."

"I'll start researching it now." Yulisia added. "But meeting with Jinir and Myriam and Rewil?"

Nollew slowly nodded, his mind exploding with options and possibilities. "Fine. Take care of it."

Yulisia's smile fell. "Take care of it? Nollew my love, we are partners, but you do not get to tell me what to do."

Nollew felt the laughter come fast, erupting. "By the source, Yulisia, that's exactly why I love you!" when the laughter ended, he was pleased to see her face had removed the frown. "How about we will make it happen. I'll write a letter, but you and your section have far better contacts outside the spire than any of us. What was the word again? That something?"

"Thaumaturge" Yulisia's eyes rolled as she said the word. "You're not going to start using that, are you?"

"Why not? It gives an air of mystery. It's a lot better than 'Caster' at least." Nollew sat back down. "I'll write the letter, and you, with your connections, get it to Jinir and Rewil. If you are sure this Lord is him."

"A fair arrangement, my fellow Tarn." Yulisia lowered her head in a mocking bow.

Chapter 40.

Myriam watched Ralta unpack supplies in silence. She'd slipped back into this safe house not even a full bell before Ralta appeared. No apologies or even mention of what the delay had been came from the Trinil. Myriam was left guessing as usual, which had become a kind of game for Myriam. But she never voiced any guess out loud, she was never sure if Ralta was going to find it funny or not. There was a new tear on the leather vest she wore over her shirt. Not a large one, but it hadn't been there two days ago.

So, some fresh trouble? She knew Ralta could use those knives she carried everywhere, but more telling was that Ralta never needed healing. She never got hurt. And that made Ralta one very dangerous opponent. Or at least she never an injury, and she was sure Ralta wouldn't allow her to delve her without a good reason. "What did you bring this time?" Myriam finally asked. Her stomach didn't hurt with hunger anymore, but it would help allay suspicion.

"Food. Drink." Ralta answered and fell silent, with a slight glare at Myriam.

Myriam felt a moment of panic at the short answer. Did she already know? She wasn't a prisoner, exactly, but... her fears died as Ralta smiled at her. "Ha." Myriam croaked out.

"Several dried meats, fruit, beer bread, jam, fresh butter... which is NOT cheap here, and even this." Ralta threw a small paper-wrapped package to Myriam.

Myriam caught it without a problem, if only because Ralta's aim was always very accurate. The smell was sort of familiar, but she couldn't place it. But she'd smelled this before. A strong smell, very garlicky. Then she remembered. A kitchen in the Guild. William, making a dish...

"KLAH!" Myriam unwrapped the package, tearing the paper off. She was right. A small box of the strong garlic paste from the Reach. "But how?"

"Is that what that stuff is called? There is one merchant in the Middle City, whose parents came from Palnor. He makes the stuff sometimes.

It's not a great seller, but his parents made it, so he makes small batches from time to time." Ralta cocked an eye at the box. "You actually like it?"

Myriam smiled. "Well, I didn't grow up with it. But William, he loves the stuff. I grew to like it more when I was in the Reach for a while." Myriam closed her eyes and the smell of the Klah wafted up to her. Her mind drifted back to the Golden Chisel, sitting on the steps, talking to Regin, or even William. A good memory, before the insanity that came after. At the time, she thought her life couldn't get any stranger.

"Well, I'm glad you like it. No one else will at all." Ralta's voice broke into her daydream. "And I got this to drink. Just more water, and some juice. I know you don't like to drink any alcohol when healing. But I got one bottle of Jasmine wine."

Myriam placed the lid back on the box of Klah, limiting the smell, but not ending it. "Thank you. Oh, I need more honey juice."

Ralta stopped in mid-movement. "You need an entire bottle?" Her voice, warm and friendly a few moments ago, was whip sharp now.

"I dropped it." Myriam answered smoothly. "I had a patient who needed it, and after giving him a dose, I left it on the table over there. She motioned to a small table she kept by the place she examined those who came to be healed. "I bumped it and it broke."

Ralta still didn't move except for her eyes, which darted to the table, the floor, and back to Myriam. "That was not cheap." Her voice was flat and her mood had changed in an instant.

"I am sorry. It won't happen again." Myriam looked away, hoping now that she appeared embarrassed by the accident, not the fact that she was worried that Ralta could see right through her story.

There was a long silence, and Myriam's mind was repeating. *Please don't know, don't know, don't know.* Then Ralta spoke in a voice that Myriam noticed was controlled. "Of course. It won't." The words were almost a statement of fact, and Myriam's heart froze.

She didn't see Ralta approach, but she found herself looking eye to eye with the Trinil. This close she could see a faint long healed cut under her eye. "I'm tired. I think I will go take a short nap, in the front room. While still wearing my clothes. In case you are wondering." Ralta made the words a slow mocking speech. "I will be right next door to you. In case you drop anything else and need some help." Myriam forced a smile onto her face and nodded. Sparks burn her for a fool. She had often wondered if Ralta still had the Trinil gift to tell if someone was lying or not. Truthfully, she still wasn't sure, but the more she thought about it, the more her story didn't make sense, even to herself.

One, there was no scent of Honey juice in the air. If she'd spilled the whole bottle, there would be. And the floor was dry. And no evidence of broken glass. Honey juice was slightly sticky, the floor would still have some evidence, even more so here where there wasn't a broom or mop to be found.

Myriam watched Ralta leave, knowing that it might be a long time before she could leave a safe house again.

Will turned three corners and pushed on a section of a lower wall, watching with some satisfaction as the opening slid free to show another hallway. Pulling out a parchment that had more than a few notes and half drawn maps on it, he made a note of this location.

In the past few months, outside his crafting work and repair work on the quickways, Will had spent any free time finding and mapping every hidden entrance or exit from the hallways and rooms used by the people who aren't in the sections.

He'd started the project simply as a way of dealing with his anger and frustration with everything that had happened. The meeting with Yulisia, the investigation with Rewil, and the dead ends that both things had wrought. He should have told Rewil what Yulisia had said, he now admitted to himself, but now it was too late.

This mapping project helped him take his mind off things. There were no maps that anyone knew of already. Those in the sections sort of either shrugged him off or, worse, looked at him as if he had an illness for even asking. If he asked any of the people who used them, they usually ignored the question.

Only one had said anything. Will had been somewhat stunned by her answer.

"Look lad. I'm only saying this once. You know where you need to go for your job. No one maps them. No one cares. And stop asking. The questions get around. It makes people nervous to have one of the spire folk looking into how we live our lives. You lot have your world, we have ours. And that's the way it should be." The older woman made food in the crafters section and had waved a spoon at him the whole time.

He'd protested, of course, but she'd ignored him from then on. So, he'd made a map himself. He'd wondered if anyone would try to stop him, but true to form, he was ignored. At first, he'd had some level of excitement, but now, a while into it, it didn't feel quite as adventurous.

Still, it gave him something to do. So why not? Will paced down the hallway after closing that last hidden door. There was only one question in this part of the spire left. There was space for a room. A large room. But he'd not been able to find out if there was one.

He'd found other hidden rooms before. Some small, other's large. Almost all of them had been totally empty, dusty things full of stale old air. Only two had held anything. One had a pile of cloth so old it was falling into dust from age. Its original color couldn't even be seen, so much time had passed.

The other room was more interesting. It was on the smaller side, but held a desk, a chair, a cot, and letter. He'd learned to find rooms by using his boon, feeling the rock for voids or gaps that were regular in shape. Using the power, he'd found the way in with some surprise, as unlike most other places, the place to open that room had been not in a spire hallway, but in a Greystone hallway that was itself hidden.

The letter had been the major surprise. Written nearly three hundred years ago, it was an apology to a lover for not coming to see them the night before. But why it was here, and who had left it, was a mystery. It had not been signed, and whom it was for was not written anywhere on it.

The room he was searching for now he didn't know how to get in, or that there was room there at all. But based on the mapped-out floor plan, it fit. But how to get in? He reached out with tendrils of his power. He still felt weird about it. And this wasn't a normal use for him. He used his boon as little as he could, to reinforce things he was making. Still, he managed. Will reached out more, feeling the power flowing around him, and then, suddenly a feeling like a spark hitting bare flesh ended his concentration, and he dropped the power. *There.* Will found the white polished stone section and felt around it. The panel popped out with a push, but only a small amount, but enough for it to be rotated. The door to this room appeared as he did so, moving in time with his rotation. *That's different.*

Will twisted the panel until it opened fully. The room beyond was dark, and the air held an old, dry smell, but that wasn't unusual. But what was usual was the stacks of ingots all over the room. Will was a Reacher. He'd grown up with mining, smelting, and forging. He'd been, at least for a short time, the Forgemaster of Amder. He knew metal. And this, this was a prize.

He shouldn't be surprised. This room he'd uncovered was almost directly under the Crafters section, so its location made sense. But to abandon a storeroom like this? Will kept a portable glow with him for exploration reasons, and he shook the glow to start it working. Light bloomed, an orange yellow glow.

For a moment, he wondered why the glows here were orange red, and the glows were silver white in Ture and the Reach. They looked the same, but had that one difference. Something to ask Rewil about at some point, or one of the other older crafters. It wasn't something worth spending a lot of time on, anyway.

The light shone out, illuminating a trove of metal he'd not seen in a very long time. Bags of silverlace and goldlace, bars of Drendel steel, a small bag of crimsonlace even, and more. It seemed like every metal he'd ever heard of was here. Not in large amounts true, but even so, this was a treasure. He was about to leave and report his finding to Rewil, when his eyes fell on a set of seven ingots.

They shone with a faint white glow, their surface appearing almost ethereal. Wight Iron. Seven ingots of Wight Iron. Large ingots. Will slowly approached them, his thoughts running back to the Reach. To home. The sound of Wight Iron in a bag that Duncan threw on the table with a smile. One of the last times he saw Duncan smile. Before the Blood Curse, before dead gods and anvils, before any of the thousand strange and terrible things that had come into his life.

Will reached forth, his hand he noticed was trembling slightly. He took a breath and let it out, feeling some of the nervousness subside. He tapped an ingot with a finger. The low moan echoed around the room in such a way it seemed to be made louder. Will felt his skin reacting, covering itself with an array of prickly bumps. Wight Iron.

Chapter 41.

Three days had passed before Myriam felt somewhat at ease again. Ralta had stayed in the front room as much as possible since her lie about the honey juice. She had left a few times but had assigned some local to 'keep watch' on the door. The man let people in but didn't even pay her any attention except when she tried to leave. She'd taken two steps after a patient left, and the man held out a thick arm and stopped her, wearing a scowl that made her step back inside.

Finally, though, Ralta left without a word one night while Myriam slept. But this time she'd left a note.

"Myriam,
Jinir needs me. Something has come up. Stay here. I know you won't, but I'm still asking you to stay here. It's not to control you, but it is for your safety. It's good you only spoke to Teren the cook, down the road. He's a good man, and not one to make trouble. Though he cheated you blind on the honey juice.
—Ralta"

Myriam read the message twice. She knew, and of course she knew, the man who she made the deal with. But why for her safety? She'd left. It wasn't dangerous. No one knew who she was, but Mikol didn't know she lived. Right? The more she thought about it, the more she didn't like it. Ralta could have least said WHY it was for her safety. It made her feel like a prisoner without bars. Unsure and fearful. Maybe that was the point, though. She stared at the front door for a good half a bell. Leave or stay?

There was the chance that Ralta had left someone watching her. That man who had been guarding the door had left a day before, after a brief conversation with Ralta. Myriam had not been sorry to see him go at all. Myriam pushed the door open slightly, peeking her head out. The new day was still dawning, and the city was waking up. In the distance, she heard a few merchants calling, and some carts moving around. A cat hissing and then a series of yowls and banging as it fought some unknown adversary. But no one was in sight that she could tell.

Closing the door, Myriam took off her robes, dressing again in plain clothes. This time she took some of the food and water, putting it in a small pack. She would not be gone long, but long enough to see if Ralta found out. She still had those free meals at that one stall, but knowing that he worked for Jinir and Ralta, she wasn't sure she'd ever go back to him.

Stepping outside after putting her hair back, Myriam blinked in morning sun, now having risen above the edge of the City wall. She could see the huge white marble wall circling the city, its arc vanishing in the haze and distance. And as always, towering over the city, the pure white stone of the spire. At this distance, she could barely make out the thin coppery lines of the quickways, which had finally started back up in operation recently.

She'd only known because a man came in to be healed who spent the entire time complaining about it. He was not fond of anyone from the spire and viewed the quickways as an insult to those who didn't live there. "Always keeping themselves out of the actual City, aren't they? Spire dwellers. Section folk. Not down here, with us. Just cause the source gives them a 'boon' and not a knack, they think they are too good for us." The man had ranted.

Myriam had kept her mouth shut and healed him, a series of tiny breaks in the bones of his right hand and wrist. She had no idea how it had happened, and she didn't ask. After he'd left, though, she'd thought about what he said. She'd never thought about the fact that the sections kept themselves separate from the rest of the city.

And the quickways allowed them to travel around the spire and even to the walls without setting foot in the lower or middle city. The thought made her uncomfortable. It wasn't like the spire folk even thought about it, it simply was. Maybe that was the problem. They didn't think about the rest of the City or the people who lived in it.

Myriam found she actually rather liked the lower city, and she would probably like the middle city as well. It reminded her more of home, or

Ture. Some of the people were strange, races and groups she'd never have imagined in a thousand years. Even so, it was a city. It breathed, it lived. The spire was… so different. The magic that suffused this place was concentrated there, and it showed.

You never saw constructs outside the spire. Or anything else overtly power based. Everyone had a knack, of course, but most were not useful. The rare cases like Ralta were of course, but most were not. She'd had one woman come in whose knack was the ability to make anyone sneeze out purple smoke with a touch. That was it. A sneeze with three or four spurts of a purple smoke each time. Useless in the great spire. Even so the woman had found a use for it, by entertaining children with stories about dragons and other monsters, using the smoke for effect.

And yet some in the spire could work massive amounts of power. Even in the Librarians, who many in the spire considered the weakest. They used their connection to the power to make and transcribe multiple tomes of knowledge. They also used their power to gather information from the world outside that wall.

The frown stayed on her face. The way the city worked was… she didn't know. On one hand as far as she knew, or at least as far as anyone had told her, the power gift, boon or knack was random. Pure chance. It wasn't like anyone was picking who got what gift. But how it organized itself was very tiered. But so were a lot of places. Even in Ture, there had been the Priesthood, the Guild, and then the King and the Nobles. Above everyone else.

Myriam's thoughts were interrupted when she ran into a man who had stopped to look at a merchant stall. She stepped back, feeling somewhat flustered at her error. "Very sorry." She mumbled out and reached out a hand to the man who had fallen over. He was older, tall. He looked human, but there was a hint of something else, a cast to the face that wasn't quite like other people. Just different. His hair was gray, but flecks of a dark black still mixed in. He appeared fairly nondescript except for the cast of his face and the large stringed instrument he carried on his back.

"Thank you. I hadn't expected to be run over today." The man took her hand as he stood. "Though in truth, I never expect to be run over."

He *was* tall. On the ground Myriam had thought him tall, but standing, she realized how tall the man was. He was two good handspans taller than she was, and taller than even Ralta. He didn't have the long face of the Trinil race, however. "Very sorry, was deep in thought." She smiled trying to find a way out of this conversation. The longer she stood here, the higher the chance that Ralta or someone with Ralta would see her.

"I am fine. Though…" The man pulled the large instrument around off his back and examined it. It was a shocking mix of strings, levers, bellows, and one long reed. He brushed some dirt off a few places, frowned a tiny bit as he plucked a single string, nodding as the tone came. "Well, she seems fine. So, no harm done." The man smiled. "Rauger. Rauger Manter. Bard, storyteller, and…. long-term resident of the fair City." He put the strange contraption back on his back.

Myriam nodded. "Very sorry again." Taking a sidestep, she hurried on and away. She was going to complete a long circle, and then back to the safe house.

"You're in a hurry. Need company?" the tall man, this Rauger, walked beside her, his strides easily able to keep up with her. "The lower city may not be a safe place."

"No, I'm fine." Myriam glanced at the older man. She flicked a tiny tendril of power at him, but it failed. Strange. She tried again, harder this time, and yet, it failed again. The power flowed from her, and then… she stopped. Was this the right way?

"Ah, I'm afraid whatever you're trying to do with magic won't work. I have a few tricks up my sleeve." Rauger smiled. "I know who you are, Myriam. I'm a friend of Jinir." He spoke in low tones, even though there were still few around and out yet.

Myriam felt her heart drop. Of course he was. They knew, so they sent this man to watch her. Great. "Who?" she managed to say. If she was caught, she would not make it easy for them.

Rauger lowered his eyebrows. Great bushy things. "Pretending you don't know doesn't help anyone." He lowered his voice even further. "There was some concern. I agreed to…. Well, I agreed to keep watch."

"Fine." Myriam finally said, disliking the fact that Jinir and Ralta had sent this man. "But how did you find me?"

"A good guess. I saw you coming. You were so wrapped up in your thoughts you did not spot the two men behind you. I made sure I was in your path. I didn't expect to get knocked over though." Rauger lowered his head. "You are made of stronger stuff than you appeared."

Two men? "What two men?" Myriam glanced behind her, not seeing anyone. "I don't see anyone."

"No. They slipped away after you knocked me over." Rauger shrugged. "Easier targets elsewhere."

Myriam wasn't sure if this man was being truthful or not. There were ways to tell, but most used the power, and she had never really learned them. "What did they look like?"

A shrug was her only answer. "Come. I'll escort you back to the safehouse." Rauger gave her a half bow, arm outstretched for her to lead the way.

"How did you know I was going back?" Myriam asked as she started walking. "Maybe I was leaving for good."

"I don't think that would be a good idea." Rauger smiled. "I'm sure Ralta and Jinir would not be pleased. And a displeased Ralta is not a good place to be at, she can be scary if she wants to."

Myriam didn't answer. What could she say? The feeling that she was more a prisoner than anything else came back with a vengeance. Or maybe less like a prisoner, and more like a useful tool. Healing those that Jinir wanted healed, to keep his base of power strong.

There was no more conversation between them, and they walked in a long circle, passing houses, merchants, and various stalls. Everything looked older and somewhat worn until they came to a large bridge. It was quite telling the difference to Myriam. On one side of the bridge, this side, was the same older shopworn style. The cobblestones were cracked and dirty. Worn smooth in many places.

There was a small shop here, with a weathered sign so old that the name of the place couldn't be made out, though by the smell it served food and drink. The bridge itself arced over a swirling mass of water that flowed in a strong current.

"That's magic you know." Rauger finally spoke. "It marks the line between the lower and middle city. It flows in a complete circle. It's also clean. Which is strange considering how much gets dumped into it. The power at work."

Myriam looked across the bridge, and the difference was striking. The streets were clean, spotless even. Every building was in good repair, at least for what she could see. And even the people were better dressed. "But why?" she whispered.

"The great divide." Rauger answered. "There are three divides here. The lower from the middle, the middle from the spire, and the spire from everyone."

Myriam nodded but didn't answer. It added to her thoughts about the place. What was Jinir trying to carry out? She realized she didn't really know, and that bothered her.

Finally, they arrived back at the safe house, Rauger stopping at the door. "This has been enjoyable. I wish you a good day." He bowed again; the thing strapped to his back threatening to fall sideways.

"Thank you." Myriam finally replied, not sure exactly what to say. She turned and entered her prison, closing the door behind her.

"Myriam!" Ralta came rushing out. "Where have you been?"

"I went for a walk." Myriam shrugged. "You don't need to worry. Your friend Rauger found me, took me back here. A guard for the prisoner."

Ralta's face went pale at her words. "Rauger? Rauger Manter?" the words leapt out of Ralta in a rush as she raced for the door, throwing it open with her knives in her hands.

"Yes? Why??" Myriam was confused, then awareness came with a cold rush. "You didn't send him, did you?"

"No. Rauger Manter is a dangerous man. A very dangerous man. A man who wants nothing more than to keep Jinir out of power." Ralta looked both ways out the door, but the tall man was gone.

Chapter 42.

Will couldn't help but smile as he searched for Rewil. All those metals, sitting there! And Wight Iron! He reached down, fingers brushing the hammer at his side. It still didn't feel like his. He knew it was a gift, despite that, it wasn't his. He had to make a new one. And with that Wight Iron, he could. He didn't HAVE to use Wight Iron, but it felt right. A link to the past. But he needed to find Rewil first.

After searching through several parts of the crafters section, he finally found the Tarn pretty much where he should have started, in his private workshop. As usual, he was tinkering with something, but it must have been something unusual. The power was thick in the air here, a feeling that was different for this place. Rewil, like anyone else in the spire, had the boon. The ability to use the raw power in whatever way they were best suited. As the tarn of the Crafters, it was to make things. But Will realized over the last few months that Rewil didn't use the power all that often. He'd usually use one of the stored power sources, rather than work the power himself.

So, it was all the stranger to enter here and find him working the power. Whatever he was doing wasn't all that large. Rewil was completely blocking the worktable, his shoulders hunched over as he worked. Will wasn't sure if he should interrupt or not. Rewil was working on something important, or at least something out of the usual.

His dilemma was solved when Rewil dropped a tiny blade, its edge glittering, and when bending down to get it, saw Will. He quickly threw a nearby cloth over whatever he was working on and stood. "Will! Didn't hear you come in."

Will decided it was better not to ask what Rewil was working on. If he wanted it to be a secret, Will was fine with that. He didn't need any more secrets or drama in his life. "Sorry to bother you, but I found something. You know how I've been mapping out all the hidden entrances and rooms in the lower parts of the spire?"

Rewil nodded, wiping his hands on his leather apron. "And remember how I told you it was a waste of your talents? I know it's something to occupy your time lad, but you're a crafter of the spire, you can make things!"

Will nodded, keeping the frown off his face. He didn't agree with Rewil on this. Mapping the passages and rooms made him feel like he was doing something, anything, to help bridge the obvious problems in the City that no one else seemed to even see. Not that it helped the lower or middle city folk, not yet at least. "Well, I found something. A room full of metal ingots. Rare ones as well."

Rewil frowned for a minute, then his eyebrows shot up, with a laugh. "Oh! The storeroom of Tarn Salik."

Will felt a sinking feeling. It wasn't a surprise? "Who?" he said, not keeping the disappointment out of his voice.

"Oh, cheer up Will. I had forgotten about it. Tarn Salik. He was the crafter Tarn, what… five Tarns ago? He decided that each section should have an emergency storeroom. He made one in the crafter section as an example. It never really went anywhere, though. The other Tarns pointed out that they didn't need them. It was a point of contention for a while, but after the events of the Curors, it wasn't a question anymore." Rewil smiled. "But we could use those supplies, so that's an excellent find."

Will knew about the Curors. Not directly, but it was one of the strangest stories he'd ever heard. The City was under attack from followers of Valnijz. And instead of fighting them, they simply left. They moved the entire city. It made no sense to him. And the source moved with them. It was… hard to understand.

"Ah, so you've heard the story then? How Jindo and the Curors attacked?" Rewil shook his head. "Nasty business that."

Jindo? A fragment of a memory came to Will. Jindo. He knew that name. The man who had killed Regin, sort of. The man who had cut him, or something, with that long spike. Things were not clear still to him about that day. But for once, he could clear enough of the fog in his mind to remember more. Oh, sparks. He remembered now.

Jindo had been about to kill them. Valnijz was returning to full strength, and they were trapped in the Anvil. And Myriam... did the only thing she could think of. She placed the crystal on the pillar and brought forth the new god. A deep sense of shame hit Will then. He had forgotten all that? He'd yelled at her. Berated her. And... he'd been in the wrong.

"Will?" Rewil asked, concern touching his voice. "Are you all right?"

"Yes... I... that name. Jindo. I know that name. In the Anvil. I remembered. He killed Regin. He was about to kill Myriam and me. When she did, whatever she did. She saved us. She saved me. And I screamed at her. I was so angry. But none of it was her fault." Will frowned. "I wish I knew where she was."

"I do as well, I do as well." Rewil shook his head. "Jindo Halfman is a nasty piece. I didn't know he was still living, though connections to the former Blood God would make him live longer. Do you remember what happened to him?"

"He's dead. The Blood God said something about needing his blood and killed him." Will closed his eyes, remembering. "The blood mist had come, somehow. It was so... loud. A thousand thousands screams were going off at once. She saved me."

"We will find her. Somehow." Rewil shook his head.

Will knew Rewil wanted to believe it, but Will wasn't so sure. Maybe think about something better. "Can I use some of the ingots? The Wight Iron in particular. And the use of a forge? An actual forge if there is one around here."

"Well... there is, but why not have the constructs do it? They are faster, and better..." Rewil trailed off at the sour expression that had appeared on Will's face. "Noted."

"No offense Rewil. But I need to do this myself. Me, a forge, an anvil and tools." Will looked down at his hands. How long had it been since he'd swung a hammer at a forge? "I need to reconnect. The wonders of this place are still new to me, even now. I need something simple. It will help me think."

Rewil smiled and nodded. "A good explanation. And yes, though I doubt they have been used much in the last hundred years or so."

"That's fine. As long as it all works." Will tapped his mouth. "Well, I might need one construct."

"Oh?" Rewil smiled. "For what? Delicate work?"

"To run the bellows." Will laughed then, pushing his shame down about how he'd acted towards Myriam. If he found her… no, WHEN he found her, he'd apologize. He'd make it up to her. But for now, he needed this.

"I am sure we can find you what you need. Give me till morning though, I'm in the middle of something, and it's getting late. I don't think you want to be working the forge at night." Rewil stepped in front of his workbench.

Will wondered what Rewil was working on. He obviously didn't want Will to see it. But he was the Tarn, and if he wanted to work on something without interruption, there wasn't much Will could do about it. "Yes, true. Gives me a chance to think, anyway." Will nodded. "I'll leave you to your work."

"Good." Rewil said the words fast. "No, I mean, thank you."

Will shook his head and left. He had to think. The walk back to his room was quiet. Most crafters were already in their rooms, or in a public area. Will had never felt comfortable doing that. He didn't know them. He didn't know what to say. He didn't think they would be angry with him or anything, but he'd never been one for much of a social life. He'd not been great at it at the Guild either. Myriam had, of course, been the bridge between him and the rest of the apprentices.

He paused though as the sound of laughter came from an open area ahead that young crafters congregated in. There was another reason he kept a distance. He knew they had questions. Who wouldn't? No one had actually said anything, but everyone knew some of his background. He'd brought Amder back to life and been named the youngest Forgemaster ever. He had been there when Amder was destroyed, again, and come here from the Anvil of Souls.

Even without all the details, it was an insane set of events. And Will did not know how to actually talk about it. Without sounding like he was bragging, or worse, saying something that would make people upset. He'd realized that talking about the Gods made people in the City give you strange looks. Will had only ever been devout to Amder, and even then, it was more a conversation than worship. But here, in the City, that was strange talk.

Maybe, one day, he'd be able to go in and have some of the confidence that Myriam had, or more so, Duncan. He tried not to think about his cousin much, but the resurfaced memories of that day brought back thoughts of Dunc. By the sparks, Duncan could win people over. He'd heard an old trader once say that Duncan could work a room. He'd not understood what he'd meant until several years later. Duncan had been at the Golden Chisel and brought the inn from a sober mood to rousing song and laughter.

Will wished he had that power. He didn't, though. He had skill in other places, but not that. Will resumed his walk, the laughter and talk fading away behind him. Soon, silence reigned again, only broken by his boot steps.

Will entered his room and sat on the edge of his bed, his mind moving on to the task he was going to try tomorrow. It felt right, somehow. He placed the hammer Amder had given him, its surface golden and yet, it carried a blue swirl, and if Will concentrated, he could still see the power moving in it. The same bright blue specks that had been there since the Anvil.

Standing, Will took out some more items out of storage. One, his old armor, and two, the circlet. The bracers were fine still, the fine work Myriam had done on them still as fresh as the day she had finished. The breastplate was also perfect, except for that long gouge. Will frowned at it. A symbol of his failure.

The circlet was another story. He'd had nothing to do with the making of that. He'd watched Amder do it. Will wished he'd somehow taken the shackles when Valnijz freed himself. That metal was special to him. But it was long gone. Probably still laying on the floor in that forsaken cave.

The circlet was made from that disturbing black iron dagger that Valnijz had been carrying. Amder though had changed it, formed it with his own hands into a thing of dark beauty. It had been meant to bind the spirt of the Blood God to it. Freeing Duncan.

Instead, it sat here. Somehow full of the power, but useless. Its purpose unfulfilled. An idea came to Will that he at first discounted. But the more be thought about it, the more he liked it. Looking down at the hammer, the armor and the circlet, Will had a plan. It would be a start. A way of putting his past life behind him.

Chapter 43.

The Unnamed God sat on the same throne that he had been on when Taltus had come to see him. Now Grimnor was coming. But unlike the last time, the formerly sundered god knew exactly why one of his brothers was coming. The reports had been clear. Famine gripped the Gorom world. Without the Vinik beasts to supply milk and meat, the Gorom were running out of food. He'd gotten his revenge on the creatures, and their miserable race was gone. And if things worked out the way he expected, he would have the Gorom with his army.   All that was left was the City. The so called 'City in Blue'. He had his weapons. He would soon have all his anchors. Then, with the Palnorian army, and a conscripted force of fighters from other human lands, he would lead them on a crusade to end the blight of magic on this world. Or at least magic in mortal hands. Grimnor and his creations would make an excellent addition to his forces.

As usual, he felt Grimnor long before he saw him. A force, moving through what amounted to rock and stone here. Erupting short of the dais, Grimnor formed himself from rock and stone as he always did. "Brother." The Unnamed God nodded at the form, wondering if Grimnor ever did anything different. Not that it mattered. All that mattered was why his brother god had come, and the Unnamed God could guess that with little effort, all he had to do was detect the feelings coming from the form that stood in front of him.

The feeling of anger was there, but joining it was desperation. A twinge of fear and sadness. A god without his followers, his believers, wasn't much. And Grimnor's people had never been many. He couldn't afford to lose more than he already had. The Unnamed God felt a twinge of guilt for that. But that one holy city of the Gorom had stood in his way, and that was not allowed. Ever. He'd given them the chance to make it right. His hands had been forced.

"Speak Grimnor. I do not desire to spend forever trying to decipher your feelings." The Unnamed God pushed that guilt away, scowling. They had forced him to act. He'd not taken any pleasure from it, he wasn't a monster.

"Brother." Grimnor spoke, a voice like grinding rocks and shuddering magma deep in the world. "I need help brother."

"Yes?" The Unnamed God remained sitting. "I offered help before. I told you this was going to happen."

"Please." Grimnor spoke. "My people suffer. And I falter."

The Unnamed God said nothing for a long while. He did like Grimnor. But the old offer of help was now not good enough. Things had changed. The end of the City was drawing close. He needed more from Grimnor now. Much more. "I will help. But the conditions have changed, my needs are different now." The Unnamed God stood, walking towards Grimnor. While his brother god dwarfed him in size, it was he who anyone could see was far more powerful. "Not only will you swear fealty for as long as we are in this world, but your people will also serve mine. That is the price."

A wave of anger came from the form, bringing with it a change from hard gray rock and brown stone to near red molten lava. Grimnor kept his shape, but a few errant drops of melted rock dripped onto the dais. Heat drove off the figure of Grimnor in increasing waves. "Serve??" The voice of Grimnor rose to a crash of an earthquake, or a collapsed tunnel, echoing around them. "The Gorom do not serve!"

The Unnamed God shook his head. "They serve or they starve. Before, I would have been content with your fealty. But now, since I must fix the error you and the others allowed to fester, I need more. They will serve."

Grimnor did not respond, his form still glowing white and bright red in spots. But slowly, ever so slowly, the heat lessened. As it cooled, the colors dropped from white, to yellow, to red, then a dull orange. Finally, Grimnor stood unchanged except for one thing. A hand now was closed, grasping something tight. "What will you do with them? With me?" Grimnor spoke again. Its voice lower now, the sound of wind moaning through an ancient cave.

"They will serve the Palnorian army. You will swear yourself to my service while we are in this world. You will back any decision I make, and work to your full ability and power to make sure anything I plan becomes real." The Unnamed God couldn't help but smile. He had won this battle, at least.

"You ask much." Grimnor spoke in the same low tone. "Yet my people will live?"

"I will make sure they do. Food and supplies will be given, this I promise." The Unnamed God thought for a moment and then, with a frown, pulled a thin blade from out of the thin air. "To remove any doubts." He breathed, and with one motion, sliced his arm. Blood flowed, a blood unlike any other. Copper and brassy looking, it dropped on to the dais, giving a sizzle where it met some of the still hot drops that had fallen before. "I swear by my blood, shed freely, that I am not lying." The Unnamed God flicked his hand, and the knife vanished, but the wound remained, a slow drip of brass like liquid.

Grimnor didn't look any different, but surprise was probably beyond what a bunch of talking rocks could show. But the feeling was obvious. "You would swear on the blood? That my people will not die?"

"I swear." The Unnamed God replied. "Do you accept?"

Grimnor opened the clenched fist and laying in his hand was a twisted stone ring. Reaching out, Grimnor dropped it onto the dais, into the blood that had spilled. "I do." The voice came again, sounding more like the grinding of rocks than anything else. For a moment, nothing happened. The air went still. A tingle of excitement and change gripped the Unnamed God. In all the long eons, across multiple worlds, this had only happened once. It was why there was a goddess of the sea and air. Grimnor had agreed to be bound to him. Just for this world. Or at least that's what he thought.

The ring melted into the spilled blood, the color of the blood changing as it did so. What had been a coppery brass was now a glistening black with flecks of gold. The blood flowed upwards, back into the Unnamed God. It hurt. The pain of binding. Had Grimnor betrayed him somehow? Everything burned. He could feel the blood of the world, the deep lakes of fire and rock, the twisting lines of metals and earth. It burned into his mind with a fierceness that made him shudder.

And there, pulsing through it all, was the power of this world. Magic. A heartbeat. Tightly controlled. For the smallest of moments, he could see all of them. All the other gods see them tethered to the world by the lines of the power. Their food, their desire. Alos was rich and full, even now, after so many years.

And yet, there, in two places, things were different. The Anvil of Souls was one. A crack in the protection magic spilled out. It remade the world in that location to reflect what the wild power wanted. That was acceptable. A minor issue. No mortals lived there. Just animals and plants. Some now intelligent, knowing, but still acceptable. They did not seek to use the power; they were created by the power. The distinction was important.

But the other, the City was not. A fierce, powerful glow lit the location, and even with the binding, The Unnamed God could not see it. It resisted him, even now. Somehow, the power there the mortals had harnessed resisted even him. For now, he was the God of Humans, and Gorom. Grimnor's form fell apart in front of him.

The Unnamed God reveled in this added power. He turned his gaze into the world again, studying the location of the City. No one should be able to turn back a god, and yet, they did so.

His anger grew. His army was nearly complete. He would feed the Gorom, and they too would join his crusade. For the might of the new god was great, and he would put an end to this abomination.

Master Trie Reinhill watched as the man screamed. The scream did not last, however. What had been the Anvil room was now a factory for making her lord's anchors. Each required an exact number of metals, the correct procedure, and, above all, a living mind to link the magic to the rest of the world.

Making the link required a death, of sorts. Their minds lived in the anchor now. She could feel them. Though not what they thought. Most were screaming. A few wept or gave off sorrow. One even laughed in your mind when you touched it. A laugh that was hysterical, but still a laugh. The sounds faded out over time, a few days in total.

Could these people not see they were giving their lives for the good of the great one? The Unsundered one? The Unnamed? Her lord was an excellent master. He had given her the gift to make his anchors. She had bent the Guild to her will, and the craftsman made what was needed. A flicker of her eyes landed on the first collection of anchors. More than a few of those minds in those early anchors had belonged to less enthusiastic members of the Guild.

A blinding light filled the room, and Trie Reinhill and the rest of the workers in the room dropped to their knees as one, bowing their heads. Their Lord had come.

"Master Reinhill. Your work has been exemplary." The Unnamed God spoke, a soothing balm to her mind, easing the memory of the screams.

"Thank you, my Lord. We are nearly done." Trie kept her face down. She was not worthy of looking upon the glory of his form.

"You are done, actually. It is time. Send word. Gather the armies. Give them the weapons. Keep the anchors separate. I will instruct my forces what to do with them once we reach the City. We must end the stain the City makes upon this world." The Unnamed God's voice reverberated through the chamber. "Look up Master Reinhill." The voice commanded.

Master Trie Reinhill, Guildmaster of the Smithing Guild, did so, for she was sworn to serve. The shining form was like the other times, but yet different. Stronger. More real. "My lord?"

The voice spoke again, in low tones. "Only you can hear me now. I am sorry Master Reinhill. I am not an evil god. But the blight of the City forces me to take actions that I normally would not. You must understand that."

"My lord?" Trie did not understand at all. This was the Unnamed God. Her god. She lived only to serve him.

A long silence greeted her before a sound like a sigh came from the glowing form. "Go, gather the armies. The crusade begins."

Master Reinhill stood and walked out of the room. She would do as her lord commanded. Her footsteps echoed down the cold stone hallway. Each step muffling the faint screams of horror that lived in the far reaches of her mind.

Chapter 44.

Will stood in front of the forge, feeling oddly nervous. But then again, he was about to do something, or at least try to do something that to many would be foolish. *And they might be right.* Laid out next to him were the circlet, his old armor, and four large Wight Iron ingots. His base materials were ready, or at least as ready as they would be.

He was alone, as asked. A simple construct was at the bellows, silent and still. He wished for a moment it was Duncan. Or Regin. Or Myriam. But they were gone or missing. But the construct was quiet at least. He could concentrate. He checked the flux and other components. The forge wasn't coal fired, instead it used the power, like everything else here. He wasn't clear on how bellows actually worked with that, but decided not to worry about it too much.

Everything was well stocked, true to what Rewil had told him earlier. Rewil had tried to come along, or at least hinted that he wanted to. But this was something that Will needed to do alone. Picking up his hammer, he hefted it. The golden surface marred by the same bright blue stains that had been there since arriving here. It still sparkled if he concentrated enough.

He knew he was wasting time. He wanted at least the first part of this to be done today. He would need the results for the next part, anyway. He'd not used a power lit forge before, but Rewil had told him what to do. He reached for his boon, feeling it coiled up in the back of his mind, and reached out to the forge with it. True to Rewil's instructions, there was a... something there to link to. The moment he made the connection, the forge lit up, heat blooming. A heat that somehow vanished out of arm's reach of the thing.

Hotter. He needed it hotter. He nodded to the construct, who used the bellows to good effect. A regular rhythm blew the bottom of the forge, and it changed. Soon the orange red had grown to a white hot and bright thing. *Good enough to start.* He wasn't sure what the exact temperature was going to need to be, but this was a good place to begin.

He took out a large crucible, and placed two of the ingots in it, and carefully, using the tools, placed the crucible into the forge. Within moments, the Wight Iron melted, a faint whisper of sound escaping the melt. Soon the crucible vessel was half full of melted Wight Iron, its silver color now brighter, shimmering hot.

Will picked up the circlet, its shining black surface smoother than anything he could make. God made and God touched. He'd kept the thing only because he hadn't known what to do with it. Its purpose was lost in the aftermath of the god's cave. The Anvil of Souls.

A thought came to him as he held the circlet. He didn't like it here. It was all... too strange. He was meant to work a forge, not fiddle with strange machines and use magic. He'd been dancing to someone else's tune for so long. Gods, friends, family, enemies, it didn't matter. He'd spent forever... reacting to other's needs, other's wants. But what did he want? He put down the circlet and picked it up again with a set of tongs. *I very much hope this works, and I don't die in some catastrophic explosion.* Carefully, and trying very hard not to breathe, Will added the circlet to the crucible.

He was somewhat disappointed by the initial reaction. The circlet sat there, half submerged in the molten Wight Iron, doing nothing. No reaction at all. Will frowned and considered raising the temperature even more, when a thin black thread of liquid started flowing. Followed by half a dozen more, the circlet submerged in the Wight Iron. There was a reaction then. Will had to step back as the crucible trembled. A howling sound came, a vestige of an ancient scream. For a moment Will blanched, convinced that the sound was the Blood God, returned to life. But no, the sound faded quickly. It was more an echo of what had been, not what was.

The metal continued to mix, a war of silver light and black emptiness. Slowly the war ended, becoming a uniform dark silver that, to Will's magic sight, gave off silver sparks. Not blue, but silver. *Odd.*

"I liked it better when you did this back in that forsaken tower." A voice whispered behind Will.

Will turned around in shock. And there, standing before him, but not fully, was Duncan. A Duncan like he had been. Healthy and strong. He wasn't solid though; he looked misty. As if he was standing in deep fog. But it was him. *Duncan*. Will couldn't believe what he was seeing. "Dunc?"

"Sort of. A memory. A tiny echo of what was. I carried that knife the circlet was made from for quite a while. Or at least my body did. I was there. Trapped in my own mind." Duncan raised himself up to see into the crucible. "I cannot say I'm sorry to see it gone."

"Duncan!" Will stepped forward. "I am so sorry Duncan. I thought, back in the Anvil…." Will stopped as Duncan held up a hand to silence him.

"That doesn't matter. I don't even remember it. I'm… I don't even know if I am really Duncan, or a memory of him." Duncan settled back down, looking at Will. "But you cousin of mine. Look at you. Here in this place. Gave up on all the Guild nonsense finally I see."

Will shook his head. "That's not fair Dunc. I …It all sort of happened."

"No, you made choices. Will, you were always far too eager to go along with people. It worked in the Reach because you were liked. Respected. But out in the world, you ended up following people around. You know it's true." Duncan shook his head.

"Yes. I thought that." Will frowned. "Maybe you are only a memory."

"I never said I wasn't. But if I am, it's because you need to talk to me. You are at a fork in the road, Will. One that will be a deciding one." Duncan smiled. "You seem to get these decisions often."

"I hate it." Will frowned. "I don't want any of it. None of the pressure. None of the repercussions. None of it."

"I know. I know you. It's not in your nature to do things to hurt people, and all these choices you've had to make, all these decisions have always had someone in pain at the end." Duncan frowned. "But this one Will, this one will be the last."

"What do you mean?" Will felt a chill touch his skin. *I'm not ready to die. I hope he doesn't mean that…*

"No. Not death. Well, I can't say, actually. But I don't THINK death." Duncan smiled. "Yes, I know what you're thinking. I'm a memory, right?"

"Then what do you mean, Duncan?" Will was conflicted. Talking to Duncan again was something that felt right. Like he had missed part of himself and never realized it was gone. Yet, he had sort of forgotten how maddening Duncan could be. He'd often taken a great deal of enjoyment out of frustrating Will by not fully explaining things at first. More than once he'd let Will get furious with him, only to diffuse it all by being straightforward.

"That soon you will have to make a choice that will be the last one you will be presented with. At least the last one that will change things for other people." Duncan's brow furrowed. "A huge choice."

"That's not very helpful." Will cracked a smile. "Care to be clearer?"

"I can't. But you will know it. You have already made the choice, but you don't realize it." Duncan seemed to fade some, looking even fainter. "Ah, well, I guess my time is ending."

"Duncan!" Will yelled as the form flickered before staying, but still less real than before. "I'm not good with this, but... I miss you. You were my best friend. My only family. And I'm sorry."

"Bah. Will, you always were the good one. I was only there to keep you normal half the time. No one should be as *good* as you were as a kid. And remember, I'm a memory, so I'm always there, and always will be." Duncan's form faded and was gone.

Will felt himself choke on the next breath. He did not know what that was, but he'd... needed it. It made what came next somehow easier. Turning back to the forge, the crucible was still now, the dark silver color seeming more real, stronger. It was time.

Will searched through the molds, finally selecting two and were close enough to the final size he would need. Taking care, he took the crucible in its holder and poured the metal into the molds. He could use help, but he was strong enough, if only barely, to do this alone. The metal sang still as it poured, but instead of the low moan of Wight Iron, it was a song of something new. The sound brought a smile to his face, reminding him of brief summers in the Reach when the small meadows would explode in grass and clover. It felt *right*. The metal flowed into the molds, and thanks to years of practice, not a single drop spilled onto the stone floor.

Will placed the crucible down to one side, letting out a held breath, glad to be rid of that step, at least for today.

The newly molded metal cooled quickly. Far quicker than he'd expected. Not that anything about this was probably going to go as expected. Will flicked a drop of water at them both, watching it bead up but not hiss or dance. Cool already. Taking them out of the molds, he gave them both a careful inspection. One thick, one long and thinner. Everything looked exactly as expected, though. Now for the next part.

Will slid a large anvil over, giving it a frown. Anvils were supposed to be... not this. The anvil that was here was obviously made of the same stuff as the quickways. Will knew a lot more about the alloy now, but still, wondered why that for an anvil? His sight was still in effect, and he grimaced now, the thing was charged full of the power. *Not what I want.*

Will searched through the forge room, and even the nearby supply area. *Great. I want a normal anvil; I get an anvil that is charged to the brim with the power and is made of the one metal that can explode under the right circumstances.* Will looked back at the recently cooled forms. Did he really want to hammer on this? He knew he didn't. He'd take anything other than this coppery anvil. Even a large hunk of iron rock. Anything. But this was what he had. He could walk away. Right now. Walk away and find a proper anvil, then come back to it.

It wouldn't mess anything up. Well, nothing that he was making. But would he be all right? The whole reason for this was to make a choice. To stay or go? Even if he went, he'd not leave until he got an answer on where Myriam was. Yet, the choice needed to be made. Did he want this life? Will knew he had to move forward. With a sigh, he cracked his knuckles, gave a smile, and placed the first larger squat shape in the forge. It was time to find a fresh path.

Chapter 45.

Will watched the metal glow, looking for the signs that it was ready. Whatever this mix was, it was taking longer than he'd thought to get to the place it needed to be. So many unknowns. It felt good, though. This was what he was meant for. Him, a hammer, a forge, an anvil. Even if they were all somewhat different from the standard, it was still something he felt perfect for. A place he belonged.

The metal glowed the barest white hot when he pulled it out. He had to test it. He placed the billet on the anvil and steadied his nerves. He had no idea what was about to happen. He raised his hammer and struck, guided by talent and more practice than his years would have shown. The hit pealed around the room. It started low but grew into the same sound as when it was poured.

It also drew a shower of sparks. Sparks that went from silver to blue to gold. More sparks than he'd expected, but not enough to make him stop. He dropped the hammer again, knowing what he needed to make. This City. It wasn't home. Too many people wrapped up in power and fighting for whatever bit of magic they could get. Was this the right way?

The billet took shape; he squared off the head more and slipped it back into the forge to reheat. Out of the corner of his eye, he noticed the anvil looked different. The power that flowed through it was less now. Odd. But it didn't matter. Not now. Not to him. Will watched the metal, careful to make sure it didn't overheat or deform.

Satisfied it was in the right heat again, he pulled it out and resumed the shaping. His hammer blows brought the same sparks, but the blue was growing less and the gold as well. The silver sparks were almost white and growing more numerous. No matter. He had to create. Once again, his thoughts turned to trying to decide where he belonged.

If the City wasn't right though, was Palnor? The Reach? He loved his home. The feel of it was etched into his heart and mind as surely as any metalwork he had ever done. It was *home*. It always would be, but was that where he belonged now? He wasn't the same William Reis who had left the Reach, heading for Ture. That version of him was as vanished as the mist that burned off in the mornings.

Ture wasn't much better than the City. Or it hadn't been. His hammer blows grew harder as the remembrance of the dungeons under the Temple of Amder filled him. A different goal, but the same path. Power. Will didn't understand why people simply couldn't just be. Why destroy what was around you to be better than your neighbor. It made no sense.

The billet had cooled too much, and Will placed it back into the forge. It was almost done. The front side was made. Clean lines showed the head of a new hammer. Only the other side needed to be finished. But should it be like the other side? Will didn't think so. He wasn't making a new blacksmithing hammer. There was more to this.

Removing the piece one more time, he started shaping the other side. He'd made an approximation of Amder the last time he'd done this as decoration. Amder. Will had been devout, in his own way. But he'd seen too much of the gods. The same petty fighting seemed to plague the gods and mortals. Amder was gone. The Blood God was gone. This Unnamed God remained. And yet, Will didn't like him. If Amder had never died, would he have followed him? He wanted to say yes, but the longer he was here in this place, the more he wasn't sure.

He couldn't answer that, and it made him frown. If the world of the City wasn't the right answer, and the lands of Palnor weren't the right answer, what was? He was being pushed into picking a side in a fight where he didn't like either now. He raised his hammer, and looking down, stopped. He had finished. One side was a solid and even blacksmithing hammer. But the other was a chisel. Tapered with a strong edge. But what was it for? Will didn't know. Wasn't sure he wanted to know. But it had a purpose. The surface was the smooth dark gray of the metal, but something pulsed inside it.

Will was no healer, but it felt like a...heartbeat. It wasn't alive, though it seemed to call to something. Then the feeling faded, leaving a slight sheen on the otherwise unremarkable surface. He snorted for a moment, kicking himself. He'd forgotten a step. There was no hole for the handle. He'd have to reheat the whole thing.

It hadn't been heat treated though, so he could wait till he made the handle. Might be for the best, anyway, considering he wasn't sure yet how long the handle was going to be. He needed leverage. He needed a hammer that would accentuate his already powerful blows. Placing the hammer head off to the side, Will picked the longer thinner billet and placed it into the forge.

He watched it, and knowing it was going to be longer wait now, watched the construct work the bellows. The forge light reflected off its surfaces, accentuating the angular and foreign shape it held. Constructs. He didn't mind them, but…again, it wasn't him. This wasn't his world.

The billet drew his attention back, he watched the final color change, its near white color showing its readiness. He placed it on the anvil which now seemed almost dull to Will and began to shape it. The sparks still flew, but more silver again than any other color. Lengthening the haft, Will lost himself to the work.

Each hammer blow sang as Will fell into a rhythm. He needed no sharp edges, or blister causing roughness. Faster than he'd expected, he had a haft that seemed correct. He placed it back into the forge for a moment. He needed to flatten the pommel more, and it would be done.

Removing the haft after a few minutes, Will did what he needed to do. The haft was long, longer than this hammer at least, but still strong. He placed it off to the side, and reheated the hammer head, enough to start the hole for the haft. Grabbing the boring tool and placing it nearby, Will removed the hammer head. He placed it on the anvil so that he could find the right spot to begin the last step. He took the haft and moved it where he wanted it with a practiced hand and a lifetime of experiences.

The reaction was nothing he had expected. The hammer grew silver bright for a second, and to Will it felt like the anvil was about to shake apart, and then suddenly, as fast as it had started, it was over. But there was no need for the hole. The haft was now joined to the rest of the hammer. No seam was there, no trace that they had been two separate pieces recently. It was as if they had always been one. They always had been in his mind. Will pushed the thought aside. He put down the hammer he'd been using and picked up the new one. Knowing somehow that it wouldn't burn him. It was warm, borderline hot, but still not painful.

Will made a hammer blow in the air, testing the balance and strength. Even a practice swing told him that this would work better than the hammer he'd made with Duncan back in the Reach. There was something of that hammer in this, but also of the City, and of the Gods. Will knew that this hammer held a part of his past, all of his past. The chisel edge was wickedly sharp, even though he'd not even gotten it close to a grindstone. Nor had he hardened anything yet. He placed the now formed hammer into the forge again and gave the construct the hand command to raise the temperature even more.

Heat bloomed again, hotter still. The hammer held its shape but glowed a grayish white. It shimmered in the heat, and the rare silver spark flew off with a high-pitched whistle. Will turned to the quenching equipment, selecting the right size vessel, and opening various large urns of liquids, checking what they were.

Water, oil, some kind of strange solid fat, one even held what appeared to be blood. Will did not examine that one further and closed the lid and put that one away. Finally, he narrowed it down to two fresh oils. Will didn't know exactly why these two, but for this day, he'd given up questioning things.

He poured half of each urn into the vessel, watching the oils, one a rich golden color, mix with the other, a purple plum color. A hint of a sweet smell wafted up from the mix before fading into the background. The hammer glowed the perfect temperature. Will couldn't say why, though. He knew it was right. Normally, it would have to stay this way for much longer, yet his gut told him it was almost ready. Almost.

A memory came to him. Not one he could talk to like before, but one that was old. One he hadn't fully remembered until now. He was young, very young. His Da and mother were still alive. He was four or five, watching his father work in the family forge. His father was making shears. Simple shears. His mother needed new ones.

"William. Remember this." His father took the quenching vessel, filled with water and placed it nearby. "I am going to show you something." Will's father looked around, and picked up a sharp thin metal burr, and swiftly poked his finger, forcing a large drop of blood to the surface, and he let it drop into the quenching water.

"Do you know why I did that?" Will's father asked.

"No, isn't that wrong? The bad god… the monsters, they like blood. Isn't that wrong?" Will had answered.

"Ah. They crave blood, to feast. To take. This blood, this is different. This is a gift. I give a speck of myself to the work. I mark the metal as ours. The world is a living thing, Will, and the metal is part of that life. I give a drop of blood as a way for it to know me. A drop to say, I am here. To say a thank you." Will's father pointed to the quench water.

"But… what about Amder?" Will had asked.

"Amder is a good god. Our god. But the world is good too. We take part of it, and we give back to it in thanks." Will's father had smiled. "Just remember."

Will shook himself. He'd never done it. He'd never offered a drop of his blood to any of his work. He'd not remembered until now. The sadness at the loss of his parents soon after had pushed those memories deep inside. Survival had been the goal then.

Yet now… he could do it. He took a small sharp knife, used for carving bone or wood, and pushed it into the palm of his hand deep enough to draw a bead of red. He held it over the quench, and watched as it fell into the oil, and mixing with it as well. A gift to you, Alos.

Will turned back to the forge. The hammer was ready now, though usually it would need to be there longer. The quench was ready too. He removed the hammer, the heat near to unbearable off the thing. He could feel his skin dry and heat as he moved it, the tongs almost feeling sticky as if they were going to melt being near the hammer.

The quench brought a pillar of silver and gold flame out of the oil. It leaped up, the tips of it brushing the ceiling, leaving Will worried he was going to damage the place. Nothing thankfully caught fire and it slowly died, the flame vanishing. Leaving the oil to sputter a few more times, the surface roiling with heat before it slowed and stopped.

Reaching in with a new pair of tongs, Will pulled the now complete hammer out of the oil. It was done. Will wondered at his new creation. It was unlike any other hammer he'd ever made. The design was similar in some ways, but in others, not so much. The biggest difference was the chisel end on the one side of the head. He'd never made anything like that. He'd never seen a blacksmithing hammer like that. This was a hammer made for a purpose. Just what that purpose was remained to be seen.

Chapter 46.

Will didn't know what time it was, but he wasn't tired, which surprised him. If anything, this had rejuvenated him. He felt... real. And since the construct wouldn't get tired at all, Will could keep going if he wanted. And he very much wanted. Giving the construct the signal to lower the temperature. He cleaned up a few things from the making of the hammer, and then turned his full attention to what was next.

He placed his old hammer down. Its gold and blue surface felt less real now. Less alive. At least compared to the new one. Next to it, he placed the last two Wight Iron ingots, and finally his old armor. Will traced the decoration with his finger. The filigree work was immaculate. Myriam had done an incredible job. The symbol of Amder still glowed in the forge light. The silver hammer over the golden anvil, wreathed in copper flames.

The bracers as well, with their own work. He'd not worn it all that much, but then again, he'd told them all he didn't want to. Regin, Vin, Myriam. Regin had insisted, and Vin had backed him up. And in some ways, they HAD been right. It saved his life in the Gorom caves, and in the Anvil. That he had died anyway and then was brought back wasn't the fault of the armor. It was wrong, though. It wasn't his anymore, though that made little sense. Like the old hammer, its time had come and gone. Yet he needed armor. He wasn't sure why, but he knew. So new armor had to be made. Armor that reflected who he was now. What he was now. Where he was now.

Pulling out the largest crucible he could handle, Will placed it on the forge's edge. This would not be easy to do alone. As before, he placed the last two ingots in the crucible, then the old hammer. Its gold and blue surface making an odd crackle as it touched the Wight Iron. Finally, he removed all the straps and leather from the armor and placed them in the crucible as well. It was full and was going to weigh a great deal when he had to pour it. Will moved the crucible into position, straining with the effort. But with some brute strength and bit of leverage, he could get the vessel into where it needed to be. He watched the Wight Iron melt first, taking on its characteristic silver white glow as it did so. The hammer was the next to go, giving off more of those crackling sounds as it melted away into the growing pool.

At last, the armor relinquished its form, the liquid metal changing color as the materials joined together. The silvery white of the pure Wight Iron turned a coppery yellow when the hammer melted. And then as the armor fell apart, the color became almost a vibrant golden yellow. It thrummed in a way that was unlike anything Will had ever heard before.

It roiled and churned, and Will took the opportunity to skim the surface of any impurities. There wasn't much, if any. But far be it from him to not follow blacksmithing procedures. Though, to his momentary embarrassment, he had forgotten when making the hammer, not that it seemed to have made much in the way of a difference. Will pulled out the two largest flat molds they had here. It was close, but he felt like it would work. Smith born indeed.

"Yes. You always knew exactly what you needed when you worked the forge, didn't you lad?" the voice was one that was long gone. Haltim.

Will turned, surprised but not completely after his visit from whatever or wherever Duncan had been. There now stood Haltim. Mentor, father figure, friend. Wearing the robes of the eight, and as old but wise as he'd ever been. "Haltim!" Will moved to embrace the old Priest but stopped. He wasn't there either. The same shimmer and foggy haze clung to the image of the man.

"Will lad. Or I should call you sir now. The Forgemaster of Amder. I wish I could have been there. What a marvelous accomplishment, Will. Truly." Haltim smiled for a moment before sorrow appeared on his face. "And I am very sorry about how it all ended for you. Amder gone. Duncan gone for good. Here in this… place."

"It's good to see you. Or remember you." Will felt a sense of calm envelop him. Haltim. How many times had he asked for advice from this man? Haltim was one of the people in the world that Will trusted down to the bare ends of his soul.

"Yes. It's good to see you as well." Haltim sighed and locked eyes with

William. "Duncan did not deserve his fate. I think we all didn't understand what was happening. How far everything had gone when the blood curse took him." "Some tiny part of him survived Haltim. I don't know how, but a speck, enough to remember him by, made it through, and got to the end. "Will shook his head. "I could have never done that."

"Duncan always was a strong young man. A little brittle in some places. Despite that, he would do anything for you, and you for him. It was that strength, more than any other, that kept you both alive in the face of so much pain." Haltim rubbed his eyes, raising them again. A transparent glimmer showing in them both.

"But that's not why I am here, lad. I'm here to give you some guidance. I think so at least. After all, I am only a memory." The smile that came to Haltim's face was one that Will had seen a thousand times before. One that he'd missed so much.

"Advice is something I need." Will looked back at the crucible, its golden metal still glowing in its place. "What am I doing Haltim? Why am I here? I feel like a mummer's puppet most of the time now if I think about it. Moving around by having my strings pulled. And I have a lot of strings on me."

"Why did you want to join the Guild?" Haltim folded his arms, taking on the pose he had used to teach Will and sometimes Duncan a life lesson.

"To fulfill a promise. To Da. To be the first Reacher to ever get into the Guild." Will answered right away. That was a straightforward question.

"No. Why did YOU want to join the Guild?" Haltim asked again, his voice louder. "Think Will."

Will thought about the question. All those things he'd said had been important, sure, but were they the real reason he'd joined the Guild? Partially, yes. But also, he'd joined the guild for himself. He'd wanted to be the best version of himself that he could ever be. The Guild was the way to get that. To be honed, hardened, remade into something more than he'd been when he'd left the Reach. "To become the best version of me." Will answered with some trepidation. He wasn't sure where Haltim was going with this, not that he ever had known where the old Priest was going with any of his questions.

"Good. Now, why are you here? Not here in this Forge. I can see the impish streak still lives in you young man." Haltim gave a brief smile, cutting off the oh too clever answer Will had been tempted to say.

"I didn't have a choice." Will shot back. "I escaped the madness of the Anvil with Myriam, and we ended up here. Someplace safe, supposedly."

"Think Will. You really had no choice? None?" Haltim lowered his eyes and waited.

Will paused, thinking over what he had said. He'd not had a choice, right? But the more he considered it, the more he realized that wasn't the right answer. He HAD been given a choice. He didn't have to join Myriam; he could have stayed in the Anvil. The remade god, or whatever he was calling himself, had brought him back to life. He'd been safe, or at least not in any immediate danger. So why had he come?

"Because I needed to be there for her." Will finally knew. "Even after everything, I had to be there for Myriam. She'd lost Regin and been fooled by the spirit of the new god. She had lost everything. And yet, I turned my back on her as well. I blamed her."

"Yes. You did. Now, that anger was justified somewhat. Yet, when it had cooled, you ignored her. But yet, you stayed. You stayed for the knowledge and the wonder. You stayed because in your heart, you knew she was here, and you needed to be here too." Haltim smiled. "The heart can be a hidden place Will. Sometimes we do things and make decisions based on that heart that the rest of us doesn't even know."

Will nodded, the words sinking in. "But where does that leave me now? She's missing. And I don't want to be here anymore."

"And if she wasn't missing?" Haltim asked once more.

"I'd… still leave. This isn't where I belong. I'd…" Will looked deep into himself. "I'd ask her to leave with me."

"Exactly. The two of you are the two sides of a coin now. Before it was you and Duncan. But his part is played. But for you and Myriam, it's not over yet." Haltim was fading now. "Be good lad. You will know the path, just, focus. Remember who you are."

Will watched his mentor fade away. It may have only been a memory, or some vision brought about by the strange combination of forces that he'd joined here. But it was good to see his old mentor. And he was right. He and Myriam had something yet to do together. Will didn't know what it was, but like the hammer, there was a purpose, even if it was hidden from him right now.

Will turned back to his work, losing himself to the metalwork. While he struggled with the pours, he managed to get both done without making a mess, or worse, an injury. This new alloy gave off golden sparks as it cooled, finally settling down into a pair of large and relatively flat sheets of metal. Will stood there for a long while, looking at them. The strange conversations with Duncan and Haltim had only begun to sink in. Had they been real? He was more than somewhat confused by his own lack of reaction. Had he really become so used to the strange and bizarre after living here for most of a year that this was normal?

Did it matter, though? Both visits had shown him something. In himself. Something he needed. He would finish, then find Myriam. And work harder than he ever thought to get her to leave this place with him. None of this was right. This PLACE wasn't right. Different players, but the same game as Ture. A game he didn't want to play again, ever. Will finally began moving again, taking the cooled metal alloy and fashioning armor again, but different from his old. The new hammer sang as he worked. If Will had to put a name to it, it sang of the joys of a simple life. A life that did not need power, or danger, a life that he discovered he not only craved, but needed.

The new breastplate was simple. He'd still need to line it with leather for a better and closer fit, but the new hammer made quick work of the shaping needed. The bracers were more of the same. Simple, clean armor. No more strings. Will still felt like it needed something, though. Some kind of decoration. Various symbols came into his thoughts, and he discarded those out of hand. Too close to this city or to some other power. No, he needed something new. He was no expert at inlay work, but a glance over at the first crucible gave him an idea. There at the bottom was a small flat disc of hard metal, leftovers from the pour for the hammer. Not much, but enough.

The breastplate and bracers had cooled now and had lost much of their gold color. Now if anything, they were a dark copper. Still shiny, and nevertheless, thrumming with some kind of link to whatever power this place held. Will turned the hammer, and using the chisel point he'd made on the other end, etched three lines, all starting at a single point, all going up at angles. He could not guess what it meant. Or why it was the only thing that felt right. He worked quickly, as the long day threatened to catch up with him. He forced the thin disc of leftover silver alloy into thin strips that he placed into the lines he'd made. The dark silver color shone with its own light in the breastplate.

Will knew it was right. He'd decided and knew what to do.

Even if he did not know how to start it.

Chapter 47.

Jinir stood still and scowled at the door, and at Myriam. Ralta had told him everything. About Myriam leaving the safe house, her run in with Rauger, all of it. He looked less than pleased to Myriam's eyes.

"Rauger." Jinir forced the word through clenched teeth. "Rauger is a blight. Cunning, respected, and as wrong as they come."

"He led me back though." Myriam spoke and regretted it at once. Jinir's expression grew harder still. "He could have made other choices, but he led me back."

"He led you back to make a point, Myriam. That nothing is safe from him. No one." Jinir removed his hood and rubbed his scalp. It had finally begun growing hair again and was covered with a thin layer of white blond hair. You could still see the fresh pink of his scalp in places, but that last piece was coming along.

"Why is he so bad?" Myriam asked again, meeting the glare of Jinir head on, and ignoring the slight noise from Ralta. "You keep saying it, but not saying why."

Jinir's face turned dark, and for a moment Myriam wondered if she was going to have to heal him because something might break inside. Then the man relaxed, giving himself a more normal cast. "Rauger Manter was an associate of mine. And of Ralta's. If she's my protector, he was my informant. Until one day, he decided he didn't need me, and could do the work himself. I suspect, but have no proof, that this was a Mikol thing. But now, Rauger stops me whenever he can, and works to undermine me." Jinir scowled. "And now, he knows about you."

Myriam paused for a moment, thinking over what Jinir had said. Which, while a lot of words, wasn't much. "You didn't answer the question." She finally let out. "What did he do? Stop you? Stop you from what?"

"REGAINING MY POSITION." Jinir yelled finally. "He gets in the way. I find a way to feed thirty people. He feeds fifty. I help five families get better housing; he helps ten. I take two steps, he takes three." Jinir clenched a fist and punched the wall, hard.

"I had hoped that with you, I had finally found a way to free myself from him. He didn't have a healer, see? With you, I could win. I could get enough support and backing from the Lower city to push into the middle, and then force the issue, and return to my place as a Tarn. Getting my revenge on Mikol as well. And kicking that toady of Mikol's the current Tarn Grib to the side with him." Jinir kept his fist clenched and raised it.

Myriam stepped back, out of his fist's range. "So that's it? That's his crime? That's why you saved me? Why I'm here? To give you power?"

"Of course it is!" Jinir screamed. "I will have my revenge on that man. That so called gentle soul, Mikol. And you should want it too! He tried to kill us, Myriam. BOTH of us. And men like Rauger, they stop us!"

Myriam didn't join Jinir in his hate. She realized that right away. There was a darkness here that she hadn't guessed at. She watched as Jinir, now trembling with the released emotions, let go of his fist. He didn't look at her, but turned to Ralta.

"Rauger has gone too far. He dies." Jinir turned to Myriam now. "You will be moved. One bell. And not see anyone until Rauger has been removed from his life." With a jerk, he pulled his hood back over his head. And with a fake limp, Jinir lowered one arm, and shuffled out of the building, and into the street.

"Ralta, you can't do this." Myriam finally looked at the Trinil. Ralta's face was... shaken. That was the only word Myriam could put to it. Pale, and somewhat gray, she was torn between her deep love and loyalty to Jinir, and the order she'd been given.

"He gets so angry." Ralta's voice was a whisper. "He wasn't like this before. But ever since Mikol tried to kill him, there's a rage there that..." Ralta stopped and shook her head. "Why didn't you listen? If you'd never left this place, Rauger would not have found you. This is your fault."

"Ralta, you can't believe that." Myriam protested. "You keep me here, almost a prisoner, of course I'm going to want to see more than these walls."

"No Myriam. You brought this. Now I must kill Rauger. My second oldest friend. Even though we haven't spoken since he betrayed Jinir, I have avoided this moment. But thanks to you, I cannot anymore." Ralta let out a long-ragged sigh. "A fate I do not wish."

"He's being blind, you know. You **KNOW** he is Ralta." Myriam stepped in front of the door. "I don't know if Rauger did what he did to track me or send a message or whatever other reason Jinir believes. But I know he got me home safe, and he had every chance to NOT do that."

"Move Myriam. I will not ask a second time." Ralta's voice had lost its sorrow. The edge in it now was only matched by the knife she held up. "I won't kill you, but if you force me, I will hurt you."

Myriam's palms went sweaty as she considered the warning. She knew Ralta was more than capable of hurting her. "Don't do this Ralta. You know it's wrong."

Ralta stepped forward and pushed Myriam out of the way. "It doesn't matter what I think. I have pledged myself to Jinir. Always." Ralta hesitated for a moment, then stalked out the door, leaving Myriam alone and afraid.

A bell. A single bell. Myriam gathered a few things in a rush. She was sure the place was being watched, but the fact was she would not stay here right now. She had a lot of thinking to do, and all of it needed to be elsewhere, away from Jinir and Ralta. She took her rucksack, crammed with as much food as she could carry, another bottle of honey juice, and a few things that had some valuable metal in them. Nothing crazy, but if she could get access to a decent heat source, she could remove the inlay from a few bowls and utensils. She did not know what the worth of materials was in the City, but it was worth a try.

Selling the whole thing would be worth more, but it would be easy to track back to her. Assuming she pulled this off. *Which I don't think I will be able to.* Myriam headed out the door. While there were people here and there, the day was ending and the streets weren't crowded. But they weren't empty either. Myriam set a brisk pace, turning through main and side streets at random. She avoided alleys and darker areas where the houses blocked all the light. She didn't know if they were dangerous, but again, it wasn't worth the risk.

Her plan was simple. Find that water that separated the lower and middle city, find it and follow it to a bridge, and sneak into the middle city. It was her best bet. Jinir had even said he had to 'push more into the middle city.' She wasn't sure, but it seemed like Jinir didn't have as large a grip there. She kept listening, hoping that soon the rush of water would come. But the City was a maze, and soon she realized that she'd passed that same butcher's shop. Or she hoped it was a butcher's shop, three times.

"Follow me." A voice whispered. "Rauger would like to talk to you."

Myriam turned to see a tall figure covered in rags. They hid almost all the man's features. She had no desire to get any closer to see them, though, because of the smell. A midden heap on a hot summer day would smell better than this man.

"What?" She managed to say, before her stomach stopped her desire to talk. The stench threw the rest of her into a desperate attempt not to lose all her food on the stone road. The figure said not a word, but took off in a quick gait, leaving Myriam taking large breaths of clean air as the man left. Myriam watched him, but with no other options, followed. It wasn't hard. The man made a trail that would have led a rock to follow. Anyone else in the street found rapid reasons to move out of the way and stay away from the stench.

Finally, she heard water, and saw the bridge. It wasn't the same one as before, but still it led into the middle city and that was good enough. The man was standing at the edge of the road, staring down into the swirling water. He pointed to the other side of the bridge, saying nothing. He was standing in such a way that none of the guards standing on the top could see him. The figure nodded at her, then the man jumped into the black roiling water, vanishing.

Myriam rushed to the water's edge, but the figure was already gone. Pulled into the dark water, he was nowhere to be seen. She didn't think him dead. Why lead her here to meet with Rauger, and then end his life? No, there was something else going on. The lingering odor made it hard to look for him, it clung to the place he had jumped from. She'd never smelled anything that foul.

Standing here was dangerous, though. She felt eyes on her; she was sure of it. And recent events had shown her eyes were dangerous. It would be better to cross the bridge and enter the middle city first, before she took time to think. She ran her fingers through her hair, making sure there were no obvious knots or tangled mats. She fixed her clothing as well. Pulled it tight in a few places, let some others relax.

She didn't like that sort of thing, but she enjoyed being a prisoner even less. Or becoming a liability, and meeting Ralta's knives. Not that she thought it would really come to that. Jinir had been furious with her though, and she wasn't one to leave things to chance, not anymore. Myriam took a quick pace onto the bridge, feeling like she was being watched intently from behind her. The urge to look over her shoulder was large. Who was it? Was Ralta there, wondering if she threw a knife, could she wound Myriam enough for her to give up? Was it Jinir? Was it someone else she'd never met?

She resisted the urge and calmly walked onto the bridge. The guards were attentive, but not overly concerned, it appeared. One held out a hand for her to stop while the other waved something at her, then with a nod, he moved out of the way and let her pass. Neither said a word to her. She wanted to know what that had all been about but didn't ask. She had to figure what to do next. If this Rauger person wanted to talk to her, she'd listen. Though she hoped it wasn't a trap. Maybe a public meeting. The middle city was already proving itself a far nicer place. The streets were all well-kept, and even the alleys were well lit because of no overhanging buildings.

"Ah, so she comes at last." A voice she knew whispered from beside her. Rauger. Dressed in somewhat the same clothes she had seen him with last. But not carrying that strange musical instrument he'd had last time. For an idle moment, she wondered what it sounded like. But that was not important, not now. What was also obvious was the man was also wet. His clothes weren't, but his skin and hair were.

"You were the man?" She took a sniff but not a hint of the earlier smell remained.

"Yes. I told you the water cleans things, right? If you know the way to make it out, the water will remove any dirt any smell. Useful to know." Rauger leaned forward, arm outstretched. "Come, let's talk."

Chapter 48.

"I imagine you have some questions." Rauger spoke his voice not exactly low, but not loud enough for anyone to hear much.

"Yes. What exactly is the history with you and Jinir? And Ralta? He made some claims." Myriam walked beside the man staying close but keeping her eyes in motion. "Is it safe here?"

"As much as Jinir runs the lower city, I hold sway here. Though I'd rather not." Rauger shook his head. "I'd rather be a bard, play music, tell stories, and generally not be part of all this. But, you know, things happen."

Myriam found herself smiling. If anyone understood that saying, she did. "But what is the history? If I'm going to decide, I need to know."

"What's there to decide? If you want to be a puppet? A toy he can take out and use to get attention? Because that's what you are right now to him." Rauger frowned. "He wasn't that way, before."

"Before the accident? Or I mean before Mikol tried to kill him?" Myriam said the Tarn of the Healer's name quieter than the rest, almost feeling scared doing even that.

"Yes. So, I imagine he told you I was a friend of his. An associate even? I was, he wasn't lying. Jinir, Ralta and I were a powerful trio. Jinir was the Tarn, Ralta was the muscle, and I was the information. And then everything went bad. When Jinir was aware enough, he blamed me. Said I hadn't told him out of spite, or I was in the pay of Mikol. Something. I was the one who TOLD him it was Mikol, after the fact." Rauger grimaced. "Those were bad times. But I was going to stay, I respected him."

"Then, he changed. He became obsessed with getting his position as Tarn back. It became all he wanted, that and revenge on Mikol. I pointed out that he could do as much good, or even more good now, that he wasn't tied by the politics of it all. That made him angry. We argued for days. Then, one day, he ordered me to leave. Gave me two bells, or he'd have Ralta take care of me with those knives of hers." Rauger shrugged.

"I came to the middle city. Jinir's base of power has always been more in the lower city. And I'm not in a section, so I couldn't go to the spire."

"But he says you stop him? That you keep him from getting more power?" Myriam felt sure there was more to all this. So far, Rauger had spoken the truth. She just felt it.

"Yes. But that was a hard choice. He started using people in ways I didn't like. Trying to find lower city folk who work in the spire to do things for him. Dark things. Steal things. To put this or that into someone's drink or food. And to pay for all this, he leaned on people. Took from them. If someone died or vanished doing work for him, he confiscated everything they owned. I had to step in." Rauger shrugged. "I knew Ralta wouldn't."

"Why not? She doesn't seem like the type." Myriam rather liked Ralta, even if she found the Trinil rather dangerous.

"You need to ask that? You know it." Rauger looked at Myriam with a smile that did not reach his eyes. "She's devoted to him. She's bonded herself to him."

"She's what? Bonded?" Myriam hadn't heard that used before.

"You don't know?" Rauger for once looked less grim and more surprised. "Well, based on what I know, I guess you wouldn't have heard that before. It's also not done much, it's frowned upon. Back when Jinir was still Tarn, she had herself bonded to him. Meaning, she can't go against his orders. Ever. I think Jinir was always annoyed that I never wanted that."

"Ever? For anything?" Myriam at once didn't like the idea. "That sounds... wrong."

"Yes. If he orders it, she must do it. For her, it was a simple decision. You know the way she looks at him?" Rauger sighed. "Hopeless."

Myriam knew what he meant. Ralta was utterly and totally in love with Jinir. Even if Jinir didn't feel the same way. Myriam was sure he liked Ralta, and saw her as useful, but he didn't love her. She still felt a level of pity for the Trinil. *A bad way to be.* "All right, but what does all this have to do with me?" she finally asked. Rauger paused and turned towards a nearby baker's stall. "Are you hungry? I'm hungry."

Myriam didn't care for the fact that he was not answering, but getting closer to the stall brought a grumble to her stomach that she couldn't ignore. It smelled incredible. "Yes." She managed to say as her eyes took in the display. More sweet pastries than she'd ever seen in her life. As well as breads, rolls, many things and all looked delicious.

"Ah Madam Pelit. May I buy two of the hidden boxes? And two crocks of the cold water?" Rauger asked of the woman behind the counter, who smiled at Rauger with a look that screamed she was thrilled to see him.

"Of course. 1 silver for all of it." This Madam Pelit held out a hand. "Please."

"But of course." Rauger pulled out a bright bit of silver, pressing it into the woman's hand. "Thank you, and pick two good ones. Please."

Madam Pelit nodded and rummaged through a counter that Myriam couldn't see in the back. She turned around with two perfect cubes of some kind of bread, crispy brown, and multi layered. She handed each of them to Rauger in a small piece of parchment. "Here, I'll be right back with the water."

Rauger handed her one cube. "If you've never had this, you're in for a treat. Pelit used to bake in the Librarian section until she did some work for Jinir and got caught. She was expelled from the spire and ended up here. I helped her, and here she is."

Myriam was surprised by the texture of the outside, sticky and crunchy. She tore it open to reveal layers of soft white bread filled with cream. One bite later, she was grinning from ear to ear. "This is delicious." Madam Pelit reappeared and handed over two large blue ceramic bottles. Both were ice cold. She nodded and turned away, vanishing back into her stall.

"Madam Pelit is impressive." Rauger agreed as he ate his bread as well. "But I took you there for a reason. I like Jinir. I do. And he does good, he helps many people. But his help always has a price these days. A price that he never thinks about. Madam Pelit is a good person. She helped Jinir by making copies of things she heard while working. Jinir did nothing to help her after she got caught." Rauger shrugged. "I can't work that way."

"But Jinir was a better Tarn than Grib is turning out to be, by far. Grib is… Grib. He is never concerned with most people at all. At least Jinir helps those around him, in promise for future help if he needs it." Rauger took a last bite, finishing his bread before taking a long drink out of one bottle.

"And that leads me to you. I had to do some work, but I know you're a Healer. A powerful one. I know Mikol tried to kill you. I know you are not from the City, you're from the north somewhere. You came here under mysterious circumstances with another person. A William Reis, who is in the Crafters. He is also powerful." Rauger smiled. "How close am I?"

"Very." Myriam answered in between bites of her bread, savoring the taste and texture. "William and I are both well… he's from Palnor. The Reach. I am from right on the southern border of Palnor, so I don't know if I am really a northerner."

"Myriam, anyone born on the other side of the blood sea is a northerner. Anyone." Rauger laughed. "But what now? Jinir knows you met me."

Myriam felt the blood drain from her face. "Ralta! Rauger, I forgot, I didn't think… He's ordered Ralta to remove you."

Rauger's eyes opened wide for a moment. The first time she'd seen him have that reaction to anything. "That could be a problem. What was his exact words? Quick now, tell me."

"He told her you die." Myriam answered, keeping her voice down. "I tried to tell her she didn't have to, but she said she must. She didn't look happy about it. She called you her second oldest friend."

"Did she now?" Rauger's mouth curled up for a moment before he slapped his thigh. "I need my Lutrain. I need to think."

"Lutrain?" Myriam had no idea what he was talking about. "My instrument. The one you saw me with last time. Custom made. I need to think, and plan." Rauger started walking, his pace quick.

Myriam followed. She had nowhere else to go, and despite anything Jinir had said, Rauger so far had been more than helpful. She finished the last scrap of her bread, licking some sticky residue off her fingers. Bad manners, but she was hungry, and it was delicious. They passed through several archways, taking a route that led deeper into the middle city. Each step took them closer to the spire, a place she no longer desired to return to. The buildings grew grander and larger along the lane as they walked. She saw more fine clothes, and people who were servants running here and there on whatever chore they had.

The pace was brisk, and by the time Rauger stopped in front of an inn that was three times larger and grander than any other inn she'd seen, Myriam was winded. She was happy that this place was where they were going. She still hadn't recovered her full strength since the healing. She doubted she ever would.

The inside was as impressive as the outside. Myriam had an eye for a well-run inn because of her family, and this place was perfect. The wood floors were mirrored bright and clean. The furniture showed the signs of careful care and polish, and the bar was waxed and cleaned regularly. And the smell…. No trace of refuse or heavy perfumes that poorly run inns used to mask less savory odors. Just the clean smell of wood, and a slight smoky smell from the fireplace. She smiled at that detail. In a place like the City there was no need for one, yet a fireplace always gave a feeling of comfort, safety. It was a good business decision, and Myriam approved.

"Untis!" A smiling woman came from behind a partition, wiping her hands. "I was hoping you'd be here soon. The afternoon crowd will come in soon." The woman blinked a few times, looking at Myriam with some surprise and a touch of shock. But like a good merchant, the emotions slid away to show a serene smile. "And who is this?"

"My…niece. Gali" Rauger smiled, putting a hand on Myriam's shoulder. "She lives on the eastern end of the lower city, normally."

Myriam swallowed at the small lie but gave the woman a smile. "Pleased to meet you. Your inn is… perfect." That brightened the woman's expression quite a lot. "Why thank you! My name is Vinli. And this is the Whitestone Quarry." Vinli waved her hand around the place. "Started by my husband and I."

"Very pleased to meet you Madam Vinli." Myriam liked this woman right away. "It truly is an inn worth visiting."

"Untis. Why did you hide this dear girl away in the lower city? She has far too good manners to be in that rough place." Vinli pulled two chairs out and sat herself down in one. She pointed to the other chair, eyes on Myriam. "Be a dear and sit Gali, was it? Gali."

Myriam did so, enjoying taking a rest after the stress of the day so far. "It's quite a large inn." She finally said, eyes moving around.

"Yes, well, my late husband believed if we could be big enough, we'd be the finest inn in the whole City." Vinli shook her head. "I agreed, fool that I was. The finest inn needs the best staff, and about three times the work."

Myriam suppressed a laugh at that. It was good for a few minutes to escape everything. Talking to Vinli was like talking to an aunt who was whip smart and friendly. "Does the inn get crowded in the afternoon?" Myriam could see how many empty seats were here right now.

"Oh yes. Well, when Untis plays. The things the man can do with his musical machine. I can't remember what he calls it." Vinli shrugged. "But the man plays and the crowds come."

As if on command, Rauger came back into the large common room, the 'lutrain' in his hands. Stringed with a small bow, it also held a series of keys, like a harpsichord. Rauger held it carefully and smiled, and without a word broke into a multilayered song.

Chapter 49.

Myriam had heard a lot of music in her time. Lutes, pipes, violas, horns, many things. But whatever this lutrain was exactly, she was very impressed. Rauger obviously had years of practice, and playing the complicated thing seemed to be second nature to him. The bow flew across the strings, and his free hand moved across the keys in a complicated pattern, drawing a wall of sound out of the thing that dwarfed its size.

"Untis is so good, isn't he? I mean, you must have heard it a thousand times, being his niece." Vinli smiled and nodded her head in time to the music. "What is your favorite song he plays? Mine is the one he calls the 'Crafter's lament. So sad, but haunting."

Myriam's skin turned cold. She didn't have an answer. "Oh, um… anything he plays. But he never really played for me much as a child. I was always busy, trying to make a living." She did not know if that sounded right or not. Why couldn't have Rauger said he was a friend, or someone he was helping?

Vinli didn't answer, but stood up and swayed to the music. Myriam found herself grateful there wasn't further digging. Whatever song Rauger was playing suddenly ended with a flourish, and he stood quickly. "Vinli, I will be right back. I need to get Gali something before I send her back home."

Vinli's face fell, but she nodded. "Fine. Just fine. I'll check on the cook."

Myriam watched her leave, heading into the back of the inn. She didn't see what was being made, but the smell that came out of the door as it opened was enticing. "Why say I was your niece? She started questioning me."

"Anything else and she would have considered you a rival. Vinli is a bit stuck on me, I am afraid. Or on Untis Treim, at least." Rauger gave a small smile as he looked at the way Vinli had gone. "I am rather fond of her as well, but things are what they are."

"Wait, you use a custom-made instrument as both Untis and Rauger?

And no one puts it together?" Myriam didn't get any of this. "How does that work?" Rauger's small smile broke into a chuckle. "Myriam, in a City full of wonders, no one looks twice at a man carrying this…" Rauger hefted his lutrain. "Besides, my knack helps. I can make people dance."

"Dance? How does that help?" Myriam thought about what Rauger had said. It was true that in a place like this, no one would even think twice about the thing he carried. It just seemed, too easy.

"Ah. But when you're listening to music, and dancing, you don't think about other things. You get lost in it all. At most, all you remember is having a good time. You can't always even remember the player or the songs." Rauger put the lutrain down. "But that's not important now. What is important is what is next."

"But what about Ralta?" Myriam lowered her voice as she spoke. "She's dangerous."

"I know she is. But there's something you're not understanding. Jinir ordered her to kill me, yes? But not WHEN to kill me, correct?" Rauger pointed a long finger at Myriam. "Words matter with bonds. She will eventually have to kill me though."

Myriam paused, thinking what the exact words were that Jinir had used. "Yes, but he said I couldn't see anyone until you had died. And why? What if you died tomorrow? Got run over by a wild cart or something."

Rauger frowned. "That would have been good to know at the start." Rauger's voice tightened. "But you are not bound. His words are just words. I do not know if Ralta will be bound by them, though. As for why, if she doesn't kill me herself, she will die at the same moment I do. That's the nature of a bond, and an order. Now you see why it's rarely done now."

"Sorry." Myriam mumbled. "But what do I do next?"

"You come with me." A voice carried from the front door. *Jinir??*

"Jinir." Rauger's voice was flat. "What are you doing here?"

"Protecting her from you, Rauger. Be glad I do not know where Ralta is right now, or I'd order her to kill you right here, right now. Come Myriam, something interesting has happened." Jinir reached out with a hand. "Something very interesting."

Myriam looked at Rauger, who stood, stone faced, staring at Jinir. Then she turned to Jinir who, while he was mostly hidden by the hood, was smiling as if he had found the key to the house he needed to get into. "Maybe I want to stay here." She stood. "I'm not a pet, you know. I'm not a servant, I'm not bound to you like Ralta is."

That shattered the look of satisfaction on Jinir's face. That same anger as before, a dark, violent anger appeared. "You are MINE. I saved you. You would be dead without me. You owe me EVERYTHING. I may no longer be Tarn, but you forget who I am, little healer."

Myriam didn't flinch. She thrust her chin forwards. "No, I'm not yours. You don't own me. I healed you Jinir. I brought you back to this, and yet, you order me around like an indentured servant?"

Rauger moved at that, stepping between Myriam and Jinir. "Jinir, You are not Tarn. You are lost. You are nothing!" He pointed at the door. "You leave. Now."

Jinir took a step backwards, then stopped. He reached into a pocket in the robe and held up a folded parchment. "No. Because she will want to come with me."

"I will not." Myriam scowled at Jinir. "I trusted you. I even liked you some, but your temper is…"

"I have been called to a meeting. A special meeting. Your presence is needed. AND your friend William will be there." Jinir shook his head. "Myriam, I wish I could make you understand. What all this has done to me, why I do the things I do."

Rauger broke in. "Who is the meeting with?"

"Old friends. You were NOT invited, Rauger." Jinir placed the parchment on a table. "This came from the spire. You, Myriam, can read it." Myriam reached out and took the parchment, feeling the smooth nature of the stuff. It had come from the spire. That was true. Opening it, she skimmed the words; not sure she was believing them. She read it three more times before putting it back on the table, folded back up. "I see."

"Rauger, I have to go." Myriam turned to the bard. "I will, however, find you again."

Chapter 50.

"If you go with him, you may never see daylight again, Myriam. He will lock you up and keep you as a prize." Rauger spoke quickly, ignoring Jinir's grunt. "He's not right in the head."

"He might not be, but I still have to go." Myriam wasn't sure if she believed all that was in the letter, but the chance to see William, talk to him, outweighed the risk. "I wonder how he found us though."

"Do you think that Rauger is the only person I ever had being my ears? He's good, but not the only person capable of listening." Jinir's face held a smile that didn't come close to reaching his eyes. "I've long suspected he was here, but until now the risk didn't outweigh the reward. That letter changed that. And I knew he'd be after you Myriam. Your too good of a prize." "I don't use people like you do, Jinir. I never have." Rauger took a half step towards the former Tarn. "Gods take you Jinir! It doesn't have to be this way between us!"

"Oh, we have a visitor?" Vinli burst from the kitchen. "I'm sorry sir, but the inn doesn't open till another half bell."

"That's fine. I am here for her." Jinir pointed at Myriam. "We are leaving."

"Goodbye Vinli, it was very nice to meet you." Myriam smiled and gave the inn one last look. "I fully approve of this place."

"I will see you soon, UNCLE Untis." Myriam emphasized the Uncle, trying to make sure Jinir picked up on it. The last thing she wanted was to ruin all the work that Rauger had put in here. But Jinir held his temper and questions in check and said nothing. Rauger, for his part, shook his head as if to tell her no. After a moment he locked eyes with Jinir, neither man looking away for a long span. Myriam wondered if they were going to fight like a pair of tomcats after a piece of food. Rauger, however, finally dipped his head. "I will see you soon, far sooner than you think."

Myriam nodded and turned with Jinir towards the door. "I hope so." She added as they walked out into the fading light.

"You did not listen to me Myriam." Jinir kept his voice low, and his hood up, but each word could be heard. "I had hoped you'd learned your lesson."

"What lesson? That you own me? That you control me?" Myriam did not yell, but the steel in her voice was obvious, all the same. "I am not a pet Jinir."

"It was for your safety!" Jinir waved one arm at her, momentarily forgetting he was not supposed to be whole, not yet at any rate. "I can't protect you out here. Not yet."

"Protect me from what? Mikol? He doesn't know I'm alive. Rauger has shown me nothing but kindness. The only person since the day of the accident that has even threatened me has been Ralta." Myriam raised her voice now, not caring if anyone heard them. "I don't care about your power. I don't care about even getting revenge on Mikol. I'm coming for one reason. William. That's it. Be clear Jinir. I will take my chances out here in the City rather than be nothing more than a pawn for you." Myriam growled the words. Her anger boiled up. Anger at the whole stupid situation.

The Unnamed God watched as his army gathered. Legions of his people, men and women, were camped in tight rows, each area flecked with the standard and colors of whatever country they were from. The reds of Palnor dwarfed the rest, but there were large contingents from the Stael to the west, their greens almost blending in with the grass of the field. Yellows marked the expanse of the Silt Islands. There was even a contingent from far off Bimnia, their purple coursers matching the paler purple armor. And mixed throughout were the sigils of various noble houses and powers of his creation.

The unnamed turned to the largest tent canopy he'd ever seen, even in the distant memories. The Gorom. Hiding from the sun, but still here. The agreement he and Grimnor had made was binding. The generals were meeting, coordinating their strategies and designs for the assault on the City.

None had fully understood why they were attacking it, but like with Master Greenhill, the Unnamed has his ways to change that. He didn't enjoy doing things that way, though. Why couldn't his creation be more... devout. Maybe that was being unfair. They had been split for so long, and then without a god at all for generations. They weren't used to the facts of his ascension. They would learn. The crusade would help. Nothing united a people more than war.

Rauger slipped into the shadows, taking a quick path through a series of alleys and then into a stream of people heading towards the spire. That was the third time in a week he'd had to slip away from one of the three men who seemed to appear near him. Two were normal human men, one dressed like a well-off merchant, and the other as a cook's assistant. The kind that went out and about during the day picking up food and whatnot for a kitchen. Normal, safe, and utterly boring jobs.

Yet there was something off about both. The cook's assistant, his work clothes, were always spotless. Rauger had been in enough Inn's to know that was never the case. And the merchant never carried a money pouch. Another sign that he wasn't who he appeared to be. The third man, that was the interesting one. He was dressed like a food stall runner in the lower city. He was greasy and smelled like roasting meat. He stood out some here in the middle city, though not enough to ask a lot of questions.

And more to the point, Rauger had seen him before. Selling a sandwich to Myriam, back when he'd been watching. That one was getting too close. Dangerous. Yet that was the one who Jinir claimed worked for him? Rauger laughed. They all worked for Grib, they had to. No one in the spire would need them, and they didn't work for Jinir, he was sure of it. That left Grib. Poor Jinir, being outmaneuvered by Grib for once.

Rauger would be willing to bet his lutrain that Grib thought he could use Rauger. Rauger had no intention of signing onto that headache. He'd have to make a deal to get Grib's men off him. And there was only one person he could make that deal with. Rauger spat at the thought. Deals like this made his stomach sour. There was too much going on, though. He had to have room to maneuver. He hoped he didn't get stuck in the mud when all this was over.

Chapter 51.

The thumping sound that interrupted his sleep was not welcome. Will lifted his head, gritted his teeth for a second and then threw it back down, hoping that whoever it was would give up and go away. His hopes were not to be fulfilled as the sound grew louder. Whoever was knocking was doing a sparks lot of it. At last, Will sat up. "WHAT?" He grumbled. He'd spent twenty bells at the forge, and he was tired. It was that simple.

"I need to see you. Now." The voice was one he knew well. Rewil. Will rubbed his face, wincing at its unshaven skin and knowing he badly needed to clean up. But he threw on a clean shirt and opened the door to find the Tarn standing there, his expression one of irritation.

"What is this?" Rewil said, thrusting a parchment at Will, who took a step back at the sudden movement. "I thought we discussed this, and you would not talk to her."

"Who?" Will wasn't sure what he was being asked. "Her?"

"Yulisia! In the Chamber of the Source!" Rewil pushed past Will into his room, closing the door behind him as he did so. "I told you not to go."

Will felt the blood drain out of his face and fully woke up. How had Rewil found out? "I… well… I…" Will didn't know what to say.

"Will, I like you. But this is… now what am I going to do with this?" Rewil threw the parchment down on Will's desk. "Read it."

Will picked up the parchment letter, adverting his eyes from Rewil's angry frown. He opened the letter and began to read.

"Tarn Rewil,

While you didn't listen to what I told William Reis, I hope you listen now. I request a private meeting of all parties. You, me, William, Nollew, and two old friends to some of us, Jinir and Myriam. And yes, they are alive. Both of them. We must discuss the truth and make decisions. We haven't been kind to you, Rewil. I know that. But we had reason. Please meet with us and listen. We shall meet in the middle city, the canal underground, in three nights. Ten Bells.

I am still your friend,

Tarn Yulisia."

Will read the second line twice. "Myriam! She will be there?"

"What did Yulisia tell you that you did not mention to me?" Rewil pointed at Will. "I considered you a friend, and a bit of a personal apprentice. This betrayal of my trust, though, it bothers me, Will. As your Tarn, I order you to tell me." Rewil poked Will in the chest with a large finger. "All of it."

Will nodded. "I owe you that. She told me that the person behind the attacks was Tarn Mikol. That no one knew how old he was, or how long he'd been Tarn. That the reason she and Nollew had turned their back on you was because Mikol had influenced them to do so. They hadn't wanted to. And when they ended his control, they put in protections to stop him, but kept up the charade so he didn't suspect." Will blanched. "I am sorry, it sounded so… crazy."

Rewil's scowl had grown while Will talked. "Tarn Mikol is a great man. A good friend. I wouldn't still be Tarn without him. To say he was behind the deaths of Myriam and Jinir…" Rewil frowned. "And Mikol is old. Does it matter that no one knows how old?" Rewil shook his head, closing his eyes as if trying to shake something loose.

"Who is Jinir?" Will pointed to the name in the letter. "It sounds familiar, but I can't place it."

"Former Tarn of the lower city. Grib's predecessor. I liked Jinir. In some ways, he was almost a Crafter. He could use his boon to fix things. Not make new things mind you, but fix things. Just about anything. He couldn't improve it, but he could use his boon to make it as if it was new." Rewil sighed. "Source soured fool went and didn't check a vat in a cloth dying factory in the lower city. Was full of caustic chemicals. There were a dozen vats, but whatever worker had been assigned to empty that one prior to Jinir's work hadn't done so." "It exploded. Jinir was killed in a horrible, painful manner." Rewil frowned and took the letter back from Will. "Why would they claim he was alive? Unless they used his name to get me there, and Myriam's name to get you there. But what game are they playing?"

"Are you sure they are?" Will pointed out. "Part of that seems true, based on what you said. You don't know how old Mikol is do you? Or how long he's been Tarn?"

"It doesn't matter that I don't know." Rewil snapped back. "Mikol is a GOOD MAN."

"Think Rewil." Will stepped back, hard to do in his small room with someone the size of Rewil standing in the middle of it. "If that's true, why couldn't more of it be true?"

"Because." Rewil muttered. "Just…because."

Will felt like he was balancing on a narrow ledge, something he was very much not good at, but he had to keep going. If there was any chance that Myriam would be there, he needed to be there as well. "Listen, when I spoke to Yulisia before, in the chamber, she said when you try to think about those things, Mikols age and how long he'd been Tarn, the thoughts sort of skitter away. Then you can't think about them anymore. Is that how it works for you?"

Rewil did nothing for a long moment, then nodded. "But that could be Nollew doing that to me. That man is cunning. This could all be a trap."

Will shrugged. "Yes. It could be. But it also might not be. If there's a chance that Myriam could be there, I must see. And you, I know how much you have felt the betrayal of Yulisia and Nollew. If it really was Mikol's influence? You could get back two of your oldest friends?"

Rewil finally sat down on Will's bed. "I don't know Will. Going to the canal underground? Late at night? It's one of the places where it's very hard to read things. The water and the power makes things muddled."

"Isn't that good, though? Would that keep Nollew in check some?" Will knew Rewil was close to accepting the need to go, but he needed a push. "And you said you liked this Jinir? Why not go. We will be careful. I'll wear my new armor." Will pointed to the copper gold breastplate and bracers. "That might help."

Rewil nodded. "Fine. But I'm putting a few construct guards as near as I can." He looked at the armor Will had pointed at. "You made that yesterday?"

Will pulled out the new hammer. "Yes, and this. It was time to change. I am no longer the Forgemaster of Amder. I'm just Will now."

Rewil laughed then, the first laugh Will had heard in a while from the man. "You are nothing simple, though. What is it made of? Both of them? I thought you had a hammer?"

"I did. But none of it was right. I used Wight Iron and an item that came with me here, from the Anvil, to make the new hammer. Then I melted down my old hammer with Wight Iron AND my old armor to make the new stuff." Will shrugged. "Honestly, part of me is surprised it all alloyed well. It was a strange mix." Will thought about the conversations he'd had yesterday. Duncan, and Haltim. They seemed too unreal now. They had been memories. Brought on by the release of so much mixing of powers.

"I would say so." Rewil thumped the breastplate, listening to the vibration with a surprised expression when he heard the sound it made. "What was that...?"

"It does that." Will blurted out, now suddenly not wanting Rewil to investigate the items. "So, are we going? I've never left the spire the whole time I have been here. Might be fun. What's this canal?"

Rewil stood and ran a hand through his hair and beard. "Ah yes, I forget that. The lower city is surrounded by a wall, right? In between the lower and middle city is a circular canal. It's ancient. There's a room, the canal underground, where the power and machines that make it work are located. It's an old place. But it keeps working. I once assigned a few crafters there, worried that it was going to break one day, but they did nothing for an entire year before I recalled them. Sent no one else, was a waste of time."

"But why does it need the power?" Will asked. "It's water."

"Well, actually it's not. Well, it is, and it isn't. It's fast, very fast. Keeps people from crossing it except for the bridges. Also, it's got unusual properties. Any trash, waste, anything like it, that ends up in the water is gone. It vanishes. The water is permanently clean. What happens to those items is a mystery. We've tried to find out before. Well, I haven't, but other Tarns have. No one ever has figured it out."

"Sounds well worth seeing at least." Will threw in. *Even if I don't plan on being here much longer.* He would tell Rewil, but not yet. Not yet.

Rewil fell silent long enough that Will wondered if he should say something. "Fine. We will go. But Will, if you ever keep things like this from me again, you will no longer be welcome in the Crafters section. Do you understand?"

Will resisted the urge to cheer and only nodded.

Mikol reread the letter one of his fingers had brought to him. The man was a vermin killer, making sure no mites ate the older books in the library. Mikol doubted if any Librarian ever learned the man's name. They simply ignored him. Though Mikol didn't know his name either, he didn't really matter, except for what he could bring to him.

And this time he'd brought a letter. A letter that had been on the desk of Yulisia. A letter that spelled out the meeting between Yulisia, Rewil, Nollew, William Reis, Jinir, and Myriam. A great assembly of powerful and notable people.

And a meeting that he was determined to disrupt if possible, or at least listen in on. They had chosen a place he couldn't listen to though. The canal underground was one of the handful of locations where the power was too wild, too concentrated for him to be able to work his skills.

Mikol needed quiet to work. He was no caster, using brute force and direct methods. His use of the boon required great skill and a delicate touch. Places where the power rushed around made it impossible for him to concentrate. Thankfully, there were only a handful of them, and only the underground was outside the spire. He wouldn't even be able to get close enough to make sure Jinir died. *Not in the underground at least, but maybe outside it?* He'd need maps of the area; he had not left the spire in many long years. What memories he had of the middle city were fuzzy. But maybe, if he could get close enough as the meeting broke apart, he could remove Jinir.

He would be free of the potential problems that Jinir being alive would cause and bind Grib even closer to him. The Gorom was showing more of a spine than Mikol wanted him to have, and the death of Jinir, for real this time, might push that Tarn back into line.

There was one problem, though, one that he had no way of knowing the answer to. If Myriam HAD healed Jinir, she might have found his little gift he'd left. Myriam might be young and inexperienced, but she was very talented, and had an eye for detail. And if she had found it, all this planning would be for nothing.

He needed more information. A lot more information. And he would need it quickly. But his list of people he could influence was small. Rewil was a possibility, but Nollew might be on the lookout for that. Nollew and Yulisia were out. He couldn't get close enough to either Jinir or Myriam. Which left, William.

Based on what he knew, the odds were high that William had been warned about Mikol. It would be a foolish risk to think otherwise. Direct influence was out then. With someone as full of the power as William was, and with forewarning, there would be no way to turn William into a puppet on a string.

It had to be something more subtle. He needed information. Mikol wracked his memory, trying to think of how to use the boon to get what he needed. Right before dawn, the idea came to him. He wasn't sure it would work, but if it didn't, he wouldn't pay the price. He'd have to move fast, though. The meeting was soon, which didn't give him much time.

Chapter 52.

Will hated waiting. After meeting with Rewil, he had spent hours nervously thinking of what to say to Myriam when he saw her next. *Sorry, I blamed you for everything. Let's leave this place because it's crazy.* Yes, that would be a good idea. Will knew he had to come up with something better than that.

Will knew the wait would be better if he had something to work on. But he had nothing. He'd not returned to the construct project after the explosion of the quickway. And the investigation with Rewil into that explosion had hit a dead end. They had their resonance theory, which fit all the information they had, but they still didn't know one important piece. Why had the construct drawn in the extra power in the first place? He had no idea. Rewil didn't either. Though Rewil hadn't seemed to want to push the investigation much further. He had been happy to realize that the quickway itself wasn't the cause.

Soon after, the quickways had been put back into use, and the damaged one repaired and rebuilt, and that was that. Will had been asked to help with the repair, but he'd declined. Then he'd thrown himself into his mapping project and helping others with their work. The only real crafting he'd done as of late was the hammer and the armor. He knew Rewil wanted him back in the workroom. That was obvious. Several of the older crafters he'd run into had dropped hints about it as well. 'Idle hands lead to dangerous decisions.' One senior crafter had said, wagging a finger at Will. While he had appreciated that little piece of advice, Will still couldn't bring himself to return to the workshop.

Even if he thought about it, all he could think of was Myriam. Myriam falling, trying to save her life, the utter terror of it. How he couldn't have done anything to help, but still the idea haunted him. He had hoped the feeling would lessen now that he knew she was alive. Sadly, it hadn't. Bored, Will decided to recheck all his maps, at least in his section. It was something to do, and he felt more relaxed when he worked alone. And it helped him feel better about the situation here. Seeing the people who live in the rest of the City, actually seeing them, felt good. Even if most of them never spoke to him and gave him odd looks if he appeared in the hallways and secret ways if he was wearing Crafter garb.

Will looked down at himself and grimaced. As a matter of habit, he always wore his crafter's leather apron. He took that off, placing it to the side. He looked more like anyone else, except for the hammer. This new hammer drew attention, somehow even more than the old one. And that one had been golden with the mark of the power on it!

This one was gray, and shimmered, yet it drew the eye right to it. How that worked, Will didn't think he wanted to know. It was special, that's all he knew. But should he leave it here? The idea of leaving it behind did not appeal to him. He knew he would not be gone long, yet the desire to keep it with him grew.

Finally, he placed it back on his hip. No, it needed to stay with him. He wished he had a coat, or some other covering that he could wear over everything that would hide it at his side. He had none, however. The thought made him grin in spite of himself. A Reacher, without a coat.

He left his room, making his way down a quiet hall. One thing he did like about the Crafter's section is that everything here was very self-determined. Back at the Guild, there had been so many classes. Group instruction, and then having the student do it. Here, it was 'go do it' and let us know if it works. Older crafters were always around to help and give advice, but Rewil very much wanted everyone to try anything they could think of.

The hall ended in a staircase. Not the main one, but still large enough. Will made his way down into the lower parts of the spire, careful to stay out of the way. He didn't know why; it felt like he should. No Crafters cared, it seemed, as he passed some others that he knew, and they all ignored him. At last, he came to a wall down a short side hallway that had a panel that would allow him access to one of the main Greystone passages. He didn't know what they were called, but if those who lived in the spire lived in the whitestone hallways, then this was the Greystone.

He pushed a small section, and it sunk in, opening a door that he never would have known was there if he hadn't marked it on his map. He wasn't even using the power to find the openings, if only to say to himself he didn't need it. Stepping through the door, he found himself in an alcove he'd been in a few times. An alcove that opened into a wide Greystone hallway. There must have been three dozen people he could see heading one way or the other.

 Some were deep in conversation, others walked alone. A few glanced his way, gave a nod and then, their eyes drawn to the hammer for a moment, gave him a confused look before heading away. Maybe he should have left the hammer behind as well.

 He stepped into the flow of foot traffic, not sure of where he was going. He'd never actually followed one of these passages very far. He knew they exited somewhere else outside the spire, but that was it. Rewil hadn't even expressed any curiosity about it. Will frowned, and neither had he. Why had he never wondered what was on the other end? He walked, watching people come and go through various doors and hallways that connected to this main one. He could hear in the background a larger hum that got louder the more he walked. Soon he could see why. This hallway was merging with another, one that was filled with three times as many people. It was huge in comparison. Still the same basic gray stone, uncarved and solid.

 But it was not undecorated. There were scrawled pictures and words often. None of them complimentary about the spire or those who live there. He often saw the words 'boon baskers' or 'spire lords' written, usually with mentions of anatomy. It wasn't everywhere, but it wasn't rare either. Will actually felt some relief at seeing it. So, at least someone cared about how screwed up this system was. No one in the spire seemed to even understand the problem.

 Most of the pictures and words attacked the Casters, and in second place, the Crafters. He frowned at one picture of what was supposed to be Tarn Rewil. Eating people while the city burned in the wreckage of what had to be a quickway. It was the first sign that the accident was being thought of differently in the City than the spire. "I don't think they got Rewil's nose right." A man's voice came from behind Will.

 Will turned around to see a tall man, thin, with greying hair and a pleasant smile on his face. Plain and simple clothes, except for the strange instrument on his back.

"My name is Rauger. It is a pleasure to meet you." The man spoke in a low voice, leaning in so other Will could hear. "Yes, the nose is wrong."

Will didn't know what to say. This was unusual. Why was this man talking to him? It felt off. "I wouldn't know." He answered, deciding to pretend he knew nothing about the Crafters or the spire.

"Yes, you do William Reis. You know very much. Did you think that your activities here would go unnoticed?" Rauger nearly touched the hammer at Will's side, but kept a gloved hand off it. "And carrying that?"

Will felt the blood leave his face. "How do you know my name?"

"Well, for one, I've been watching. And two, I've spoken to Myriam lately." Rauger stood up straight, a full hand and a half taller than Will. "She is an interesting person, Myriam VolFar."

Will didn't know what to say. Excitement and a twinge of fear filled him. What was the game this man was playing? "And?" he managed to say.

The man gave him an odd look, as if that was the last thing he expected William to do. "And she is safe. For now. I am not so sure about in a few days, after this meeting."

"How? How do you know about that?" Will was confused and felt like he was slipping on ice. The last thing he expected was to have a conversation like this.

"I have an interested party, let's say. I mean you no harm, or Myriam, for that matter. But I need to know what will happen in the meeting. I need to hear it." Rauger looked around, the workers flowed around them. "Maybe let's get a place a little less busy. I'll explain."

Will realized that the man was right, this Rauger. "Follow me." Will headed back the way he had come. He mentally recalled his map, and soon found one of the smaller alcoves that led to a door under the librarian's section. "This should work."

Rauger's expression was amused now. "A good choice." He finally said. "I am Rauger Minter. I have had several positions over the years, but I am currently a solo player in the play that is the City in Blue." Rauger gave off a small bow. "Bard, friend to the City, and occasionally, collector of information."

"Spy?" Will retorted. "Why, by the sparks, should I give you any information?"

Rauger shrugged and was silent for a moment, looking out into the Greystone hallway. "I was approached about getting information. I was offered a handsome reward to get it. A reward I could use to help these people. You can see it, can't you? You're not of the City. Spire folk don't even think about this place. I doubt even half know it exists. The place is cracking. The lower city is roiled by turmoil brought about by Jinir's desire to return to power. Your friend, Myriam, is in the thick of it, though she truly doesn't want to be."

"She wouldn't." Will replied. "She'd say she was an innkeeper's daughter and none of this has anything to do with her. Though she knows as much as I do, that means nothing."

"Innkeeper's daughter?" Rauger smiled and shook his head. "That explains it."

"Explain what?" Will questioned the man. "You still haven't answered my question. Why should I give you any information?"

"Spoken like a Crafter, straight and to the point." Rauger fell silent for a moment, then shook himself. "I am not your enemy. I am, however, trying to stop Jinir. He was my friend once. A good friend. But after his accident things changed."

"Accident? You mean when Mikol tried to kill him?" Will crossed his arms, taking a step back from Rauger. "You aren't doing very well at this." Rauger nodded. "It can be difficult you know, with people like you and Myriam. Your attitudes are different, harder to predict. Yes, when Mikol tried and failed to kill him. I don't like Mikol either, but that's not the point here." Rauger paused and stepped deeper back into the shadows. "And now, your part is here."

Will was about to ask what he meant when suddenly, he couldn't move. A feeling like raw ice shot up his spine, and his body jerked into place. He could see Rauger take the thing off his back and lean against the wall.

"Tell me when to play." Rauger said to someone that Will couldn't see.

"Keep quiet. This is hard. He's far stronger in the power than anyone else I've ever done this to. Our mutual friend had better appreciate this." The voice was unknown to Will. But he had worse things to think about. His vision doubled, and an echo seemed to book around him. It hurt. By the sparks, it hurt. He felt as if he was being torn in two.

A groan slipped out of whoever was behind Will. "It's done. But I'll never do that again. Tell our friend that our debt is over. I don't know why he wanted such a tiny simulacrum, but it doesn't matter. Play now."

"He is not my friend." Rauger said, taking a small glowing orb from whomever was behind Will. And then he played. A soft tune, then faster. It soon became a whirlwind of sound that Will was sucked into.

Will couldn't think. Everything was the music. Will danced to the tune, body swaying and tapping in time to a rhythm that was more felt than heard. He'd never danced before in his life, but now, now he had to dance. He HAD to. No fear, no embarrassment, nothing but the dance. And then it was over. Will panted, sweat clung to him, and an exhaustion he could feel in his bones. "What, wahhh.." He managed to say. He'd been looking at some pictures and then… he was here.

"I'm glad you are all right. You slipped and hit your head. I brought you here and played you some music to make you feel better, to calm you. I'm glad you are doing better." The man nodded to Will. "I'd better be on my way." "Who… are you?" Will managed to say.

"Untis. But it doesn't matter. Have a good day, sir. And I'd go rest, you hit your head rather hard." The tall man, this Untis, gave one last look at Will and left, walking out into the hallway and disappearing.

Will felt horrible, and his head was screaming at him. Yes, a bed sounded good. Maybe he shouldn't explore too far down those tunnels. Will made his way back to the crafters section and finally to his room, head still hurting, and a strange echo in his ears.

Rauger watched Mikol approach. He did not like the man. In fact, he rather hated him. But sometimes, arrangements had to be made. He would pass over the tiny simulacrum that caster person had made, and in return, Mikol would pull Gribs hunters off things. A deal he didn't like, but one that was needed.

"Do you have it?" Mikol spoke from under a dark brown hood. "Was he able to make one?"

"Yes. But he said to tell you that things are even. He had a hard time making it, he said." Rauger pulled out the small green orb that glowed and shifted as you looked at it. A tiny thing, not sure how it could be useful.

"He doesn't get to decide that. I do. But that's not your worry. I will make sure Grib drops his investigation and questioning." Mikol reached out. "But that is mine, now."

Rauger hesitated. How sure was he that Mikol would follow through? He'd only dealt with him twice before, and both times, he had, yes, but the stakes were higher now. MUCH higher. "What assurances do I have?"

"The assurance you will get is this. I will do it. Grib is wearing on me some. I wonder if he should step down. Who could I setup as the next Tarn of the City?" Mikol pulled his hood down. "But I do need that."

Rauger almost laughed at the offer. "And tie myself to you? I think not. But you have held onto your bargains before. You had better again." Rauger passed over the tiny orb. "I don't see the reason for such a tiny thing. It will only last a week, or less."

"Keep to your own thoughts, Rauger." Mikol pulled his brown hood back up. "You don't need to worry about it."

Rauger watched the man go, wondering if he had made the right choice. He'd liked Will as much as he liked Myriam. It was refreshing to find people that had their outlook. Mikol was dangerous, but predictable. He'd bought himself some time, and Rauger planned to make use of it. Ralta was out there still, and while not exactly hunting him, he knew her well enough to know she was keeping an eye out. Dangerous times in the City. Dangerous times.

Chapter 53.

Mikol held up the tiny orb. He was pleased, though he'd hoped for a larger one. Considering how much power that William held, though, it had been a hard job to even make this one. He had always found it strange that the stronger the boon, the harder it was to make a simulacrum. A tiny simulacrum was the best he could hope for with the boon that William had.. A fraction of a copy of William Reis. Enough that he could, he hoped, use it to spy on William and the meeting.

Mikol put the orb away and made his way back to near his section before removing the brown robe and leaving it on a chair in an empty room. The healer's section had several of these, unused. Still, as he ascended back to his office, he passed others and was forced to nod and acknowledge people as he went. Thankfully, he avoided any of the older healers. They often wanted to pin him down about when he was going to step down, and then he'd have to waste power on them. Pushing their concerns away with a feeling of certainty that Mikol was still in his prime. The workings weren't hard, yet he didn't want to waste the time.

His office was empty, and he ordered the dull looking young man at the door to make sure he wasn't disturbed. Mikol closed the door behind him and sat at his desk, gathering his thoughts and his boon. This would not be an easy working. Mikol had never actually tried this, at least not this way. When he'd influenced the construct, that had been a hard leap to make happen. The only reason it had worked with the fact that it was run by a simulacrum. A copy of a lower city worker. Or a copy of his mind, and only partially. Enough to operate the machine.

This was a tiny copy of William Reis, and he was going to try to link it back to the real William Reis, and then, using his boon, listen through Will's ears. Thankfully, he knew where Will could be found. He'd been very clear to Rauger to make sure that William went back to his room afterwards. Rauger was useful. Once he was done with all this, he'd need to devote some time to making sure he was more under control. Mikol had always rather discounted the middle city and lower city as not worth the attention. Recent events had shown though that they needed more hands-on direction. Regardless of what Rauger wanted, he'd make an excellent Tarn to control.

But that was in the future. Right now, he needed to focus on this. Mikol gathered his boon, building it up as much as he could. It was an irritation to him that these two outsiders, William and Myriam had access to far more of the power than he could ever hope for. With their connection to the source, and his years of experience, no one would ever stand a chance against him.

Yet, this was how it was, so he'd better move forward with what he had. Carefully, he reached forth with a featherlight touch, feeling out the tiny fragment of William Reis. Mikol jerked back, nearly dropping the orb. His head echoed with the scream of anger that had responded to his touch. Mikol readied himself and reached forth again, trying for an even smaller feeling.

He had to find it. He'd examined half a dozen of the simulacrums, as carefully as he could, of course. He wished he'd thought of using his boon to control them when they had been in higher use. With the advent of the constructs, they had fallen out of favor. Yet, all the ones he'd investigated had a single spot where he could overlay his power. An artifact of their creation, somehow. He'd even compared the person and their simulacrum once. The same point didn't exist in the actual person, at least not in the same way.

No, it was something unique to these creations. This was going to be the hardest one yet, he could already tell. For one, this tiny thing had been made in pain and hurt, which already clouded its patterns. The other was that it was weak. That had been the tradeoff. Having something like this made would normally be considered useless, a strange and silly waste of power. Yet, for Mikol, it was the answer. He pushed, ready for the spike in emotions this time. The scream of pain and hurt was strong, but now that he was prepared, Mikol could brush it away. He'd have to lower that soon. If he was successful in the binding, that amount of raw emotion would make it too hard to listen.

He pushed in further, the feather of his power becoming a needle. Razor sharp and so thin, it might not even exist if it had been a physical thing. He pushed, searching for the one area he could connect to bind to. Minutes passed, and Mikol blinked as the sweat started rolling down his face. He wished he could wipe it off, but he had to concentrate, fully. He shuddered as he sent a working into his own mind, one that allowed him to ignore the sensation.

Where was it? Mikol felt the tiredness seep in. This level of control was exact and could exhaust him if he wasn't careful. Still, he pushed, and finally he got a sense of something. Something warped, something off, a minor fracture in the wholeness of this tiny copy. *THERE!* Mikol latched onto that speck and threw the binds onto it. He had to work fast; the exhaustion was growing, and the anger and rage that lived in this tiny mind was fighting back. A lurching, falling feeling came, along with a rush of power that made Mikol grunt in agony. A storm of raw power swirled around his connection, threatening to destroy it.

For a long moment, Mikol was sure it had and that this plan of his was lost. Yet, the storm died, and his connections stood. Not his best work, but it held. Mikol gathered what power he could and used his new connection to calm the anger, feeling the tiny fragment of Will that he held respond. The rage ebbed with some effort. The pain was still there, but less raw, less present.

He had done it. He was now bound to this simulacrum. It would hold long enough for this without him having to remake it, a fact he was very pleased about. He wasn't sure he could do that again. Working with such a tiny target was hard enough, but one so steeped in the power, and so full of sorrow and hurt…

It didn't matter. He had done it, and that was good enough. He released the power now, still feeling the connection. Good. Mikol wiped his face with his robe, surprised at how wet it was. This is the most exhausted he'd been in years.

He couldn't rest, though. There was still more to do. Mikol gathered himself again, hoping this would be easier. He'd not exactly tried this before. The thought had only come to him after healing a young caster who had made a simulacrum of herself. The young lady had made the copy and forced a crude connection to its mouth.

It had been a prank, one that would have allowed her to have the silent simulacrum speak with her voice. She'd think it, and the copy would say it. Of course, it had gone bad, but that was more because of her lack of control than a flaw in the underlying working.

Mikol's new working would be far more passive. He would link the simulacrum to Will's hearing. Meaning anything Will heard, the simulacrum would hear, and through the connection, Mikol would hear. If it worked, it would open up a whole new way to keep things in control. No more having to wait for reports, no more information filtered through other's feelings and judgements.

If it worked. Mikol paused and then, knowing the path from his office to William Reis's room, sent out a tendril of power. Searching the way, keeping it small and unnoticeable. More often than not, he used the pathways the power always used; it was far easier. When Will left the city for this meeting, it would not be as easy to keep the connection, but he was sure he could manage. Even through the headache noise of the canal underground.

The tendril flowed under the floor and into Will's room. He could sense the man asleep. Good. That would make it simpler. Sleep turned off some of the normal defense the mind used on its own to stop this sort of thing. Mikol wasn't completely sure why, but the mind asleep was almost a different person. The tendril gathered and struck, hitting like a viper. It flowed into Will's ears, his body and unconscious mind not even registering the power.

Mikol quickly pushed and made his way to where hearing lived. His age gave quick and careful movement, and the connection bloomed. Mikol felt his stomach lurch as the link formed. For a long moment, his vision doubled. But it was Will's room overlayed on his office. His mind stretched and nearly snapped with the strain. But as fast as it came, the feeling faded. Mikol took a deep breath, releasing his off-hand. Speck of red appeared where he'd clenched his fist hard enough for his fingernails to draw blood.

But he had done it. Mikol focused, and he could hear everything in Will's room. Not that there was much to hear other than the man's breathing. It made Mikol's head hurt some, a dull ache. He could live with it, though. He could now hear everything said in this meeting. Mikol was back on top.

He pulled his power back with a sigh; glad he'd not needed to do this with a conscious Will. This had been a particularly rough working, but a good learning experience. He wasn't sure he'd be doing that again in a hurry.

"You have all been gathered for a single purpose. In a land far away, there lies a city. A City that spits in the face of the gods. A City that dares to play with powers beyond what any mortal can control. A City that even now, gathers its strength, so that one day, it can control all." The Unnamed God hovered a few feet off the ground, clad in glowing armor again. "We must strike before they do so."

The Unnamed God looked at the assembled force. Forty thousand fighters. Men and women. Another fifteen thousand Gorom. All armed with weapons made by the Guild. While not anything equal to the power the Priesthood used to sell things at too rich nobles, all these would take three times longer to dull, and wouldn't snap without a mighty effort. Even the arrows were blessed by the Unnamed.

"Spare no one, but one. There is a woman, Myriam VolFar. She must be spared and brought to me." The Unnamed God sent a vision of Myriam to all who were gathered. A strong woman, dark haired and green eyed. "All others may meet the end they so deserve, if they get in your way."

Off to one side sat huge piles of dark black rods. Anchors. And with them, Gorom wearing thick leather gloves. They would plant the devices on the battlefield. The bare metal touching the skin caused problems for most mortals. Humans very much so. Gorom, much less, even so, problems. With his creation, holding the anchors with bare hands for any length of time could kill, though for some, it drove them insane.

"We leave now. My brother Grimnor has made a tunnel, a special tunnel that will allow us all fast passage to this evil place. When the sun rises, we strike, and when the sun sets, the City will be no more!" The Unnamed raised a hand, the roars from his people, his creation, echoed around him.

Chapter 54.

Will stood in the hallway outside Rewil's private workroom, trying to keep himself calm. He was not, he decided, doing a very good job. After wiping his hands on his pants for the third time, Will wondered if he should knock. Rewil was taking his time. The meeting was tonight. Soon. He'd finally get to see Myriam again.

I have no idea what I will say to her, though. Will considered actually talking to her with some fear. If she was angry with him still for his foolish anger when they arrived here, this could go poorly. Though Mikol had said she was coming to see him when the whole quickway explosion happened, right? But could he even trust Mikol? The whole thing, all the confused backstabbing and blame, gave Will a headache. Rewil's door opened, revealing the Tarn standing there, clad in more formal garb than Will had ever seen him in. Still the standard crafter gear, but for once a robe, dark gray with silverlace accents. Rewil also had a bracer on. Just one bracer. Will wasn't sure what to make of either change.

"Will." Rewil greeted him, his voice lacking the upbeat tone it normally held. "Let's get this meeting done."

"Yes, Tarn Rewil." Will could tell that Rewil had no desire to be part of this. "Thank you." Will finally added.

Rewil said nothing back, but did nod, and looked to relax after he touched the bracer on his wrist. Rewil closed his eyes and kept a finger on the bracer for a silent moment before the first grin Will had seen that night appeared. "It works!"

"What works?" Will asked as they started walking. Will followed Rewil, mostly because he did not know how to get to this canal underground that he'd heard so much about.

"Ahha! You don't know, that's right." Rewil held up the wrist with the bracer. It was thick and smooth, except for a few carvings that made little sense to Will. "This Will is something new. Remember our discovery that the reason the quickway had exploded was the construct had an error and had overloaded on power?" "Yes." Will still knew they were missing something. Something obvious. It still bothered him if he allowed himself to think about it.

"This little device allows me to check all the remaining simulacrum constructs. I tied them all together, at least enough for me to read them. But I wasn't sure if it would work away from the workshop. The early version was powered the way most things are now, with a direct power source. It didn't work when I was outside the workshop, I couldn't get one to fit in this bracer. BUT I had a simulacrum made for this… and it works!" Rewil lowered his arm. "I feel better knowing I'll never be surprised by that again."

Will understood the idea, but didn't like it. He found simulacrum to be… disturbing still. He didn't discuss it with Rewil, or anyone else, but the thought of making a copy of someone. Or a magical 'version' of someone and forcing it to do something until it faded away seemed cruel. Slavery almost. Will's thoughts were stopped when Rewil turned a corner and paused in front of a blank wall. Will looked around. He wasn't sure he knew where they were. He'd not paid close attention as they had walked. It hadn't been far, yet none of this looked familiar.

"So, mapper of the Greystone ways, do you know this one?" Rewil touched the wall and pushed. Hard. The wall flexed in a way it shouldn't have, and then, with a very loud pop sound, sprung open.

Will felt the pressure change. "No. What was that?" Leaning forward, Will traced the edges of the door at the door itself. While it looked like the same material that was used everywhere in the spire, it wasn't.

"That is a rarity. In fact, it's the only door I am aware of that does that. It's known only to Tarns. Well, and you now." Rewil paused and frowned. "I shouldn't have shown you that, I suppose. Don't put it on your maps." Rewil stepped through. "This is the direct way from the spire to the canal underground. It's a straight line. No connections to the other Greystone ways. As best we can tell, it was made at the same time the canal was."

"Why is it a secret?" Will asked as he followed Rewil. The Greystone passage looked like all the other ones he'd seen, at least at first. Plain, dark gray, and sparsely lit. That was the first clue that at least something was different. While the normal passages were torch lit, this used glows. The other difference was the smell. The air was damp, wet even.

"The canal underground isn't well understood, as I explained. It's a strange place. The power flows strongly there, and in unpredictable ways. It does, however, make working the power, any working, hard. The main reason we keep it a secret is simple, it's dangerous." Rewil led the way on as the passage stretched on behind them.

Will reached out to touch the wall, surprised at the level of wetness. For a moment he remembered being underground, in the Gorom caves, and then the Vinik hive. He suppressed a slight shudder. He'd never felt comfortable with the Vinik, the superficial but real resemblance to giant insects still bothered him.

"Will?" Rewil had paused and was waiting for him to answer.

"What? Sorry, I was thinking about the time I spent in the Gorom caves. And with the Vinik." Will wiped his damp hand on his pants again. "What was the question?"

"If you were ready to meet Myriam, we are almost there." Rewil asked. "You know, I never asked, what were the Gorom areas like? My grandfather, or it was my great grandfather? I can never remember. He was a Gorom."

"Odd." Will answered without much thought. "Imagine coming from a world of forest and mountains. And entering a world of strange purple light, glowing tattoos, white glowing skin, and fearsong. Strange creatures attacking you…all the while trying to follow a Gorom who doesn't like you much."

"Doesn't sound like much of a fun trip." Rewil shook his head. "Sounds rather strange."

"It was. I don't think you all in the City understand how different things are here. Out there, Gorom are white, covered with glowing skin lines, and talk about Grimnor, constantly. Here, Gorom have normal skin, no tattoos, and even have hair. Out there, Trinil are a forest dwelling people who can tell if anyone is lying. They never allow outsiders into what cities they have. Here, they are tall thin people, though they have some affinity to the power that others don't from what I've seen." "True. Maybe we should have people leave more, explore outside our borders. The outside world might do some good." Rewil frowned. "Though it could as much open up more problems."

"That it could. The idea isn't a bad one, my Tarn." Will smiled despite himself. "We are close, you said?"

"Hmmm? Oh, yes. Yes. Further down this passage, and then through a door. I find myself nervous Will. Nervous and worried. If this is a trap, we've walked into it. If it's not, then I've been wrong for years about things. Both thoughts don't make me look all that wise."

"But, standing here and talking about it doesn't get us through that door." Rewil smiled. "Come. Besides, I want to test the bracer on the construct there. It's also an old simulacrum model."

Will didn't answer, but followed Rewil all the same. Soon, looming in front of them in the dark, was a huge gray and blue door. The colors swirled in whatever it was made of, for all the world looking like moving water, which Will assumed was the point.

Rewil paused before the door, taking a moment to gather himself. Will was surprised at how nervous Rewil appeared to be. He'd never seen Rewil be this out of sorts. He watched as Rewil smoothed his hair twice, straightened his clothing, and even wiped his hand on his pants several times. Even when the quickway accident had happened, he'd not been this unsure. With a shove, the door swung open, and a bright light bloomed from the open door. Will followed Rewil in, taking stock of his surroundings. The room they were in was large. Very large. On the far side was a canal looking structure, full of raging twisting water. There was little sound coming from the canal, despite the churning blackness it contained. Will found that strange.

Near the water were enormous cylinders of different metals and glasses. Some tinted, some not. He could see liquid in a few, but all seemed to thrum with power. Will shifted his perception a bit and closed his eyes as the sudden blue glare shocked him. This place was bathed in the power, literally. It flowed around him in patterns that were unlike the ones in the Source's Chamber. There the patterns had been many, but gentler. A feeling of age and waiting had hung there. Here, the power may have been less by a small amount, but it raged. A crashing, sweeping torrent. He understood why working the power here was dangerous. You could never tell what was going to happen in a place like this. Finally, farthest from the canal, sat a circle of chairs. Six chairs. One obviously sized for Rewil. So, someone was already here.

"Hello Rewil. Hello William. I'm pleased to see you. And regardless of what you may think, I do mean that." Yulisia stepped out from the far end of the chamber, from where Will couldn't see. There must be a door hidden by the cylinders. They hadn't come in the way he and Rewil had entered, he was sure.

"Good evening, Tarn Yulisia. And Tarn Nollew." Will said, guessing that the Tarn of the Casters was here as well.

"Good guess, Crafter Reis." Tarn Nollew appeared as well, right behind Yulisia.

Will had not seen Nollew before and found himself disappointed with the man. This was the mighty Caster? Will thought he looked more like a frumpy, middle-aged bureaucrat. He was the man who drew so much respect? Will bowed, though, if only because he thought it was expected.

Nollew paid him no attention and instead approached Rewil. A Rewil who stood shock still, towering over Nollew with a very unpleasant expression on his face. "Rewil. You may not believe me. But before anything else, I want to apologize. At first, I was under the thumb of Mikol, and I couldn't, well, I couldn't stop myself. Then, after I discovered the truth, I played the part to keep Mikol from guessing we had broken free. But Yulisia and I hurt you, old friend. I hurt you. And I am sorry. I wish I could say more, but a sorry will be all I can say."

Will watched Rewil, curious to see how he would react. It had been obvious that he thought of the betrayal by Nollew and Yulisia as a very painful event. People he'd been close to attacking him not for his work, or his opinions, but for who he was, for the very blood that flowed through him. It had deeply hurt the man. Rewil, however, had dropped the frown, and even relaxed enough for it to be seen. Will watched him take a shuddering breath before speaking. "I don't know what to say, Nollew. To either of you. I want to believe you. Wanting to think that you didn't insult and demean me because of what you think, but because you were under some kind of influence. I'm not even sure why I came." Rewil finally added.

"To find out the truth, I assume." A new voice came. Walking in from the same direction as Yulisia and Nollew had come stood a smaller man, hooded, and behind him, a young woman.

Will broke into a smile that faded almost as soon as it appeared. It was Myriam, but it wasn't Myriam. Gone were the muscular arms and shoulders of the woman he had known. Gone was the simple black hair bun and blue-green eyes. Now, a thin silhouette greeted him. Thin to the point of almost being gaunt. Silver white hair, and even stranger, silver eyes. It was Myriam, but not Myriam. Was this someone else?

"Hello William." Myriam's voice removed all doubt. It was her.

Chapter 55.

Now that the moment was here, Will didn't know what to say. He wanted to apologize, he wanted to ask how she was, he wanted to say something memorable. He opened his mouth but all that came out was a fumble of sounds that weren't words, prompting him to close it again.

"Really?" Myriam arched an eyebrow at him with an expectant look.

"Sorry." Will spat out. "Hello Myriam. You look…" Will wasn't sure how to talk about how she looked. "Different." He finally spat out the word, regretting almost instantly the tone he was sure it sounded like.

"What? Thin, silver, waifish?" Myriam smiled. "It's ok, I don't even look in mirrors anymore, I don't recognize myself!"

A throat clearing brought William back to the now. Nollew and Yulisia were sitting in two of the chairs. Rewil was in the one that was for him, leaving the other three for William and Myriam, and this Jinir. A man who William didn't know. Jinir sat down and removed his hood, revealing a young-looking man, but a second look would show an age and a wariness that screamed of pain and anger. The youthful appearance was because his skin was smooth and pink. So, this must be the former Tarn of the City. Jinir. The one Mikol had killed, or at least tried to kill.

Will blinked in surprise as the man looked at him and gave a thin smile. "You must be William. Myriam has mentioned you. I'm sure the two of you have a lot of catching up to do. But first, sit. Your part of this too, both of you." Will watched as Jinir pointed at a chair next to him while looking at Myriam. There was a hardness to his Jinir person. Will could feel it, an angry edge. Brittle. Like untreated metal. The look he gave Myriam as she sat was unsettling. His brows had furrowed, he had locked his sight on her, and a frown had played on the edges of his mouth. Anger. Anger or contempt. But what worried him was the fleeting glimpse of fear that Myriam held when she sat next to Jinir.

"We are here to discuss a problem." Nollew looked at each of them. "A problem named Mikol. A problem that runs the healer's section, and in reality, the entire City."

"Please. Not this again, Nollew. You keep saying this but present no evidence." Rewil answered, his voice hard to hear as it mixed with the ever-present thrumming.

"It's true Rewil. He tried to kill me. He tried to kill Myriam. I survived by luck. I lived in agony for years. Body twisted, throat destroyed, skin warped and burned." Jinir chimed in. "And it's good to see you again. All of you."

"And you have evidence it was, Mikol?" Rewil shifted in his seat. "I know you believe it, but can you prove it?"

"It had to be him. He set that vat to explode or had someone do it. I know it. I was a threat." Jinir's voice grew hard. "I would think a friend would trust me."

"Jinir… I am your friend. I am. And it's good to see you as well. But that doesn't change that I need evidence. I am not going to work against Mikol, against the person who put me in this position, without some kind of proof. Or at least even a solid idea of how that I can verify!"

"Rewil, I know you feel strongly about it. I understand." Yulisia broke into the argument, her voice calm. "But the fact remains that it is true. I know he influenced Nollew and I. Did you never wonder why we started acting that way towards you?"

Rewil didn't answer and locked his eyes downward, toward the stone floor. Will could see his struggle with the question. Their change in behavior had made a deep wound in Rewil. He could see it every time it came up. He hated the idea that Mikol was behind it. Kindly Mikol, Tarn of the Healers, was some kind of evil ruler? It did sound ridiculous, though Will believed it.

"Proof. I need proof." Rewil crossed his arms, as Jinir, Yulisia and even Nollew, who had said little yet, all started talking at once. Will glanced at Myriam and motioned that they should move away. One because the talk was getting heated, and two, because he wanted to speak to Myriam more. Thankfully, she seemed relieved at the prospect. And they both got up and moved away from the four Tarns, who were all yelling or pointing fingers.

"Not going well, is it?" Will asked her once they were far enough on the other side of the room.

"No, it's not. It's a hard thing to realize. I didn't want to accept it either. Some part of me still doesn't. Mikol is almost a kinder version of my grandfather. Who wants to think a person like that would try to kill you? "Myriam sighed. "How have you been? You look worn."

"Tired." Will shook his head. "Look, Myriam. I need to apologize. I was not myself the day we arrived here. I was angry, and I didn't deal with it well. I took it out on you because you were there. I AM sorry."

"I kind of deserved it." Myriam answered back as she looked at the churning water in the canal. "It's true. If I had told you all about the crystal, about the voice, about it all. We wouldn't be in this mess. Amder would be alive. Your cousin would be alive. Regin might even be alive. Vin could be as well."

Will wanted to tell her she was wrong, but she wasn't. But she also wasn't the only one to blame. He bore a large part of it as well. "Why didn't you?" he asked, searching her profile for an answer.

"I've asked myself that a great deal. I was scared. You were the Forgemaster. You had a GOD in your head. Regin was a Guildmaster. Even Vin was a decorated veteran of the Palnor army, and your bodyguard. And there I was. A barely trained first year apprentice guild smith with a talent for inlay and jewelry work. I was nothing. My parents ran an inn for traders on the southern road. That was it." Myriam frowned as she spoke. "I didn't want to be anything worthy. If that makes sense." Myriam sighed. "It made sense at the time. Somehow."

Will said nothing. He knew that feeling. He'd had it when he realized what Amder wanted from him. What they all wanted. He'd not desired that fate and had wanted to hide from it. He'd refused the idea because it was a dream he didn't have. And yet, he'd still found himself in that forge under the Temple with Myriam, remaking a god. "I understand." Will finally spoke. "I do. And I bear some of the blame as well. I was so wrapped up in my personal quest to save Duncan that I didn't pay attention. I didn't see it, and I should have."

"How could you have seen it?" Myriam smiled. "It was all in my head."

"I didn't see you and Regin either." Will answered. "I should have.

Again, too focused on myself." Will wondered if he'd gone too far for a moment as a look of genuine sadness crossed Myriam's face. "Sorry." He finally said.

"No, it's fine. I wonder what he would make of all this. This place." Myriam looked around, squinting. "About the power, about…" Myriam paused, staring at the lone construct in the corner. "What is that?"

"It's a construct. You've seen those before." Will shrugged. "It's an older one."

"No. I mean… with the sight. Our sight. It's different." Myriam looked at the construct again. "It's… like it's a person. But not a person."

Will wondered what she was talking about, and with some effort shifted his vision so he too could see the power. It tore through this room, its pattern shifting and swirling. It clung to the Tarns who were still arguing in thick clumps. Mostly the same blue, but there was a tinge of green on Rewil's wrist, and then as he examined the construct, he knew what she was seeing. The same greenish tinge lay on the thing. *Simulacrum.*

"What is that?" Myriam frowned at the thing. "It feels… wrong. Twisted. Lost."

"The early constructs used simulacrums. Magical temporary copies of real people if you want to know. Before they found a better way. It gave the constructs power, and a way to reason, sort of." Will pointed at Rewil. "He made that bracer, it's got a simulacrum in it as well, apparently."

Myriam frowned at the construct all the harder. "It's in pain." She finally said. "It's not aware, not all the way, but it hurts." "What do you mean?" Will didn't know what she was talking about. "How could it be in pain?"

"It is. I can fix it, let me try…" Myriam pulled in her boon, gasping as the power here tore through her. Instantly, Myriam hunched over as she spasmed in reaction to the wave of power. Thankfully, she hadn't made a sound, and the Tarns didn't notice in their argument.

"Let it go!" Will whispered urgently. He leaned down, grasping her shoulders. "Let it go Myriam!"

Thankfully, she listened and released her connection, except for the vision. "What was… I didn't expect that. I saw how wild the power was here, but I didn't think it would do THAT. Thank you."

"It's fine. Rewil said this place made it hard to work the power. But you working on a construct? You should have been a Crafter after all." Will smiled and looked at the construct, and nearly fell to his knees as the realization came to him. "By the sparks, that's how he did it!"

Will turned to the Tarns, his voice loud. "I know how he tried to kill Myriam!"

Will swallowed a sudden lump in his throat as the Tarns nearly as one stopped their argument and looked at him. Jinir, Nollew and Yulisia looked hopeful. Rewil looked more annoyed than anything else. "Well?" Rewil finally said. "How?"

"Rewil, the rail riders. They are older constructs. They use simulacrum to make the pattern, right?" Will pointed at the construct in the corner. "Just like that one."

Rewil frowned. "Yes, but what does that have to do with anything. All the older units do."

"The simulacrum. It's a copy of a mind. A living mind. Bound to the machine. It's not a full person, but it's like one, right?" Will slapped his hand against his thigh, hard. "Can't you see it? Mikol. He's a powerful Healer. He used that. They carry enough of a living mind for him to use his power, his boon, to make them do what he wants." Will grinned, lost in the understanding. "He used that to make that one quickway construct take in too much power and form the resonance. That moved under the carriage with Myriam in it and caused the explosion. Nobody saw, and unless you looked for it, and had the skill to look for it, no one would know. Ever."

"Do you think he could have done that with me as well?" Jinir asked. "It's hard for a construct to operate in the lower city, we don't see them there, at least not with any kind of regularity."

"I guess not. But it makes sense. You said you wanted proof, or at least an idea you could investigate, right? Rewil here it is. Mikol used his boon to influence simulacrums." Will pointed at the bracer on Rewil's wrist. "And if he can do it with constructs, I'm sure he can do it with that as well."

Rewil frowned, taking a long look at his wrist bracer. He said nothing for a long minute before standing. "Will, can I see your hammer?"

Will hesitated but handed Rewil his new hammer, feeling like he was handing over part of himself. It glinted a silvery black almost in the light here. He knew Rewil would not hurt it, but it didn't feel right, having someone else use it.

Rewil removed the bracer and placed it on chair he had been in, and with an overhead swing, crushed the bracer with a single blow. A shower of silver fire seemed to burst from the impact. The sound echoed around the chamber far longer than it should have before fading off.

"There." Rewil handed Will his hammer back. "Nice hammer. And I agree with you. That makes sense. I don't like it, but it makes sense. That leaves the next question. What do we do about it?" Rewil looked down at the twisted remains of his bracer.

Mikol kicked his chair, sending it flying across his office. This was intolerable. He'd not heard everything since the fool William had talked to Myriam, each apologizing to each other in some ritual of worthless self-pity. And then William had figured it out. All his work now threatened.

If Rewil, Yulisia, and Nollew came against him in a Commons, Grib would cave and side with them. He knew it. Grib was a weak fool. Even if Mikol used Jinir's presence to push Grib to support him. Grib was ambitious, but not stupid.

Everything was falling apart on him. He couldn't even do much more than listen. The power in the room they were all in made it hard to do even that. His head pounded from the effort. He had spent years, decades, working to keep his position safe. And now some northern child and his foolish friend were going to undo all his effort!

There had to be a way to salvage this. There had to be.

Mikol stormed towards his door, ready to march down to that canal underground himself when the spire shook. A sound came, a warning. It reverberated through the walls, the floor, and pushed Mikol's rage to the side. A sound he'd never expected to hear, a sound no Tarn ever HAD heard.

The wards had fallen.

Chapter 56.

The Unnamed God watched in silent satisfaction as his army, his people, swarmed across the valley floor. Even the Gorom were being useful. Now that night had fallen. Set back far enough, the camp was still within sight of the walls of this accursed place. He also was silent for good reason. He was exhausted. The wards this place had been covered in had been formidable. All the more reason to wipe this aberration from the face of this world.

Grimnor flowed out of the rock next to him, an aura of disapproval and sadness came from his rocky form.

"This is the right thing to do, brother. Don't worry, I won't throw your people into the fire too much." The Unnamed could already see the changes in Grimnor since the signing of the pact. He was smaller, less powerful. In a few hundred years, he wouldn't exist anymore, subsumed into the Unnamed. He wondered if Grimnor understood what he had agreed to. But did it matter?

Turning his attention back to the City, his mood darkened. It was awash in power. A blasphemy. And somewhere in there, in that evil and madness, was Myriam VolFar. He could feel it. He'd been able to feel her since he tore the last of the wards down. His namer was here. He couldn't see her yet, though. Which was another irritation. If he tried, all he got was a swirling madness of magic that made everything out of focus and blurred. "She's in there, brother. I know it. I WILL get my name from her. Then, I will be complete." The Unnamed God watched his forces at work. "Your tunnels worked well; they never knew the truth." Grimnor didn't answer, only nodded.

Force marching his men into the tunnels had been hard. But the working of the power to shift all the equipment and soldiers here had been seamless. He'd had to make sure the anchors were last though, as the shortcut was pulled apart by the things as they passed through it. He'd considered using the anchors to pull the wards down as well. He could have saved some strength that way, but had discarded the idea. Better to have them be a surprise. He looked forward to seeing the arrogant fools try to work the power against them, only to see it vanish before it could do any damage. "Magic is for us, brother. Tomorrow, they will know it too." The Unnamed raised a hand, and a new dais and chair rose out of the ground. Mirroring the one in the godshome, if somewhat larger, the Unnamed God sat and waited. He would win. Tomorrow he would have a name, the City would be gone, and all would be right with Alos.

Will opened his mouth to say something, but couldn't, as Nollew, who had been silent, gave a great bellow of pain. He sank to his knees, grasping his head, followed by a hissing sound from between clenched teeth. Chaos erupted. Jinir jumped back, as if he was about to be attacked. Yulisia dropped by Nollew, trying to help stand him up, murmuring something that Will couldn't hear. And Rewil stood in silence, staring at Nollew in obvious shock.

"The wards." Nollew finally managed to say, still not standing. "The wards are down."

Rewil joined Yulisia and tried to help Nollew up. "What? Explain yourself." Rewil's voice broke over the sound of Jinir trying to open the door and run away.

"He's here." Myriam yelled. "Will, I don't know how, but HE'S here."

Will, for a moment, didn't know who she meant. Then he understood. "By the sparks… HIM?"

"What is going on?" Rewil looked at them. "Someone explain??"

"The Unnamed God. He's here." Myriam shuddered. "I can feel him. He's here. For me."

"Don't worry, Myriam. We will keep him away." Will stood by her side. "I am not going anywhere."

"You don't understand Will. He's stronger now than at the Anvil. I can feel him trying to find me. He will tear this place down to the bare rock if it gets him his name. He will end the life of every being here. He wants to." Myriam closed her eyes and shuddered. "I never should have run."

"Nonsense." Will grabbed her shoulders. "We will make it through this. We survived the Anvil, we survived the attack at the Reach, we can survive this."

Myriam didn't respond. Will could see the terror in her, though. Her body scrunched up, as if to hide from whatever she was feeling. What could have caused this? Why now? Will had always sort of considered the threat from the new god remote. He'd put it out of his mind, mostly. There had been nothing he could do about it, so why try? He regretted his own blindness now.

"He's strong. So strong Yulisia." Nollew spoke again, rubbing his head. "My head hurts as if you'd hit it with that hammer, Rewil."

"Hmmmmm." Was all Rewil said in reply. Will could see how conflicted Rewil was. He'd been angry at Nollew and Yulisia for so long, it was hard to let it all go. Yet, the theory on how Mikol had worked the quickway explosion seemed to have shifted something in his Tarn. Some level of acceptance.

"We need to get out of this room." Yulisia spoke. "Myriam, I know you are afraid. I don't blame you. But outside of here can you examine Nollew. I don't trust taking him to Mikol."

Myriam was still frozen but gave the tiniest of nods. "I will do what I can." Her voice a whisper, cracking in fear.

Will helped her move as they all exited the canal underground. Rewil led the way, followed by Myriam and Will. Nollew and then Yulisia brought up the rear. Will hadn't been this way before, and didn't know it, though he spent much of his focus on helping Myriam. Her body had relaxed some. Her eyes remained shut tight, however, as if closing them would hide her from whatever was looking.

A few minutes later, the tunnel opened up into a room, gray and dim. "Here, this will do." Yulisia helped Nollew against a wall. "Can you please help him?" she asked Myriam. "Let me help her first." Nollew croaked out, his voice low, dry. Will hadn't released his sight yet and was rather taken aback by the display he saw now. A fountain of power flowed from Nollew, stretching and shifting with the delicate motions of Nollew's outstretched hand.

"What are you doing?" Will asked, not sure if he should trust this man. Myriam wasn't fully aware of what was going on, and he had to do something.

Nollew lowered his hand. "Small ward. It will keep his eye off her, at least for a while." He managed a small smile. "Don't worry, she's not harmed."

"Can't the Unnamed get rid of it? Like he did the other wards?" Will's sight could see the ward now, a tiny fabric of lines and points, sitting on Myriam's skin. It seemed connected to her somehow. It was complex and delicate, and despite his fears, he was impressed. Nollew had done this, even in his state, with no preparation and no time.

"Smaller target." Nollew released his hold on his boon. "Now, please. I feel like my head is about to split open. Makes it hard to concentrate."

Myriam opened her eyes, one at a time, blinking. "I can't feel him. Not like before. Thank you."

"Are you sure you're fine to do this?" Will whispered in her ear. "You know what's out there."

"Yes, I'm fine, Will." Myriam nodded. "Let me work please."

Will sat back, keeping a close watch on her and her patient. But he need not be concerned, he realized. Myriam's control over the power rivaled Nollew's in touch. Her work was a thousand tiny threads, each tipped with a tiny feather of the power, seeking injury and pain, and quickly removing it. Will had seen nothing like it.

The effect on Nollew was as dramatic. The man relaxed fully, and his face, moments before locked into a grimace, smiled now. "That was fantastic. You truly are one skilled healer. I can see why Mikol was threatened by you." Yulisia poked Nollew and whispered something that Will couldn't hear to Nollew, who nodded, and the smile left his face. "Sorry, I wasn't thinking. This isn't the time." Standing, he brushed his robes and looked around. "What happened to Jinir?"

"He ran. He went the way we did, but I haven't seen him." Will looked around. "I don't know this place."

"It's not used. Which is why we took it. There are several other

Greystone passages that are no longer in use, for various reasons."
Nollew frowned. "We probably should find Jinir."

"No need. I'm here." Jinir came out of the passage across from them, hard to see in the dim light. "I was scouting. Scouting ahead."

"You were running." Yulisia threw the words at him. "When did you run from danger?"

"After I got nearly killed by not being careful, Yulisia. But now is not the time. What do we do now?" Jinir walked over to Myriam. "If the city is under attack, my friend and I here need to return to the lower city."

"I am not your friend. I'm staying with Will." Myriam moved herself out of Jinir's reach. "I don't know if I can trust you."

"I found you. I brought you somewhere safe." Jinir answered back, ignoring the others. "If Ralta had left you there, you wouldn't be here now."

"And if she were here, I'd thank her. SHE saved me. Not you. But isn't she out hunting Rauger? Your onetime friend, now enemy?" Myriam's voice was low, still it carried around the chamber. "I want to be free of you. And him too. I'm done with all this nonsense. The city is about to be attacked by a GOD. A God who wants me. If I give him what he wants, maybe he will leave."

"An excellent idea." A voice came out of the shadows. "But not the only option."

Mikol was here.

Chapter 57.

Mikol watched them as each tried to make sense of him being here. He'd had to rush once he realized where they were. Even better, the tiny simulacrum of that fool boy William was far easier to get a focus on now that he had left the chamber. It was the only reason he had known where they were. His fury rose at seeing them all together, plotting against him. He was Tarn Mikol Nese. They were nothing!

Fools, the lot of them. Nollew and Yulisia, the pair who think they could dislodge him. Rewil had been useful, but now he was a ruined resource. Jinir and Myriam, they both should be dead. Something Mikol might finally be able to make happen if he managed this right. Or at least one of them. And that left his unwitting spy, William. He'd about broken a fist, hitting a wall when Will had left the discussion to talk to Myriam. The two of them were obnoxiously dense. All that fumbling, apologizing, and not wanting to say too much, without even knowing what too much was.

Not that any of it mattered, not right now. The board they were all playing on had changed. "My fellow Tarns, it seems there's been a commons called, yet no word reached me, or Grib it appears." Mikol kept the smile on his face with some effort.

"Mikol." Nollew broke into a broad grin. "What a wonderful surprise!"

"No, it's not." Mikol dropped the smile. "You were all in the canal underground, plotting against me. Do you think anything you do escapes my notice? You, Nollew the unimpressive. Waving your hands around, making things explode. But can you use your boon to bring life? No. Just a glorified killer with a lecherous appetite."

"And you Yulisia. Yulisia, the leader of the leftovers. You knew that, though. If someone gets the boon, and isn't a Crafter, a Caster or a Healer, they go to the Librarians. The so called 'Keepers of knowledge' who don't even know what's in the books they guard so carefully." Mikol scowled now, caught up in his anger.

"And you Rewil. I MADE YOU. You would have been passed over a dozen times for Tarn if I hadn't stepped in. I put up with all your silly machines, your priceless 'constructs'. And yet, you turn your back on me all because of some young stupid crafter who isn't even one of us." Mikol turned his ire on Jinir. "You, Jinir. Or should I call you the 'Downtrodden Lord' now? Always trying to be more than you are. Always trying to be the best. Do you know how easy it was to pay someone to rig that vat? One of your precious lower city street rats. Do you want to know how much it cost? Five copper bits. That was all. Your own people betray you for FIVE COPPER BITS." Mikol could feel his body shaking with anger now, the pent-up irritation and rage spilling out.

"And the two of you. Myriam and William. Outsiders. Your presence isn't wanted here. You have done nothing to help this city. You've been granted amazing access to the power of this place, and what do you do? Heal worthless lower city trash, and whine about everything. And you, William, 'oh look I made a hammer… aren't I an amazing Crafter." Mikol clenched his fists, the skin turning white.

"I have been balancing the City on my back for longer than any of you know. Either secretly, or openly as Tarn. And I will NOT have my work, my plans, my position torn down by you lot. Not now, and not ever." Mikol released his hands, flexing them to return the blood flow.

"But now, none of this matters. You hate me, you want me gone. But to save the City, you need me. There's no time to remove me and pick a new Tarn. Not now, not with the God these two self-absorbed headaches brought back to life and straight to our doorstep." Mikol paused, waiting to see if anyone else was going to talk. Shock and some anger were all that seemed to come, so he resumed talking. "Myriam. You will name the God. The rest of us, or at least the rest of the TARNS, will do what needs to be done and move the city. It will buy us time. Maybe we can get a Tarn of the Casters who can make wards strong enough this time."

Nollew's skin took on a dark red cast, but he said nothing, only exchanging glances with Yulisia. In a few moments, they both nodded. Rewil still had a rather shocked expression on his face, Mikol noted. The man was far too old to be this innocent. Still, Rewil finally nodded as well, and lowered his eyes. *Good, maybe Rewil won't have to be replaced quite yet.*

Jinir kept his mouth shut and took a few steps backward, keeping his eyes on Mikol. "Gracious speech. But your days are numbered, Mikol, you know it. We know it." "Fool. Even now you're backing away. I don't have to use the boon to see your fear. Wishing your pet Trinil was here to protect you? Wishing she was here so she could stick one of those knives of hers between my ribs?" Mikol almost pulled up his undershirt to expose his side. He thought better of the idea, though. "Your little knife wielding friend is in her own trouble right now. She's not coming to save you." Mikol waved his hand in dismissal. "But I don't need to deal with you now. So, run. Go hide again. But I know you're here now Jinir. And once this danger has passed, I will hunt you down properly this time."

Jinir didn't say a word, but turned on his heel and left, half walking, half running down a long Greystone tunnel. Mikol watched him go. Such a simple man to fool. He had no idea where the Trinil was. She'd vanished from his watchers as much as anyone else's. She was out there somewhere, but the City held dangers, if you weren't paying attention to them. "Now. Myriam. You will leave the City. Your little creation out there will not harm you. Not now. You will give him a name. If all is well, he will leave. If he doesn't, we will move the City, and find a new way to stop this foolish being. This is the CITY. We do not bow." Mikol waited. He had released some of his pent-up frustration with these fools, and he felt better for it.

And as much as they all hated him, the other Tarns knew they needed him. To move the City required all the Tarns, working together. A relic of when the process was made. Mikol wondered if it was time to adjust that rule, but it would have to wait. Mikol knew his fellow Tarns were onboard, but the namer and her unwitting friend, Will, did not yet seem convinced. Will proved it. "Tarn Mikol, your actions have brought this…" Will stopped in mid-sentence as Rewil held up a hand.

"Hush Will. I don't like it. None of us do. But the fact remains, the City comes before us all. And without him, we can't save it. It takes all of us to do the move. After this, we will see what will happen. But for now, we must be united, or the City and all its people could fall." Rewil's voice was low, quiet. Mikol almost burst out laughing, though. The idea that the

City could even come close to falling was silly.

"We could send out that Construct army of yours, Rewil. Send them out to make drinks and clean up tents." Mikol needled Rewil, watching the man frown. *Good, now he knows I'm not cowed.* Mikol looked at each of them, trying to bore a hole in each skull. The only one he could read was William right now, and all that came through was confusion and fear. *Lots of fear. He could use fear.* "After the City is safe, we will meet to discuss recent events." Mikol frowned at each of them. "My fellow Tarns, I believe we are needed at the top of the spire. Myriam, fulfill your end of things." Mikol turned and left the chamber, satisfied by the utter silence behind him.

"He's a hateful man, a fool and a tyrant." Nollew spoke first. "In this case, he is right. The safety of the City comes first."

Will felt his stomach lurch at the thought of sending Myriam out there, into the path of that thing that had been made in the Anvil. "There's no way Myriam can go out there alone."

"I can speak for myself, Will." Myriam placed a hand on his arm. "I appreciate the concern, but they are right. If I name him, he might leave."

"And if you name him, he will get more powerful, remember? Giving him a name, finishes him, somehow. And once you say that name, he will have no reason not to kill you. Or this City." Will pointed in the general direction of the valley. "He's out there right now, waiting. Let him wait."

"William. They are right. I know you are worried about your friend. But if it buys us time, we can move the City, and come up with a better plan. Everything is in danger right now. Like a spring wound too tight. You're a Crafter, you know how to see problems." Rewil shook his head. "I rather wish now I hadn't come to this."

"Oh, please." Yulisia walked over and, much to Will's surprise, embraced Rewil. "You foolish giant of a man. You know you missed us. Mikol's days are numbered now. We will move the City, set new wards, and continue. But we need you Rewil. The City needs you. If you hadn't come tonight, William wouldn't have come either. This is all as it should be."

"What do you mean?" Rewil stepped back, breaking the hug she had been giving him. "Yulisia?" "I have always found it interesting that the rest of you never thought to ask. Part of the library is dedicated to, let's say, looking into the future. Using the power to see what may come. An inexact practice, despite that, useful." Yulisia pointed at Will. "His job isn't done. But if he hadn't been here tonight, and you as well, the future was bleak. I don't know exactly why, but this was needed."

Will didn't like the way that sounded. He was so sick of anything having control over him like that. Destiny, being a 'chosen one', being special. He hated it. "I don't know about any of that, nor do I care." Will turned to Myriam. "If you are really doing this, I am coming with you. Let me grab my armor, and let's go face this thing, together."

"Will…" Myriam looked ready to argue, her face set with a disapproving glare, before she simply gave a sigh and nodded. "I would be happy to have you with me."

"Then it's decided." Nollew went and stood next to Rewil and Yulisia. "We will do our parts, it appears. Good luck, to both of you."

Will watched as Nollew and Yulisia left. Rewil started after them, then paused, turning back to Will and Myriam, his face dark. "Yes Tarn Rewil?" Will found himself saying. His annoyance at Rewil not stopping this stupidity surprised even him.

"Be careful. Both of you. I don't like the way this all feels. A day ago, I would have told you the City was safe, and everyone was overreacting. Now, the City is under attack, Mikol is feeling betrayed, and I don't know what's true. But be careful." Rewil took a few more steps before he turned around one more time. "Will, I believe you. Which means all this time, I've been played for a fool by Mikol." Rewil left them, hurrying after the other two Tarns.

"Well, let's get this done." Myriam looked around. "Do you have any idea which way to go, Will? I mean from here."

Will tried to remember his maps when the realization struck him. "You called me Will. In fact, you've called me Will this whole time, well, I mean today. At the meeting, and now… and… I'm babbling."

"Yes. I realized something. I was being an idiot. You asked me to call you Will. I called you William because I was mad. It was childish. You hid your true self at the Guild for good reasons. I should have understood. You're the same person you always were… right, Markin Darto?" Myriam threw the name out with a smile.

"Never say that name again…' Will made a fake gagging noise. "Well, I think we both have acted like fools in the past, and it looks like we are about to again. This plan… I don't know how many holes are in it."

"We can be fools again together." Myriam gave Will a shrug. "But none of this gets us out of here. They are waiting for us to do what we agreed to. To face down that thing outside."

"True. And I know the way, follow me." Will pointed and Myriam followed.

Chapter 58.

Will walked next to Myriam, pointing where to turn as they made their way back to his rooms to get what gear he had. The halls were silent, the silence of a breath holding far too long. He saw a few other crafters, but all were running, either carrying blueprints and plans, or in one case, a rather large bottle of firewine.

"One moment Myriam. It won't take long." Will kept his voice low as they entered the hallway outside his room.

"It's fine, Will. Truthfully. Honestly, this helps. It keeps my mind off the insanity of what we are about to try to do." Myriam gave a tiny smile as she looked around. "Ah, I love all the white stone. I haven't seen that in every other strange corner of this place."

"Ha ha." Will threw back at her. "You want to know something? One reason I enjoyed mapping the hidden passages was that they weren't this same bland and cold white stone. I wish I knew who made it all white. It seems off to me. I mean, they call this place the 'City in Blue' and yet, it's all white. I get the blue means the power, but really, call it 'City of Magic' or the 'City of Power' or something…" Will stopped at his door. "Here we are."

Entering the room felt odd to Will. It had only been a few hours, still it felt like it belonged to someone else. He wondered if he'd ever see it again. He didn't care if he did. It had been a home, though, for a while. A place to rest, a place to put some of the past madness behind him. So, it had been worth it. Mostly.

"Ah, nice place you have here. Very cozy." Myriam looked around the austere room. "I can see you've tried to decorate."

"It wasn't in my mind." Will answered back as he pulled the breastplate and bracers out from under the bed. "Now that's odd."

The armor was different. It was still his new creation, but it looked different. The same golden copper color, but it shimmered a blue green now. A full touch brought a hint of vibration, almost. "That's very strange." He added.

"That's not your armor." Myriam pointed at the gear. "Where's the armor we made in the Reach?"

"Gone. I melted it with the hammer Amder had given me. I needed a fresh start, Myriam. Amder is gone. I'm not the Forgemaster anymore, I really never was one, in my heart." Will put on one bracer, then the other. "This feels different. I should leave it I think."

"All that work I did you melted away?" Myriam frowned. "And you melted the hammer Amder gave you? With the power bonded to it, with the god touched armor? You do realize how dangerous that was?"

"Yes, and No. I knew there was the possibility of danger. But I also knew I had to. It was time. And besides, with the damage the breastplate had, I didn't think it would help me too much." Will stopped, holding the breastplate in one hand. "Oh, I'm sorry Myriam. I wasn't thinking."

"No, it's fine." Myriam remembered that moment all too well. The spear flying through the air, Will being pushed into the way. The spear tearing a gouge and splintering apart. Regin falling, a long section of broken wood fully embedded in his side. "Maybe we all should have worn armor that day." Myriam blinked a few times, and Will could see the wetness there. "Wear it Will, even if it feels different, I'd feel better if you did."

"Should we get you armor? We could try the small outriders' posts." Will put on the breastplate, letting Myriam help him with the buckles.

"No. That life is behind me. I'm a Healer now. You wouldn't think it, but they are similar. At least healing with the power makes it so, for me." Myriam finished the last buckle. "There. You do look plain, but it should help."

Will tried to think of something to say but couldn't. There was a lot of history between them now, and yet, he still found himself unable to talk to her. Or at least not knowing what to say. Leaving the room, Will leading the way to quickway out to the city walls. "I know you may not want to take it, but the quickway will give us the fastest way out. If we have to go through the middle and lower city, I don't know how long it would take." He didn't get a response right away. One look told him why. Myriam looked pale and was chewing her lip before she finally nodded. "I agree." She smoothed her hands on her robe a few times, nervous. They approached the quickway, finding it waiting and ready. "A stroke of luck." Will opened the door, leading the way into the carriage. It was empty, as he'd expected.

Myriam followed him, looking pale, and biting her lip once more. As soon as she noticed him looking, she stopped and gave him a thin smile. "I'm fine. But the last time the thing exploded."

"I don't think Mikol can pull that off again, at least not on short notice. And he needs us to do our part." Will sat, offering Myriam the seat next to him. "And I'm here. It will be ok Myriam. I know it." She didn't answer, but much to his surprise rested a hand on his arm with a firm but not tight grip.

The quickway lurched forward, bringing forth a tiny gasp from Myriam, but nothing else untoward happened. The City flew by under them, looking normal, and quiet to him. Myriam, however, seemed surprised and muttered a few things he couldn't hear. "What was that?" Will asked. He wanted to continue to repair their remade friendship, so he asked questions. *Hopefully, I don't ask too many.*

"It's the lower city. The streets are full of people. Far more than I've seen in the past. I never got out a lot, but a few times. I imagine they are terrified." Myriam shook her head with a smile. "Or angry. The City folk are an interesting group. I wish the spire treated them better."

"I agree!" Will blurted, happy to finally find someone who saw it too. "None of them seem to understand that they need the City, more than the City needs them. The Spire hoards all the power, all the true wonders. They call the lower city folk 'knackers' and look down on them as something to be pitied. At least most of them do. The ones who don't, don't even think about them. It's infuriating after a while."

For once, Will knew he had surprised Myriam, who gave him a look that he couldn't read. "Well, you aren't the same shy young man who never said what he truly thought that I met on the way to Ture."

Will laughed. Still, the fact of what was about to happen killed his humor. The quickway stopped at the wall, bringing forth a fresh wave of nerves. One look told him Myriam wasn't much better. "I'm scared Myriam."

"Me too." Myriam released his arm and stood, if unsteadily. "You don't have to do this, you know. It might be better if you didn't. I don't know if after I name him, he will kill me where I stand. At least one of us might live through this."

Will stood, pushing his fear away for now. "No. We do this together, Myriam. We have to. For Duncan, for Regin, for Vin, for everyone. If we are lucky, you name him and we both are free. Everyone leaves, and that's that. I won't stay in the City, I'll leave. I decided a while ago. This isn't the right place for me. I belong back in the Reach. Or someplace like it. I'm going to be a simple blacksmith, and for once I'll be happy. No more Gods, No more magic, none of it."

Myriam nodded. "I know. I want to go as well, but I also want to know more. There's… something else. Something keeping me here. I can't describe it. But it doesn't matter if this goes badly."

Will led the way out into the wide hallway that circled the City in the outer wall. Unlike the nearly empty spire and the crowded but chaotic streets of the lower city, this was more like he had expected. Teams of outriders moved in groups, and groups of ten of the large guardian constructs moved together, all heading in the same direction.

"What's going on?' Myriam asked. "I didn't expect the constructs."

"Remember what Mikol said? I guess the constructs do have a role in the city's defense. That's good. Those things are tough. Power soaked, strong, and fast. They wouldn't bleed in battle either." Will led the way, stopping at a door that looked familiar. "I think this is the place. But before we go in, one last question, do you know what name you're going to give?"

A nod was the only thing Myriam gave him. "Care to share it?" Will asked. "Because if it's William Reis, I'd like to try to talk you out of it now. Or Markin Darto. Both of those are off limits."

Myriam did finally give a slight chuckle at that. "I promise it's neither of those. I picked one on the way here. I don't think it really matters, though. As long as I do it and it's a name. But where are we? This looks slightly familiar." "This is Ride Captain Julis's office. At least I think it is. I figured why not leave with the person who brought us into this place." Will shrugged. "She also is the only person I could ask how to actually leave the City. I realized; I don't know."

Will knocked, and the door slid open, revealing an office that was a mess. "Leave the report on the table with the others. I will get to it if we live through this day." A voice came from the far side of the room, behind a divider.

"Ride Captain Julis? We are on a… mission, from the Tarns." Will glanced at Myriam, who shrugged in response. "We need to get outside. Into the valley."

A silence greeted them before the divider fell over to reveal Ride Captain Julis, armored and with an expression of total surprise on her face. "You want to what?" she managed to say.

"Leave the City. Go into the valley." Myriam blurted out before Will could say it. "The Tarns sent us."

"It might stop them, our mission." Will added. "Do you remember us? The two who appeared in the valley?"

Ride Captain Julis still wore the same incredulous expression on her face. "The two of you are going to stop the army out there? There are near fifty thousand people out there. And another large group of Gorom. GOROM! I don't know what this madness is, but there's no way the two of you are going to be able to stop it."

She paused though giving them each a look before her expression finally changed. "I do remember. You both look different. William, right? And you are… Myriam?" the Ride Captain shook her head. "I don't know what the Tarns told you, but this plan, it's suicide."

"No, please. The Unnamed God, the one who leads them. He wants something from me. He NEEDS something from me. If I give it to him, he might pack up and leave." Myriam took a step forward. "I have to try. I don't want anyone to be killed."

"No one, a god included, brings an army like that one someplace to turn around and leave." Ride Captain Julis snorted, but Will watched her sigh. "This is from the Tarns? What are they doing about this?" "Move the City. If this doesn't work, and he doesn't leave, they will move the City." Will explained. "But if what we do works, this shouldn't happen again. We hope."

"I should have expected them to try to move the place again. It's running away, you know. Eventually it will be found again." The Ride Captain walked over to a desk that stood in the corner and pulled a large red key out of a drawer. "But if you can end this before it starts, I guess I shouldn't stand in your way."

"Thank you." Myriam gave a slight bow. "I hope so too."

"Thank me when make it to a new day dawning." Ride Captain Julis led them out the door and then through a succession of doors to finally a staircase leading down. "Down here." She explained as they decided. Will could feel the cool stone pressing in on them. A growing pressure that he couldn't put his finger on.

The stairs ended at a door of some black metal that the Ride Captain opened with her key. It slid open without a sound, showing, for the first time in a year, the outside world.

Chapter 59.

Will enjoyed the feeling for a moment of being free. He had missed this lightness. That only lasted as long as it took him to grasp the army that lay on the horizon. Will had spent little time with armies. None really. "A whole City appeared here." Will had a hard time grasping the enormity of what he was seeing.

"A new city that wants to kill and raze the city we got out of." Myriam whispered. "You still can't ride, can you?"

"Well, if you rode, I might be able to ride behind you and hold on." Will felt a rush of heat. He swore to himself that if they made it through all this, he'd learn how to ride a horse, finally. It hadn't felt fair to the horse before. But he was lighter now. Maybe it was time?

"Faster than walking, at least. But we will have to stop when we get closer to them and walk the rest of the way." Myriam stuck her head into the still open door. "Can we get a horse?"

Ride Captain Julis appeared shading her eyes from the sun. "Blasted sun will be right in our faces soon. Bet they attack then. But yes, I can have two horses made ready. See that large door? Down the wall? Knock there, they will bring them out."

"Just one." Will shook his head. "I'll be riding behind her."

For a long moment he wondered if the Ride Captain was going to laugh, but she nodded, face still grave. "One horse then. Do you want a stunning rod? It's poor equipment, but while William is armed, you, Myriam, are not."

Myriam frowned and turned to Will. "I don't know. I don't want to appear threatening but going out there unarmed. I didn't even think about it."

"Bring it." Will shrugged. "At worse it sits there. But I know how they work; I might be able to increase its effect some. And if things go bad, it might let us escape from this."

Ride Captain Julis took the rod she carried at her side and handed it and the belt it had hung on to Myriam. "If it stops this, you can keep it." She nodded to them both and then closed the door.

Will was surprised to see the door they had exited meld into the stone as if it had never been there. But it made sense. "I was wondering if the doors made sense. Now I see. They meld back into the wall. Impressive."

"Magical even." Myriam remarked, throwing Will a thin smile. "Come on. I can feel him still searching for me. I don't know how long this protection Nollew gave me will last, and I'm already feeling like I'm unraveling inside. The sooner this is done, the better."

Making their way to the large double doors wasn't hard, and it finally gave Will a chance to examine the outer wall. It stretched out, a long massive curve that faded out of sight in the distance. He could see no other doors than the one they were approaching, but based on what he had seen, that made sense. Must be part of the defense for the City. Give them no easy way in. The double doors opened as they got close, and a young woman clad in the outrider's armor led an enormous horse, as horses go, out of what must have been stables. Will couldn't see too far into the space, but it was large, and the faint sound of animals and people talking came from the crack.

"Here, take him. He's strong but refuses proper warhorse training." The young guard handed the reins to Myriam, who had stepped forward. "Good luck." The young guard nodded to them both and returned to the doors, closing them behind her. They too melded into the stone as if they had never been there.

Myriam climbed on first, getting the rod tangled up in the folds of her robe, but managing to free herself in short order. She reached down to Will. "Come on." Will took her hand, surprised by the strength that still lived there. This new Myriam looked so different, but it was still her, after all. He settled in behind her as she prodded the horse forward, the animal moving forward at a brisk trot.

"So, why do you look this way now?" Will blurted out, trying to find something else to think about than the approaching line of pickets and tents. And men, lots of men, all armed. Inwardly he cringed though, of all the ways to ask that question. "I healed myself. I don't know why it ended up this way. I was very injured by the explosion. When Ralta and

Jinir got me to a safe house in the lower city, I was in poor shape. I, however, pulled enough power to heal a small thing that helped me pull more power to heal more. But when I was done, I looked like this."

"I thought healers couldn't heal themselves?" Will tried to search through his memories. "I am sure I heard that somewhere in the spire."

"They aren't supposed to be able to. But I did. It wasn't without its problems, though. It was painful, excruciatingly so. But I kept going. I did it. I'm not sure I could ever do it again. It changed me, and not just in ways you can see. I don't know how to describe it, sorry." Myriam tensed under Will's hands. "They have spotted us."

Will leaned over a fraction to see what she saw. A group of six soldiers were approaching them on foot. He didn't recognize the colors they wore, but each was armed with a spear, overlapping plate armor, and a small Warhammer. *A spear and a hammer, obvious, nevertheless, proper.*

What concerned him more was that both weapons were… god blessed. He'd never seen felt anything quite like it. He knew that was what it had to be. He reached in and opened himself to the sight. The spearheads glowed an almost sickly yellow, and the hammer heads did as well.

"Will? The weapons…" Myriam squinted at the approaching soldiers.

"I know. God touched. And if I'm right, so is every single weapon in the entire army." Will leaned in close. "Let me see the rod. Stop here."

Myriam halted the horse and pulled the rod from its holder. "What are you going to do? You don't have any tools or anything else you need to work the power."

"For this, I don't need tools. Wait." Will bored his sight into the rod, seeing the connections inside it. It held stored power. Closer to the City it would repower itself from the surrounding power. But out here on the valley plain, it could only use what it held.

It was full, at least. That would make it more useful. Will gathered his power and quickly doubled, tripled the connections to the power it held. It wouldn't last forever, and the rod wouldn't be able to take it for too many uses, but now it would send out a blast stunning any attackers for a suitable distance. Not a useful weapon of war, despite that, it would give them a chance to escape it need be. "It can only be used five, six times, but the rods effect will affect everyone near you now." Will handed it back to Myriam. "If you use it, think about the enemy sleeping when you strike. The power should take care of the rest."

"Only five or six times?" Myriam took the rod and placed it back at her side.

"Try doing that on horseback with no tools! It's an escape tool. Blast as many as you, we, can and run. Not the most elegant of plans, but we are out of options." Will could feel his skin chill, and a thread of fear wound its way up his spine.

"Yes. You are." A whispering voice swirled around them. Will knew that voice. The Unnamed God.

"What you propose, Mikol, is madness! Betrayal!" Nollew stood at the Commons table. "To move the City like this? When we have sent two of our own to try to stop this? Leave them here to their fate?"

"I agree!" Yulisia stood, followed quickly by Rewil. Only Grib and Mikol remained sitting.

"Sit please. We do not have time for your theater." Mikol cleared his throat. "Please?"

Nollew sat, red faced and angry. "You would betray the very people we sent out there?

"I take no pleasure in it, Nollew. But the facts remain. If they fail, and the Unnamed God attacks, the City could fall. If we wait till they are done, the City could still fall. But if we move the City now, while the Unnamed is busy, the City will not fall today." Mikol looked around the table, face calm.

"They are not of us. They have been part of us for what, a year? Less? Are their lives worth the lives of everyone in the City?" Mikol leaned back now, his voice becoming louder and surer. "I know you all hate me. I know none of you trust me. Maybe not you Tarn Grib, but the rest of you do."

"But tell me I am wrong. Explain, logically, why we should not trade the lives of two outsiders for the City itself." Mikol waited, his eyes darting from face to face. He fought the temptation to reach into their minds and fiddle with their feelings.

Yulisia was the first to nod, her eyes downcast. "May the power protect us from this decision." Nollew shot her an angry look, but after a long moment, he nodded. "I can find no fault in the logic, but I hate you even more now, Mikol. Forcing this action."

The other four turned to Rewil, who sat, arms crossed. Silence fell, and all watched the Tarn of the Crafters. The enormous man's discomfort was obvious. To leave Will and Myriam here, to their fate, so that the City might escape.

"We should have asked them. If they had known, and still gone, that would be one thing. But to leave without telling them on purpose?" Rewil's voice grumbled over the table.

"Rewil, Do you know how much the move last time changed the lower and middle City? It took months to rebuild new sections outside the spire. And we were ready for it then, and it still broke things. Now? Without warning? The lower city and the middle city will burn. I know it. And yet I'm still going to say yes. Not because I want to, not because I dislike Myriam or this William, but because the City comes before all of it." Grib rapped his knuckles on the large table. "We must move it now."

Rewil gave a slight nod. "May the source protect us. We will move the City now. And may William and Myriam understand."

Chapter 60.

Will froze, then slid off the horse. Myriam followed suit, landing softly compared to the audible thud William made when he landed. "Show yourself." Will managed to say, his voice dry and cracking. "Show yourself." He repeated it, this time with more strength.

"William Reis, Forgemaster of Amder, giving me an order?" The Unnamed God's voice floated around them. "You should be dead, you know. You're only alive because I was trying to make the namer happy. I picked the wrong one to bring back. I should have raised the other one, Regin? She loved him. Far more than she ever loved you."

"Show yourself." Myriam repeated. Will couldn't detect any fear in her voice. It was stronger. It wasn't loud, yet a steel was in it. "I am here to do my duty as your namer."

"Now that's worth being here for." The Unnamed God's voice echoed around them.

Will's skin chilled as the air grew cold. A certain thickness came. The air felt slick, heavy. For a moment, Will wondered if the Unnamed was going to suffocate him with the very air around him. But the feeling passed as the air swirled and from the ground speared a figure. Clad in golden armor, the Unnamed God.

"Myriam, you've changed." The Unnamed God's smile turned to a scowl as he peered at her, then he turned his attention to William, his scowl only growing. "I see. You've been corrupted by that foul place. Using the power. Magic. It is not for you."

"I am here to name you." Myriam kept her gaze on the Unnamed God. Will could tell she was scared, though. He'd missed it before, and none of the fear appeared in her voice, but her hands were gripping tight enough to be bloodless. "But before I do so, we will make a bargain."

"The only bargain you will get is this. You will name me, or Will dies. You name me, or your family dies." The Unnamed God spat the words. "I am done with this farce. Do your duty, namer." "Promise you will not attack the City. Promise that you will leave after I do this. Promise that you will not kill my family or friends. Promise me this, and you will have your name." Myriam's voice cut through the air.

The Unnamed God stared at her. "That is a bold request." The Unnamed God examined her again. "I wonder if you understand what you are asking."

"I am asking to trade the name you want, for freedom from you." Myriam took a moment to look at Will, giving him a nod. "For both of us."

"I do not care about William Reis. He was a poor Forgemaster, anyway." The Unnamed God circled them. Will noticed he left footprints, but no dust rose from his steps. "But you Myriam. My namer. I made a mistake there. I didn't realize how much the Anvil would change you. I should have killed you both as soon as I was reborn and found some poor beggar to name me. A name for a loaf of bread."

"Yet I didn't. I chose you." The Unnamed God stopped his circle. He turned towards Myriam and cocked his head to one side. "Fine. I promise that I will not attack the City. I promise that I will not kill your family or friends. I will do none of those things."

Will saw it at once. This Unnamed God had said HE wouldn't attack the City. He didn't say anyone wouldn't. Will raised a hand... "Myriam!"

Myriam paused and raised her head. "I name you Sartum."

Mikol reached out with his boon, feeling the surrounding air grow wild with the power. The Chamber of the Source was full of the power. Standing around the well, his fellow Tarns with him, Mikol could barely believe they were doing this. To wield this much of the power was intoxicating. Torrents of it flowed around them, each of the other Tarns adding their boon to the mix.

The air shuddered with its majesty. His only regret was that he needed the others to do this. Something to investigate once all this was over. For now, feeling it around him was nothing short of ecstasy. He could see the same rapture on the other's faces. Nollew and Yulisia held hands, but their expressions held the same joy that he did. Eyes wide, they both looked at the edge of tears. Rewil was more sober, his guilt over making this decision still wore on him. Mikol had felt it on the way here. A deep gnawing guilt. Mikol hoped he got over it. Rewil was still useful. As it was, Mikol planned to remove Nollew and Yulisia from the board as soon as this was over. The game would continue, with some newer and easier to control players.

He was close enough to them to activate his little security measure. The poison wouldn't take effect immediately. A day or two, and then a silent death. No pain, no awareness of what was going to happen. Just a slip into a darkness that did not end. But first, the City had to be moved. He did not want to risk it, not yet. Even Grib looked on the edge of nearly bursting into laughter with the joy of the power here. The air shuddered with its growing might. This moving working was a complicated one. One that every Tarn had to commit to memory. One mistake, and who knows where the City would go?

They already had the place picked, of course. The Tarns kept a group of five or six locations, and memorized not only the description, the location on a map but also committed to memory a picture of the place. A very well-paid artist from the lower city with the knack of making a drawing look real. A magical knack. The City would move this time to the far side of the eastern continent. Far away from this Unnamed God. And crossing an ocean that wide would be difficult for his army. Hide, rebuild the wards, and bolster their defenses. If all went well, the City should be safe for another hundred years.

The power continued to grow; the air went from a shudder to a whine, the very rocks in the walls vibrating. The light from the well grew in response, becoming so bright Mikol had to look down so as not to be blinded. Still, they built the power. A shudder sliced through the room, and for a moment the whine faltered. A far-off sound like a scream of joy seemed to echo before the power grew again, erasing anything else. Mikol did not know what that had been, but the fact that it had interrupted the rite worried him. One look at his fellow Tarns showed they shared his concern. Yet the power still flowed. Something to be looked at later. They were ready. "Now!" Mikol yelled, as each Tarn released the power, all feeding the same location, the same picture, Willing the mighty City to move.

A rumble came, drowning out even the whine, the sound of rocks and earth tearing free. They had done....

Silence fell. The power that moments before had been reaching a crescendo of might to the point of turning one mad with pleasure, was gone. The boon snapped back into Mikol with a force that brought him to his knees. Gasping, Mikol tried to make sense of the failure. The others fared no better. Nollew was prostrate, grabbing his head. Yulisia sat next to him, holding her stomach and grimacing. Rewil WAS getting sick, the huge man retching and pale. Grib was also grabbing his head with both hands, breathing through clenched teeth.

Mikol tried to think, but the snap of the boon made him unable to string too many thoughts together. "What happened?" He finally forced the words out.

"It failed." Yulisia spat, wiping her mouth. "It broke."

"That can't happen." Mikol growled. "It was perfect!"

"That noise. Did that do something?" Grib let go of his head. "I heard something, did you?"

"Yes, but..." Nollew shook his head. "By the source, I feel awful."

"What happened?" Mikol asked again. "Did one of you try to break the working? You Rewil? All guilt ridden and angst laden over leaving your prize pupil?" Mikol clenched his jaw. If the City didn't move, it was too risky to remove Nollew and Yulisia. If Rewil had ruined his plans, the man would no longer be considered useful.

"I did nothing." Rewil answered, still clenched up and giving the occasional dry heave. "I had the place in mind, and then... it shattered."

Nollew raised his head. "We have a problem." His face was paler still now. "Something bad."

"Of course, we do! The move failed and we don't know why!" Mikol shouted.

"No. The Unnamed God. The working I put on Myriam. It's broken. The Unnamed God isn't unnamed. The God Sartum now stands at our door." Nollew placed a hand on Yulisia, trying to comfort her, or himself. "He is here."

Chapter 61.

Will grabbed Myriam, pulling her back from the form of Sartum, as the now named God seemed to get larger. "We have to run. NOW." Will took out his hammer, holding it as if to ward off the light that was expanding off the God.

Without warning or fanfare, the glow faded, and the newly complete God stood in front of them. "Thank you, namer." Sartum was different, in several ways. His voice had changed. It was closer to Amder's now, at least to Will. Confidence projected from every word. *Maybe, maybe this was not a good choice.*

With a flourish, the God stood carrying a hammer and a shield. The sight of both brought Will some worry and a flush of fear. The hammer was bad enough, spiked, bloody. It had been used, and used recently, and not cleaned. But it was the shield that scared him, Large and shaped as a single large piece, it was the coloring that threw him off. Golden swirls, like the shell of the Vinik they had met in the tunnels. Exactly like the Vinik they had met in the tunnels.

"Yes. I had to punish them, you see? They broke me. They shattered me. If they had not done so, none of this would have ever happened. No Valni, no wars, no destruction. No City either, no mortals using the powers reserved for the gods alone. They were the root of all the evil in this world." Sartum looked at the City and fell silent.

"Will…" Myriam whispered. "I don't feel so good. Did he say he killed all those Vinik?"

"Yes, namer. I did. And all the rest of that misbegotten race. Oh, I'm sure in some dark and lost side tunnel there might be one or two chittering in the blackness. But they are a pitiful footnote. I have ended the Vinik. Even the ones in the Gorom cities. Slaves no longer. Death was fated, for all of them." Sartum raised a hand, and a stone chair rose from the ground as if it had grown there.

Will didn't know what to think. He'd hated what the Gorom had done to the Vinik, but to end them all? To kill a race? Madness. This new God didn't seem mad, though. If anything, he was calmer than Amder had ever been. "All of them?" he managed to ask, the thought bringing a wave of revulsion.

"Yes. Grimnor, of course, complained. 'My people will starve! What will we do!' But eventually we struck a deal." Sartum raised his head "Come brother."

A fresh form walked out of the ground, the dirt and stone sticking to it as it appeared. More rock than anything else. It stood next to Sartum, smaller than the new god, somehow reduced next to him. "Grimnor." Sartum smiled.

Will couldn't process this. One God was bad enough, but two? Grimnor differed from what he'd expected, less impressive somehow. But he was still a god. But why two gods? Why was he here? In his mind, the thoughts clicked together, and a sickness filled his stomach.

Myriam must have come to the same conclusion. Her face pale, she stood finally, holding the stun rod that Will had changed tight in her left hand. "You can't. You promised!"

"I promised that I wouldn't attack the City. Of course, that was the unnamed me. I'm not sure it even counts anymore. But I know it doesn't cover Grimnor here." Sartum snapped his fingers at them both. "See, to save his people, to save his world, Grimnor made a deal. He and his people serve me for the rest of the time in this world, and in return, I keep his people alive, and therefore him alive as well." Sartum stood and the throne he'd made melted back into the ground as if it had never been there.

"So Grimnor leads your war for you?" Will gripped his hammer with all his strength. He wasn't sure what, if anything, it would do to a God, but he wasn't about to let this go.

"In this case." Sartum answered without even looking at Will. "He will lead my army to victory. I'll not enter the battle, though I might yell a few orders." Without a word, Sartum took a step forward and faded away to some other place.

Grimnor stood there, unmoving. Will wondered for a moment if this thing was Grimnor. Sartum wasn't exactly truthful, or hadn't been, or...

Will gave up trying to think about it. Either way, they had to escape and right now.

What did move then was a large group of soldiers. A group of twenty were approaching now at a fast run. Spears drawn and speeding up. Will hefted his hammer, wishing he had a shield of his own.

Myriam held the stun rod and nodded at Will. "We will not die here, I promise you." Her voice low, Myriam forced herself to not look at the form of Grimnor. In silence the form stood, looking more a statue than a god. It bothered her, it standing there.

Then the soldiers were upon them, and there wasn't anything else she could pay attention to.

"That's impossible." Mikol spat the words. "How could you even know that?"

"You SENT them to name him, remember? And the ward I drew on her, it takes power, but I can listen, if I work at it." Nollew spat and made a sour face.

"Power? So, you weren't using all your might here? To save the City? You are the reason the move failed!" Mikol was yelling now, but he didn't care. "Tarn Nollew, you are not worthy to be Tarn. I will see you removed, and your life forfeit as a traitor!"

"Don't be a fool Mikol." Grib cut him off. He was standing now, but obviously unsteady by the way he was hunched over. "Something else blocked our working. My bet is on that new god, Sartum. Your 'grand plan' may have cost us everything."

"You sent them out to name a god. You sent them out to complete him. Well, now he's complete. Done. And we are stuck here. It seems your plans need work." Yulisia added. Her face was still pale, but she, too, was standing now.

"Yes, I agree. A foolish plan." Rewil joined the others. "You let the god get a name. You sent them. "

"And you all agreed to it, do you not remember?" Mikol wanted to reach out with his power and explode the tiny lines of blood that filled the brains of all of them. To explode the poison in Nollew and Yulisa, right then and there. "I am not at fault here. You thought the plan was wrong? Yet you all went along with it. So, you are all cowards then I see."

Silence fell in the chamber. A sullen, angry silence. "Do we try again?" Nollew asked finally, breaking the hold the silence had. "I don't think it will work though."

"No." Rewil paused. "We prepare for war. Nollew gather your casters, I will ready the constructs. Yulisia, find a way out of this. Search the library. Something, anything we can use. And Grib? Ready your people. I fear if the walls fall, the lower and middle city will be torn apart. Get as many as you can into the Greystone ways, sealing them behind you."

"I am in charge Rewil, not you." Mikol yelled the words. "I will set the defense of the City. Your constructs alone should do it, assuming you haven't switched sides."

Mikol's anger grew as his words were totally and utterly ignored. Nollew and Yulisia left the chamber, ignoring Mikol. Grib followed soon after, giving Rewil a nod, almost a bow. He, too, refused to even look at Mikol. *Ungrateful wretch.*

That left Rewil and Mikol alone in the chamber. The blue light had faded some since the other Tarns had left. It was always brighter around those who held a boon. "Well, Rewil? Are you going to strike me? Yell at me?" Mikol refused to look at the man.

"No. I still have a hard time with this, you know that? That you, my friend, my mentor, you were pulling all these strings. You ruined my friendships, you tried to have people killed, you? Mikol?" Rewil sighed, looking back at the door. "Get your Healers ready. I know you want to argue, but I don't think you'd like to be neck deep in dead bodies if you don't offer healing."

Mikol wanted to argue, but Rewil was right. With the City not moving, the attack was now imminent. "Fine. When the army is gone, torn apart by the casters and your constructs, we will have a commons that will decide my fate, and yours."

Rewil turned and left, his shoulders slumped. Mikol watched him go, still angry. Why hadn't it worked? What had gone wrong? Could this named God stop them? The thought made him uncomfortable. No, one of the others had to have lied or interfered. Nollew, it had to have been. How had he been able to tell what was going on out on the plain?

Working the power here was very hard, outside of the one thing they had failed at. Even gathering his power was hard here, not doing anything with it. It made little sense. The City would stand, and Mikol would deal with those who stood in his way. For their own good, of course. Between Nollew's casters and Rewil's constructs, no normal army could stand against them.

He would hold his healers back, of course. Unlike Rewil and the others, Mikol knew there was no way the force arrayed against them would be successful. They couldn't. The City was eternal.

Chapter 62.

Will smashed his hammer into the closest soldier, trying to remember all the training he'd ever had in warfare, which, granted, wasn't a lot. Still, he could hear Vin's voice telling him to pivot at the hips, snap the hammer, don't try to use his arms and shoulders. Faster hits, more control. And it worked. The blow sent the soldier down, crumpling as he grabbed his side.

Will pushed the silver and white flash that had come from the hammer out of his mind. No time to think about that as he swung again, trying to knock the spear from another attacker's hands. An attacker that he could see was a woman. Will wasn't a fool; he knew it was common for armies to have women soldiers. He knew she would have no second thoughts about stabbing him in the gut with her spear that he was desperately trying to disarm her of. Yet he felt strange about fighting her.

He could see Myriam wasn't faring well, either. She was currently trying to escape a pair of green clad warriors, who, unlike the ones he'd been fighting, were clad in armor that he recognized. Lotin, a northern land that bordered the western sea. *Sartum had been busy.*

Why wasn't she using the rod? She could have stunned them both. Yet she continued to run, dodging in and out of the increasingly crowded group of the enemy. Will didn't have time to think on it, as his breastplate took a blow from behind from one of their attackers. The sound was horrible that it made, and the reverberations in his chest felt even worse. But it held, and he was thankful he'd made a backplate to go with the breastplate.

He slapped the spear away again, trying not to trip over his feet or any stones or earth they were churning up. Hints of fatigue were already hitting him. Desperately trying to keep everyone and everything in front of him, his blows were now more to delay than attack.

"Will... run!" Myriam's yell gave him a slight surge of energy as she finally used the rod. He saw then why she had waited. She'd gotten almost all the soldiers close enough together with her running and by using him to help gather them. Only one had escaped, but he'd caught the edge of the effect and while he was not out cold, he could not hold his weapons as he stood there, mouth agape.

"Run!" Myriam yelled again. Will did so, once again hating it. He'd lost some weight in the city, but the armor and the hammer somewhat made up for the missing amount. They made a straight line for the horse, which had moved back away from the fighting. "Faster!" Myriam yelled again.

Will's feet felt like hammers themselves as he ran, each step hitting the ground with force. A sharp pain traveled up his right shin and grew with each step, but he couldn't stop. He wouldn't stop. Reaching the horse, he tried to thank Myriam, who had already gotten there and was astride the animal, but his gasping didn't allow him to do so.

He reached out his hand, and she helped him up. Settling into the saddle, Myriam started the horse at a fast trot and then, as soon as she was sure he wasn't going to fall off, into a gallop. The ground sped away behind them. For whatever faults this horse might have had, it was strong and fast. The distance was eaten up as the walls grew closer. Soon the only thing Will could see behind them was the form of Grimnor, who still had not moved.   "I don't know where to go!" Myriam yelled as the walls began to loom over them. But it didn't seem to matter, as the horse knew. It stopped its mad gallop at one spot and waited. It didn't look any different than any other part, at least as far as Will could tell. Same smooth white and green marble. Yet… The wall shimmered and then, growing from the middle out, stood a pair of doors. Stable doors. The door opened and the horse, without waiting for Myriam or himself to do anything, entered.

The door closed and vibrated behind them as soon as the horse's tail cleared the opening. "Well… we lived." Will slid down, carefully. His legs were already sore from that gallop. Sore legs were a small price for escaping that madness.

"Yes. I wasn't sure we would." Myriam dismounted as well and set to unsaddling the horse. Unlike before, there was no one else here, only a door on the far side and, of course, other horses.

Will kept a firm grip on his hammer and looked around, searching for any waiting attackers. He didn't expect to find any, yet he was still on edge. "Myriam, what does Sartum mean? Where did you get the name?" Pausing, Myriam lowered her head. Will couldn't see her face and he wondered if he'd said something wrong. Better to apologize now, though. "I'm sorry if you don't want to talk about it. I won't pry!" Will blurted the words out, hoping that Myriam wasn't about to burst into tears. Instead, a peal of laughter burst from her as she raised her head. She was laughing so hard, her eyes were watering. "Will... Sartum is the name that Dileres traders give to donkey droppings."

Will stood still. Shock warred with humor and a tinge of fear. "You renamed the new god of humans after... donkey droppings?"

Myriam nodded as she still laughed, wiping her tears away. "Take that, oh great God of Humans." Myriam wheezed out as the laughter trailed off. "By the sparks, laughing feels good."

Will looked at Myriam with even more respect than he already had, which was considerable. She had gone right up to a god, a GOD, and named it after donkey droppings. He never would have had the strength to do that. Ever. "Myriam, you are one of a kind."

"Thanks, Will. You're pretty unique too." Myriam gave her eyes one last wipe and finished with the horse. "Let's go. I imagine the city will be moved soon."

The door to the room burst open at that, and Tarn Rewil came storming in. "There you are."

"Rewil? What are you doing here?" Will was confused. "How did you find us?"

"Nollew. That ward thing on Myriam. It's mostly gone, but he could tell me where you all were." Rewil paused, eyes darting around the stable. "No use for it. Come on. We must hurry. Will, I might need your help. Myriam, I'm sure you don't want to go back to the spire. But your gifts will be needed in the lower and middle city, I'm sure."

"What's going on Rewil? Is the move going to hurt people?" Will and Myriam exchanged glances. "The City won't be moved." Rewil hurried them through the smaller backdoor, and into a narrow tunnel and more stairs. "We tried. It failed."

"What do you mean you tried?" Myriam stopped on the stairs. "You tried to move the City when we were out there? Just leave us to the mercy of a god who hates us?"

Rewil didn't answer. He shook his head and refused to make eye contact with either of them. Will could see the pain on his face. "You did, didn't you?" Will added. "You tried to leave us behind."

"It was Mikol's idea. He pointed out that if you failed to survive, you'd still make the named God. What was it, Sartum? You'd make Sartum more powerful. And the City would be at greater risk. And if you did survive, the City would STILL be in more danger." Rewil's face had grown sourer as he spoke.

"Either way, we were in trouble. But move before he could be named? We'd buy space. Mikol is convinced there is nothing that this Sartum could ever do against the City. I am not so sure." Rewil turned back to them both. "I am sorry. I never should have gone along with it."

Will could feel the bile grow as Rewil had spoken. Tarn Rewil, one of the few people Will considered an actual friend here, or really, in the world, had betrayed them. Betrayed them both. Will was about to yell when Myriam rested a hand on his shoulder and squeezed it tight.

"We understand Rewil. The safety of the City comes first. Always." Myriam's hand squeezed hard again, cutting Will off from talking. "You didn't like it, that much is obvious."

"I didn't. I wanted to take it back as soon as the vote was cast. But it didn't matter. We can't move the city." Rewil pushed ahead again, and this time Myriam and Will both followed. Will still was angry, hurt. The idea of being left behind had never occurred to him. *I'm a fool. A thrice blunted fool.*

"We went to the chamber of the source. We began the working. The power had grown to a near crescendo. The very ground we stood on was shuddering and tearing free. We would move the City halfway around Alos. And then, on the cusp of success, it failed." Rewil slapped his bare hand on the wall.

"Why?" Will croaked out. He wanted to scream it in Rewil's face. But now was not the time.

"We don't know. Nollew thinks that the rebirth of Sartum broke the working, he wanted to try it again." Rewil led them on until they finally entered one of the main halls that stretched the length of the City walls.

"Here we are. We don't have much time. With us unable to move the City right now, we must fight. Will, I will need you to help me activate the constructs. I don't talk about it much, if at all, but each of the human sized or large constructs has a way of being used for defense. Every single one." Rewil gave a halfhearted smile. "We are going to be busy when this is over, repairing things after this Sartum attacks."

"Sartum and Grimnor." Myriam added.

Rewil stopped his stride and whirled around on Myriam. "What?"

"Grimnor. Sartum and I made a deal. A poorly worded one on my part, I admit, though I didn't know about Grimnor when it was made. I gave the name, in return for Sartum not to attack the city, and not kill any of my family."

"And it worked." Will added. "She made a bargain. But then, Grimnor appeared. Sartum said that Grimnor was now sworn to him, and that Grimnor would run the attack."

"So now we have to face two gods? Not one?" Rewil stared at them both. "You do not bring good news. The situation grows dire."

Chapter 63.

"Brother. Why did you let them escape?" Sartum appeared before Grimnor, forcing down his rage. "They were right here. And yet, you did nothing when they stunned my warriors. You stood there, like now."

Grimnor didn't speak, but a feeling of confusion filled the area. Confusion and sorrow. "Enough of that." Sartum snapped. "I'm done playing 'Guess what Grimnor means.' Speak."

"You didn't say to. You said to run the war after the agreement with the namer." Grimnor's voice was still the same harsh sound, filled with stone and rock.

"Do I have to tell you everything to do?" Sartum for a moment debated smashing the figure in front of him into shards and dust. He could kill Grimnor. He wouldn't put up much of a fight, not anymore. Every time they spoke, Sartum could feel his brother growing weaker. Though if he took that step, the others would not let him be. Grimnor had angered him. That was true, but it wasn't worth fighting a war with all the others over. Sartum knew that even after being named finally, he could not take them all on. Not at once. Named. The moment of being named had been incredible. Even now, afterward, he could not put it into context. Feeling parts of him merge and join in ways he never thought.

He had no memories of the last name he'd been given, or what that world had been like. The others all did. One more thing those horrid Vinik had stolen from him. But they had paid their price. Now, it was the City's turn. His connection to the namer had vanished once she had named him. So, he couldn't find her as he could before. While he had no sorrow at her upcoming death, he would have spared her and even the other one, William. He would have spared both, but they were now tainted. Cursed by their lives in the City.

"Gather the army, Grimnor. Gather your Gorom. Attack today." Sartum raised a new throne sitting on it. "I will watch you tear the place to the ground."

"My Gorom, the sun…" Grimnor pointed up at the bright clear sky.

"The dark will come." Sartum waved him away. "I will see this done brother."

Will followed Rewil, if only because he had no other choice. His shock at Rewil going along with moving the City still clung to him, but was turning into something darker. He was mad. Hurt. This bothered him, though. If he was going to leave anyway, why was he mad? Because they tried to leave him with the one being in Alos who wanted them dead. At least after it had gotten what it wanted. Now, the one thing the Tarns wanted to avoid was going to happen. Rewil had said that Mikol assumed they would win and defend the City easily from the massed attackers. Will wasn't so sure. If every one of those soldiers carried a god blessed spear, and hammer, on top of whatever the Gorom were doing, that was dangerous.

Yet, the City had the constructs, and the Casters. The thought of a moving mass of the constructs killing and destroying every enemy in their path was not one Will relished. But the arrogance of Mikol and the others didn't sit well with William. He wasn't about to downplay the threat they were under. In a detached way, he wondered what a god touched hammer would do to a construct. How the forces would interact. But that wasn't important, not really. And some of those people out there were from Palnor. He was sure of it. And that many god touched weapons had to be made somewhere, and the Guild was the most likely place. The Guild. Will didn't enjoy thinking about his failure there. He'd run so far after Duncan and turned his back on the one thing that Amder had asked of him. If I had done as Amder asked, none of this would have happened. None of it.

Will took a glance back at Myriam, who followed along for now. Her face set in a frown. She was deep in her own thoughts. Soon, though, she would leave them, heading into the lower city. It would keep her away from Mikol, it was true, but it would also put her in danger if the walls fell. Not that he expected them to fall. Nevertheless, the chance did exist. "Are you sure you want to do this?" Will slowed up to walk closer to Myriam. "You could come with Rewil and I. We will only be in the Crafters section for a small time, then back to the walls."

"No, I'm not sure. But there are things I need to try and fix. Jinir is out there, Ralta is out there, hunting Rauger. And Rauger is out there. They all have their problems, but I don't want any of them to die. Nor anyone in the lower city. They don't deserve this Will. Most of them are normal people, trying to make a living in this strange place. They all have a tiny fraction of the power, but for most of them, it amounts to nothing. Less than nothing." Myriam's frown deepened. "It all seems so unfair."

"I know. I don't understand it either." Will knew they would be separating soon. They were close to the junction where Myriam would go her own way, as he followed Rewil. The Tarn was setting a fast pace, so he didn't have much time.

"Myriam. When this is over. Leave with me. This place, it's wrong. The same lust for power that ruled Palnor rules here. I know I don't have the right to ask, but come with me." Will couldn't look at her, he was too nervous. "You should know, this would mean the end of our boon. Or at least most of it. The amount of power we'd been able to draw, out there, would be miniscule."

Myriam didn't answer. Her face had gone from a grim frown to what Will could only describe as blank surprise. "Will, I don't... I mean, I don't like this place much either, but I didn't..."

"Myriam. Go that way." Rewil had stopped, a side passage leading off to the right. "Will, follow. Quickly."

"Stay safe. If we live through this, let me know." Will spoke before she could. He paused for a moment, then reached out and hugged her. Feeling her in his arms brought back a slew of memories he'd tried to forget. The smell of flowers in the Guild garden. Quiet laughter, and a sweetness that never really left him. "Stay safe Myriam. Please."

Will ended the embrace and rushed after Rewil, a small smile on his face. Myriam had embraced him back.

❖

Nollew paced around his study, tearing through notes and ripping pages out that might have usable workings on them and stuffing them into his pockets. He'd already gathered the best of the casters together. There were fifty-three of them, all waiting. The nervous energy was impossible to ignore, though. Sweat and fidgeting hands betrayed it in all of them.

And why wouldn't they be? They had practiced for this, made new and terrible ways to use the power to kill and maim in defense of the City, but they had never actually used it. They had never had to. Every time it had been to the level where they would need to, the Tarns had moved the place somewhere else.

But that was no longer a possibility. Fighting a war had not been something he'd ever expected in his time as Tarn, yet here it was. He tore out another page covered with notes on how to change a fire rain working into a deadly ice rain working. Nollew had no idea what to bring.

"You're going to make a mess of your study. And when we win, I'm not cleaning this up you know." Yulisia entered the room, side stepping several notebooks that lay open and torn. "And you better not be tearing up any of MY books."

Nollew paused. He had been a superbly lucky man the last few years. Even with all the political intrigue and infighting, having Yulisia by his side had been the one thing that had kept him going sometimes. "Yuli, what are you doing here? I thought you were overseeing an emergency storage of the library?"

The library kept its own secrets, and one of them was that in the event of a direct and serious threat to the City, the library, and those who were sworn to that section would work to save as much of the knowledge as possible.

"The process is started. They can continue without me for a while. I came, because I found this." Yulisia held up a scroll case. Wooden, cracked and dusty. "While we were starting the storage, this scroll was found behind a set of the "*Wonders of the Southern Bloodkiss.*" Six volumes, each as large as an anvil."

"What is it?" Nollew took the scroll case from her, handling it carefully.

It was old, ancient. And two, Yuli only ever brought him things if they were important. There had been one thing he'd been after for years. Even before all this mess with Mikol. One scroll. "Open it." Yuli was obviously pleased with herself.

"I'd love to, but I've got all this preparation to do. We don't know how long we have until this Sartum attacks." Nollew tried to push the case back to her. "If I had time, I would. But right now, I'm not in the right state for this."

"Open it. It pertains to all this." Yulisia sat on the edge of a chair, avoiding knocking over the stack of notes that sat behind her, precariously balanced. "Trust me Nollew."

Nollew wondered what game she was at, but carefully opened the case, and let a very old and very thin parchment slip into his hand. A quick glance and all thoughts about the upcoming battle left his mind. This couldn't be what he thought it was, could it?

Chapter 64.

Will followed Rewil into the Crafters section. Thankful they were using the Greystone passages that only the Tarns used. He couldn't see anyone, but in the background, the running of feet and the occasional yell, muffled by the stone, were plain. It sounded like panic had already taken the spire.

"What are we after here again?" Will asked Rewil, trying to sort out his feelings. He was still surprised and angry that Rewil had voted to leave them behind, even if he had to admit that the idea made sense, at least logically.

"Something I thought I'd never need." Rewil said, but not following up. Will hated it when Rewil did that. They stopped at a side passage, and Rewil pushed sideways and then raised a small panel that slid open a larger door they could exit through. Will had been right. The panic obviously had set in.

He was looking down on a hallway from a balcony he hadn't even known was there. It was small, with one larger chair, Rewil sized. The hidden door closed behind them, leaving one other plain door on the far side. The hallway below them was chaos. Swarms of crafters moving to who knows where. A fair number carrying creations they had made. Some looked very much like weapons, others, Will had no idea. He almost used the sight to check to see how many were full of the power but knew he didn't have time.

"I used to enjoy sitting up here. I could hear crafters below me, talking, arguing. It almost made me feel like I was one of them." Rewil rested a hand on the chair. "I think those days are behind me now. Come." He opened the nearby door, showing a way into the back of his office.

"What do you mean? You're a crafter, you're always one of us. You lead us." Will was confused. Everyone, well, all the crafters, at least, liked Rewil.

"I'm the Tarn." Rewil began searching through a crate he pulled out from under the back workbench. "I'm a Crafter, but I'm the Tarn. The moment I became Tarn, a wall went up. Almost everyone in the spire treated me much differently after that. It's one reason I always liked you Will, you never did."

Will frowned. He understood that feeling. Even his short time as Forgemaster had shown him how people would treat him with that title. He'd never really thought about how it affected others, though. Will wondered if he should say something, but had no idea what to even begin to say.

"Here it is!" Rewil pulled a metal rectangle out of the crate. Bronze with a tracery of crimsonlace, it held a single black square in the middle of it. It looked utterly unremarkable.

"And what is it?" Will asked again, hoping he might get more information now that Rewil had found whatever it was.

Rewil looked at Will, his expression growing serious. "William. If the constructs are losing, this device will cause every construct in the City with the newer power sources to explode. If the City is at risk of falling, this is the insurance."

"What do you mean?" Will already hated this idea. "To blow up the city??"

"No!" Rewil shook his head. "I'm already doing a poor job at this. Every construct but a few, the rail riders and a few others, have switched to the more centralized power source. No simulacrum. Every one of those constructs that use a power source will be out there, in the valley, fighting. If somehow, they lose, those orbs of the power can be made, with this box, to explode."

Will remembered the violence of a power explosion. While a large part of that had been the quickway, the rest…." By the sparks." Will could imagine it, and it terrified him. Huge explosions of the power, each one throwing massive amounts of sharp metal and the power around. It would be chaos.

"Yes, you understand now." Rewil hefted the box. "It's not been activated yet, so it's safe. And only I can activate it. I hope I will not need to."

"Come, let's get back to the wall. The fastest is the quickway. We can use the Tarn's carriage." Rewil left the crate sitting on the floor, for once leaving a mess behind.

Nollew read the scroll three more times to make sure he understood. It was what he thought it was. At the founding of the City, before the sections, and the spire. Before the Tarns, there had been a group of people of many races, called here by the power. A call that they could not ignore. Among them was a singular person. No one knew their name, their race, or their sex.

But what was known was that this person, whomever they were, had created some of the first workings. And one of those workings was still active. Deep under the City was the source, but also there was a working known to the casters only. The shield.

Its purpose was unclear. But it sat under the foundations of the City. Many casters had spent long years studying it, trying to figure its purpose. How did it grow with the City? Why did it? How could this working still exist? And what was its reason for being there?

The only reason they even called it the shield was that it sat between the source and the rest of the City. It wasn't the cause of the hunger of the well, or the cause of the deaths, at least not that anyone could tell. The shield seemed to have another purpose, one that escaped them all.

But this scroll, this ancient scroll, gave the working to activate the thing. It maddeningly didn't say what it did, only how to start it. It was the first new piece of information about the shield found in centuries. Strange that today, of all days, it was found. Nollew did not like coincidences.

"And you found this?" Nollew put the scroll back into the cracked and dry wooden case. He didn't like things like this. Chance was rarely that useful.

"Yes. I was as surprised as you were." Yuli took a sip of water from a cup she had poured. She looked into the cup and gave a loud sigh. "I wish this was honey wine."

"Later. After this is over. I'll pay for a few barrels, and you can bathe in it." Nollew didn't like strings, and it felt a lot like someone, or something, was pulling him with this scroll.

"Promises must be kept Nollew." Yuli took a long drink of the cup and set it back down. "I must return to the library." She paused, however, her characteristic relaxed expression and almost laconic personality gone. "Be careful Nollew. We haven't fought a war before. I've only read about them, and none of them read easy. You belong to me, remember that."

Nollew smiled at her, keeping a smile on his face, regardless of what he felt inside. "Do not worry. Between Rewil's mechanical terrors, and our magic, no army of mere flesh and blood can stand against us."

Yulisia nodded, face still pale. She didn't answer at first, but came over to Nollew and kissed him on the cheek. "Be careful." Nollew watched her leave his chamber, wondering if that was the last kiss he'd ever get from her.

Rauger slumped into a corner of an alley, aware that he couldn't keep hiding like this forever. He'd avoided Ralta three times today, and all three were only because of the panic that had gripped the City. Rumors had already started flying that the Tarns had tried to save the City but failed. And the army outside the walls would burn the City to the ground. Or that the army outside was the army of the Downtrodden Lord, come to take the City for their leader, who would overthrow the Tarns. Or that the army was led by all the gods of Alos, here to take back their people, by force if needed.

Rauger did not believe most of it. He'd been in the spy business too long and could spot a lie. The only actual truths he was sure of, the Army was going to attack soon, and the City wasn't ready for it. The panic in the streets was real, even if it hadn't reached its peak. Lots of yelling, some running. But when the army did attack, panic would set in.

Grib was useless, probably holed up in the spire somewhere, hiding out. Jinir was missing in action, one reason that rumor about the army had gotten started. Either Jinir had started it himself, Rauger wouldn't put it past him, or the fact that the Downtrodden Lord was missing, and someone had put the two things together.

"You know Rauger, I thought you'd hide better." Ralta's voice was silk, with an edge of tempered fire. "Well, Ralta, I couldn't very well spend all day leading you in a chase. There's about to be a war on, if you haven't heard. I've got other things to do." Rauger gave a cheerful tone to his voice, even if he was cursing himself inside for getting distracted and not hearing her approach.

"You let me find you?" Ralta snorted as she lowered herself next to Rauger. "It's a strange day."

"Do you mean the upcoming attack on the City by the army of a god? Or that Jinir ordered you to kill me?" Rauger reached into a pocket, pulling out a small black flask. "I'd offer you a drink, but I know how much you dislike it."

"I dislike what YOU drink. That stuff is vile." Ralta pulled a knife out, balancing it point first on her finger without effort. "I imagine Myriam told you. About Jinir?"

"Yes. Nice girl." Rauger took a long drink of the flask, fighting the first sour taste before it faded into something far more pleasant.

"She is. It will probably get her killed though." Ralta flipped the knife and caught it again, point first, on the tip of her finger. "Did she explain it all?"

"He didn't include a time. You knew that though." Rauger put the flask back, careful to keep a fair amount. He had a feeling he'd need it a lot today.

"Exactly. I could kill you right now. Slit your throat, a few stabs in both lungs. Or I could kill you in a decade, when you're fat and lazy, playing that instrument of yours in some old inn here in the City." Ralta smiled. "All the same to me."

"And I didn't think you cared." Rauger snorted. "Well, are you going to do it now?"

"Not today." Ralta stood, keeping the knife balanced on her fingertip. "I think we will need everyone in this place before the day is through."

Chapter 65.

Will and Rewil stood on the outer wall. In another time, Will would have loved it. They were high up, and while he did not know how high, it was enough that he could see over the tops of the few trees in the valley. The valley spread out like a vast bowl in front of them. The red rocks were clearly visible, even in the bright sun. It was quite beautiful, if it wasn't for what else was out there. If he closed his eyes, he wouldn't even know what was coming, except for the scent of smoke. He wondered how it would look at night, thousands of campfires burning away. Or that horrid purple light of the Gorom. He didn't miss that particular shade of color at all.

They had spent the last few hours giving a visual examination of every construct they could find. The wall was full of them now. Rewil had activated some command that only he knew, and every single construct with a power source had come. With a single command, Rewil could send this force streaming out to kill the attackers.

"I don't want to do this." Rewil squinted in the light, facing the approaching army. It wasn't moving fast, not yet at any rate, but it was getting closer.

"I don't think anyone wants to fight a war, Tarn Rewil." Will wasn't fond of the idea either, maybe less than Rewil. Out there were Palnorians. Maybe even fellow Reachers. The idea did not sit well with him. *I wish Amder was here, in my head. Or Haltim appearing again. Or Duncan. Or Regin.* Anyone to give him advice.

"I didn't make the constructs to fight. They can work as guards, but to fight a war? I never wanted that for them." Rewil looked at the box he still held, the crimsonlace etching glinting in the sun.

"Wishing you had been successful in moving the City?" Will asked without thinking about the words. The realization of what he had asked wasn't a good thought.

"No." Rewil shook his head. "Yes. Maybe." Rewil returned his gaze to the approaching force. "It's complicated. But it doesn't matter. Not now."

The approaching force grew closer as a silence fell over the wall, and even the City itself. Even the air felt calmer, a stillness that settled into their bones. Rewil glanced up at the sun, then back to the approaching force. "What are they waiting for?" "Maybe for it to get closer to night." Nollew said as he appeared, climbing up the only stairs nearby.

"Why night? That could be dangerous for them." Rewil frowned. "It would be easy to blind them."

"Gorom." Will smacked his head. "They hate sunlight. I bet they want to wait till closer to nightfall. So that if they are needed, it won't be that hard on them. Remember, Grimnor is now leading the attack."

"Yes." Nollew frowned. "Word of that reached Yulisia and I. No one has seen Grib all day, and Mikol is hiding out as well. He may not know. Thank you Rewil, for sending the message."

"You're a Tarn. It's right that you should know." Rewil waved a hand. "I am not sure if that helps us or hurts us."

"We will see." Nollew surveyed the forces against them. "What are those?" Nollew pointed to a series of carts, each full of long black rods. "William?"

"I have no idea." Will really didn't know. He couldn't make out a lot of details, but what he could see, he didn't like. There were a lot of them, that was for sure. Black and dull, the surface on them made it hard to examine. "They look wrong."

"Well, whatever they are, if we do our jobs here, they will never get touched." Nollew turned to Rewil. "When your constructs attack. My casters will come out after them. We will spread out and start doing our job. I have the information you sent. How hot can the fire be? How careful do we need to be with lighting, acid, cold, mud, water, all of it. It made planning our attacks that much easier."

"I don't need you wrecking the constructs, flailing about throwing the power." Rewil almost gave a laugh. "Having that army win because of poor communication on our side would be downright embarrassing."

A horn split the air and ended the banter. As one, an immense mass of the enemy lurched forward. The army was coming. A series of war cries carried over the air. Full of anger and hate. Hate spurred by lies, but then again, most hate was. "How would they ever get past the wall?" Nollew yelled over the sudden din. "They have no siege equipment."

"Does it matter?" Rewil yelled back and with no further words, made a complicated pattern with one hand, and yelled a word that Will couldn't make sense out of in the sudden dun. Doors came out of the stone, and a whirling, crawling army of utter destruction was released.

The sun shone on the metal and claws of the larger units as they rolled forth with speed. The ground closest to the city was flat and held little other than dirt and grass, which offered no interruption to their progress. Spider legged constructs seemed to keep two legs up and used the other legs to walk.

Will wondered why until he realized they were more weapons. Pointed and sharp, they could stab through most armor, he was sure. The noise that rose from the movement of the machines was massive. Will covered his ears and winced at the mix of clanging metal and a horrible scrambling sound that reminded him of the bugs in the Gorom tunnels. It was madness.

Myriam kept her head low at first, but soon stopped. No one was looking at her, or for her. Not now. Most streets were empty here in the middle city. And the people she saw were far more locked into their own fear than to give a silver-eyed waif a second glance.

She considered looking for Rauger, but where to look? She might be able to find her way back to the inn he had taken her to, even though it was a decent walk. If she did so, it would mean leaving the people of the lower city to their own fate. The attack would come soon, she was sure.

"Hello Myriam." Ralta's voice from behind her made her stop her quick pace, nearly making her stumble. "I seem to be two for two today. Rauger didn't hear me coming as well." Ralta walked around Myriam, examining her. "Just that thin robe for protection?" "I wasn't dressing for a war this morning." Myriam felt herself relax some. Ralta's knives weren't out. *Wait, did she say Rauger?*

"You saw Rauger?" Myriam tried to keep the worry out of her voice but failed badly. "Is he… doing all right?"

Ralta smirked. "He's fine. I didn't kill him. Not yet, at any rate. I think we will need everyone with this insanity coming."

"You're not here to kill me either?" Myriam glanced around, wondering if there was any place she could hide and run. The idea was foolish as soon as she wondered about it. Ralta would have her pincushioned with a dozen knives before she could think.

"No. In all truth, I saw you. I was going to head back to stay with Jinir during this time." Ralta glanced away when she said Jinir's name, her voice softer.

"Curse my luck." Myriam took a breath. "I'm coming with you. I'm heading to the lower city in case the walls fall. I will heal everyone I can, then… well… we will see what happens."

"I wasn't going to ask you to. I don't know what happened today at that meeting, but it sure appears that things have changed all over." Ralta perked up, her long, Trinil ears sticking straight up. Ralta turned towards the wall, scowling. "The attack has begun."

"We'd better hurry then." Myriam broke into a run, hoping she didn't trip. Running in robes was a trying task. For a fraction of a bell, she pictured herself tripping and falling into the canal, being washed away before the true fight even began. *That would be my luck.*

The closest bridge came into view, for once not guarded. Not that it needed to be. The bridge wasn't there. The ends were shorn off, clean and shiny. Effectively leaving the lower city to their fate. Myriam turned to Ralta, unsure of what to say. Ralta's face was even more bleak than Myriam felt. She did not know it would be like this. How had that happened? Were all the bridges this way? "What now?" Myriam waited for a response that she wasn't sure would ever come.

Mikol wiped his hands on his robe, satisfied that he'd bought some time. He wasn't sure any of the others had even read the *Defenses of the City*, but he had. Read it three times and made notes. Lots of notes. Notes that spelled out actions that only a Tarn could take to secure the spire.

It had not gone smoothly. The writ had been vague in some parts, and the language was archaic overall. But it had worked. He had removed the bridges separating the middle and lower city. When the walls fell… IF the walls fell, the full brunt of the attack would fall on the lower city. They would be destroyed most likely, but sacrifices had to be made sometimes. He didn't think it even possible for this rabble outside the walls to take the walls, but in case the lower City was expendable.

He gathered his boon once more, seeking out his target. William Reis. The connection to the simulacrum was stretchy, at best. Its purpose fulfilled, Mikol was waiting for it to vanish, leaving poor William Reis none the wiser. But while it still existed, he would not throw away a potential tool.

Will's location bloomed in his awareness. On the wall, with Rewil and Nollew? That presented some interesting ideas. If Nollew fell today, Mikol would lose a powerful enemy, and none of the blame. It was a war, after all. People die in war.

Reaching out, Mikol touched his strained link with William. He reached out and twisted a tiny bit of the boon that Will carried and sent it to delve into Nollew. It was hard, but doable. But not yet. That was only a test to see if it was possible. Nollew was still useful.

Mikol could feel the fear grow in William through the link, a sudden spike of fear and anxiety. The attack must be starting. Mikol poured himself a glass of water and sat back. No army, even one led by a god, could breach those walls. He half wanted to go down and watch the end of the farce in person. But if he was going to make his move today, it was better he stayed here, far away from the battlefield.

Chapter 66.

Will had a hard time watching the initial clash. The constructs were more effective than he'd thought they would be, and he'd been sure they would be deadly. Seeing it though? It was a slaughter. While the army outnumbered the machines a hundred to one, each construct was far deadlier. Even from this vantage point, the ground was soon red and most of the constructs were covered in blood.

Nothing he wanted to see. Or hear. He'd expected the sight, but not the sound. Screams, oaths, the sound of breaking bones, all of it carried up this high. Mixed with the crash of metal on metal as soldiers tried to find a weak point in the things. Swords thrust forward and skidded off the metal bodies, a few times generating sparks, but usually a scraping metal noise that made Will's skin crawl. The hammers were more damaging, but even then, it took six or seven of the attackers to even dent one construct. Behind the constructs, a long line of casters filed out as the machines pushed the battle line back. Nollew had gone to join them as soon as the battle had started. They had fanned out, a single one every so often. From here he couldn't make out which one was Tarn Nollew. All the Casters were doing something, though. His sight showed him the power swirling in identical patterns around each of them, or at least all the ones he could see. And soon arcing bolts of fire sprung forth, crashing behind the front line of Sartum's forces. It pinned them between a hellish fire and a whirling machine of death.

"I can't watch this." Rewil turned away. "I'm proud to defend the City, but... that's a slaughter."

Will had to agree. The first wave of the attackers was destroyed or being destroyed. He didn't know how many soldiers Sartum and Grimnor had sent to their deaths. "They are plainly throwing them away. They can see they aren't a match for our forces. Why do this?"

Rewil shrugged, keeping his face turned away. "Hopefully they see the folly of this and leave." His voice, however, was not hopeful.

Will doubted it as well. He'd met Sartum and Grimnor, and while the mere thought of the fact that he'd met gods, GODS, of all things, his perception of them had changed. Once the thought of meeting a god would have terrified him, or at least held him in awe. Not so long ago, even looking at the busts in the Church of the Eight back in the Reach made him nervous.   Now, not so much. They were petty and scrambling things, only after power. At least Sartum was. Amder hadn't been, but Amder had only been a part of the whole, the good part. Will knew that was not totally correct, but he liked to think it. Below was quieter now. The fires still burned, a long line of red and yellow flames burning with the power. Then the actual battleground. A sight that Will had to force himself to look at. The constructs stood still except for a few of them that reformed a ragged line. None were broken, though a few seemed to move less smoothly.

The casters stood, waiting, and to Will's surprise, oddly calm. Hands up ready to work more and deadlier power. And of the enemy forces, Will could see nothing. They were all dead. Every single one. Even the ones that had tried to run were killed by a construct or died in the magically furious fire. Silence fell as both sides took a breath. "Run away, leave! Why don't they understand?" Will whispered to no one. "They are all going to die!"

"They hate us Will. Or at least their gods do. The Tarns have long known of this possibility. Yet we never wanted to fight, it's why we always moved the City somewhere else. We take no pleasure in this." Rewil hunched over, his enormous frame somehow compacted by the day's events. "I rue the day I made the constructs now, even if those they kill wish to kill me."

A horn sounded, two blasts that echoed off the rocks, a lingering sound that held harsh echoes. The blast brought forth a fresh wave of attackers, a sight that made Will sick to his stomach. He was about to turn away when something different struck him. This new wave was comprised of the same armed soldiers, but with them came a series of hooded figures holding those long black rods in gauntleted hands. Those were Gorom. He knew those pale robes anywhere. But what were the rods? The Gorom ran along, keeping up with the charging wave when they stopped, somewhat short of the fire line. And almost as one, plunged the rods into the ground. The effect was immediate and terrifying.

"Rewil, you need to see this." Will yelled as the sight before him took shape. The fire, still burning hot thanks to its connection to the power, leaped into the rods. Into and vanished, as if the rods had sucked every speck of the power away from it. The fires died down, and ultimately vanished, unable to sustain themselves.

"I don't need to see a slaughter, William." Rewil refused to turn around.

"No, you need to see this." Will was stunned by the sight. The casters below were yelling at each other, but it wasn't doing any good. Every working they made only flowed into the rods, unable to do anything else. The worried cries grew as everything they tried failed. More than half a dozen of the Caster's line had already backed away from the battlefield, and one took off at a run towards the City wall.

The constructs were another problem. They moved forward, approaching the army, but froze in place. Unable to move if they got close to the rods… William concentrated and examined the things with his sight. He instantly wished he hadn't. The rods were wrong. A twisted and dark sight, the rods had something of a simulacrum about them, but it was horribly wrong. They gave him an icy shiver if he looked at them for more than a few moments. But what they did was obvious. Every scrap of power that came near them was sucked out and sent into the ground. Into Alos.

"REWIL!" Will yelled now. "The constructs, they are failing!"

Rewil turned around, his face surprised. "What do you mean…." His voice left him as he saw the battlefield. "Oh, no." Rewil pulled the box out, the strange device and hesitated for a second, then closed his eyes and pressed the black square.

Will closed his eyes along with him and braced himself for a tremendous explosion. An explosion that did not happen. Will peered through his eyes to see. The constructs power sources were empty, dragged out of the machines by those rods. Every single construct now either lay on the blood-soaked ground, or was still upright, frozen at the moment the power was torn from them.

"We have to do something!" Will yelled, as another force started towards the City, even as this second wave surged forward. More of the casters ran, but the rest stayed, desperately trying to find a working or something they could do to stop this. Their bravery was to no avail. Will watched in horrified silence as the enemy charged at them, caught those who ran, and executed them all. Soon every Caster he could see was dead. He didn't see Nollew though, and hoped the man had made it back to the City. A few of those who had left early enough had managed to get back to the walls and back inside their protection.

"It was a trap." Rewil examined the battlefield below. "They drew us out. Get the casters to commit, get the constructs to commit, and then unleash those *things*, whatever they are. We have lost the two strongest weapons this City has." Rewil slammed a meaty hand on a nearby battlement. "This was planned well."

"But they lost so many soldiers." Will didn't get it. "Why throw away so many lives?"

"It's war William. Those fighting for the enemy are following their gods. They will throw themselves into battle without question. And I'd bet that vanguard of forces that attacked first were not their finest soldiers. Expendable." Rewil spat. "Reducing lives to pieces in a game."

They watched as the second wave got to the walls and waited. Will wondered why the City didn't have defenses for this. He'd heard cities had catapults, or giant vats of boiling oil, to drop on attackers. The answer was obvious, though. They never thought they would need them. Both were happy to see Nollew appear, breathing hard, accompanied by two other casters. One of which had a makeshift bandage on his left shoulder, but otherwise none of them had any obvious injury. "Nollew! You live!" Rewil exclaimed and helped his fellow Tarn find a place to rest.

"I can't believe it." Nollew wheezed out. "We had them, we HAD them. We had a plan of the battle; it was going to be glorious... Fire first to set the line. Not only would it harm the enemy, but it would also show us the normal range we had on workings. Rain and water were to be next. They are all wearing metal armor, soak it and the ground well, and then start the lightning. Beyond that was lava, and even a working for strong acid as rain."

Nollew took a drink from a cup offered by one of the other casters, who shared Nollew's exhaustion. "But those things, they…" Nollew threw up a hand and sat in silence. "I've never seen them before. But they appear to attract the power and redirect it into the world itself. It's an odd design." Will kept his voice low, if only to calm everyone down. "And they feel… wrong." Nollew nodded, face showing none of his normal amusement. "I know what I must do now." He finally said. "I hope this works."

"But any working you throw at them will get sucked into those things." Will pointed out into the field. "It would be a waste."

"I'm not throwing it at them." Nollew grinned then, finally. The smile held only determination, not humor. "I'm throwing it at the City."

Chapter 67.

Myriam and Ralta stood at the canal edge, both lost in their thoughts. How had this happened? Why had it happened? "Have you ever seen this?" Myriam could see the other side, and see a few people milling around, also confused. It was too far to hear anything, especially over the rushing water of the canal.

"No." Ralta frowned at the water. "I didn't even know it was possible." She walked to the edge and looked down into the black, swirling water. "Rauger knew a way to get in and get out, so maybe there's a way for me. Or us, if you're still coming."

Myriam remembered that he'd used that trick when they had met. It seemed rather dangerous, though. She'd seen the power at work with this water, and it was nothing she wanted to get lost in. The force used was far more than she could handle swimming. "I don't know. One dangerous move and that water will drag us under."

"I have to get to Jinir." Ralta shrugged. "You know that." Her face flickered with sadness and determination.

"I know." Myriam still felt pity for her. Ralta could be terrifying, with her knives and willingness to hurt, or even kill. But she was devoted to Jinir. And in love with the man. A man who did not love her back, nor did Myriam think he ever would. Jinir only loved himself.

"Stay here then." Ralta pursed her lips. "If I make it, we will try to get a makeshift bridge put up. If things go badly, we need to evacuate people."

"Good idea." Myriam wondered if she should try the same thing on this side of the bridge. She doubted she'd get many to help. Middle city dwellers didn't consider lower city folk worth much. Only their coin was useful.

"Wish me luck!" Ralta took a deep breath, and before Myriam could answer, dived into the inky black water, disappearing. Myriam watched for a few minutes, hoping to see her exit on the other side, but no such sight greeted her. She could see nothing in that frothy swirling mess. Her fear grew, but she pushed it aside. She'd not see Rauger climb out either, so that meant nothing, right? She had nowhere to go though. Ralta had said she'd seen Rauger, but not where. Will was with Rewil somewhere. Will. The thought of him was confusing. She admitted she'd been a fool with the boy. *Man.* She corrected herself. William Reis was no longer any kind of boy. The embrace had brought up feelings she wasn't sure of. And did she even want to go near that sort of thing again? Not that she was sure of anything at this point in her life. The water below raged, but came nowhere close to escaping the brick walls of the canal. An errant leaf from some plant somewhere blew against her robe. She picked it off and threw it into the water. It landed and traveled for a short time before it was washed under and vanished.

That's me. Just getting moved around, outside of my control. Myriam thought about what Will had asked. To go with him. Out of the City. Out of all this. She knew he was serious. Will wasn't one to ask things like that and not mean them. She reached into herself, grabbing the boon and filling herself with the power.

If she left with him, all this would be gone. She still might be able to work a trickle of the power, but nothing like this. The way she was now, she could heal almost anything. She had done what others had told her was impossible with the healing of herself, regardless of the side effects. What other wonders could she do with it? *But if I stay, I will always be that leaf.* Mikol, or if he was gone, whoever came after him would be pulling her strings. She wasn't City born, and she never would fit in all the way. Her power and skill made her valuable. To Mikol, to Jinir, to anyone with a want of power. And that description fit a great many people.

The ground shuddered under her feet, and she fell to all fours, thankful she wasn't closer to the canal edge. The shudder hit everything, and the shudder was repeated, harder this time. Cracks appeared in a wall nearby, adding a new sound as plaster and wood cracked in sharp counterpoint to the low rumble. Screams came as well; yells as more than a few people ran out of buildings that swayed with the shudders. Suddenly, as it came, the shaking and tremors ended. The shudders ended, leaving only a few leftover cracks and snaps, as a few other walls split in the aftermath. Myriam couldn't guess what that had been, but she had no chance to think on it as the very ground she stood on erupted into a white glow that shot upward. It was everywhere and covered everything she could see. What new insanity was this?

Nollew stood still, both of the other casters with him keeping a hand under each arm in case he fell over. The man was doing something. Will could see the power flowing out from the man into the City to something hidden. The hidden thing appeared without warning, and Will had a hard time not yelling in surprise.

It was everywhere. Under all the City, under each street, under each building, even under the wall. Unlike any other use of the power he'd seen, it felt old. Ancient. The appearance of whatever it was brought forth a shuddering that made him yell in panic, his face flushed from surprise. He stumbled off to one side, almost pushing Rewil over and down the stairs.

The stones underfoot shifted, and for a moment, Will thought they were all going to fall to their deaths. Crushed by falling stone was not a good way to go. Rewil didn't seem to do much better as the Tarn grabbed at anything to help him steady himself. "This place is going to shake apart if this doesn't stop!" Rewil yelled as the shudder grew stronger, louder. Will was about to agree when, as fast as closing a door, the noise stopped. It was totally silent, a strange feeling after the recent event. And then came the light. From the edge of the wall, all the way into the City, as far as Will could see, a white glow was coming. It filled every road, every square, every alley. It felt warm almost. Comforting. "There." Nollew said before waving off the other two casters and slumping against a wall. "I've done it."

"What did you do?" Rewil asked, his face pale as he took in the City. "It's... I've seen nothing like this."

"I don't think anyone has ever used it. I only recently learned how to make it work, and even then, I didn't know what it did. Not really. But now I do." Nollew wiped sweat off his forehead. "That, is the shield, or a shield I should say." "What does that mean?" Rewil did not keep the confusion out of his voice. Or was it anger? "You have kept secrets Nollew."

"Every Tarn of the Casters has known of it. Under the City was a hidden working. Cunningly hidden. I don't even know how the first person to figure it out found it. But the knowledge of how to find it was passed down from Tarn to Tarn." Nollew smiled at the sight. 'Pretty, isn't it?"

"What does it do, Nollew?" Rewil snapped back. "I swear, sometimes I want to throw you off this wall."

"That would not be possible, not now." Nollew laughed. "Good thing I know you're not serious. That glow, that shield. Yuli found the scroll on how to activate it. What working to make it activate. It's old, you know, placed by one of the first ones. Before the Tarns, before the sections or the spire. How it works I still don't understand."

Standing again, Nollew made a rude gesture to the far side of the valley. "Take that!" Nollew was grinning now. "As for what it does? Inside the City, right now, while the shield is active, No violence of any kind can happen. No fighting, no killing, no nothing. I didn't know it would do that, but it's a wonderful defense."

"What's stopping them from taking the rods and putting them on the wall?" Will pointed out the one flaw in this idea that he could think of. This shield was impressive, though. He'd never thought of something like it. But then again, he wasn't a Caster.

"The wall itself." Nollew shrugged. "I don't know how those rods work exactly, but I could see them in action. They need to be very close to the magic for it to work. Add in that the way the shield works. It's bound to the ground, to Alos as well. So, based on what I've seen, if they tried, the rods would take the power, feed it back into the ground." Nollew paused, then grinned with some satisfaction. "Where it would be taken in by the shield and be right back at full strength."

Rewil, for the first time since this attack, gave a chuckle. "Nollew, that is one of the smartest things I've ever heard. You saved the City."

❖

Mikol sat in stunned silence. What was this? First the whole spire shook, enough that for a moment his unbroken faith in the place's power had faltered. Then the shaking had stopped, and everything was now bathed in a soft white glow. Everything. The entire city. Mikol tried to use his boon to figure it out, but it made no sense to him. What was this? If he tried to find its source, it flittered away. If he tried to find its function, his mind got hazy, peaceful. Who had done this? Was it some attack that this Sartum had found? But it didn't seem to do anything. It all just glowed.

He raised his hand to slam onto the desk in frustration, but much to his surprise, he couldn't. He wanted to, but his arm wouldn't do it. Mikol broke into a delve, using his book to find the problem. This he could do. He was the Tarn of the Healers; nothing was beyond his skill. At first everything seemed normal, but then, faintly, the lines were plain. It was thin white lines. Every time he tried to slam his hand down, they appeared and stopped him. *White lines, white glow...*

It was some sort of defense then. A defense he had never heard of. It wasn't in any of the records of the City he'd ever seen. A working that prevented all violence in its area. It was a genius idea. He had to admit that. But it might make his plans of removing himself from Nollew and Yulisia difficult. Plans could be remade, however. The only thing that still worried him was where had this come from, and who had made it. But the answer was obvious as soon as the question formed. There was only one person who might have the skill, Nollew.

'Well played." Mikol lowered his hand and watched the glowing City below. Nollew had made this working. But why? Between his casters and the constructs, there should be no need for this. Something had changed out there on the battlefield. The link with William was still there, but it was growing fainter as time passed. The tiny simulacrum would not be around too much longer. But he might listen in, at least for a short time.

Chapter 68.

Sartum could feel his anger growing. Everything had been perfect at first. The fraction of the army that Grimnor had sent first was dead. A high cost, but they had removed the two largest threats that the City could use. It appeared so, at least. Those machines had been worrying at first, and a part of him was curious to see how they worked. But the casters had always been the one threat he'd been most worried about. Even if they were blasphemous. The anchors had worked exactly as designed and had also taken the constructs down. As whatever power that they ran on was sucked away. He hadn't expected that threat, but they had been rendered powerless, so the threat was over.

"But now, we are stuck." Sartum muttered and swung his hammer, slamming it into the ground. The mortals inside the place had done something massive. A ward that covered the entire city, that made violence impossible. What was worse was the way it was made. It drew from the magic of Alos. Meaning his anchors would do nothing to the ward. "Grimnor!" Sartum yelled, slamming his hammer onto the ground again. Grimnor flowed out of the ground, silent as always. "What are we going to do about that?" Sartum pointed at the City with the hammer. "The anchors are useless. It feeds the power back into the thing."

Grimnor was no use. Never one for quick thought, he stood still and contemplating. It was one of his major faults, as far as Sartum was concerned. "Useless." Sartum threw down his shield and hammer, frustration growing. "I want one of those machines, though. I might do something with that."

"I never should have agreed to that mortals' terms." Sartum wanted to hurt something, kill something. His gaze fell on Grimnor, but he decided not to take his frustration out there. Grimnor was a fading god, and soon enough, wouldn't even exist. And regardless of anything else, he was sure the others would not accept him taking that step. An enormous pile of anchors still stood nearby, unused. But they were useless now. Sartum studied them, feeling the faint, almost imperceptible tugging they gave off. The anchors can't be used to end the ward, because they feed the magic back into the world. *But could they feed the power into something else?* The constructs? Possibly, he would have to have some of the things saved for study. But that would take time. Time he didn't have and didn't want to take. The anchors fed the power back into the ground because they were placed in the ground. But what if they were held? Could a mortal be used to hold the power like that?

"I need a champion!" Sartum's voice rang out, echoing around the encampment. "Soldiers, strong, and pure of heart. Come to me!" Mortals came. Sartum did not care one bit about the purity of their heart, but they seemed to like that kind of nonsense. His creation had grown strange to him, without him there to guide them. One more thing he'd have to fix over the coming decades and centuries.

A group of fifty soldiers finally had gathered. Enough for this test, at least. They seemed to be led by a large man wearing leather and chain. Older, the man was kneeling, head lowered. At least some mortals knew how to behave. "My lord. You have called us?" The man kept his face down.

"Yes. The foulness in the City has an unexpected defense. One that we must find a way to remove. I have an idea. Each of you will take two of the anchors. Barehanded. And attack the City with them. If this works, the power that hides the doors, and that cursed new defense should be drawn into the anchors." Sartum flicked a wrist towards the waiting devices.

"My lord..." The man's voice was confused, unsure.

"Are you refusing to follow the desires of your god? Your maker?" Sartum lowered the pitch of his already low voice, but made it louder, more for effect than anything else.

"My lord, will that not hurt? Will the power not be drawn into your holy miracle, and then into us? Magic is not meant for us. That is a central truth, you taught us." The man finally raised his head. A few gray hairs mixed with the brown and red on his face and head, but he appeared strong, healthy to Sartum's eyes.

"Yes. It will hurt. And yes, that is true. But for this purpose, it will be different. You will not be using magic; you will drain it. You will be part of the anchor itself." Sartum liked the idea. It would burn out these dedicated mortals, but there were always more mortals. A minor sacrifice for the end of the City. The man bowed and argued no more. He approached one wagon that still held the anchors. Removing his heavy leather gloves, he took a deep breath and, with no more wasted time, grasped an anchor in each hand. The effect was instant. He went rigid, his face tight, and locked into a scream that had no sound. Slowly, his back arched, and he held that pose for a while.

Sartum wondered if the mortal's back was going to break when the solider returned to normal and turned towards the god. Normal was the wrong word to use. While his body was back to normal, his mind obviously wasn't. A madness clung to his mind. Sartum could feel the gibbering and howling that echoed in the soldier's head.

"Do you understand what you must do?" Sartum asked the man.

"Yes, my lord." The voice was unfamiliar now as well. Before, low and confused, it was higher, each word almost ending with a hiss.

"The rest of you, go!" Sartum waved his hands as the rest of the assembled soldiers took their anchors. Six of them did not survive, and died right there, their bodies unable to process the pain and power that the anchors offered. But the rest made it through the initial contact. Though all now seemed to join the first of their kind in his madness. "Attack! And may the City fall beneath your might." Sartum waved his hand forward, sending his new weapon forward, and into the fray.

Will sat back against part of the wall, full of relief. Somehow, someway, they had outmaneuvered two gods. The City was safe. This shield that Nollew had made work was incredible. Sartum could scream all he wanted, but his army couldn't breach the walls, and couldn't even commit violence to them.

"Nollew?" Tarn Yulisia appeared at the top of the stairs, relief obvious on her face when she saw him, sitting down with the other two casters.

"I'm fine, Yulisia." Nollew grinned. "It worked! The complete city is protected. All of it."

"It's incredible, Nollew. Though it might have been a good idea to warn some of us about the shaking. About a third of the remaining volumes fell off the shelves, and more than a few people in the spire, and outside the spire, ran for cover."

"You felt that even in the spire?" Rewil's eyebrows shot up. "William, it looks like we will need to do some clean up."

"The spire was the worst for what I understand." Yulisia sat next to Nollew, resting her head on his shoulder. "The rest of the City had some cracks and minor damage, but nothing else. Though we do have one issue. Outside the quickways from the wall, the lower city is cut off."

"What do you mean?" Will blurted out. "Myriam went to the lower city to help people in case the walls fell, and to find Ralta and Jinir, and Rauger."

"Why would she want to find them?" Yulisia frowned. "They didn't exactly treat her all that well."

"It's who she is." Will decided not to get into it much. He doubted they'd ever understand. "But what do you mean, cut off?"

"Somehow, all the bridges are gone. And the Greystone tunnels that go under the canal are sealed. Can't open them. It sounds like a defense, like the shield." Yulisia's frown faded. "But it's only the lower city. The spire is safe."

Will waited for someone to argue with her, but none of them did. Even Rewil didn't raise an objection. *One more point of proof that leaving this place is the right idea.* Rewil, in fact, was standing facing the valley. The light was dim and growing darker by the minute. "Will, what color lights was it again the Gorom use?"

"Purple. Days of purple light were enough to make me hate the color." Will shifted, trying to find a more comfortable spot for his back. "Why?"

"You should all come see this. I don't understand what I'm seeing." Rewil's voice betrayed something Will had hoped to not hear for the rest of the day. *Fear.*

Will and the others stood and rushed over to the wall, looking below. It was a strange sight. A small group of soldiers were running as fast as they could at the City, and each was carrying two of those evil rod looking things. But they wouldn't do any good. Nollew had explained that. Behind them came a large group of Gorom. Nearly six times as many, but each was carrying what, in the dim light, looked like a horn, or some kind of musical instrument. And a glowing purple orb tied to their belts. Awareness crashed into Will. As a remembrance of blind terror, a scrambling run through pitch black caves, a falling over into a monster filled nightmare gripped him. And the death of Vin. "FEARSONG!" Will's voice came louder than he expected.

"What?" Nollew looked at him oddly, as did all the others. "What's fearsong?"

"It's a Gorom weapon. It's not magic, it doesn't use the power, at least not as far as I know. The Gorom discovered a way to make a sound that causes anyone who hears it to fall into a blind panic. You can't control it. You MUST run away. It's horrible stuff."

"But we are safe, Will. We are decently far away, and they can't breach the shield. Don't worry." Rewil frowned at the Gorom, thumbing his face. "I'd like to get a look at one of those things they use, though. Might be interesting uses."

Will wanted to scream. They didn't understand. "If we can hear it, they can use it." Will pointed down the stairs. "We all need to get out of earshot. Now."

Chapter 69.

"Will, you are overreacting. Look, they don't have them ready to play."
Nollew pointed below. "They have them all on their backs. When the
rods don't work, they will pack up and leave. We've won."

Will didn't agree. One, something about the soldiers carrying the rods
bothered him. Some detail. Two, if Grimnor was in charge, he wouldn't
send his Gorom into the battlefield without good reason. Why were they
carrying two rods? Before, the rods had been placed one at a time by the
Gorom, covered head to toe, and thick gauntlets. What was he missing?

"Rewil, the ones carrying the rods. Are they wearing gloves?" Will didn't
dare look. He wanted to be close to the stairs when the horns sounded.
Maybe he could get far enough out of earshot that way before it got bad.
He hoped so.

"What does that matter?" Rewil frowned. "Will, I understand your
reaction to the horns, but I agree with Nollew. It's a pointless attack on
their part."

"Look, now!" Will closed his eyes, hoping to hear that yes, they did.
Sartum couldn't be that wrong, could he? To make living people do that?

"Fine." Rewil peered over the edge. 'No. But they are almost…"

The words died on his lips as the first of the enemy carrying the rods
reached the wall. Instead of planting them in the ground, they used them
both as a tiny ram, slamming them into the outer wall. The effect was
instant. The wall shimmered and glowed as the door, magically forced to
be absent, appeared. All along the wall, the same thing happened. Each
soldier carrying the rods screamed in pain but kept going.

"What?" Rewil yelled, his voice full of shock. He didn't get to say
anything else as the doors, also closed with magic, were rent open. As the
soldiers swarmed in, everywhere they went, the glowing shield vanished.
It was obvious the pain was terrible, as a few of those carrying the rods
collapsed. But some ran on, grimacing, screaming. Or, sometimes,
giggling and open laughter as the pain drove them into madness. Huge
swatches of the shield were already gone, as whatever working that made

it unraveled under the rods. Soon, over half the city was no longer under the power of the shield, and the rest was falling apart in front of their very eyes. The moment of victory was fading. "What happened?" Nollew's voice, only moments before calm and almost cheerful, was now torn into panic. "How can this be happening?" his voice rose with each word, his face growing red with either fear or anger.

"Sartum! He's using people to hold the magic, instead of it returning to the ground. He's killing them, or at least hurting them, but it worked!" Will looked at Nollew, Yulisia, Rewil, and the others. "Come, we must get out of range!" Will's voice barely had reached them, when the horns sounded for the first time. Will's world vanished. In a torrent of utter terror, he threw himself down the stairs, along with the others. *Escape! He had to escape! He had to run, hide, dig a hole and hide. Never come out, run, run, RUN.* He plunged down the stairs, ignoring every elbow and thump, every knock and kick as he and the others ran. He could feel the armor take a massive hit as he slipped on the stairs. There was a horrible crunch sound nearby, but it didn't register as he had to run, he had to run, he had to...

Silence.

Will took a huge breath, gasping to find air and clear his mind. He was on a landing; the stairs continued downward. Rewil, pale and still was unmoving nearby. As well as one caster he'd never learned the names of. "Rewil?" Will ran over to the Tarn, shaking him, but one look was obvious. Rewil was dead. The back of his head was smashed in. In the panic, he must have fallen and landed right here. Will couldn't process this. *No, No! Rewil couldn't be dead, he couldn't be... NO!*

"Yulisia? Are you all right?" Nollew's voice came from farther down than Will was. "That was..." Nollew stopped. "William? Rewil? Hodge? Vimil?"

"I'm here." Will closed his eyes. How could Rewil be dead? It... made little sense. He couldn't accept this. Not now. Not like this. "Rewil... he is dead." Will couldn't grasp it. Rewil, dead. His mentor, his friend, his Tarn. Just dead. How had it happened like this? Will's breath caught, and he tried to take a deep one to steady himself. But his breastplate restricted it, and it led to coughing that warred inside with the sorrow and fear that gripped him. Rewil was gone.

This armor had saved him. He'd hit the stairs hard, but most of the blow had been in his chest. Not a single mark showed on the stuff. He wished Rewil had been wearing it. It might have saved him. It might have taken enough of the blow. Might. How could this happen??

"What??" Yulisia's voice broke, and he heard running steps up the stairs. Yulisia and Nollew appeared from lower down, running to Rewil's body. "How??"

"He must have tripped in the panic. I don't know what his name is, but that caster friend of yours, Nollew, he is over here." Will pointed to the Caster, whose neck was at an angle that no neck should ever be. Will felt himself going numb and tried to feel something. Anything. But he felt empty now. Some giant pit was opening in his heart, and every single thing he could ever feel was being sucked away.

"Hodge." Nollew's voice broke. "I couldn't even think. I had to run... I had to escape."

"Fearsong." Will explained. He wanted to yell at them, tell them he had told them so. That if they had listened, Rewil and this Hodge person would be alive. But that wouldn't do any good. Sartum was winning. The city would fall. And there was nothing he or any of them could do about it.

Mikol sat, grasping at his robes. His mind was still fighting off the effects of that sound. Fearsong? Will had called it. Even through the link he shared with the boy, the panic had come close to making him run from his desk. A blind, unthinking panic had almost overcome him. He guessed the only reason it hadn't been he was hearing it through the simulacrum, and not in person.

All of this... Rewil was dead? The city was going to fall? How had they been beaten? The city had stood for thousands of years. A bastion to all who sought the power. And it would fall? Now? In a single day? Mikol couldn't imagine it. Everything he'd spent his life on swept away in an instant. Nollew and Yulisia would get what they wanted, at least for a short moment. Mikol wouldn't run anything when there was nothing left to run.

He could see them through Will. A pair of sad faced fools. This was their fault. He was sure Nollew had stopped the city from moving. Just to spite Mikol. Serves them both right, the City will fall all because they didn't understand the truth. Leading a place like the city requires a single firm hand. It was that simple. It was his fault. Her fault. If they had done what they were supposed to, the city would be safe. Mikol would be safe. Instead, it was all ruined. Ruin and death. Death. Mikol smiled. At least he could make sure he lived longer that they did.

He reached out through Will's still terror addled mind, a feat which was surprisingly easy. The panic and its aftereffects reduced the resistance to his working. With a pair of thin tendrils of the power, he thrust them deep into the bodies of both Nollew and Yulisia. Activating the tiny poison ball that had been placed there a few years ago was trivial. He could feel the poison crack open and release the death into their bloodstream. He followed it with a second, working to speed up the effects. He wanted to watch them die. They must all die. The poison worked fast with the second working. He could feel them shut down, the poison killing all communication between the parts of the body.

Both were taken so quickly they couldn't even yell or process. Through Will's eyes, he saw them try to stand, to talk, but ultimately convulse. A black foam on the lips and then fall, as if a puppets string had been cut. The satisfaction he felt was worth the risk. The city would fall, but he would standalone this time. And Mikol Nese would rebuild the City, his City.

Myriam had been trying to understand the glow when it left. The power she could feel being wrenched from it, and flowing in torrents into the lower city, and towards the far city wall. *What was going on?* Whatever was causing it was spreading. She watched as the white glow vanished, unraveling as if a cord had been pulled. A thought of Will came unbidden to her. He might be dead. The wall had fallen, and he might be dead. *No, don't think that. You can't think that.* Yet the thought persisted. That she'd never see him again brought a deep pang of sorrow. A sadness that surprised her.

She'd only registered that when the sound came. She was far, but still even here, she heard them, and knew what it was. Panic filled her, her breath caught, and she fell into a ball, desperate to try to hide. Some part of her stayed aware, maybe because of the distance. Fearsong. That was fearsong. The walls had been breached then. They had to do something. Anything. Her body trembled as the echoes of the fearsong washed over her. A tiny rational part of her was thankful she was so far away. She never wanted to hear that again.

Her boon burst forth, uncalled for, and settled into her like a blanket. The fear vanished, and she shivered as a feeling of ancient waiting and cold settled into her. Myriam stood, blinking. What had happened? Why had her power come like this? *Come. The Chamber of the Source. It is time.* A thin and breathy voice echoed in her mind. All other thoughts vanished, as did her confusion, and she took off in a run, heading towards the spire.

Rauger pulled himself out of the canal, shaking. Below in the dark water that was still for the first time in his life, was a few dozens of middle and lower city folk. All who had thrown themselves into the water in a mad dash for escape. He'd wanted to run too. He'd never been so terrified in his life. To his sorrow, none of the others who had thrown themselves into water still moved. They had all drowned, flailing in their induced fear. *A horrible way to go.* His own survival had been a surprise, but he was grateful to still draw breath. He was on the lower city side now. The canal had stopped moving at the same time the glow had stopped, and it never stopped. He hadn't known it could stop. Something was terribly wrong. That belief was proved true when a roar came, a triumphant roar from a thousand throats. He knew then; the walls had been breached; the enemy was inside the city.

Rauger wasn't a soldier, he wasn't a great fighter, but he would not let his home go without resistance. He pulled a long knife out from under his coat, along with a short club. "May fortune give me blessings tonight." Rauger whispered before he turned towards the sound and ran. He did not have far to run before he found his first match. Three soldiers carrying long spears and strange armor came around the corner. They spotted him, of course. He had no interest in hiding, not now. With a roar, Rauger ran at them, half yelling, half singing the ballad of the Swordsman of Avrunil. A tragic tale of blood right and betrayal. It seemed to fit, given the day.

The enemy in the lead lowered his spear and ran at him, screaming words that Rauger didn't understand. The spear tip flicked forward, cutting Rauger on the cheek, but not deep. Rauger choked down the panic he felt and swung his short club in a long arc, soundly hitting the upper arm of their attacker. He could feel the bone snap as his opponent gave a mighty yell and grasped the injured area in their other hand.

Before he could ready himself, the other two soldiers ran at him. Rauger backed up, trying to find a way to not have to face both at the same time. The sound of hoofbeats almost made him run before he realized that the hoofbeats were not coming from the direction of the attackers. But horses were forbidden in the city. Who could that be?

His answer came faster than he knew. A group of eight riders, all wearing the uniform of the Outriders, came bursting around the corner, waving short swords and in a mad charge at the enemy. Led by a copper-skinned Ride Captain who was screaming something as she directed her force. He barely jumped out of the way in time, as the group that attacked him were run down. One taking a sword blow in the face, the other being knocked over and trampled by several of the horses. The outriders did not stop, however, and were quickly gone, running towards the sounds of battle that were louder now. He paused for a moment, unsure if he should follow or run. His own brief battle had already shown him that while he might be useful, it was more as a target. So that someone, anyone, with more combat skill could take care of the attacker.

No. No running. Rauger let out a breath, steadying himself. The one attacker he'd hit was still alive, having been knocked over but otherwise unhurt by the outrider's charge. Rauger's luck seemed to have held, because it appeared the man had landed on the same arm Rauger had broken. The enemy had sat up, but that was it. The man spat as Rauger approached. "Do your worst." The man's accent was thick, but he could understand him. It barely registered that his accent was like, though much stronger than, Myriam's.

"Why?" Rauger stayed calm. "Why do this? The City just existed. We are no threat." He knew the answer wasn't going to make sense to him, but he had no choice.

"You use the power reserved for the Gods! The reborn god, Sartum, demands the end of this abomination!" The soldier tried to push himself up with his legs but gave up after a few moments. "Do it. Kill me with the power then."

"I can't. That's not what I can do with the power." Rauger felt some pity for this man. He'd been lied to, manipulated, and turned loose to kill people who didn't hate him at all. "It never had to be this way."

"You're a fool." The man spat again, but a trace of blood in the spittle gave Rauger pause. Something inside the man might be broken. If so, he wouldn't live that long.

"I am sorry." Rauger raised his knife to end the man's suffering. Then something hit him. It was quiet. Silent, in fact. Rauger looked towards the place where the fighting sounds had been coming, but heard... A new sound, one that instantly made him retch. Great waves of nausea covered him. He collapsed to his knees on the street, unable to stand as his body convulsed. For once, he was thankful for being a somewhat picky eater, because if his stomach had been fuller, it would have been even worse.

Head pounding, Rauger tried desperately to not be ill. He couldn't help it. The sound made his whole body want to rid itself of everything. Sweat already clung to every piece of skin, and his muscles trembled as the new blast came. He looked at the soldier he'd been talking to with some effort, but the man was already dead. He'd been sick too, but whatever injury he'd had inside been made horribly worse by whatever this was. The man was lying face down in the street, blood covering his face and chest. Rauger felt one last swell of sorrow for the man. None of this had been his fault.

"Kill him." A voice spoke, one he did not know. He focused enough to realize that a set of boots, several pairs of them, were walking towards him. His stomach lurched again, and Rauger closed his eyes, unsure if he could even raise his voice to protest. He did not, as a dagger came down, severing his spine as he hunched over. He wished he'd let Ralta kill him. She would have been spared her fate. Rauger fell into the welcoming darkness.

Chapter 70.

Ralta thrust forward, using her knack to keep her balance on an already blood slicked stones. She didn't fight with people wearing full armor often, or at all. Not that hard, though. She learned to strike the right places. Under the arm, the face, the wrist on one soldier who hadn't been wearing gloves. She'd cut both wrists, leaving him to bleed out. She had to find Jinir. He was somewhere here, in the lower city. Probably at a safehouse. They had several scattered across the parts where he held sway. She'd already checked three of them before she had run into the fighting. She could have avoided it, but the enemy was attacking a group of men who had nothing more than a few cleavers and poles to defend themselves.

Ralta had leaped into the fray and helped turn the battle. The men had thanked her and, much to her surprise, run towards the fighting, not away from it. She had done the same. Any idea of leaving the fighting to find Jinir had been pushed aside for the moment. She cut again, ducking behind a woman who swung a hammer at her, leaving her guard open. An opening that Ralta took full advantage of. The sounds of fighting fell silent from the main line, and for a moment, Ralta wondered if they had pushed them back.

The new sound that came was a horror. Before it had been terror, but now? Sickness. Trinil don't get sick often, and only a handful of diseases could ever make a Trinil throw up. But now? Ralta found herself hunched over, her body trying to empty itself of everything it could at once. Her knack kept her upright, but only barely. Even with her knack powered balance, she stumbled as her body reacted to whatever this was. Ralta had to escape. She had to get out of range of whatever this was, so she could breathe. Lurching forward, her head barely able to see in front of her, a dark alley beckoned. A cool dark alley. The thought was a craving. Cold and dark. She needed that. Now.

She'd made it into the alley when a searing pain hit the back of her neck. She would have screamed if she'd not been fighting too hard to keep from throwing up again. As it was, all that came out was a series of choking coughs. Not that it mattered. Her mind cleared some with the pain. It was over. She knew what had happened. Rauger was dead. She'd left the man back in the middle city. Why had he come here? The power of the bond with Jinir was going to kill her now. She had a few minutes, but it was going to happen. Rauger's death should have come at her hands. The bond was clear. Rauger's death should have come at her hands. Or better, Jinir should have rescinded it. She'd never know if he would have, not now.

Already the feeling of something leaking out of her, some part of what made her was leaving. She wished she was with Jinir. Or even Myriam. The girl was infuriating at times, but Ralta did like her. *Jinir*. She never should have left his side. Her vision faded to a grey and then to a black at the edges. At least she wouldn't die to some northern fool, following a god who didn't even care about him.

"Source be gone Jinir, why did you have to order me to kill Rauger?" She pushed the words out, each one harder to say than the last. It wasn't fair. She deserved more.

She gasped as the last of her breath fled, her hands still gripping her knives.

Will tried to make sense of what he was seeing. Rewil lay dead, and without warning, Nollew and Yulisia lay dead. They had been mourning the loss of Rewil when both had convulsed, and black foam had erupted from their mouths. Then, death. Will felt the blackness in his heart grow even more. So much death. Three dead Tarns. All within minutes of each other. All right in front of him. And that caster, Hodge. The other one, Vinil? Viril? He couldn't remember what Nollew had said. He was missing. Will hoped he'd made it somewhere safe. If there was a place, that was safe.

Nollew and Yulisia were dead. How? Rewil's cause of death was obvious.

But they had been fine! Well, not injured. Then, simply… dead. Was it some kind of weapon of Sartum or Grimnor? Some fresh attack? Was he next? The thought should have terrified him, but he felt cold, disconnected. Maybe it was better if he died. Right here. Right now. The City was falling. Myriam was probably already dead. The walls had fallen. The lower city had been in the thick of it.

Mikol had held his healers back to 'care for the few wounded' after the battle. He'd been so sure that this would be over and over soon. Arrogance was the death of fools. And Mikol was a fool. Myriam probably died doing what she was best suited for. Healing the injured. But she knew Fearsong. She knew its dangers. He hoped it had been quick for her. Nothing painful. Nothing like Nollew and Yulisia. Both still lay where they had collapsed, eyes wide, pain and surprise on their faces. They hadn't even gotten to say goodbye to each other.

Closing his eyes, Will waited for the death he was sure was coming next for him. He was stuck here. He should have done something, anything else. He'd been through so much, all to die here, in a stairwell in an outer wall of a City of Magic. Halfway around Alos from the Reach. Haltim. Master Jaste. Vin. Regin. Reachers and normal townsfolk. All the innocents who had suffered and died for him, one way or another. He'd failed to honor what they had given him. All this death. It was too much.

Come to the Chamber of the Source. It is time. An unfamiliar voice echoed, thin, almost like wind through the spruces back in the Reach. A voice he had to obey. Will stood, and after one last look at the dead, headed the calling.

Jinir didn't feel pain from the bond failing. It was more as if he'd forgotten something important but couldn't even guess what it was. A sense of missing. A sense of emptiness. Ralta was dead. Jinir shivered. She couldn't be dead. It was Ralta. His friend. Always at his side. Always there with him. She had sworn a bond with Jinir, and she was dead. He should have stayed with her. He never should have sent her after Rauger. He'd been so angry at the man. Rauger had put his nose into Jinir's business one too many times. In a fit of anger, he'd ordered his death. He didn't want the man dead. He'd been in a rage. And even then, he'd never said when, only that Ralta had to kill him. *Ralta had to kill him.* Awareness settled over him, his skin turned cold, and a tremble started in his hands. He'd done this. He'd ordered her to kill him. But he'd died elsewhere. And... the power of the bond killed her. She'd not obeyed. It had to be true. His words in anger had killed her. Rauger was dead. Ralta was dead. The lower city was full of soldiers. Those horrible sounds had blasted across the lower city, destroying any semblance of a resistance. It had fallen. Jinir had never thought it would have been possible for the City to fall in a single day. Never. And yet, here they were.

Jinir had run and hid. The lower city was gone. He should have been out there, leading the fight. Instead, he'd hidden. A coward. A coward who was now alone. Jinir wept. He wept for Ralta. He wept for the anger and hate he'd held onto. He wept for his city. He huddled into a ball, tears on his face, and hid. He was a coward and deserved a coward's death.

Let the soldiers come. Let them find him. He would welcome the end of this pain. Pain. Jinir reached into a small pocket on the inside of his robe and pulled out a tiny pouch. He could do this. Upended the pouch into his palm, there lay a tiny brown and black ball, slightly oblong. The poison. Poison put there by Mikol, most likely. Poison to kill. He could take this and be done with it. Take this and atone a little for his lack of bravery. His failure to help those who cared about him. Take it and be free.

His hand trembled as he took the small pellet with two fingers. Be brave. One swallow. That's it. Only one swallow. The shaking got worse, and his breathing turned uneven along with it. Just a swallow. Jinir stared at the pellet and finally threw it across the room. He couldn't do it. He knew that when the soldiers came, he'd beg for his life. He'd offer whatever they wanted. He'd show them the Greystone passages. He'd give them every secret he'd known as a former Tarn. Simply to live. He'd hate himself for it. But he knew he'd do it.

Bitter tears came, and Jinir waited for his fate.

Sartum watched with satisfaction as the outer walls fell. His plan with the anchors had worked. Those who had taken up his command were now tainted, of course. He had kept track of them as they entered the city. Eight of them had died. The buildup of magic had burned their minds out. Others had collapsed from the same power. They lived, but whatever had made them, them, was gone now. But a few, a few, were interesting. They had absorbed huge amounts of power, yet they lived. They ran. They even fought. The one who had done the speaking, whatever his name was, was one of those. Even now, Sartum could feel him smashing the anchors against heads and necks. Crushing bone, smashing weak tissue.

He was mad, of course. Of those who remained, they were all mad. Some screamed, some wept, and others, like the one Sartum had been watching, was laughing. A crazed giggle. It had the added effect of utterly terrorizing anyone who stood against them. It was the power, of course, it had broken them, but for some reason, in some way, they had a link to the power. Not that they could use it, but they could hold it. Sartum wondered if he could use that. But not now, now was a time for celebration. The city was on the brink of collapse. And the Gorom had proved very useful. Grimnor should be commended, but it didn't matter in the long run. They were his Gorom now.

Those songs of theirs were wonderful. No use of the power, nothing to taint them. They exploited a flaw in his creation that he'd not even been aware of. Sartum wondered if he should be angry about that, but truly didn't care. It was something he could use here, and in other places. What other songs were there?

"My lord Sartum. God of us all. We have your prize." A group of five soldiers approached, leading a wagon that had something in it covered.

"What prize?" Sartum didn't remember asking for anything.

"The machine? We heard you say you wanted one." The lead soldier went down to a knee and motioned the others to do the same.

"Yes." Sartum hid his surprise. He was going to get one anyway, but it was a good sign that these mortals who had only recently accepted him as the true god of their kind were already showing this level of obedience. Ripping the cover off the wagon, he could see the creation up close now. A wonderful device. Its artisanship was fine, better than fine. It was intricate and ornate but sacrificed nothing for function. It was one of the medium-sized ones. The ones that crawled along with spiked legs like an insect. Or a Vinik. The memory of those things brought a flare of rage that he worked to subdue. They were gone now. All gone.

Still, this thing was special. Powered by magic, though, but he could use it. He was sure. "That will be taken back to Ture when this is over. To the Guild." Waving the supplicants off, he found himself pleased. Soon the spire would fall. The city would be gone. And magic would be in its rightful place, under the control of the gods.

Chapter 71.

Will made his way across the ruins of the lower city. Many buildings were gone now, burned to the ground. He could hear fighting, but not close. He tried to move against this strange compulsion that overtook him, this demand that he go to the chamber, but couldn't. He could not get there, though. The bridges were gone, and the tunnels were caved in. Or sealed. It was hard to think, and Yulisia's words were only dimly remembered. He struggled against the compulsion again, but soon gave up. But why the chamber? What was going on? His worry spiked when a group of five soldiers wearing the livery of Palnor came stomping by. Each showed some wounds, and their spears were bloody.

Will braced himself for whatever was going to happen. Would they kill him right here, right now? Would they ask him questions? Could he convince them not to attack, based on his status as the former Forgemaster? Would they drag him off to Sartum? He still felt a surge of amusement at the name. Even with everything else. He was glad that one of the last things Myriam did was name that thing after donkey droppings. Will waited for them to stop him, but they walked right by him as he moved. Ignoring him. The one thing he hadn't expected. Or even thought possible. He was even more confused now. He was riding along in his own head, his body moving on its own, and being ignored by the enemy. None of this made sense.

He wondered if this was what it was like for Duncan. Watching, but unable to do anything about it. Thankfully, his body seemed to be walking somewhere. Poor Duncan had to watch as his body did unspeakable things and wasted away at the same time. His trip got stranger when his body turned down a side street and opened a cellar door, descending into the dark. This wasn't the spire. It smelled of rotten vegetables and old leather. Lit by a single torch, the room spread out, though shadows of shelves and boxes could be seen. The floor was covered with flagstones, most of them huge and old. In places they were worn smooth, and generations of steps had made paths in the rock, noticeably carved in arcing curves.

Yet his body stopped by one wall and smashed the flagstone that lay there with the hammer. It broke away, revealing a passage. A passage that was dimly lit, with no source for the light. Unlike the cellar, the light was white, though dim. Crawling down into the passage, the other part of it became plain. This wasn't a carved tunnel. It wasn't a Greystone passage. The tunnel was round, though the floor was flatter. The walls were smooth, with the occasional bump or ridge. The light sprung from all parts of the tunnel, giving it a moonlight like radiance. It felt to Will like a burrow, not a tunnel. But it went off into the darkness, and Will had to go. The tunnel ended in the room he had been in, so there was only one direction to move.

It was tall enough for him to walk, though often he was stooped over. His back arched to keep his head from hitting on the ceiling. He walked for a long time, the only noticeable thing being the occasional change in the air temperature. He'd passed through a section that was much colder than before or after, and the walls in that part of this strange tunnel were damp. But it didn't last long, and soon he was back in the cool, dry air of the rest of this strange location.

After walking for longer than he liked, Will spotted a blue tint ahead. The chamber? His steps, not under his control, quickened. And at last, the tunnel ended, and Will stepped out into the Chamber. Three things happened at once. One, he suddenly had full control of himself again. It made him gasp as whatever it was let go, his legs shaking. Two, the tunnel behind him closed. He didn't know how else to describe it. A noise came, a grinding noise, causing him to turn to get a glimpse of the wall melting over the opening. No heat, no glow, but the solid stone still moved like water, closing it off.

The third was the awareness that he wasn't alone. Standing in the chamber with him, right at the far edge of the light from the well, stood the one person he'd never expected to see there. She wasn't dead! Myriam!

❖

Mikol groaned and kept a two-handed grip on the pounding in his skull. He'd been watching and listening through William. The link kept growing weaker, which had been annoying, but it was useful still. When suddenly he wasn't alone. It was almost impossible to explain the sensation, but there was something else in William's mind with him. It wasn't William. It was something *other*. Ancient. Sorrowful. And not human. Nor any other race Mikol had ever touched. No, this was something else. And it knew him. It took Mikol a moment to grasp, but he knew, whatever this was, found him amusing! He, the Tarn of the Healers, the leader of the most powerful City on Alos, was amusing!

The ire was short-lived though, as pain shot through him in levels he'd never imagined. He couldn't sense anything through Will. He couldn't even make sense of his own surroundings. All he could feel was pain, and all he could hear was a high-pitched buzzing sound that never ended. A hellish sound that he couldn't make stop.

Mikol screamed as a fresh wave of white-fiery agony tore through his mind. His first real scream. It brought a lone healer rushing into the room. "My Tarn! What can I do to help? May I treat you?" The young man was earnest enough, but Mikol was in no mood to even try to explain. Mikol pushed the man back and howled again. As the intensity of the sound grew, it doubled in on itself, echoing over the sound. Mikol pushed his head up off the floor and wished that window was breakable. He'd throw himself out of it if death would stop this noise! His face was wet with sweat, and even breathing brought pain with it. He was going to die. Right now, right here.

As suddenly as the pain and noise started, it ended. His link with Will was gone. No surprise. He wiped his face with his robe sleeve, only to see red stain on the cloth. A quick check showed his nose was bleeding. He must have hit it on the floor when he'd been trying to crawl into a ball. "Tarn Mikol?" The young healer had fallen when he'd been pushed and was now on the ground. "Are you all right?"

"Do I look like I am all right?" Mikol coughed, trying to get a good breath. "I am not doing well."

"May I?" The healer stood then, raising his hands up to try to delve Mikol's injuries.

"No. I will see to finding them myself." Mikol realized something with a slight edge of alarm. "Where are the others? Why did only you come?"

The young man dropped his hands and his eyes. "They fled my Tarn. We may be the only people left in the section. When the lower city burned, most of the healers ran that way to help any survivors. I argued. I reminded them you had ordered us to stay. But they had to go. It wasn't right, they said. So, they left. The rest that stayed went elsewhere. I think some went to the crafters section. They were setting up defenses in their section for when the fighting gets there."

Mikol stared at the young man, blinking the now cold sweat off his face as it tried to get into his eyes. "Are you saying the section disobeyed me?"

"Yes, my Tarn. I stayed though. You ordered us to stay back, so I stayed back." The healer nodded. "I hope it pleases you."

Mikol was not pleased at all. His own section. His Healers. His chosen. They had betrayed him. Most were dead now. The fighting in the lower city had been a slaughter based on what he'd heard through William. By now he was sure the middle city was almost reached. Then the spire. Led by those rod wielding fools, and that strange Gorom sound. It was inevitable. So, the City would fall. But not Mikol. Mikol would live. He doubted even the fool of a god out there could get rid of the source. No, Mikol would hide and live. Then when the dust cleared, Mikol would have full and solo use of the source. All the power that ran this place would be his alone.

Yes. That would be perfect. He could still make something out of the failures of Nollew and Rewil. It was their fault this turn of events had happened. Not his. If they had done their jobs, the city would stand tall. Any other survivors would have a single choice, swear themselves to Mikol, or be banished and lose access to the power. No more Tarns. No more Commons. Whatever he wanted would be the rule. Mikol would be the only power now. He realized the young healer was still watching him, waiting for some sign of approval. "Yes, you did well." Mikol waved the man away. "I feel fine now."

He felt better than fine. He might still feel odd from whatever that had been, but the new plan was a good one. No more subterfuge. Mikol would rule.

Myriam blinked in surprise, her eyes adjusting to this strange blue light. Where was she? She'd been in the middle city, and then she was here. A wisp of a memory came to her, one that felt strangely familiar. She couldn't put her finger on it, though.

"Myriam!" Will's voice broke into her thoughts.

"Will!" Myriam ran over to Will, grateful to see him. He was all right! For a few moments she'd wondered if he was alive, when the wall fell. She had feared she'd never see him again. Without a thought, she threw her arms around him, feeling the realness of the man. A stability she craved, now more than ever.

"Are you all right? I heard the lower city was cut off; how did you get here?" Will held her as well for a moment, then released her. "Do you know how you got here?"

Myriam struggled to find the words to explain it. "I, I don't know. I was in the middle city. The bridges were gone. I heard the fearsong, and then,... I was here."

Will frowned. "I remember the trip, but I wasn't in control. I was being forced to come here. Whatever was controlling me ended as soon as I got into the Chamber." As his frown deepened, and he lowered his eyes. "Myriam, I have bad news. Rewil is dead. And Nollew, and Yulisia."

"What??" Myriam couldn't grasp it. "Three Tarns? All at once?" How?"

"Fearsong for Rewil. We were on the wall, no one wanted to listen to me about the fearsong. When it started, we all ran down the stairs in a blind panic. Of course, we fell. This breastplate saved my life. Will rapped it once. "But Rewil hit his head, crushed the back of his skull."

"Oh Will. I am so sorry. I know he meant a lot to you." Myriam hadn't met him much, but she liked the giant man. He wasn't crazy or evil. He had simply been himself. He'd also been one of the brightest minds she'd ever encountered when it came to melding machines and the power. A loss the city would never recover from, she was sure. "And Nollew and Yulisia?" Myriam pushed to find out. She hadn't exactly liked them, but after she had learned the truth of them, and their situation with Mikol, much of her earlier animosity had fallen away.

"I don't know. It happened so fast. They were examining Rewil, crying over him when both started shaking, floundering right there on the stair landing. Then a foam came from their mouths, black, brown, something. And then they died. It happened so fast." Will shook his head as if to erase the memories. "It was horrible."

Myriam let her skin turn cold as she listened to Will. Her mind jumping back to the small piece of poison she'd found in Jinir. Mikol. She was sure of it. How, she wasn't sure. But they had been poisoned. It shouldn't have acted that fast, but it was him. She knew it. "I am sorry Will, that would have broken me." Myriam was trying to figure out how to explain why it was Mikol when there was a loud grinding noise. Her attention turned from Will to the center of the room.

There was a well. Or at least it looked like one. Waist high, round. Open top. And instead of water, bright blue light spilled out. Strong light. Yet even as she watched, the well changed. It slid and flowed, and a stairwell formed, leading down into the place where the light came from. "I was told that whoever ever tried to go down there, they died." Will whispered, his eyes on the well with a look of what Myriam could only call longing. And maybe dread.

"But we are supposed to go." Will added. "Can't you feel it?" Myriam could feel it. A longing. A sense of countless time and patience growing then. Whatever had called them was down there, and it wanted them to come farther. If they didn't go, eventually this place would be found, and they would be killed, she was sure. Especially when they discovered what Sartum really meant. That brought a tinge of a smile, at least to her heart.

"Let's go then. Together." Myriam took Will's hand, and without further discussion, they walked down into the light, hand in hand. The walls were smooth, no trace of grit or texture. The stairs themselves had a sandy feel underfoot. They spiraled down, the light growing perceptibly brighter the further they descended. They turned their tenth round to see an opening. The light was dazzling now, and it made it harder to see where they were going. They shaded their eyes, and finished their descent, entering what for all the world looked like a forge. A strange forge. This was strange enough.

Yet sitting in the middle of the room were two things. One a huge blue crystal that shone like the noonday sun. This was the source. She knew it. The true holding of power. She didn't need to touch her boon to know that working any power here would be hard. The air was alive with it. The second thing, is what gave her and Will a great deal of pause. Because sitting over the source was a form. A form they had seen before. Just as blue as the crystal, though this one's outside held a slight transparent shimmer. The form raised up, and eyes they thought they never would see looked at them.

A Vinik.

Chapter 72.

The Vinik was smaller than most of the ones they had seen before. But it carried a feeling of age and power that dwarfed even the one that had spoken to them that one time. "You are here. Finally." The voice was thin and reedy, a voice that they knew from the call. This Vinik had called them here.

"You're a Vinik." Will pointed at the creature. "But you're blue."

"Yes." The creature Vinik seemed to cock its head at Will. "This is not a good start." The Vinik stated. "I called."

"Right." Myriam tried to process this. "Sorry we weren't expecting a Vinik."

"That I understand. I will be the last Vinik you will ever see. The rest are dead. Dead by the hand of your creation, Healer." The Vinik gave a long buzz. "I was always going to be the last."

"What do you mean, dead?" Will shook his head. "Sorry, let me start over. You called us. Why? What is a Vinik doing here? Who are you?"

"Better questions." The Vinik sat back on its back legs. The voice was still thin and reedy, but they could understand it well enough. "I am the last. My name would not make sense to you. My time is up. You were told, yes? Of the history of my people? Of the failure we had to stop the gods from destroying our world? What the elder you spoke to didn't know was this. A few of the creator Vinik, those who could use the magic directly, had a backup plan. We made this." The Vinik tapped the glowing orb crystal, the sound bright and pure.

"We made this and let it grow. I was appointed its guardian. We waited. The new creations of these gods came, those who rejected the flawed hunger of the gods. The excess power that spilled out the city used. I let them. It was good to have others use the power of this world, even though they were not here at its birth. I waited as the crystal grew. I waited and watched. For the two of you." The Vinik made a quick series of movements with one arm and the forge sprung to life.

"I saw you bring Amder back. I saw you reform the sundered god. And I knew the time was soon. I brought you to the city. I needed you close. It was always going to come to pass that the remade god, this 'Sartum', would destroy the city. But soon there will be a new City, a new way." The Vinik made a keening sound, one that brought sadness and sorrow.

"The remade one. He sought revenge on my kind. He killed them all. Including doing a mercy to those held by the Vzzzderrrrttsskilk. A small mercy, but a mercy still." The Vinik dragged itself off the orb. "But now, your true purpose is here. It will require the two of you both. You will give the world what it truly needs. What will save the world of Alos, our world, our home, is simple. A new god. A god of magic itself. This orb has absorbed more power than anyone knows. Power that will give life to the new god."

Myriam blinked in confusion. "You brought us here? And you want us to make a god??"

"Yes. The wild power of the Anvil would have torn you apart if I had not." The Vinik reached a pair of spindly blue arm leg things towards them. "You, William, will make the body of the new god. You, Myriam, will bind the power to this body. The crystal will give it life. You new creatures think of it as male and female, yes? The words you use… I do not know."

Will rubbed his forehead. "You mean father and mother?"

"Yes. That is the words." The Vinik's voice changed, giving it a reverberation to go with the whistle. "You will be father; she will be mother. You will make a new god. A god of magic. A god of power. To stop the stranger gods. The ones who came from elsewhere. A god for Alos."

Will was stone faced, staring at the orb. "I don't know. This is…" Will looked at Myriam, his face pale. "What do we do?" he mouthed to her.

"There is no other way, human William. To save magic, to save the world from the coming ravaging, when the interlopers you call gods will suck the world dry of its power. Then will move on, like locusts." The Vinik shook suddenly, a pitched whine erupting from it that echoed around the chamber. "NO! YOU MUST NOT!" it yelled into the room as power erupted from the creature. This close to the source, it was visible with no boon. It flowed outward in an immense sphere, protecting them all. William thought it looked like they were inside a soap bubble. The same shimmer clung to the protection.

"HE DARES TO STRIKE. I GO. I WILL END HIM. MAKE THE NEW GOD. I LEAVE NOW. MY WAIT IS OVER." The Vinik shimmered and then, with a sound of escaping steam, collapsed, the blue shimmer fading away to nothing. What was left of the body of the Vinik went from bright blue, to pale, to gray. Will and Myriam watched in stunned silence as it cracked and crumbled away, leaving dust and more questions than answers.

Mikol delved into his body and was thankful that whatever that had been, it did not seem to have caused any actual damage. A few very minor injuries had caused the blood, and the rest had already stopped hurting. Good. He did not have time to deal with an injury right now. He would not lose. He could not lose. "Leave this room. I must do something. Mikol ordered the younger healer who, while now standing, had stayed in the room in case he was needed. "Go. We will leave soon and head down into the chamber of the source. We will be safe there."

He watched the younger man bow twice and leave. *Useful, could have a future in the new version of the city. My city.* Mikol now had to tie up a loose end. Or two. One, he needed to rid himself of William, and, if possible, Myriam, for good this time. And second, Grib. The only other Tarn out there. He had fled to the middle city and stayed there by all reports. Grib had been a useful scapegoat for things and had played his part well. But the situation no longer required Mikol to have any need for him. Grib was a potential rival in the new order of things. Something Mikol would not allow. But he didn't know where Grib was, not fully. It would take time to track him down. And time was something he had little of. Will was first, then. Then Grib and Myriam. Will he could find.

Mikol gathered his boon and pushed through, finding the still existing though almost gone link. He braced himself for whatever that sound had been before, or the attack. Or the *other* he had felt. Yet none of that was there. What was there was something that made Mikol almost drop the connection in surprise. One, Will was with Myriam now, somehow. That was useful. More than useful. Fate smiled on Mikol Nese today. Two, he didn't know where they were until he saw it through Will's eyes.

They were under the well! The one place no one could go, and yet, they were there! Mikol watched, barely able to breathe as the Vinik appeared and started talking. The surprise gave way to anger and fear. This thing, this creature, was going to take the magic away! The power would be gone! Mikol could not allow that. Would not allow that! He had sacrificed too much, fought too hard to have it ripped away from him by a mere insect. Anger boiled over in Mikol, anger that gave force to his working.

He had to kill them. Right now. He pushed as hard as he could. He would stop Myriam's heart and force the blood in Will's head to harden. That would kill them both. No one would ever take the power away. Not now, never. Mikol threw everything he had into his attack. If this failed, he would have nothing. He would be normal, just an old man with no particular skills or power. He reached out, ignoring the Vinik, and the power swarmed out, reaching towards Myriam when the Vinik exploded into action. The thing screamed something that Mikol couldn't understand, the sound sharp and painful. With a huge bright explosion that Mikol more felt than saw, it battered away the working Mikol had created. Not just pushed but brushed away as easily as Mikol would brush off a leaf.

He could feel it, the presence. He was pushed out of Will's head, his awareness snapping back with such force he doubled over. But it was not enough. The thing was in his mind now. And it was angry. Mikol tried to push it away. He used all his years of skill and power, but the thing removed his attempts without effort. A kernel of panic formed in Mikol's gut. He was Tarn Mikol Nese; he was the most powerful Tarn in the City's history. But this thing was overwhelming everything he tried, without apparent effort.

You will not interfere. The voice echoed in Mikol's head. *You are nothing.* The voice spoke one last time as the blackness erupted around the edges of his vision. He could feel his heart pumping harder and harder as the presence pushed it to work more. He tried to stop it, to call out to the young man who stood outside his door, but it was to no avail. Mikol could feel the pain in his chest grow, and then, like cutting a string, it stopped. Blackness washed over him, and Mikol, Tarn of the Healers for far too many years, lay dead.

Jinir shuddered and wept as he heard the door come down. He raised his head, expecting to see armed soldiers. Instead, he saw a pair of large men with crowbars, and a Gorom. And not any Gorom, but Grib. "Grib??" Jinir croaked out, taken aback by this turn of events.

"Jinir." Grib walked in, nodding to the two men, who turned and watched the door. "This was the fifth place we looked for you." The Gorom pulled a chair over and sat, but it wasn't sized for a Gorom, so he looked somewhat silly sitting in it, not that he seemed to care. Jinir would have laughed though, if things had been less serious.

"Why? How?" Jinir wasn't sure what Grib was after. "I mean. Why are you looking for me? How did you find this place?"

"Well, in truth, I've known where some of your safehouses were for some time. But things were too tied up in the Commons for me to make a move. They refused to let me kill you. Did you know that? Nollew, Yulisia, and Rewil. Mikol, of course, would have voted yes. You know how it is." Grib gave a broad smile. "I don't think I'll need to worry about that anymore."

"What do you mean?" Jinir pushed back from his successor, very slowly. "Why not?"

"The city is over. I've had a few reports that say the others are dead. Rewil, Nollew, Yulisia. Mikol is hiding in the spire. I'll deal with him later. But you, you Jinir, I can take care of. Do you know I found Ralta's body? Strange, she died. I couldn't find anything other than a single scrape on her. All the blood must have been others. There were over a dozen soldiers dead nearby. She was one wonderful fighter."

Jinir nodded, the pain of that fresh in his mind. "She was."

"But without Ralta, you have no one to help you now, Jinir. You know I would have not cared if you had kept to yourself down here. After Mikol failed to kill you, you should have just stayed low, out of sight. I would have left you alone. But you had to try to get your position back. You had to turn parts of the city against me. I admit the whole Downtrodden Lord bit was quite a stroke of skill." Grib flicked something off his boot with a thick finger that landed on Jinir's robe. Blood. Thick, congealed blood.

"The city is over. When this is all done with, there will be two Tarns left standing. Me and Mikol. I don't plan on letting Mikol take over. I've danced that tune before, and I was already sick of it." Grib smiled a bleak smile. "And I will not allow you to interfere, not this time."

"I won't!" Jinir blurted. "I can help you! I'll throw in with you! I'm sure some of those who follow me have survived. They will follow my lead. Otherwise, you will never be sure if they are plotting revenge, right? You won't know who they are. I can help." Jinir's hand shook with the nervous energy he felt flowing through him. "I can advise you."

"You want me to trust you?" Grib snorted. "Jinir, you are a fool if you think I'll ever trust you."

"But how will you know?" Jinir pressed the issue again, knowing his death might be soon if it didn't work. "I have followers who will kill you if they found out that you had removed me. They would do it without question." Jinir knew that wasn't true. None of his followers even really knew who he was. They knew the Downtrodden Lord, but didn't know it was Jinir, former Tarn. But Grib didn't know that. At least he hoped Grib didn't know it.

Grib sat in silence, his smile gone. He stared at Jinir long enough for the man to break into a second sweat. "If I do this, you must promise not to raise a hand against me." Grib pointed at Jinir. "You will have to bind yourself to me once this is over."

Jinir frowned. Binding was... but if it was binding or death, he'd choose to be bound. "Yes. Fine. I agree with those terms." Jinir stood, feeling every muscle groan from his several hours hiding in a ball. He gave a stiff bow. "I will bind myself to you Tarn Grib."

"So be it." Grib slid off the chair, instantly looking less foolish to Jinir's eyes. "Come, advisor. We must get someplace safer. There are still a great many soldiers here. They have built makeshift bridges over the canal, and the middle city is a killing ground. We will have to travel fast."

Grib motioned to his men, and all four walked out into the city, into utter destruction. Jinir stunned by the damage. The safehouse was one of the few undamaged buildings on this street. Most had some evidence of violence, broken walls, smashed windows. Fire damage as well. And more than a few were just gone. Reduced to rubble or embers. He could see most of the wall now, even from here, and the wide open tunnels that led to the valley below.

Jinir didn't know how that had all failed, but it didn't matter now. He was alive, and if he played his part, he would continue to live. That was all that mattered. The pace was swift, as Grib led the way, moving through a series of alleys and destroyed houses and businesses. "We must stay out of sight as much as possible." Grib told his men, and Jinir, who he glared at. "Our lives depend on it."

They did not see anyone else at first, though they passed a great many bodies. The smell was already growing sour off most of them. He could hear moaning once as someone struggled in a building that had a broken second floor, but Jinir didn't see the person. Not that he could have done anything. He might have been able to help with his knack, but there wasn't time. His safety was the most important thing. And he doubted Grib would bother for anyone in the lower city.

They crossed over one of the repaired bridges, a ramshackle affair, into the middle city. The sound of fighting was becoming clearer now. Or killing was more likely. Merchants and well-off moneylenders don't put up much of a fight. "Why wasn't it guarded?" Jinir whispered. "You'd think they would watch it."

Grib kept walking but shrugged in response. "There is no danger. The lower city is gone. The middle city will be. You know this place. We based everything on the power. A small force of Outriders tried after the walls fell, but that was a paltry defense. Without the power, this place fell quickly. Enough talk, we are almost to safety."

Jinir knew that was true. It had come up a few times even when he was a Tarn. But everyone always thought the power would save them. Now they saw the price of that belief. Making their way through a small street, past a banker, they turned and stopped. In front of them stood six soldiers. Soldiers who looked at them with a fury and hatred that made Jinir cold.

Chapter 73.

"What have we here? A false little man, two morons with crowbars, and a balding thin man?" the lead solider gave a half laugh while taking the sight of them in. "Out for a little looting? Trying to dig up some money while we destroy your pitiful city?"

"Out looking for survivors. Take pity." Grib replied, an almost plaintive tone in his voice that made Jinir wonder for a moment.

"That would be worse. Our lord Sartum, the reunited god, has ordered this city destroyed, and all who live in it." The lead solider, his rank unclear, hefted his spear. "You're all going to die, you know."

"Please. No one has to know." Jinir threw his own pleading in. "We want to go on our way. We never liked it here." Jinir was acutely aware of the ice glare of Grib's that appeared and vanished before their captors could see it. *I'm not dying here, you fool.* Jinir wanted to yell at Grib but kept the thought to himself.

"No chance." The one soldier who had been speaking lowered his spear. "But we will make it quick. Be happy about that. I hear some of the force has taken to seeing how you false people deal with fire coals in your boots. Made them dance."

Jinir felt a drop of sweat trail down, washing away in a single line the layer of dust, soot and ash that coated his skin. He couldn't die like this. Spitted like a pig at a roast. What to do? What to say? His eyes touched on Grib. His old enemy, Grib. *I might be about to die, but he's going first.*

"Take him!" Jinir pushed Grib forward into the enemy force. "He's a Tarn. One leader of the City. Take him!" At the same time, he pushed himself back, hoping to the source he didn't trip. He wasn't about to take his eyes off the enemy, not yet, at any rate.

The effect was immediate, as Jinir hoped it would be. The enemy flinched, and then grabbed the Gorom, pushing him to the ground. Grib's two bodyguards, or hired muscle at least, ran after their boss. But their efforts amounted to little. Two thugs trained to crack skulls were not much use against trained and hardened soldiers. One was writhing on the ground in moments, a spear thrust deep into his abdomen.

The other actually managed to hit two of the attackers before falling over, his head bleeding. One of the enemy had smacked him in the back of the head with a hammer, spitting on the corpse for good measure. "Blood take you Jinir!" Grib yelled as he struggled. "He's a Tarn too! He's got connections!"

"They said one of the leaders of this place was a false Gorom. Take him to Sartum and Grimnor. I'm sure they BOTH would like to talk to a false Gorom." The lead solider turned away to watch Grib, struggling in midair as he was held up by his guards. Jinir wasn't being watched, at least for this moment.

This was the only chance he was going to have, Jinir knew that quite well. He turned and ran. He ran as fast as his legs could carry him these days. He flew over the wreckage, and in desperation, looked for a place to hide. Some kind of safety where he could gather his thoughts. If there were any to be had in this ruin of a day. His eyes lit on a small building on the edge of the alley. It was a shop, the "Lucky Coin". The door was closed, but not locked. What luck. He dived through the door, and he heard the sharp cry of the lead soldier. "He's in there! After him!"

Jinir scrambled up into the building, taking care to shut the door behind him. He searched around, taking a loose piece of stone, and pushing it against the door to keep it closed. Where was he? He looked over the place, unsure of what kind of business this was. There was no doubt it had been ransacked, but there was something else. He wasn't sure what it was at first until he followed the smell. There was blood. It was underneath everything, but there was definitely blood there. He had smelled enough blood for one day, but it couldn't be helped. Jinir was about to check the stairs when a glint caught his eye. A small coin. A silver coin. A silver coin with a likeness he'd never seen.

"Hello Jinir." A man Jinir had never seen before appeared behind him. Jinir hadn't heard him come in, but what gave him a cold shudder was the man himself. Clad in golden armor, the man was handsome. Jinir wanted nothing more than to fall on his knees and worship this man. This man, who was on the coin…

"Jinir Yellow." The man spoke again and began circling Jinir. "Former Tarn of the City itself. Marked for death by Tarn Mikol. Survived, built a new life as a 'Lord' in a place with no nobility. Healed by… Myriam VolFar. And had your attempt to take back power interrupted by the attack. Am I missing anything?"

Jinir wanted to run again. His head felt fuzzy, unfocused every time he looked at this strange man. How did he know all that? He didn't look like…. A clenching hand of fear squeezed his heart as the thought died. He knew who this was. This was the new God. Jinir would have gotten sick right then, if he hadn't already have emptied his stomach earlier.

"Very good." Sartum stopped circling and pulled a huge hammer from out of nowhere. Its huge, spiked head shimmered with a faint red glow, the red of fresh blood. Sartum waved the hammer and the room, this 'Lucky Coin' shop, came back together. The table fixed itself, the chairs reformed back together. Jinir watched with amazed horror.

"Not too far off from your old… curse. And it was a curse. You're a mortal Jinir. You are nothing. To use the power like that, magic, is not for your kind. You know that, right?" Sartum sat waving at the empty chair. Jinir wondered how far he could get if he started running. Could he outrun a god? He was sure he'd die before he left the room, though. He'd never seen the power used like that. He could fix things, but not at that speed. Not even close. One glance showed him that this god was watching him with an expression that grew darker with each passing moment. *Sit.* Jinir sat, watching the anger melt away in a moment.

"Now. Do you not see how it has brought ruin here? It pains me. A great many of my people died here. Humans like you. Real humans. Not some disgusting crossbreed. True, and pure humans. Pure Gorom. Even some pure Trinil, like your late friend. Ralta? Right?" Sartum raised a hand and the ash and dust on the floor flowed onto the table, forming the image of Ralta.

"I failed her." Jinir whispered at the sight. Her image burned into his mind, bringing sorrow and despair with it.

"Yes, you and all the rest. The arrogance that the power was for you all to use. You forced me to come here. Her death, and all the others are on your heads." Sartum slapped the image down, the ash floating away, leaving a slight gray mark on the wood. "But you Jinir, you're a survivor. You could be more. I have seen you."

"What?" Jinir's throat was dry, and the words came out harsh and cold. "What do you mean?"

"I will make you an offer. You crave power. When today is over, the city will be gone. Gone. No more magic. No more source. But there may be those who survive. You will lead them. You will teach them the truth. That magic isn't for mortals. You will make sure no one ever tries this again. The source, whatever it is, will no longer be here. I will make sure of that. Yet, I know my creation, and I know some will seek it still. You, Jinir Yellow, will be my voice. I will give you enough power, through me, to make sure that does not happen." Sartum stood, his face nearly glowing as bright as his armor.

Jinir didn't know what to say. If he understood this, he was being offered to be a what, priest? Acolyte? A follower of this new god. He would have power. He would be placed in charge of any survivors. He would have access to the power again, but only through this thing. Did he want that? Jinir, like anyone in the City was not a believer, but after seeing the day's events, that might be something to change. But if he didn't take it, he would be dead. That much was obvious. His eyes fell on that hammer again, the spikes almost glistening. Serve or die. Jinir stood as well, and went down on his knees, lowering his head. He would serve and live.

Will and Myriam stood in silence, bathed in the pure blue light. Will's skin tingled with it. Every so often he almost felt a rush, a moment of pleasure from it so strong his eyes rolled back into his head. It reminded him of eating a butter roll from the Chisel back in the Reach. Rich, fatty, honey laced. It made him shiver with the decadence. This light, this source, brought the same feeling.

"Will?" Myriam's voice was tight, and with a look he could tell this giant crystal thing brought the same feelings to her that it did to him. Her eyes were wide, her lips slightly parted. Passion, desire. Writ large on her face, and his as well, he was sure.

"Yes, I feel it too." Will forced himself to move away from the actual source, thankful that the feelings subsided enough for him to think clearly. "This is..." Will shrugged, unable to come up with the words. *Make a god? A new god?*

"Insane? The strangest thing yet?" Myriam said as she walked away from the crystal herself. "And yet, it makes sense. A strange and possibly ridiculous sense, but sense."

Will shrugged. None of this made him happy. He'd done this. He'd brought Amder back. He'd been there when Sartum was remade. He wanted to leave, and yet here he was, again. Facing the same decision. Or really being pushed into something he did not want.

"Well? I guess we should get started. I do not know how I'm supposed to do whatever it is I'm supposed to do. Bind the source to the body? What does that even mean?" Myriam shook her head. "I hope it is clear once we start."

Will looked around the room. Everything he could need, again. A God of Magic. A God from Alos. Was that the answer? He gazed at the true source. He could feel the vast amount of power it held, even from here. Enough power to reshape the world. Enough power to give magic back to the world, widespread. Too much for Sartum to stop. He hoped, at least. Will was surprised to notice the hammer, his hammer. The new one in his hand. The idea grew in his head. This was what it was meant for. This was why it had needed to be made. It was right. Or at least it felt right. Pure.

"Will? The longer we take, the more damage Sartum does. Shouldn't we get started?" Myriam waved her hand at the forge. "Get the tools ready, all that."

"No." Will finally said, looking at Myriam. He hoped she would understand. "We will not do this."

Chapter 74.

"What?" Myriam frowned, and she took a step back. "What do you mean? The Vinik said to save everyone we had to do this."

"No." Will shook his head. "Don't you get it? Since the day I took that crystal from the Mistlands, I've been a puppet on a string. First it was Amder. Then, chasing after Duncan. Then here, and all the stupid politics and infighting that remind me so much of Ture. The whole time we've been dancing to someone else's tune."

"I get you're angry, and I understand Will. I do. But the Vinik said…" Myriam stopped mid-sentence as Will shook his head with force.

"It doesn't matter what he said. It said. Whatever. It gave us the only choice it wanted us to make. Don't you get it? Do this, or Sartum will win and take the source for his own, or close enough. But that's not the only choice. Making a new god or letting Sartum win. Those aren't the only choices." Will held up the hammer in his hand. The blue light almost seemed to cling to it like a faint flicker of flame.

"When I made this hammer, this new one, I knew it was for something. I didn't know what at the time. But it had a purpose. How I knew that I'll never know. But it was as clear as the sky overhead on a summer day. Making yet another puppet master to pull the strings is not its purpose." Will hefted the hammer, remembering that final conversation with Duncan. Or a fragment of a memory of Duncan. The thought brought a smile, tinged with the sorrow that Duncan always brought.

"Then what are the other options? If making a new god, isn't it, and letting Sartum have it, isn't it, then what is?" Myriam's voice was full of concern. Will could hear it on the edges of her words. A worry tinged with fear. *I don't blame her; I just might be mad to even consider this.*

"We break the crystal." Will looked at the thing, pulsing with the power. A beacon brighter than any he'd ever seen. "That holds enough power to remake the world. To give the magic back to Alos itself. No gods, no strings. Too much power for Sartum to handle."

"How can you know that?" Myriam's voice was calmer. Will could hear it. *Good, she did not reject this plan outright.* He didn't bother looking at her. The crystal in front of him was everything right now. This had to be the way. This MUST be the way.

"I know. I'm sick of being a puppet. I'm tired of running through hoops for something that calls itself a god. I want to be Will again. William Reis. From the Reach, Palnor. No strings, except the ones I choose and place on myself." Will finally looked up at Myriam. Her face was a mix of emotions. Fear was still there, but so was surprise, and something else. Affection. Deep affection. And one day, it could be more.

"Will…" Myriam closed her eyes for a moment and smoothed her robes. She looked down at them, frowning. "Will, let's say I agree. What would that entail?"

"I break the crystal. You bind it to Alos. All of Alos. Return the power to the place it came from. No gods, no super powerful warriors and casters. For good or ill. Let Alos be as it was meant to be. There will be challenges and terrors. But blessings too." Will shrugged. "I keep thinking back to the Anvil. That wonderful and strange world that exists outside the cave. The world of Alos as it was, as it was supposed to be."

"Do you think doing this will bring that world everywhere? Are you sure that would even be a good idea?" Myriam tapped her chin as she spoke. "Outside the City, no one knows what magic is. Even those who are blessed by the gods don't really know what it is they are doing."

"I don't know. I don't have all the answers here, Myriam. I only know that making a new god isn't the answer." Will let out a long sigh and locked eyes with her. "Myriam. We've seen countless friends die. Untold numbers of people, innocent of anything other than being on the wrong side of some fight between powers far above them. It isn't right. If we do this, if we make a new god, we are adding a side. But, if we break the crystal, return the power to Alos, we change the board. We change the very nature of how things play out."

"You make it sound like a card game at an inn, Will." Myriam gave a small chuckle. Some of the tension in her shoulders fell. "But I understand where you're going with it. And I do understand. I don't want to put those same innocent people in more danger, by releasing the power back into a world that no longer understands it."

Will nodded. "I know. But I'm still sure it's the right choice. Or at least a better choice than the one they are trying to make us make. So, it comes down to this. Do you trust me?"

Myriam smiled and slowly nodded. "You know I do. So, I guess… we do it."

Will hefted his hammer. "I don't know if we will live through this, you know. There's a good chance that the power will wash us away. Utterly destroy us."

"I guessed that. But since I met you, the risk of me getting killed has risen all the time. I'm at peace with that." Myriam laughed then, for real. "My old self would think this is a very silly thing for me to say."

Will didn't answer. She was right. Death and danger had become far too usual for him and those around him. All because he'd insisted on following a dream. But he'd never have met her if he hadn't. Nor any of the other people who had helped him become who he was now. Most of them were gone now, though. But she remained.

"Myriam. After this if we live through it. Come with me. I'm not good at this, but I still… I mean, I'm not Regin, but I… "Will mumbled and let it drop.

"Silly man. Will, I know you're not. Nor do I want you to be. I was angry with you for a long time. Angry at you, and even more, at myself. I don't know what will happen after this, but I'm willing to find out with you. Of course, I'll come." Myriam walked over to Will and kissed his cheek.

Will could feel that twinge of panic as she got close, the nerves grabbing him. The smell of her, the softness of her lips. How could she still manage to smell like honey and soap after everything they had been through today, he had no idea. But she'd come. She'd said yes. That was enough.

"Well then, let's remake the world, shall we?" Will grinned at Myriam. "Be ready to channel. I'll break it, then take my boon. Use it. You do whatever you can to return this to Alos. I'll help. I saw how those things Sartum used pushed the power back in. That was nothing compared to this, but hopefully the idea is the same, only on a much larger scale."

Myriam reached out and took her boon. She gasped. "This is… strange. It almost seems eager Will. If magic can have feelings, that is. But I'm ready." Will could see a tremor in her eyes and the tightness of her smile. She was scared, but she was ready to follow his lead.

Will nodded and grabbed his boon as well. He could see what she meant. A torrent flowed through him, around him. Like a mighty snowmelt of a river. Capable of washing him away, but yet, it seemed too not. It didn't want to. He hefted his hammer. "Now."

And the hammer fell.

Sartum watched as his new recruit, Jinir, spoke to a group of survivors. Humans, of course. The few Gorom who had lived were going to be given over to Grimnor. Even though they were now technically his, it would be useful to let them be handled by the old Gorom God.

Jinir would be useful. Someone the fools from this city knew. And the man was a coward, through and through. He'd never stand up to Sartum. He was good at fooling those around him, and that was enough. All that was left was this spire, and the real purpose, the source of magic here. Sartum could feel it, underground. It was protected, though.

He'd tried a few times to go there and had encountered resistance. Some kind of protection that was keyed to particular people. Who he didn't know. Anyone else, it was like sliding off oil slick glass. There wasn't any way to find a purchase. It was infuriating. He was a god, and yet, somehow, these mortals continued to defy him, even now with their city in ruins.

Pain.

Every inch of Sartum exploded into a blue-white fire. Every thought was agony. Sartum screamed, a scream that rolled over what was left of the city. Buildings were flattened, people, including Jinir, went down as well. Grabbing ears and heads as the scream continued. What was left of the outer walls cracked in fresh places, the white-green marble falling in chunks, crashing to the ground.

A low bellow of pain joined his scream as Grimnor's voice joined in the distance. The same white blue flames covered the thrashing stone form out in the valley. The very ground shook in counterpoint to the thrashing. Rocks shivered and splintered. Faint blue spider webbed cracks spread wildly through the red stone walls of the canyon, spreading outward in an adding crescendo of sound.

A jet of light, blue and pure, brighter than the sun in the sky, filled the air. It burst out from the ground by the spire, if not exactly next to it. With it brought a new sound, one that drowned out any screams. A pure tone. A sound that brought Sartum to awareness. His scream stopped as the pain faded away.

The very world seemed to soak in the single note that traveled throughout Alos. From the far northern wastes to the depths of the caves that lay far beyond the reach of any Gorom. From Ture to a tiny village of an unnamed race on a tiny island in the Deepening Sea. The very world vibrated with the sound, a vibration that brought a feeling of excitement with it. Change had come.

The sound reached a point of nearly madness, as a single moment of joy filled the mind of every creature on the planet, and then it vanished. Gone, along with the light. And silence fell. A silence that was shocking in its purity. For several long breaths, nothing moved. No birds sang. No stray animal rooted for food. No predator attacked prey. A pure silence rested over Alos like a blanket.

Sartum had somehow stayed upright and blinked in surprise to find a wetness in his eyes. He was undamaged, yet things were different. The wonder of that single moment was hard to shake off. As his eyes fell on the remains of the city, a great sense of shame overtook him. They had not deserved this. He'd only wanted to take the power back. But he'd gone wrong in destroying the city.

The source. Sartum realized at once. It was gone. More than that. It was no more. He had no idea how, but the very ground beneath his feet pulsed with power that was uncontrolled, pure. It was like the lands outside the Anvil. Wild magic. Unrestrained. But so much of it. More than he could ever take in. More than any of them could. What had happened? It was clear that somehow, the source had held far more power than he'd ever thought. And that it had been transferred into the world itself. This would be a problem. No place would have the pure concentration that the city had been, but now it was everywhere. Still, he had won. The goal had been the end of use of power here. The end of this… wrong. And it was done.

Sartum looked once more over the fallen City. His desire for its end was satiated. There wasn't much left, anyway. Only the spire, and that was cracked already from the recent changes. He wanted to leave. This fresh problem was going to take some thought and planning. He had the machine from the city as well. He could use that design, improve it. Would anyone dare to stand against his new faith if each temple was protected by a mechanical killing machine?

Sartum looked over the wreckage one last time. This war was over.

Will shivered, his eyes closed tightly. He was stunned to even still draw breath. He'd taken the hammer and struck and then…. His memories did not make sense. Joy, pleasure, pain, sorrow… the feelings had overtaken him in a way he couldn't even describe.

Myriam! Will pushed himself up, feeling the sandy dirt under his hands. He forced his eyes open, hoping that they still worked. The light had been intense. A reddish green afterglow stuck to everything, but he could see. But what he saw made him question his sanity.

He was not in the under chamber anymore. He wasn't even in the city anymore. Or the south. He knew where he was. The air was cold, an icy chill clung to it that brought a smile to his face. The forge in front of him was as familiar as his own hands. It was his family forge. He was home. He was in the Reach.

But Myriam? Where was Myriam?

"Will?" Myriam's voice came. Weak and unsure, but it was her. Will turned towards the sound to see Myriam leaning against the doorframe that led into the house proper. She was trembling and unsteady, but it was her. "Myriam!" Will pushed himself all the way up, his legs wobbly as well. He slowly made his way over to her. "Are you well? Feeling all right?"

"I think so. I… none of it makes sense. You broke that crystal and then… I can't think straight. Everything was everyone. I was trying to drink the ocean. It was too much, and then you were there. You helped. We directed the power back into the world. And that's all I know until I woke up here. This is your old house, right? In the Reach?" Myriam looked at the anvil that sat, dark and cold in the forging yard.

"Yes. I don't understand why, or how, but we are here." Will leaned against the wall near her. "I can't even remember as much as you do."

"Did it work?" Myriam looked down at her hands. "Did we do the right thing?"

"Only one way to find out." Will reached out and found… nothing. Not in him. Wherever the boon had been was empty now. "I can't find any connection. The power, it's not in me." Will's voice was rough. "We did something, but…"

"I can't either." Myriam was full of sadness. "I can't feel the boon."

"Maybe that's for the best." Will sighed. "No more power." Myriam nodded, but with a frown on her face. "But…." Will watched as she closed her eyes, and slowly, a blue tinged glow formed on her hands. She reached out and touched Will. The effect was gentle, and slow, and welcome. It spread through him, a warmth that was light, but still powerful.

Whatever she had done washed through him, removing the after images that clung to his sight. And more, his exhaustion faded away, and strength returned to his legs. "What?" "We did it. The boon is gone. But the power lives in the world now. It can still be used if you know how to touch it. And it can be used everywhere. It's not as strong as it was, it's more spread out, but it's right. We did it, Will. You were right. We did it." Myriam grabbed Will, hugging him tight. "We did it." Will joined in her relief. What it meant in the long years to come, he didn't know. He couldn't even begin to guess what the things he'd done today would bring. But the future would take care of itself, and he would no longer do anything to change it. Right now, he was here. And she was here. His time changing the world was over. Will was what he wanted to be. William Reis, of the Reach. Will bent down, and raised Myriam's tear-stained face, and without a word, kissed her. A kiss she returned. And Will was happy.

THE END.

Thanks to all who have supported me in this endeavor. Special shout outs to my wife and kids, my mom for instilling in me a love of books, and to all my old friends who put up with my crazy D&D adventures.

If you enjoyed this book, and the others in the series, a review on Amazon would be much appreciated.

Thank you for reading!

--Joshua C. Cook
https://www.joshccook.com
Nov. 5, 2021

Printed in Great Britain
by Amazon

19674021R00243